AMERICA, AMERICA

THE LAND OF DREAMS

D. Drew

IS Books

International Society Press

Boston   Beijing

America America, The Land of Dreams reflects the lives and stories of Chinese in Boston during the 1980s and 1990s. Yet it is a fiction, people's names, places, events, names of establishments except for those of the well known educational institutions, are imagined and created by the author. Any resemblance to reality is completely coincidental.

Library of Congress Control Number: 2011941553

ISBN 9781928730033

Published by International Society Press

Web address: www.internationalsociety.us

Printed in the United State of America

to YJ

Character Chart

Ah Tu	A cook who married ill-fated Ailing
Allan	An actor, played Tiger in *yuan ye* (*The Wild Land*)
Ai-ling (Chen)	A Chinese dancer who won first prize in China's National Dance Competition; married a cook, Ah Tu, for a green card; abused by the mother-in-law; rescued by Ying Ying and Pei-hua; joined a dance studio as instructor; won grand prize in a ballroom dance competition; in the end married her student and admirer Anthony.
An Kai	Married to Hu Ning; managed properties for Dai Tong.
Anthony	Ailing's dance student and admirer, married Ailing in the end.
Andrew Johnson	Chairman of International Foundation's Board. Helped Meilan by giving her a high-paying job
Beth	Head seamstress constructing costumes for *Intrigues in the Manchu Imperial Court*.
Betty	A female actor, played Jin-Zi in *yuan ye* (*The Wld Land*)
Brandon	A professor of Classics; married to Dong Fei-yan who betrayed him by having a love affair with a Russian musician.
Brigitte Walker	A Trustee of China Society, young, beautiful and wealthy; suggested to the Board a fashion show or antique show as a fundraiser.
Bruce	Visual arts coordinator at China Society, successor of Denis
Chen Lo	Chinese Cultural Attaché of the Consulate General in NY.
Ching Ju	A grand prize winning dancer originally from China but met her husband, a rich industrialist, Jack Morrison in Japan.
Chen Yin	A college teaching assistant, one of Ying Ying's suitors
Chong Teng	A trained musician, a graduate of Shanghai Conservatory and Boston University turned carpenter, built stage sets for China Society's play production.
Chris	Ching Ju's son
Dai Tong	A bare-foot peasant in China, became a billionaire in the mid-1980s. He hired An Kai and Hu Ning to manage his real estate in Boston.
Deng, Professor	China Stage's committee member, played Chang Wu in the production of *Yuan Ye* (*The Wild Land*)
Denis Lambert	A staff member of China Society, married an older Chinese woman to help her obtain a green card. Later he finished his Ph.D. in Chinese history and taught at a college; became Pei-hua's soulmate in the end.
Dong Fei-yan	A guitarist married to Brandon, felt in love with Russian musician Ivanov.
Du Hang	A Chinese student living in a house as bird and dog caretaker
Eric	Missy's boyfriend

Fang Kuei	An artist Ying Ying invited from Italy to exhibit at China Society's gallery; entangled with Dong Fei-yan, married to an art consultant, Kathy; patronized by Ching Ju and her husband Jack Morrison; became an internationally renowned artist, married Susie, died in a plane crash.
Fran	An female actor, Played Mrs. Jiao in *yuan ye* (*The Wild Land*)
George Hemmingway	A wealthy businessman, in love with Meilan and proposed for her hand but failed; supported Meilan's touring performance in China.
Gong Heng	An artist who came to America with the help of an American artist travelling in China.
Han Tu	An exceptional baritone who won the most prestigious vocal competition and a contract with the Met; later engaged in import and export business and opened a music training school in China to make a quick buck.
Herald Schmidt	President of International Foundation
Hou Shang	A sound and lighting designer graduated from Beijing Drama Institute and studied at Tufts University's theatre department; designed sound and lighting for *The intrigues in the Manchu Imperial Court.*
Hu Ning	A non-professional female actor playing Empress in *The intrigues in the Manchu Imperial Court.* Married to An Kai; had a short-lived love affair with Meng Song.
Huang Nan	One of Ying Ying's suitors when she was 13, a student at Qing Hua University
Ivanov	A Russian Saxophone and Bassoon player, Dong Fei-yan's lover
Jack Morrison	Ching Ju's husband, President of JM Bio Medical
Jason	A journalist and a wealthy Bostonian, married to Meng Lingzhen
Jenny	An American-born Chinese, a work-study at China Society, played Lady Zhen in *Intrigues in the Manchu Imperial Court*; went to London to study stage design.
Joe	An actor, played Da-xing in *yuan ye* (*The Wild Land.*)
Jonathan	A friend of Pei-hua's
Joseph Lee, Dr	Director and Visual Arts Curator of China Society
Kai-de (Wang)	A businessmen sent by an American company to Beijing; fell in love with Meilan; married Meilan in the end.
Kang Wei	Ying Ying's boyfriend in college, married to Ying Ying years later.
Kevin Hong	A physician/actor, played Emperor *Guangxu* in *Intrigues in the Manchu Imperial Court,* an admirer of Jenny's
Kung Lang	A teaching assistant at Normal University in Taiwan, one of Ying Ying's admirers
Liang Hai	A writer in resident at China Society

Liang Ken	A son of a general, living across the street from Ying Ying's home in Taipei, an Air Force Academy student, then a pilot, persistently pursued Ying Ying for seven years until she left for the U.S. after college.
Louisa Kingston	Chairman of China Society's Performing Arts Program Committee; brought Yan Dan to China Society's attention
Lu Wen	An artist, painted decorative motifs on the theatre costumes for *The Intrigues in the Manchu Imperial Court*. Later he established himself as a renowned mural artist and a designer of special visual effects.
Ma Ya	A young violinist, a first-prize winner of an international violin competition
Malone	A piano professor at New England Conservatory.
Manna	A mediocre dancer originally from Taiwan, married to an American businessman, Roger, who divorced her for her debauched behaviour; later lost custody of her two boys to Roger. Continued a debauched lifestyle, exploited the welfare system; mired in a cult practice and tried to destroy Ying Ying
Meilan (Liang)	A movie star and popular singer from China, became a socialite in Boston; built a business empire for herself in Beijing and Shanghai; married Wang Kai-de in the end.
Mei Shan	A friend of Hu Ning, originally a clerk of an upscale hotel in Shanghai; a black-market prostitute, married an American tourist in Shanghai. She snuck into Xi Feng's room and took pictures of her jewellery and clothing and reported to the police claiming those were hers stolen by Xi Feng.
Meng, Mrs.	Meng Song's mother
Meng Song	An abstract artist, designed scenery and painted a large banner for *Intrigues in the Manchu Imperial Court;* winner of New England Artists Fellowship competition. Founded a large arts conglomeration in Shanghai.
Mike	An actor playing "The Idiot" in *yuan ye* (*The Wild Land*)
Mike	Jenny's high school sweetheart
Missy	An MIT student doing work study at Chinese Society. Came to the U.S. from Taiwan as a child.
Old Huang	International Foundation's bookkeeper, lost his wife to a rich young Jewish guy.
Pei-hua (Liu)	Ying Ying's high school and college schoolmate, studied at BU School of Law; joined Swanson, William & Murphy law firm after graduation; infatuated with actor Li Yong; married Li Yong, and divorced him years later.
Peter Si	An American-born Chinese or ABC, a college faculty, telling his experiences of being discriminated against.
Qian De	An architect of Qian/Wilson, competed for a project in China and failed to get the job because China took the designs from

the entries but did not use any of the architects.

Robert Sinclair	A wealthy businessman in Boston,
Roy Ferguson	A Korean War veteran
Ross	The Jewish young man who married Old Huang's wife.
Sally	A dancer originally from Taiwan, participated in China Society's dance concert.
Sam	The stage manager for *yuan ye* (*The Wild Land.*)
Samantha	A young pianist
Sandy Ferguson	Roy's daughter, played Juliet opposites Li Yong in *Romeo and Juliet.*
Sharon Hays	Ying Ying's schoolmate at Harvard, offered to help with writing a proposal but never delivered it.
Sidney	A dance instructor and Ailing's dance partner
Sun Sang	Came to the U.S. under a false identity, an intelligent man who despite his limited formal education and inadequate English became a successful financial manager.
Susie	A dancer from Taiwan, participated in China Society's dance concert. Bought and managed large real estates for wealthy Mr. Deng and created wealth for herself. Married Fang Kuei.
Steven	A volunteer at China Society
Tan Jin	Designed sets for *yuan ye* (*The Wild Land.*)
Tian Kun	Woolan's friend of the brick-baking days, became a very rich man in Beijing, asked Woolan to invest in Boston on his behalf and help to get his son to study in Boston.
Tonia	A work-study student at China Society, an ABC
Vladimir	The Russian director of China Stage's inaugural production., *yuan ye* (The Wild Land)
Woolan	A Mongolian from China who came to the States through marriage. Acted as Meilan's assistant in her China tour. Became rich after helping old friend Tian Kun to invest in Boston.
Xi Feng	She and her husband Jing Sheng were friends of Hu Ning's. Her valuable belongings were stolen by Mei Shan.
Yang Dan	A young pianist, a first-prize winner of a prestigious international piano competition
Yang Hui	Meng Song's friend, a medical student who came to America under the sponsorship of Pei-hua's uncle.
Mrs. Yang	Yang Hui's mother
Ying Ying	A Student of Harvard School of Design, a work-study student at China Society, later became Director of China Society, then President of International Foundation and a respected scholar; married to Kang Wei.
Yu, professor	Director of China Stage's production, *Intrigues in the Manchu Imperial Court*

Yu Xie	A woman who fled from China by swimming from Shenzhen to Hong Kong.
Zhang Ze	An artist, painted scenery for *Intrigues in the Manchu Imperial Court*
Zhi An	An accomplished soprano, winner of second prize at a Metropolitan Opera competition, whose husband gave up his career to let her pursue a career in opera.

Prologue

Where there are people there are intriguing stories.

They were all Chinese descends, from Taiwan, the Chinese mainland, Hong Kong and other parts of Asia as well American-born. Many of them were students.

China Society, a wholly own subsidiary of International Foundation for the Arts and Humanities, had the only gallery that showcased living Chinese artists in those days. It inevitably gravitated all those avid young talents.

Fang Ying Ying, a twenty-two-year-old graduate student from Taiwan, was a part-time worker at China Society under a work-study program. Her presence at the organization was an added draw to the artists and a friendship naturally developed among them. They shared dreams and aspirations; they witnessed each other's struggles, happiness, desperation, success and failure.

The organization became a stage for much human drama.

Chapter 1

"*E*xcuse me." Without a knock, Ying Ying's office door stood ajar was pushed open slightly wider. A head stuck in wearing a grin on the face. With a start Ying Ying raised her head from her desk.

"Yes?" she demanded.

"Are you from Taipei?" the grinning face asked. Before Ying Ying could give an answer he continued: "I am from Beij..." He quickly swallowed the second half of the word and changed it to "Bei-ping"

Ying Ying smiled and said: "You are from Beijing?" *The man was cautious. He was afraid to offend me.* Ying Ying thought. *But I am not that sensitive politically. The city has been called Beijing since 1949 by the Mainlanders. It's being accepted by the world. Why can't I accept it? Beside, what's in a name? Calling the City Bei-ping is a show of patriotism and allegiance to Nationalist China? I've never felt it necessary to hold such a narrow-minded view.*

At the same time the man was thinking: *Since the girl is from Taiwan I'd better respect her political sensitivity. They call our capital Bei-ping. I'd better not say Beijing in front of her.*

"Yes." He smiled and pushed the door completely open and invited himself in. "I thought you wouldn't be used to that name."

Ying Ying smiled back: "May I help you?" She asked.

"Oh, I was just passing by and thought perhaps I could come in to check the place out. What is China Society? What do you do here?'

"It's an organization that promotes Chinese arts and culture. We have many different programs. For example we showcase the works of Chinese artists, musicians and dancers. We have educational programs for elementary and secondary schools. We have symposiums, discussions, and many other activities." By force of habit Ying Ying pitched an introduction of the programs to her visitor.

"Oh, I see. What do you do here?" The inquisitive visitor asked.

"Me? I am just a work-study student."

"What is a work-study student?" The man was seriously curious.

Ying Ying glared at him and smiled again. "Work-study is a government-sponsored program. When a college student works part time at a non-profit organization the government pays 80% of the salary. The college only pays 20%.

"We don't have that in China," he said.

Suddenly he remembered that he had not introduced himself.

"Sorry. My name is Woolan. That's my first name and my only name. I am a Mongolian. We hardly ever use our last names."

"Really? You are a Mongolian? A real Mongolian from Mongolia?" Ying Ying was excited "I have never met a indigenous Mongolian."

"Now you have." The man grinned.

"Yes." Ying Ying gave him an once-over. The man was very tall with rather fair complexion, well-formed features and thick wavy hair. *Were Mongolians taller than the average Han Chinese?* she wondered. *His perfect Beijing accent sounds so pleasing.*

"How long have you been here?" Ying Ying asked.

"About three, four months."

"Which school are you in?"

"I... I... I am not in school," Woolan said. A slight discomfiture flitted across his face.

"So, you will start next semester?" Ying Ying did not notice Woolan's expression.

"No, I... I am not a student. I cannot get into any school." He admitted it honestly. That hint of abashment faded away.

"Oh. I thought all Chinese coming here now are students. I heard that the Chinese government does not allow other people to leave the country except for official businesses," Ying Ying commented. *I know this for a fact. China and the United States had no diplomatic relations for decades. It was only since 1981 that China began to allow its students to come to the U.S. Colleges and universities gladly, zealously opened their doors to welcome them. Why is this man not in school?* But she didn't feel it was her place to ask why since they had just met.

Woolan saw through Ying Ying's mind and volunteered his answer without hesitation:

"I had very little schooling in China. Because of the Cultural Revolution, you see. I was a victim of that era." Ying Ying uttered no remarks but waited for him to continue.

"You have probably heard about how it was during that time. Schools were knocked down by rebel students. Teachers were beaten up at Struggle Meetings. Red Guards ravaged people's houses, destroyed the nation's cultural legacies. Kids from the 'Five Categories-of-Blacks' were excluded from the Red Guard Corp. They hid inside the houses to avoid being beaten as much as possible. When the ten years of disaster were over and colleges were reopened some people such as myself were barred from entrance because we were deem too old, at age twenty-two."

"But there are many students from China in recent years studying here in American colleges." Ying Ying was confused.

"They must have been at least a year younger than I am. I was at the cut-off line, among the most unfortunate bunch."

"How did you get here? I thought only students were allowed to come."

The ringing of the phone interrupted their conversation.

"Yes, Dr. Schmidt. ... Dr. Lee went to meet with Mr. Fletcher. We are still waiting to hear from the Peabody Museum.... Yea, MFA has agreed to lend those objects. Okay I will tell him." Ying Ying spoke into the phone.

As Ying Ying hung up the phone Woolan got up from his chair and said:

"I'll let you go back to your work. Sorry to have disrupted it. May I come to see you again? I live close by here."

"Sure. Have you looked at our art exhibit? Please do."

Knocking on the already widely opened door, Denis popped his head in:

"Two artists just brought in their works. They asked for you."

"Thanks, Denis." She got up and strode toward the door, then turned to Woolan: "I have to take a look. Some artists just brought in their paintings."

Woolan followed Ying Ying out of her office. "Are you going to your gallery? May I go see the art exhibit now?" He paused and asked again: "Is that young man also a work-study?"

"Who? Denis? No. He is the Director of Humanities Program here. He also supervises work-study students. So he is my boss. But we are more like equal colleagues. He is very humble. He has a master's degree in Chinese history from Columbia but he said I probably knew more about Chinese history than he did."

"Columbia. That's a famous university. In New York, is it?"

"Yes."

"He wanted you to talk with the artists?" Woolan asked inquisitively.

"Oh," Ying Ying smiled: "Yes. He can speak Chinese, but not good enough."

Twenty-seven-year-old Denis Lambert has had a strong interest in China since childhood. He was fascinated by the things in his Chinese schoolmate's house in Queens. He loved the old ink landscape paintings and portraits of ancient men in exotic robes on the wall, the lacquered screens, the carved dark rosewood chairs and tables, and the curios in the glass cabinet. He wished he could read the books in Chinese characters on their shelves, or speak with his friend's parents in their language. He thought the sound of that language was so beautiful. He wished one day he could go to China.

Some of the Chinese artists were indeed still struggling with English though they were attending college here. Ying Ying often wondered how difficult it would be for them to follow the lectures. Once artist Lu Wen told her:

"We don't understand what the teachers say. But it's not that crucial since we are not required to write term papers like students in other fields of studies. And we don't have to read much either. We can get by. As long as our studio work is good, that's what counts."

"You people in Taiwan have English courses in school, I heard," Lu Wen held.

"Yes, we have studied English since 7th grade. But most students didn't learn as much as they should have. We know just enough to understand the lectures. Writing term papers was not easy for us either at first."

Woolan followed Ying Ying to the gallery door and saw two artists standing there in front of their paintings that were leaning against the wall.

"Hi." Ying Ying greeted them and introduced Woolan to them. They nodded to each other and said "*ni hao*."

"Ying Ying, when are you going to select the pieces?" Artist Tan Jin asked.

"Dr. Joseph Lee is going to select the works. Not me. If you don't know yet, he is the Curator of all six shows annually. I am not sure of his exact schedule but I believe he will do it within two weeks. You know that he already selected twenty artists for the show from a large pool of applicants. Now he is only going to make a final selection from the work you brought in."

*   *   *   *

A sumptuous reception opened the show. Hors d'oeuvres and fine wines were served by waiters in uniforms, fruit platters, various cheeses and hot food set on the tables, just like museum openings. Ying Ying, Jenny and Denis talked about how costly the reception must have been.

"I always wonder if it is necessary. The museums can afford it because their benefactors underwrite all the receptions. We shouldn't have squandered money hand-over-fist this way," Jenny commented.

"But the Trustees wanted it that way. They had discussed the issue intensely a number of times. Some suggested charging a fee to the guests. But opinions were divided," Ying Ying explained. "I overheard them at a meeting. Brigitte said the fee had to be high. She for one would not go to an event that charged only ten dollars. She said a garbage man would go to that. It has to be fifty dollars or more. Or we don't charge at all."

"What? Of course it's only Brigitte's opinion. I shouldn't say this. But she is such a pretentious profligate of a multi-million-dollar spoiled brat, never ceases to ostentatiously flaunt her pomposity whenever she can. Does she know that gallery openings are usually simple and never charge a dime?" Denis put forth his opinion on that young, beautiful but always presumptuous woman.

A girl born to a wealthy Hong Kong father and a French mother, Brigitte Walker was sent to a private boarding school in New England. After finishing college she married a rich Boston Brahmin and established herself as a permanent fixture of all high society social events. She was a glaring contrast to the other blueblood New Englanders sitting on the Board of International Foundation who were elegant, socially well-poised and polite. They were also older than Brigitte. These people gave money to the Foundation and other charities because they believed in the causes, not because they wished to openly parade their wealth.

"Mrs. Harrison said that admission might prevent some of our guests from coming. Museum of Fine Arts does not charge their guests for special viewing receptions. She said the Trustees ought to underwrite it," Ying Ying said. "Her words always carry so much weight. The other Trustees respect her opinions."

Mrs. Harrison was a renowned philanthropist, a founding Trustee of the

Foundation. While a youngster she had spent a few years in Shanghai, thus developed an emotional affinity to china. Very kind and generous, her soft-spoken words were tinged with that Beacon Hill old family accent.

"The lunches following our Board meetings are sort of extravagant and unusual, if you ask me. What other organizations would have fancy lunches and expensive wine served by a butler and maid after each Board meeting?" Denis commented. Jenny chuckled at the way he put it.

It was either Mrs. Harrison or Mrs. Saunders who donated the wine, had their chef prepare the food, and brought their butler and maid to serve them.

"I have never heard of any other organization that does this." Jenny said.

*   *   *   *

Another intern at China Society, Tonia, was a senior from Mass College of Art. She was born in San Francisco. There were about twenty Chinese students at her school. Half of them were from Mainland China, a few from Taiwan; one other girl was from Hong Kong. The rest were American-born Chinese who called themselves ABCs. That sobriquet was pretty neutral and harmless. Another often heard and more acrid label was "Banana" or *Zhu-shen,* indicating the person was like a banana with yellow on the outside and white on the inside. This irony only circled among the American-born Chinese themselves. No other Chinese ever used that term.

The native Chinese, even after becoming naturalized citizens, did not consider themselves Americans. They were so pertinacious about their Chinese ethnicity and civilization, very confident and proud of their original nationality, that they never needed to be anything else but Chinese. They took no offense when being regarded as a foreigner. Many of those from Mainland China were in fact ethnocentric, overtly loyal to their home country and its government, to the point of harboring animosity toward their adopted country, the United States, in which they chose to settle.

In general, the Chinese from Asia were not sensitive when confronted with such questions as "Where are you from?" or "Do you speak English?" or "Do you plan to go back?" They considered those questions logical and legitimate. They gave simple and direct answers without a second thought. The American-born Chinese, on the other hand, were often consumed by the issue of acceptance. They saw the American society as being racially discriminatory, prejudiced and hostile. They felt they were not being fully accepted as Americans and resented the fact. They had no close affinity with the country of their ancestors nor did they know the culture. Many did not speak the language. They were Americans just like their Caucasian, black, and Hispanic counterparts. Yet they were often mistaken, understandably, as foreigners. They felt offended, though needlessly, even insulted when being regarded as temporary sojourners. They were unsure of where they belonged or who they were. "Identity crisis," "how to be accepted as an American" were major disturbing issues that had been talked about, written about too much and too often.

One time Tonia told Ying Ying that she was very upset because some people had asked her, whether she spoke English, where did she come from, and when would she go back home to China. Ying Ying understood but was not empathetic. She chuckled and said:

"I am being asked that all the time. I don't feel a bit uncomfortable. Why would you feel offended? I think those are reasonable questions."

Tonia was even more irked by Ying Ying's lack of sympathy. She retorted:

"That's because you are from there. And you may be going back there. But I am a third generation Chinese American. My home is here. Where else would I go?"

"How would they know that you and I are different? Those are logical questions, logical errors, if you will. They took you for one of those students, or immigrants, or visitors from China who do not speak English. That's nothing to be upset about. How do people differentiate a Chinese American who speaks nothing but English, and a native Chinese who speaks no English? There is nothing written on our faces to tell people. So there is no need to be angry when you are mistaken as a newcomer." Ying Ying reasoned.

"We don't look at it that way though. I think people are just plain discriminatory. It is a major problem in this country." Tonia was still peeved.

"I don't think so. Just because people ask you some innocent questions by mistake? Discrimination is an inexcusable bigotry, no doubt. But it is not endemically American. It is everywhere." Ying Ying still did not agree with Tonia. "May I tell you a few stories? They are not concocted. They are true stories."

"Yea?"

"Yes. There was a couple. The husband David was an Anglo-Saxon American, and was a Chinese language teacher, of all things. His wife Lena was from Taiwan. Once they shopped at a store in Taipei during their vacation. The salesgirl, used to taking advantage of foreigners, quoted a higher price on an item that David was buying. Lena knew that the price was wrong and questioned the girl why. The salesgirl looked at her, puzzled, and said:

"Why do you side with that foreigner and not try to help ourselves?' The sales-girl thought Lena was a tour guide."

"Funny." Tonia commented.

"Yes. I will tell you another one," Ying Ying said: "Helen was a pianist from Hong Kong and trained by Julia School of Music in New York. Her husband, Donald, an European, was a college science professor. One year Helen was invited to give a concert in Taiwan and her husband went with her. At the Grand Hotel, the most luxurious in Taipei at that time, the clerk gave them two separate rooms. Donald told the clerk that they only needed one. The clerk looked at Helen from head to toe and said: 'You have to go somewhere else. The Grand Hotel is not that kind of a place.' He thought Helen was a call girl."

"Oh, that's rude." Tonia exclaimed.

"Right. But it was a common and preconceived notion. Mixed marriage was very rare there," Ying Ying said. "I have to tell you a different kind of discrimination. This man Steward was a son of an American GI. His parents were stationed in Shanghai in the late 1940s. In 1949, when the American army hastily withdrew from Shanghai Jim was out with his nanny. His parents could not get to him in time. And they had to get on that plane. So they left without him...."

"How horrible." Horrified, Tonia interrupted. "How could parents leave the kid behind? I would not get on that plane. I would find my kid no matter what."

"I am sure they would do the same if it were not under such extraordinary circumstances. It was on the verge of a war and the man was a GI."

"Then what happened? You said a different kind of discrimination. What about it?"

"Well, the nanny brought the boy up and he became a full-fledged Chinese despite his physical appearance. People thought he was a visiting foreigner and treated him differently. During the Cultural Revolution he was sent to the countryside for 'Reform Through Labour.' It was a time when the U.S. and China were very hostile toward each other. He was inevitably discriminated against by his fellow labourers. When China promoted 'unity among all peoples,' he was being used by his work-unit as a symbol of unity. After the Cultural Revolution, foreigners were treated favourably, with unusual politeness and respect. In a crowded bus, for example, people would give him a seat. When walking through a door people would let him go first. No one knew that he was as much a Shanghainese as any native was. The film production companies hired him to play foreigners in films. He was very happy and at ease, never took offence or complained about it. His friends often said jestingly that he had gotten a good deal. There were others like him in that city and were treated the same way. They didn't take offence."

"Somehow, it sounds different from our situation here," Tonia insisted.

"I don't see the difference. If we wouldn't get so wrought up, and accept people's mistakes with good humour, take them in stride, things would be so much simpler. And the world would be more harmonious."

"You are not us. You cannot feel what we feel." Tonia was not convinced. She sounded a little livid. "Your lecture is pointless."

Denis just walked in and heard Tonia's words. He asked jestingly: "Is Ying Ying giving a lecture again?"

"I am not giving a lecture. We were just talking about the issue of discrimination. I said we should lighten up, no need to be sensitive about a harmless mistake."

"Ying Ying has very strong views on many social issues and her opinions are often opposite to those popularly held, and contrary to what people expect of her." Denis seemed to be speaking only to Tonia.

"I don't go with the flow, if that's what you mean. I tend to form my own views independently rather than being swayed by popular buzz and media hype. I know my opinions have been attacked by some people, those special interest groups."

"I know your opinion on bilingual education is a highly controversial one. I heard that some bi-lingual teachers have complained about it." Denis said.

"Not only bilingual teachers. I heard that the Chinese community is furious. But Ying Ying has her right to voice her opinions. And I agree with her on that one," Tonia added.

"I will not change my opinion on that. Where is the validity of such a program? What is the purpose of putting children in separate class just because they don't know the language in the beginning or worse yet just because their parent don't speak good English?." Ying Ying demanded.

"But you cannot argue that the intention of the program is good. Some kids from different language backgrounds need help in school or they will fail," Denis chimed in his opinion.

"I don't agree. Not knowing English in the beginning is not the reason why they have failed. Children have amazing learning and adjusting abilities. I have many examples to prove that. I myself am an example too. While growing up in Taiwan, I quickly and easily learned different dialects from the succession of new servants working in my house. Many of the dialects were so different that they sounded like foreign languages. Over here there are Chinese families living in the suburbs where foreigners are few and the schools do not offer bilingual classes. The newly arrived Chinese children, some as young as seven or eight or as old as fifteen, not knowing a word of English, were thrown in regular classes to sink or swim. No one sank. The parents also knew that their kids would catch up in no time. For sure, the kids were fluent in English in less than a year. I knew two kids in the Wellesley school system who, coming from Taiwan, represented their school to national math and forensic competitions respectively. That was only a year after they came here."

"Forensic competition too?" Denis asked in amazement.

"Yes, I was very impressed. Competing in math is nothing. You know how many of those kids entered Harvard and MIT? The initial language barrier breaks down quickly. They soon attained native fluency and academic success.

On the other hand there are college students I have met who speak with heavy accents, broken grammar and incomplete sentences. I thought they were newly arrived foreign students. In fact they were inner-city school graduates from bilingual programs. They were deprive of the opportunity to learn the language and take classes taught by qualified teachers."

Ying Ying's argument had infuriated the bilingual teachers before.

Tonia agreed with Ying Ying on this point. She added: "Yes, I knew a woman from Dominican Republic who was born here but went back to her home country as a toddler. Then she came back to the States at fourteen. She stayed in the bilingual program throughout high school and never learned English. She couldn't get into a college because of her language barrier. She was not able to get any job either except waiting on tables in Mexican food restaurant. She is twenty-five years old, living in a ghetto and speaks no English..."

20

"You see. These prove my point. There are too many such examples. Kids coming here as young as kindergarten age, or were born here were forced by the schools to stay in bilingual programs all the way through high school on account of their Chinese faces despite the parents' objections." Ying Ying turned to Tonia and asked: " Were you ever in a bilingual program, Tonia?"

"No, because my parents were born here. But I know about those programs. The bilingual classes are usually taught by people speaking broken English with a ghetto accent, and without teacher's certificates. They also teach all the subjects." Tonia spoke of what she witnessed first-hand in school.

"Exactly. Putting kids in such a situation is to impede their ability to compete for opportunities when they grow up because of language incompetency. It strangulates their future. Beside, the segregation must be affecting the kids' psychology and self-esteem, and causing them to develop a hostile attitude of 'us' verses 'them.' " Emphatically Ying Ying stressed.

"It never occurred to me. I think your point makes sense. I wonder why the educators and policy-makers don't see it," Denis questioned.

"Why? Because they don't care. Because once a system is established it's almost impossible to abolish it. Because many people's pay-checks depend on the program. Who really cares about kids from foreign countries? It takes a powerful leader with vision, farsightedness and courage to fight the rotten system," Ying Ying held passionately.

"Is Feng Yi's boy still in the bilingual program?" Denis asked.

"I think so."

Feng Yi was China Society's custodian. The school insisted on putting his son in the bilingual class taught by a Cantonese-speaking woman. Feng Yi and his wife begged the principal to put the boy in regular classes. The school ignored them. He asked Denis and Ying Ying for help. They talked with the principal but he refused to budge. And the boy who was fluent in Mandarin-Chinese and English and spoke not a word of Cantonese had to learn that dialect in order to understand the teacher."

"You know Huang Han, the clarinettist from China? Same story. The Brookline school placed his daughter in the bilingual class. He and his wife asked me to help persuade the school to move her to the regular class. His daughter is American-born. She speaks better English than Mandarin. Now she is in this bilingual class taught by a Cantonese. Huang Han and his wife are very upset. They said the school was ruining her future," Ying Ying said.

"The schools' motivation is simple: Money." Ying Ying was not afraid to speak her mind: "They need head-counts to get government subsidies. The more students they have the more money they get. Of course they are not going to let go even one kid. Those children's future is not the school's concern. I don't believe that they haven't realized the malfeasance of the program or are not aware of how foreign kids are doing in private schools or good suburban schools."

This opinion and criticism of hers had already caused much outcry from the community that attacked her for "not caring about the wellbeing of the kids."

*   *   *   *

Fang Ying Ying was the only child of a Chinese Nationalist army general. In the old traditional culture where boys were often preferred to girls, a couple without a son was looked upon as being lacking. To make up for this deficiency, Ying Ying's father put a heavy demand on his daughter. Ever since she was in kindergarten, the father had said:

"My daughter will be ten times better than anyone's son. She will be an accomplished and useful person to the society."

She did well in school and graduated from high school before age seventeen. She passed the highly competitive college entrance examination with high scores and entered Taiwan University, the college of every high school graduate's dream. Before taking the national college entrance examination she worried about failing it and being censured by her father. *He does not know the fierceness of the competition. I must let him know,* she thought.

"Taiwan University is the most difficult to get in...." She began to put that in her father's head.

"Difficult to get in?" Before she finished the sentence her father demanded solemnly: "Will there be anyone who can get in?"

"Yes, of course. But the ratio is small," Ying Ying replied, timidly.

"If there is one, that one must be you." Father's unshakable decree drilled deep into her mind. She must not fail.

She did not fail.

In college Ying Ying avoided those boys who relentlessly pursued her. Father would not allow her to associate with them. She knew it. She was conditioned to turning her back on boys.

"You are too young. School is more important than anything else. Don't let those trivial things get in the way." She always remembered her father's precept. Some of her father's friends asked if their sons could meet her. Her father was so angry that he severed his acquaintanceship with them.

Ying Ying didn't know whether her father loved her or not; whether all those demands were simply because he wanted a daughter that was "ten times better than anyone's son." Study abroad was a predetermined course for her. She had hoped to delay it for a year or two. Then Kang Wei, the boy she started dating in her senior year, could go with her, giving her help and companionship in that strange foreign land. But her father wanted her to waste no time but to pursue the highest education.

She did not dare defy his decision.

It was when her parents saw her off at the airport that she knew her father loved her. Her father, a military man, a general who seldom showed emotions, broke down at the airport. He hugged his daughter and cried like a child. To see her mother cry was not unusual. But her father? She had never seen it in her life. This heart-renting image stayed with her forever.

"Dad, I will be back after I finish school, after I get my doctorate."
Tears streaked Ying Ying's face and stung her eyes.

As she was walking into the gate of the plane she heard her father crying:

"Ying Ying, hurry back. Hurry back." He was heart-stricken as if he would never see his daughter again.

It took Ying Ying a long while to compose herself.

$$* \quad\quad * \quad\quad * \quad\quad *$$

Ying Ying's high school classmate Ho Pei-hua was on the same plane flying to Boston. Ying Ying was going to attend the School of Design at Harvard University and Pei-hua at the School of Law at Boston University. Students in Taiwan were familiar with Boston University because the school sent a team of staff there every year to recruit students. The students thought it was one of the highest ranking universities, on the par with Harvard and MIT.

"Pei-hua, what made you decide to study law? And why BU?" While chatting on the plane Ying Ying asked her friend. Pei-hua was a journalism-major at Taiwan University. She had a passion for acting and was in a number of the school's productions. Why didn't she pursue a career in acting or continue her graduate work in journalism? True, acting was too 'frivolous,' not a career choice for a graduate of Taiwan University. Many students changed their fields of study after coming to America for practical reasons. They wanted something that would warrant jobs after getting a master's degree or Ph.D.. Most English Literature and Chinese Literature majors, for example, switched to something like computer science, accounting, etc... Science and technology students would carry on with their study and research, and finish school more quickly and easily than the humanities students. There were some who adhered to their interests without considering the harsh reality. There were stories about how students majoring in anthropology, English, philosophy and any other such highbrow but low-in-demand fields from Taiwan ended up doing clerical work, or waiting on tables even after they got their Ph.D.. These stories were enough to dismay practical-minded newcomers who were here to pursue the ultimate education and dreams.

"My mother said as a journalist I wouldn't make it in America if I were to stay there; law was a respectable and profitable field. That's what she heard from her friends. I don't know. I just have to do what she tells me."

"I thought your mother was very liberal. She lets you do what you want." Ying Ying remembered what Pei-hua had told her.

"Yeah, that's true. She said I could have all the freedom I wanted. But there are three things she must dictate." Thinking about what her mother used to say to her Pei-hau chuckled.

"What three things?"

"Oh, only three minor things. Very insignificant," Pei-hua said jestingly.

23

"Only my field of study, my career and my marriage." They both laughed.

"Right, not your whole life," Ying Ying scoffed.

"Tell me your father did not dictate your life," Pei-hua retorted tauntingly. "Remember? He wouldn't let you out of the house to do the play?"

"Yea.... I...." How could Ying Ying ever forget that? That was one of those devastating situations her father put her in. It was her junior year in high school. She was cast as the lead in a play. Of course she did not let her parents know about it since they always forbade her from participating in such "frivolous activities."

Her father was a four-star general of the Chinese Nationalist army. A well-disciplined, upright and stern man who was feared not only by his subordinate but his peers as well. Ying Ying's teacher/director was well aware of General Fang's rules. He scheduled all rehearsals immediately after school and did the scenes involving her first so that she could go home early enough without arousing her parents' suspicion. It was fine until the opening day, a Saturday afternoon when there were no classes. That meant Ying Ying had no excuse to get out of the house.

That morning she tried to figure out how to deal with the situation. Curtain time drew near. She was unnerved and couldn't find a workable excuse. Like a caged animal she paced in her room, tears brimming in her eyes. She tried to call her teacher but he was not in the office, apparently. She was in despair thinking that she would be letting her teacher and everyone involved in the production down. She could not show her face in school anymore. Yet she could not tell her parents that. To a fifteen-year-old, that was the end of the world. She just wanted to die.

Suddenly a maidservant knocked on her door and entered. Even as she announced "Young Mistress, Miss Liu..." a young girl rushed into the room. It was Pei-hua, Ying Ying's classmate.

"Why are you still home? The show is about to start. Everyone was so worried. Why aren't you there? Teacher Chen was about to have a heart attack. He sent me to get you." Pei-hua was breathless.

The Fangs had a magnificent house and garden. Their household staff included a chauffeur, a cook, a gardener, a doorman, a house cleaner and two maidservants. Though being affluent, Mrs. Fang always told Ying to be humble, never to flaunt or vaunt.

"I... I couldn't get out of the house. You know that," Ying Ying answered in despondence.

"Jeez, Ying Ying. Couldn't you have thought of some excuse? This is ridiculous." Pei-hua was more than a classmate; she was Ying Ying's best friend. Being one year Ying Ying's senior she was also like an older sister. "Let me go talk to Uncle Fang."

It was customary for people to address friend's father as uncle. In the case of these two girls it was most appropriate because their fathers were old acquaintances.

Pei-hua's father was a two-star general. He had two daughters and a son living with his estranged wife. He was involved with a Peking-opera singer. The wife found out about the affair and asked him to leave. It gave him the golden opportunity to move out and set up house with the other woman. Because of his unbridled behavior he lost the respect of his children and any authority over them. Instead, he constantly tried to win their affection by bribing them with gifts. The kids lived with their mother who shouldered the responsibilities of both parents. Ying Ying's father, being an upright and moral man, did not approve of his friend's behavior.

Pei-hua and Ying Ying made their way to General Fang's study where he and Mrs. Feng were chatting. The study was a commodious room with bookcases lining one wall, a large desk near the window, a sofa and a love seat at one corner with a carved low table in their front, a side table on which a telephone sat, a television set and sound system grouped on a custom build shelf/stand. Mr. Fang often spent time there reading or writing calligraphy. Sometime Mrs. Fang would be there to keep him company and watch some TV. When Mrs. Fang was not in the room the TV would be turned off.

The entertainment room with another TV set and sound system was for their visitors' children to enjoy.

"Uncle Fang, Auntie Fang, wish you are well. I came to pick up Ying Ying. Several classmates are gathering in my house. We wonder why Ying Ying wasn't there. So I came to pick her up. Uncle Fang, Auntie Fang, can she go?" Pei-hua's pleasant voice and beaming smile persuaded the couple. She had this talent of winning the hearts of elders. No one could turn down her requests.

"Ah, yes. She certainly can go to your house. Ying Ying, why didn't you tell me that Pei-hua was having a gathering of friends in her house?" Father scolded: "This kid, never knows when to ask and when not to."

"Oh. Thank you so much, Uncle." Pei-hua grinned widely. She then turned to her friend: "Ying Ying, hurry. Let's go."

The two whirled out of the house. Ying Ying jumped on the back of Pei-hua's bicycle and she peddled away tearing toward the school.

*   *   *   *

"Yea, I remember that," Ying Ying said in a low voice. She looked through the window of the airplane, saw the cumulus of white cloud beneath. The image of her father waving and calling, telling her to hurry back, sliced her heart. *He loves me. Whatever outrageous things he demanded of me it was from love and concern. I cannot blame him. I forgive him. And I want to return home to my parents after I finish school.* Ying Ying buried her face in her hands, sobbing.

The journey took more than twenty hours. At Logan Airport two alumni of Taiwan University were there to meet them. They took the two girls to a place where two alumnae lived. They put Ying Ying and Pei-hua up temporarily and tried to help them find an apartment.

After seeing a few places they decided to share an apartment on Babcock

Street with two Caucasian roommates. It was near Boston University thus very convenient for Pei-hua. The law school at BU ranked at the top in the nation. Ying Ying was surprised to learn that. Pei-hua defended her school and said:

"Don't think Harvard is the only good school. BU's School of Law is better." That did not stop Ying Ying from asking again why Pei-hua did not apply to Harvard Law School. Harvard was much more prestigious as a whole.

Ying Ying's father wanted her to study medicine. "Medicine is a noble career. Doctors save lives unlike soldiers who take lives," he said. That medicine was a lucrative profession was never his concern. He did not regard money as important. Morality, ethical behavior, personal cultivation, and contribution to society were upheld by him as basic convictions of every responsible individual. He often told Ying Ying: "As a person, you should always keep other people's well-being in mind. You should sacrifice yourself for others when necessary, rather than let others sacrifice for you." He wanted Ying Ying to abide to these values.

Ying Ying did not enter the medical field. She would faint at the sight of blood and there was no way she could dissect a cadaver. She loved art and was good at it. In high school her drawings and watercolor paintings had won inter-school competitions and were exhibited with other winners at Sun Yat-sun Hall in Taipei. She aspired to be a professional artist when she grew up. But she was not allowed to pursue that dream. Her father said it was a useless trade. She completely disagreed. *Only science and technology are useful to mankind? What would the world be without art?* But she could not argue with her father. Silence was her only showing of defiance. Consequently father and daughter compromised. Ying Ying ended up studying architecture in college and took some studio art courses on the side. In graduate school she took a number of art history courses and was deeply fascinated by the professors' lectures. *I wish I could lecture like that. I want to be a professor,* she said to herself.

Three semesters later Ying Ying got a part-time job at China Society under the work-study-program.

*   *   *   *

Woolan went to China Society again the day after he met Ying Ying. And every time he passed by the building he would stop by to see if Ying Ying was there. He was very handy with tools and could repair almost anything. He offered to help with various chores in the office and gallery.

"It's nice of you to help us. Volunteers are always welcome, especially people who are willing to do physical work," Ying Ying said.

"It's nothing. Don't' mention it. I like working with my hands," He said. "I picked up an old TV set on the street the other day. I fixed it. It works now."

"Where did you learn to do that? It isn't easy, is it?"

"I can fix most electronic devices and automobiles. I didn't learn from anyone. I just take them apart to figure it out. I built a house for myself in

26

Beijing too."

"That's amazing. You really did that?" Ying Ying was impressed and skeptical at the same time.

"It's a simple house. Nothing like the houses here. But it's good enough for average use," he replied.

China Society was receiving a historical documentary exhibit from San Francisco where a group of historians, research assistants, and graphic artists worked for four years to produce it. Dr. Joseph Lee had been working on a companion show for about a year. Although the two galleries were quite large yet the linear footage of the wall space was still insufficient for the two shows. As such twelve pairs of movable walls were built to augment the hanging space by 192 linear feet. They were wood structures, heavy and sturdy, covered with finely finished one-inch thick plywood. The contractor painted the panels white to match the color of the walls. Dr. Lee did not like that.

"The nail holes on wood panels would be impossible to repair; after a few shows the panels would be unsightly." He pointed it out to his staff in the gallery: "They should be covered with coarsely woven fabric to hide the nail holes"

"Hmmm. That's another expense," Denis commented. The movable walls already cost $10,000 to build."

"Will you find out how much it will cost?" Joseph Lee asked Denis. "Get a couple of estimates. If we can hire students to do the work it may be cheaper." He had to be concerned about the cost because there was no budget for it.

When Ying Ying mentioned it to Woolan he said: "I can do it for you without charge. I am happy to help."

"That is wonderful." Ying Ying and Denis thanked him. They told Joseph about it. Of course he was very grateful.

Woolan spent hours working on it each time he went there. To show their appreciation, Ying Ying and Denis would go to the workshop to chat with him whenever possible. During those weeks Woolan told Ying Ying a lot about himself and his experiences while in China.

He did not come to Boston as a student, but as an immigrant. That was unusual.

"I didn't know there were new immigrants from China. I thought both the Chinese and the U.S. governments would not allow it," Ying Ying said while watching him stretch fabric over the panels.

"It's my cousin who got me here." He said.

"I thought only a citizen's direct family could be brought here. That does not include cousins." Ying Ying was perplexed.

"Not easy, but still possible," Woolan replied.

One day Woolan had a long telephone conversation outside the gallery. "I was talking to my cousin," he later told Ying Ying.

"The cousin that brought you here?"

"Yes," he muttered and did not say any more.

Two weeks later he reluctantly revealed a secret. "Ying Ying, we are friends.

I think I should not hide things from you. But there is one thing I have not been truthful with you because it is too embarrassing for me to tell you."

"What is it?" Ying Ying asked absently.

"That cousin of mine, she's not my cousin. I made it up."

"Oh, who is she?" It was puzzling to Ying Ying. "Why do you need to create a fictitious cousin?"

"She...She...She's the one getting me out of China," Woolan stammered.

"Yea?" Ying Ying was further perplexed by his hesitation. "You already told me that. But who is she?"

"She married me in order to bring me over here." He summoned enough courage and muttered it in one breath.

It was unexpected indeed. However, even though the marriage was a means to an end rather than the fruition of love, he needed not be so secretive about it.

"So she is your wife," Ying Ying held.

"Not exactly. She was just helping me. She agreed to have a divorce as soon as I got a green card. We don't live together and aside from her mother and her son no one knows about our marriage."

"Oh, you mean the marriage is not real, not in the true sense." This was the first time Ying Ying heard of such an arrangement. "It was very nice of her to help you that way."

"She wanted the marriage to be real. Before I came, I also was willing to have a real marriage with her. As long as I could leave China, to come to America, I would do anything. Marrying her? I would be willing to be a slave of hers. She is fifteen years older than I, a divorcee with a ten-year-old son."

"Was that why you wanted the divorce?" She referred to the age difference and the woman's son. She knew most Chinese men who had never married before would not like to marry an older woman with kids. They would feel short-changed.

"But those things didn't matter to me before I came," Woolan continued, not answering her question directly.

"How did you meet her?"

"Oh, she was a tourist. That day I went to Yi-He-Yuan..."

"The imperial summer palace of Manchu Dynasty's Empress Dowager. I wish to visit that one day," Ying Ying interrupted him.

"Yes. I bumped into a group of tourists from America. I walked up to make conversations with the few Chinese in that group. There was this nice lady. We seemed to hit it off pretty well. I offered to take her to places not included in her group's itinerary. That's how we met. The next two days I showed her around. She was happy. I actually had a good time too. I told her that I wished to go to America and she said she would try to help me."

"So she decided to marry you in order to get you here?"

"The decision did not come immediately. She tried various ways for a month, without success. Marriage was the last resort, she said. But it was a serious commitment. I gave it a lot of thought. In normal circumstances I probably would not have agreed so lightly. But in that situation, I wanted to leave China so badly that I was willing to sell my body and soul to the devil, so to speak, in exchange." Woolan reminisced, spoken in a solemn tone.

"But she is not a devil." Ying Ying chuckled.

"No. Marrying her did not seem bad at all. She is a nice lady." Woolan paused for a second, contemplating, then reiterated his point. "Yes, I would marry her as long as she could get me to America."

"Was it a simple process to get here?"

"Well, we had to convince the immigration officer that we were really getting married, not using marriage as a pretext. She had to go back and forth between Boston and Beijing several times to establish evidence that we were fiancés. There were a lot of things to do, documents to prepare. It was a difficult process." He paused a short while again, and continued:

"You see, I am not working; I have all these nice clothes and free time. They are all her gifts. She pays for my apartment and all my bills; buys things for me all the time; gives me more money than I need. She has a very successful, profitable business on Newbury Street. She is not stingy about money. I guess I should be content being with her. But I am not. I have my dreams."

"I see. That makes sense. But you are not really married to her."

"Oh. We did consummate the marriage. If I did not have to live with her son and mother under the same roof things might be a little different. Living with them was frightfully awkward for me. Her mother looks at me with scornful eyes, I believe. The old lady says nothing. But I can read her mind. Her boy often wants to sleep in the same room with his mother. He resents me. She is very nice to me, generous with money. But I feel like a pet. And I am not content with being a kept man. I have my dreams and dignity."

"So you left her."

"She noticed my restlessness and let me move out. Of course I couldn't afford to pay my expenses. She pays my rent and all the bills; buys things for me all the time; and constantly gives me spending money, more than I need. She said she would give me back my freedom as soon as the Immigration Office granted me a green card. I suppose in a few more months I will have it. Then we will get our divorce."

"She is well to do? What does she do for work?"

"She has a very successful, profitable business on Newbury Street."

"She has made a lot of sacrifices for you. She must be really in love with you. Helping someone is one thing, going into such extend, through a marriage and divorce for a total stranger, is quite another," Ying Ying commented. She did not say what she was thinking: *Of course, this twenty-seven-year-old guy is a handsome devil. That forty some year old woman must have been infatuated with him. Did she think that she could actually keep her trophy?*

"Yes, I am beholden to her," Woolan muttered in a low voice as if to himself. For a moment he was lost in deep thought remembering his life back home. He felt a need to tell Ying Ying more of his story.

"Unlike you people in Taiwan, we mainlanders mostly have the most extraordinary experiences that shaped our characters and outlooks. Because my grandfather on my mother's side was a wealthy industrialist from Shanghai and my father was a son of a large landowner in Inner Mongolia I belonged to the hated, despised class labeled as 'Five Categories of Blacks' that was equivalent to criminals.

"I was not allowed to join the Red Guard.

"I was stoned by other kids.

"I was ordered to stay away from my parents.

"The Party cadre in the community demanded that I must drew a sharp demarcation line between myself and my parents."

"How terrible." Ying Ying interrupted.

"My parents were imprisoned. Consequently my father died in jail. My mother and I were sent to two different distant provinces to work in the Reform-Through-Labor camps in the countryside. We didn't know where the other was, much less how to contact each other."

Ying Ying listened in silence.

"I was sent to work in a brick factory that summer. The scorching heat of the kilns could almost set you on fire. All workmen there only covered our private parts with loincloths because there was no way we could wear more than that. We were dirty and chocked by clay dust. And we worked seven days a week and twelve hours a day with only short breaks for meals. " He pauses for a second. "Eventually I plotted to escape."

"And you succeeded," Ying Ying interjected.

"One night while going out to relieve myself I looked around to make sure no one noticed me. Then I made a run for a near-by mountain and hid there for days without food. I could have saved up some scraps of the corn bun from my daily ration, but I couldn't hide it in my loincloth," he chuckled. Ying Ying chuckled with him.

"When I was relatively certain that the factory leader had given up on searching for me I came out at night and furtively stalked to a farmer's thatched hut. I begged for help. Those simple and kind folks were sympathetic toward me. They gave me some old raggedy clothes and hid me in their hut for a few more days. Then they packed a few corn-buns for me, and took me to another village through a rarely treaded path. All the time he was looking over his shoulder to be sure no one saw us. The authorities never found me." Woolan let out a sigh.

"How could they not find you? I heard that China was extremely watchful on people's whereabouts. They kept everybody's record. No one was permitted to move without the Party's permission. Not so?" Ying Ying inquired.

"Yes. But China is such a large country. You can hide if you really want to. It's just that you would have no ration for food. No chance for a job assignment. You didn't exist. I hid in the villages doing odd jobs. The farmers could always use extra help, especially one able-bodied, adaptable, handy young guy like me. So I could earn two simple meals a day without much

30

difficulty. After two years I moved to the village outside of Beijing waiting for an opportunity to sneak back into the city. Gradually I was able to ingratiate myself with some high-up, important people and lived a pretty normal life, by Chinese people's standards."

"High-up people? Do you mean the party cadres?"

"Oh, shall I say, the daughters… and sons of some people in power." He was apparently a little abashed. Ying Ying sensed his hesitance and did not pursue further. *He must have romanced some powerful people's daughters.* She smiled understandingly.

"Huh." He knew what Ying Ying was thinking. "In China, you know, moral conduct between men and women was stringently observed. The most we did was walking in the park, having a picnic, or going to movies."

"I know. It's the same in Taiwan. If a guy goes out with different girls to the park. picnic or movies his reputation would be marred. He would be labeled as "a floor mop." Ying Ying insinuated that Woolan's reputation might not have been intact.

"You had to be discreet, of course. It required tact." He was slow in picking up Ying Ying's implication and honestly confessed his conducts.

"You mean you have to deceive them." They both laughed. Then Ying Ying wondered about the actual process of his emigration.

"But how did you get a passport if you did not exist?"

"After the down-fall of the Gang of Four people like me came out of hiding and were rehabilitated. I regained my legal identity. So I was a living person again. With the help of the lady's money, getting a passport was 'a dish of humble vegetable' to use a Beijing slang."

"People here would say 'a piece of cake.'" Ying Ying picked a perfect parallel for that Chinese expression. "In other words you bought your way? All the time I thought Mao Zedong had cleansed out all social diseases in China; people were politically, socially, economically equal; there was no corruption, prostitution, burglary or beggary. But what you just told me indicated bribery still existed."

"Money opens back doors." Woolan relived the months when he tactfully bribed an official to get him the passport. "My next step now is to make money. Lots of money."

"Making a lot of money is never my goal." Ying Ying only said this much and kept the rest to herself: *There are more lofty things to pursue. Historically and traditionally Chinese society disdained those who focused their mind on nothing but money-making: Money was referred to as 'stinky bronze coin.' Has that changed?*

It was 3:00pm. Dr. Joseph Lee should be back from his meeting by now.

"Woolan, please feel free to go home when you are ready. I am going to see if Dr. Lee has something for me to do." Then she strode back to her office.

*   *   *   *

Ying Ying passed Denis in the hallway. He said:

"Ying Ying, I was looking for you. Where have you been? There is another artist here waiting to see you."

"I was in the workshop. Has the artist waited for long? Is he in my office?" Ying Ying sped up her steps. In her office was an artist she had never met.

"I am Fang Ying Ying," she introduced herself.

"Meng Song." The artist also introduced himself.

"Oh, you are the one Dr. Lee asked me to call."

Joseph Lee had seen Meng Song's work at Hansen gallery and decided to include him in the exhibit he was curating. He told Ying Ying to find out the artist's contact information. It took her many calls and spoke with several people before she got his name and number. Then she tried four times before a voice appeared on the other end.

"I am trying to find Meng Song. Is he there?" Ying Ying asked.

"This is Meng Song."

"Thank God. I finally reached you. It was not easy to track you down."

"I am in the process of moving. This is my last trip back to this place. I was just about to step out the door. If you had called one minute later you would have missed me."

"Then I would never find you."

"Right."

"I am calling from China Society. Our Curator, Dr. Joseph Lee, saw your work and would like to include you in a new show we are planning."

"Oh. What kind of a show?" He asked nonchalantly.

"The purpose of the show is to explore the tendencies of art in China today after the Cultural Revolution. Dr. Lee is interested in showing paintings by artists from different regions in China. He likes your work. Can you bring some pieces to us? He will choose a few from each artist."

"Ah,... All right." He sounded reluctant. "After I get my apartment straightened out. It's a big mess there. You see, I am still moving."

He was not at all excited about being chosen.

Pretty conceited, Ying Ying thought. *Every other artist was thrilled. These artists were new and unknown. How often would galleries offer them outright opportunities to exhibit? How many galleries in Boston showcase Chinese artists? Practically none. Yes, he is exceptionally fortunate to be included in one show by Hanson gallery. It might be why he does not think too much of this invitation.*

Ying Ying didn't hear from Meng Song for weeks after that. She could not find him because he had left no phone number or address. She asked the other artists if they knew his whereabouts. But no one seemed to have heard of this Meng Song. Without a choice, Joseph Lee scratched his name from the exhibitors list.

But he showed up again unannounced. Unexpectedly.

"I came here to take a look at your gallery. I haven't brought my paintings because I don't have a car. I have to ask a friend to help," the soft-spoken artist said.

"Oh, okay. But before I take you to see the gallery would you please write down your name, phone number and address so that we can contact you in the future?" Ying Ying smiled as she thought about how difficult it was to get hold of this artist. She handed him a pen and a piece of paper. He scribbled something on it, stopped and handed the paper and pen back.

"I .. I can't spell it. The phone number is enough."

Ying Ying looked at the piece of paper and saw two Chinese characters, the phone number and half of an English word. The characters were his name, naturally.

"You did not write in simplified Chinese." Ying Ying was amazed, as all other people from China wrote in the simplified form coined in China decades before.

"I write calligraphy. I don't use the simplified form," Meng Song stated plainly and simply. "Is there anything else?"

Aloof and cold, Ying YIng thought. This artist's strangely apathetic attitude made Ying Ying feel a little uneasy. She did not make any casual remark like she often did with artists.

"No. I will take you to see the gallery."

The gallery passed Meng Song's critical examination. He promised to deliver a few paintings as soon as he could.

*   *   *   *

A month before the show opened, the announcements were printed. Ying Ying, Tonia and another new work-study student, Jenny, began to hand-address the envelopes and sort them by zip codes. There were over fifteen hundred envelops to address. It took them days to do it. The Trustees insisted that hand addressed mail would get more attention.

"It gives a little more personal touch. I would not open a piece of mail with a computer-generated label. I consider it junk and throw it away," Mrs. Jenkins said. Some Trustees would either come to the office or take some announcements home to address and write personal notes to their friends.

Dr. Lee viewed every piece of painting carefully and made his final selections. Denis wrote the press release, Ying Ying wrote the wall texts and labeling cards. Jenny was given the job of dry-mounting the wall texts and labels; Tonia was to prepare the press kits and send it to various newspapers, radio- and TV stations, and then follow up with phone calls.

Like Tonia, Jenny was also an American-born Chinese, a nineteen-year-old sophomore from Tufts University. She just declared her major in theatre arts and wished to be a stage designer. A stunningly gorgeous girl, her tiny waist, slender figure, luxuriant long hair and striking facial features never escaped people's eyes. They described her as a unique beauty 'possessing the best of the Asian and the Caucasian women.' Yet she was not a Eurasian, but a hundred percent Chinese. Not only men adored her but women as well. Her subtle smile would brighten up a room and arouse wistful yearnings in men's hearts and friendly warmth in women. Her presence at China Society's office stirred quite a bit of commotion. People whispered; mooned over her when she did not notice. Dr. Lee had to warn people not to be too distracted. Despite all the attention, she had not the slightest shred of presumption, as if all was normal. She was friendly, yet never flirtatious to people, and serious about her job.

She grew up in a pretty insulated environment. Living in a small town in New Hampshire near Dartmouth College where her parent taught, she was the only Asian kid in her elementary and secondary schools. Her father was an internationally renowned scientist and her mother was a well-published, highly respected writer.

Racial discrimination and prejudice were foreign to her. If she was treated differently in any way, it was her teacher's impartiality toward her because of her academic performance, her intelligence and her behavior. The kids in her school liked her because she was pleasant, friendly and generous. She fitted in comfortably and perfectly.

It was after she entered college in Boston, when Asian students asked her to join their association, that she was struck by the issue of ethnicity.

All Asian- and Asian American students belonged to this loosely formed, all-encompassing student organization. When Jenny was asked to join she coldly declined. Some Chinese guys in the school tried to ask her out. She rejected them with the same aloofness. She distanced herself from all the Asian students. People were mystified by her attitude and began to criticize her.

"Just because she is beautiful doesn't mean she has to behave like a prima Donna," some said.

"She seems to have a problem with Asians. I wonder why," others said.

For the first time Jenny left people with a bad impression. She never let anyone knew why she behaved that way. She did not feel that she belonged to that group. Furthermore, she purposely put a barrier between herself and the Asians, especially the Chinese.

She drew much attention from the non-Asian guys in the school too, no doubt. They referred to her as a "gorgeous China doll," or an "exotic beauty." That infuriated her beyond anyone's imagination.

When her father's friend Andrew Johnson, Chairman of China Society, persuaded her to do her work-study at his organization her immediate reaction was aversion. Yet Johnson's characterization of the organization's programs and activities eventually roused some interest in her. She agreed to try it. After joining the organization she developed a liking for the people there. Eventually she stayed with the program throughout her undergraduate years.

"In high school no one called me those things. I don't understand what happened in college," she confessed to Denis." I was treated no differently from the other kids in high school even though I was the only non-Caucasian there. In Boston there are Chinese everywhere, why am I called exotic?"

"Because most girls are not as beautiful as you are. Most men are visually focused. It's not hard to understand why guys are captivated by you. And when they talk about you, believe me, they must have talked about you a lot. They like to daub some colorful description for flavoring, I suppose." Denis grinned. "And you are different from the whites and the blacks. So I suppose 'exotic' is a fitting description."

"Oh, come on Denis, you are making fun of me." Jenny complained.

At age fifteen Jenny had a high school sweetheart. Kids at that age rarely kept steady friends of the opposite gender. A few weeks were as long as their interests would sustain. Jenny and her boyfriend Michael, on the other hand, were sweethearts from the time they met till college. They were two pure, innocent kids. Some people thought they were brother and sister despite that Michael was a European American. Jenny's parents were very fond of the boy and thought if the two youngsters were to marry when they grew up they would have no objection. Michael was genuinely dedicated to Jenny and treated her like his princess. Neither of them dated another person throughout their high school years. After high school Michael entered MIT and Jenny entered Tufts. They managed to get together as often as possible. Sometimes they just spent a quiet evening together doing homeworks.

There was another young man, Sean, at Tufts University, a computer science and electrical engineering major. He saw Jenny on campus. Without even speaking to her or introducing himself he fell head over heels in love with her. He had seen Michael picking her up after school a few times and felt his chances were nil. He told his father about his love-sickness.

"I saw this extremely beautiful girl on campus. What a real knock out!! I can't help falling in love with her."

"That is good. I am happy for you," his father said.

"But she has a boyfriend. I have no chance," Sean said resignedly.

"Nonsense. You are not letting her boyfriend stop you! Go for it. Even if she is engaged or married, if you truly love her, go after her. You may win her over." These encouraging words gave Sean impetus.

Sean walked up to Jenny when he saw her on campus again.

"Hi, how are you doing?" he grinned pleasantly.

"I am doing okay," Jenny smiled. It melted Sean's heart.

"Can I walk with you?" He asked.

"I suppose!" Jenny replied.

"Thank you." Sean walked next to her. "I saw you many times on Campus. I think you are extremely beautiful."

Jenny's face beamed with sweetness. Her long exuberant hair wafted in the gentle breeze. Her well-formed slender figure moved in beauty. She did not speak. But the few words she had uttered so far were lovely music to Sean. He swooned as he strode alongside of her.

From this day on Sean slowly, patiently, carefully pursued Jenny, trying to win her heart with his gentle love. Jenny felt easy and comfortable with him. They began to go to the movies, have lunches, study in the library, or saunter on the campus ground together. Jenny realized that she was in a love triangle. Michael and Sean were both deeply in love with her and dedicated to her. She and Michael had five years of history. She was Michael's first love. Sean had never loved a girl like he did Jenny, his first true love. They weighed equally on the scale. She wished not to tip the equilibrium. She did not want to lose either of them.

*　　　*　　　*　　　*

Another new work-study student, Yan, came to China Society from Mass College of Art. Yan was a twenty-year-old girl from Hong Kong. She told Ying Ying:

"I was looking for a place to do work-study and I found China Society. I thought this was exactly what I wanted. I am interested in learning how to mount art exhibits and gallery management."

"That's very good. You certainly can learn those things here. I'll take you to see our supervisor, I am a work-study student myself. So he should be the one to give you guidance." Ying Ying walked Yan to Denis's office.

"What do you think mounting an art show involves?" Denis asked Yan during the interview.

"I don't know. Just hang the paintings up on the wall, or put 3D objects in display cases and on pedestals, I guess," Yan replied.

"That is right. But there is so much more to it. I will give you a brief summary. If you still want to work here we will take you."

"Yes, Yes. Tell me about it. I am sure I will want to work here." Yan earnestly claimed:

"An art exhibit starts with choosing a topic or a theme. Over here it is the job of our Curator, Dr. Lee. Then we announce a call-to-artists. From the entries artists send in Dr. Lee will select certain number of artists. If the artists are local he usually makes studio visits to select the work to be shown. If he doesn't visit the studios he selects from the slides. When the artworks are delivered we must make condition reports, prepare a price list, and press kits. We also must publish a catalogue and prepare wall texts and signs, printing and mailing announcements, laying out the show, hanging the show, preparing an opening reception, etc.. These are all part of mounting a show. The public only sees one art show after another at the gallery. They are rarely aware of the process that goes behind each show."

"That sounds exciting. What can I do now?" Yan asked.

"Jenny is going to dry mount the wall text. Perhaps she can observe and learn how to do that," Ying Ying suggested to Denis.

"Oh, good, good. I love that. I will learn that." Yan was excited and clapped her hands like a child.

Ying Ying went to get Jenny to meet Yan.

"I am going to do the dry mounting on Wednesday. If you want to do it with me you have to be here no later than 10am," Jenny said to Yan.

"Oh, yes, I will be here. I will do it." Her enthusiasm abounded.

Despite her zeal Yan did not show up on Wednesday. Jenny proceeded with her scheduled task without thinking about Yan. On Friday Yan showed up.

She was greatly upset to know that Jenny had already finished doing dry mounting. She shrieked:

"What? You did it already? Why didn't you wait for me?"

"It was not a training session, Yan. It's a real job. We have schedules to keep. It had to be done on Wednesday. I could not wait for you," Jenny said.

Yan burst out crying. "But I came here to learn how to dry mount. You did not give me that chance. Why am I here?" She screamed louder, stumped her feet and cried.

Denis and Ying Ying heard it and came over to inquire. When they heard the story Denis said:

"Why didn't you come on Wednesday? Work-study is no different from a regular job. You are being paid. You cannot come and go as you like. Didn't you know that?"

Ying Ying said softly: "Yan. We are very sorry that you missed the chance to learn it. But there will be other opportunities. Jenny told you that she had to do it on Wednesday. You should have come on Wednesday. We got to get things done on time. You must understand that."

Yan did not understand. She continued to yell and cry: "I don't want other opportunities. I came this time just to learn that. You are not treating me right. I am not going to come back." She stormed out of the door.

Denis had the duty to send evaluations and reports on work-study student's performances to their schools. It was certainly very difficult for him to write those about Yan.

There is one other work-study student, Missy, from MIT who just joined China Society. She was a junior, majoring in physics. She chose to do her work-study at China Society to reconnect with her cultural and ethnic background. Her parents emigrated from Taiwan and settled in San Francisco when Missy and her brother were in junior high school. Her parents did not belong to the wealthy-and-leisurely class. They operated a teashop in San Francisco. Missy and her brother had to help the parents in the shop after school. A sense of duty and responsibility were firmly planted in their young minds. Missy turned out to be a very efficient and reliable worker at China Society.

*   *   *   *

Meng Song didn't deliver his artwork until after the deadline. A girl chauffeured him to the gallery and helped move his paintings in and leaned them against the gallery wall. He walked around to quickly scan other artists' pieces. From his reticence and the apparent apathetic look on his face Ying Ying perspicaciously sensed that he didn't feel he was in good company. Yet she did not express her personal opinion.

"I am going to New York today. I may be back in time for the opening." Meng Song slightly nodded and left.

Dr. Joseph Lee accepted all the pieces Meng Song had brought in. He made a final layout of the show and left the rest to the staff.

Food for the opening reception was catered. Several cases of wine donated by Trustee Mrs. Harrison were delivered from Brookline Liquor Mart. Bouquets of flowers ordered by another trustee were sent from her favorite florist on Newbury Street. Tables covered with white linen and skirts were adorned with glistening silver candelabras. Next to the fine porcelain plates, glass stemware and sterling flatware were nicely arranged; napkins printed with China Society's name and logo were neatly stacked . Waiters and waitresses in uniforms holding wine or hors d'oeuvres on small trays weaved among the guests. China Society's openings were always elegant and lavish. That was what the Trustees wanted.

There were twenty artists featured in this show. They came from some of the major art centers in China including Beijing, Shanghai, Hangzhou, Xi'an, Guangzhou, and Chengdu. Each artist's style was different. Collectively they epitomized the art milieu in China after 1977, the end of the Cultural Revolution.

The exhibiting artists arrived early, all except Meng Song. They dressed nicely for the occasion. Everyone wore a cheerful smirk on their face. They carefully looked at all the works on view and of course pay more attention to their own. When guests gradually filled the gallery the artists engaged themselves in enthusiastic discussions with some of them. Among the guests were the Trustees and their friends, those high brow wealthy ladies and gentlemen from the elite circles. Then there were friends of the artists, staff of International Foundation and China Society, and their friends. As usual, there were many regular gallery goers from the mailing list. Everyone spent a little time quickly viewing the exhibit. Then they broke into small groups, chatting about everything but the artworks on the wall. While Pei-hua, Ying Ying, Denis and the other staff member were obligated to greet the guests, they enjoy chatting with their personal friends and meeting the people brought by those friends more.

Woolan entered the gallery with a very fashionably dressed beautiful Chinese woman. They made a beeline for Ying Ying and the circle of people with whom she was chatting. He enthusiastically introduced the woman as Liang Meilan, and emphatically stressed that she was a big movie star and top popular singer from China.

"Wow, a celebrity," Pei-hua exclaimed.

"We are honored to have a celebrity among us," Ying Ying said. Meilan gave a dazzling smile showing her gleaming pearl-like teeth and said:

"I am only another Chinese girl here." But there was a haughty air about her that belied her seemingly humble remark.

When she learned that Ying Ying and Pei-hua were from Taiwan she sprightly remarked:

"I suppose people in Taiwan are not living in 'deep-water-and-burning-fire' like our propaganda led us to believe. That was in the past though. Now your singing star Deng Li-jun has swept across the whole of China. She is being regarded as the Little Deng versus Deng Xiao-ping, the Big Deng. I sing a lot of her songs."

"Deng Li-jun is more popular in the Mainland than she is in Taiwan because her style is so different from the singers in the Mainland and she is the first from outside to be heard there. This is what people have told me. I suppose it's true. In Taiwan, she is only one of many famous pop singers," Pei-hua explained.

Many people eagerly shook Meilan's hand and told her how much they admired her, and how happy, almost ecstatic, they were to have the chance to meet her. These were her fans from China. One of the exhibiting artists, Zhang Ze, peered at another knot of people surrounding Joseph Lee and saw his friend Li Yong, a theatre arts student at Boston University. When he caught Li Yong's eyes he gestured for him to come over. Li Yong found an opportunity to excuse himself and moved to Zhang Ze. He was introduced to everyone in the circle. They exchanged a few polite words. Then Li Yong turned to Meilan and said:

"Everyone must have felt honored to meet you, Miss Liang. There are many of your fans in this room, including me."

Meilan was pleased. "It is so nice to meet so many fans here. I should thank them for their loyalty. The Chinese audience is so loyal to me." She paused a second to look around the gallery to see how many Chinese were present. Then she absently asked: "You are going to be an actor?"

"I hope to be one," Li Yong replied, unassumingly.

"He is in *Romeo and Juliet* at the Huntington Theatre." Zhang Ze proudly brought everyone's attention to his friend's unusual accomplishment for a foreign student with very limited English.

"Oh, that's very nice," Meilan drawled in a patronizing voice and slanted a glare at Li Yong.

"My gosh. That's cool. What role are you playing? Romeo?" Pei-hua exclaimed zealously.

"Yes," Li Yong answered reservedly. Then he chuckled. "I had to read the Chinese translation to know what my lines were about."

"You don't know English?" Pei-hua was surprised.

"Just a little bit, far from enough to understand the script or the lectures in the classroom."

"Boy, that's something, isn't it?" Pei-hua's eyes glinted with amazement.

"How did you pass the audition then?" inquisitively Ying Ying asked.

"I read the Chinese translation before memorizing a piece of monologue. I guess my acting was okay. So they picked me."

"Just okay? You must have been phenomenal. You defeated all the other candidates, whom I assume spoke fluent English and fit the popular image of Romeo better than a Chinese," Pei-hua added admiringly

"Yes, you are right about them." Li Yong agreed to Pei-hua's point about the other actors, but modestly ignored her praise.

"What school were you from? Were you already an actor in China?" Meilan asked.

"Shanghai Drama Institute. Yea, after graduation I acted on stage and TV."

"No wonder," Meilan stated with authority. She turned to Ying Ying and Pei-hua: "If he was an actor in China he had to be good. China has the best, the most vigorous training for their actors, singers, dancers, and athletes. You name it. Chinese talents are superior to others in the world. We can win every kind of competition." Meilan cocked her head and brushed her long hair over her shoulder while giving her speech in unreserved pride.

"We are doing all right." Li Yong toned Meilan's theatrical down a notch.

Pei-hua brooded over her unfulfilled aspiration for an acting career.

"How did you become an actor?" she asked.

"I was an actor since age eleven. No, no, correction. I was picked by Beijing Opera Company at eleven. Years later I was accepted by Shanghai Drama Institute. After graduation my department kept me as a teaching assistant. At the same time I acted in a good number of major productions," Li Yong answered.

"Your parents had no objection to your choice? They let you quit school at eleven?" It seemed extraordinary to Pei-hua.

"In China, the parents have no say in their children's careers. The government and fate do. My parents belong to the ignominious *hei-wu-lei*, the Five Categories of Blacks..."

Ying Ying cut him off and said: "You too?" Because Woolan's parents were labeled the same.

Meilan did not wait for Li Yong to answer. She did it for him. "Many people were. If you were not from the classes of soldiers, peasants or workers, you would likely be one of the Five Blacks. Then you would be doomed."

Li Yong took over and said: "My father was a professor at that time. We had relatives abroad. That made us one of the "Five Categories of Blacks." I was sent to help build roads at age ten. When I was eleven, Beijing Opera Company sent for some kids in my work unit to audition. I was not being called but I went to watch. A comrade in the Opera Company noticed me. He asked me to sing a song. I sang the song I learned while building the road. They liked it and told me to stay. I was lucky."

Pei-hua was captivated by Li Yong's story. "That is fascinating. From a little road builder to a Peking opera singer, to a lead actor in America."

"I was not really a Beijing Opera singer. I did the martial arts roles, a lot of tumbling and somersaults because my voice changed at age fourteen so I could not play the female roles I studied for anymore. You see, I could not sing soprano after my voice changed." Traditionally, female roles in Beijing Opera were played by male actors.

Ying Ying had heard many stories from the Mainlanders. She said to Pei hua:

"These guys from the Mainland, every one of them has an interesting story to tell. Their lives have many incredible turns. Ours seem so bland, so boring. This tenor, Zheng Bin, has a tremendous voice, you have to hear him sing. He said his troupe, --- They called it Central Song and Dance Troupe. uh, what an ugly name! --- sent singers and dancers to entertain the peasants and solders. He was trained to sing Western opera and Chinese art songs. The peasants and soldiers had no taste for that type of music and the way he sang. His program was always inserted, as an extra, between the highly appreciated Chinese folk dances and folk songs. The audience always shouted at him: 'Get off, get off.' But he couldn't. He would be punished by the leader of the troupe if he did. He had to keep singing. That annoyed the audience who resorted to throwing cabbages and turnips at him." Everyone laughed.

Meilan said: "That was not a joke. It happened all the time."

"When Miss Liang is on stage the audience is intoxicated. They cannot get enough of her," Woolan emphatically reported.

"That is true." Li Young added.

*   *   *   *

At this point Meng Song appeared at the door, a blonde on his arm. Ying Ying noticed it was not the same girl who had helped him move the paintings. He glanced around and decided not to join any group. A waiter holding a tray walked toward him. He took two glasses of wine, giving one to his companion and sipped on the other himself. He then strode toward the fruit table and took a small plateful of strawberries and grapes to share with the blonde girl. Then they sat by an ice cream table at a corner. Joseph Lee spotted them and walked up to greet them.

"Song. I am glad you've made it. This is…?" He extended a hand to the blonde.

"Vicky." The girl introduced herself with a smile.

"Pleasure to meet you, Vicky. I am Joe, the curator of this show."

"He is Dr. Lee." Song added plainly.

"It's my pleasure to meet you, Dr. Lee." There was a mixture of excitement and reverence in Vickie's voice and expression.

"Come, join the other guests. Don't just sit here by yourselves. Come on." Joseph Lee led them to one circle of people and introduced them to some people:

"This is Dr. Herald Schmidt, The president of the Foundation. This is Mr. Andrew Johnson, a Trustee of the Foundation. This is Meng Song, our favorite artist. And this is Vicky." They shook hands.

"We have seen your paintings before today," Herald Schmidt said.

"Yes, we admired your work and would like to collect a piece or two," Andrew Johnson said.

Andrew Johnson, a wealthy, successful industrialist, marveled at Meng Song's designs and colors. He asked many questions about the artistic milieu in China; how Song learned the vocabularies of modern art and used them so fluently. Song was not able to understand all of his questions, much less give his answers in English. Joseph Lee thus acted as an interpreter for them. Meng Song's easy mannerism and calm speech invariably impressed the people standing around him. Other knots of people nearby turned their heads or walked over to listen to him although they couldn't understand a word he was saying without Joseph Lee's translation.

Meilan noticed the swarm of people, surrounding a young man instead of her. She slid a gaze over to where Song was standing and rested her eyes on him for more than a second.

"Who is that boy?" she demanded.

"Him? An artist. His work has already attracted lots of attention," Ying Ying replied matter-of-factly.

"Oh? Which ones are his paintings?" Meilan looked around with curiosity.

"Do you want to take a closer look? I will show you," Ying Ying offered. Meilan ignored Ying Ying's question and began to walk toward the wall. Like her retinue, Ying Ying, Pei-hua and Woolan followed closely. Ying Ying pointed to Meng Song's paintings. "These are his works."

Meilan fixed her gaze on each piece for a moment and did not try to hide her contempt. "These paintings? I can't see what's so good about them."

Ying Ying smiled. She was used to such remarks from people ignorant about contemporary paintings. "Yes, many people feel that way. It's because they don't understand modern art. They don't know how to appreciate it."

"I don't understand it. Do you? What was he trying to paint? What does it mean?"

"His is abstract art. You don't read meanings into the shapes and forms."

Ying Ying knew this answer made no sense to Meilan. But this was not the time to elaborate on abstract art. Or was Meilan interested in hearing it.

"I would like to meet that painter-boy." She slanted another glance in Song's direction. She was not about to go over to meet him but expected him to come and meet her, because she was a shining movie star from China. Ying Ying sensed that but did nothing. She couldn't very well barge in to pull Song away from those people. They had to wait for an opportune time. That time came when she intentionally and imperceptibly steered Meilan toward Song's set of four pieces near where he was standing. She did her very best to talk about that set to Meilan, not to interest her but to catch Song's attention. Hearing Ying Ying making a pitch for his work Meng Song turned around and grinned at her. Ying Ying grabbed the opportunity to make her request.

"Song, when you have a chance I'd like you to meet Miss Liang Meilan." Song nodded and turned his head back to his group. Meilan was exasperated at his apparent distrait manner upon hearing her name.

"I thought this boy was from China," she stated in an irate tone.

"Yes, he's from Shanghai," Ying Ying said, innocently.

"Hmm... How could he not..." Meilan couldn't understand why Song did not adulate her like everyone else. *He couldn't be unfamiliar with my name. Over a billion people in China admire me, worship me, love me.*

Woolan, Pei-hua and Li Yong wandered over to join Meilan and Ying Ying again when Meng Song extracted himself from the other knot to meet Meilan. After the introduction Meng Song politely said, "hello, Miss Liang." He was aloof and not impressed by Meilan's celebrity status. Meilan's displeasure escalated.

"So you are the famous great artist." Meilan said jeeringly in a caustic tone.

"No, I am not as famous as you, Miss Liang," Meng Song answered sardonically. He was quick in picking up signs of emotion and responded accordingly.

"Am I famous? But you don't know me," Meilan shot an acrid retaliation.

"Yes, I do know you. Who in China doesn't know you?" Song's equally acrimonious remark abraded Meilan to ire. She was about to blurt a revengeful remark. Woolan quickly interjected a downright avid sycophancy to divert the tension and placate her.

"Miss Liang is truly the most beloved singer and movie star in China. She has several platinum records to her credit, each sold tens of millions of copies. She has just been awarded the highest honor, Top Ten People's Artists of many decades." He turned to Meilan and continued. "People in every corner listen to your songs and watch your movies. We are waiting for your new movies. When are you going to make one in Hollywood?" Sincerity was written on his face and exuded from his voice.

Meilan accepted his adulation as a matter of course. She smiled smugly, took a sip of her wine, and casually disposed of the question with her lilting voice:

"Hollywood? Oh, yes. There are offers. But I have not decided which one to accept yet."

To please her further Woolan urged Ying Ying to introduce her to the "Big Heads," meaning the president and trustees of the Foundation.

"Yes, I was just thinking about doing that." Ying Ying said. "Would you excuse me." She went and asked Joseph Lee to come over. He in turn asked Herald Schmidt and Andrew Johnson to meet Meilan.

"What brought you to Boston, to America, Miss Liang?" Andrew Johnson asked with polite curiosity. Ying Ying translated the question for Meilan.

Meilan delightfully told her story: "I came because I liked America. It is the greatest nation in the world. We Chinese people think America is a land of dreams. And Boston, that's where Harvard and MIT are. It's a cultural Mecca. Everyone likes to come to America. But it isn't easy. Only those with special contacts are able to. Even I had to go through a lot to get a passport, not to mention the visa. Then you have to figure out how to bring your money out. The government only allows each person to bring thirty u.s. dollar abroad. Thirty dollars! It only lasts the first day after you land in America. If you don't have anybody to help you, you will starve and sleep in the street the second day. China has been economically impoverished for decades. The government needed to conserve U.S. dollars because it is the international currency "

"Why only thirty dollars? Does the government know that it would not last more than a day?" Herald Schmidt asked.

"Yes, the government knows. The thirty dollars is just for the first day. Because the government requires everyone to have a financial sponsor abroad."

"Does everyone really have a financial sponsor here?" Herald asked again.

"Yes. Everyone must have a sponsor in order to be permitted to leave the country. Without a sponsor the U.S. consulate would not give a visa either," Meilan further explained.

"Who are the sponsors? Are they 100% responsible for the student's financial needs?" Andrew Johnson asked this very intriguing and important question.

"In principle, yes. But not always so in reality," Meilan replied. Joseph Lee picked it up and expounded further: "The U. S. government rightfully took the precaution to prevent foreigners from entering the country penniless to become a social charge immediately. However, this measure never really worked. The sponsors are often not relatives of the students but rather nice people who are willing to help the students to come. Their sponsorship is only titular, not real. Except for a few extraordinary cases, the sponsor and the beneficiary had a mutual understanding that the former was not financially responsible. The so-called sponsorship was only to fulfill a requirement of the Immigration Office. While all the students coming from China knew it the Office of the U.S. Immigration and naturalization Service did not."

"How so?" Pei-hua asked.

"Many of the sponsors are American tourists, very kind people who are sympathetic toward the Chinese they meet. They are willing to do a lot to help them. But they are unable to lay out that much money for a stranger. Of course there are sponsors who actually do support the beneficiaries. But that is exceptional," Meilan explained.

Tourists!! Woolan's story popped up in Ying Ying's mind. She also remembered one American woman's story. She met a Chinese artist while traveling in China. He asked her to help him go to America to study. The woman, also an artist, liked his work and agreed to help him. He had no family, friends, or money in this foreign land. Once here he automatically became her responsibility. She put him in her parents' house, temporarily, she thought. But one week became one month, two months.... Five months had passed yet he had made no plan to move out.

"What about the sponsors being forced to pay? Did they sign any legal documents?" Pei-hua being a law student naturally would think about the legal ramifications.

"Not legal documents exactly, but letters to the Immigration Office and the U.S. consulate. Those could be construed as legal documents," Meilan said.

"No, if they are not written as legal documents by a lawyer and signed by witnesses, they don't hold up in the court of law. Circumstances may change to prevent the sponsor from fulfilling the financial obligation he promised. And the judge cannot and will not force him to," Pei-hua explained.

"But people don't know that. Some thought they were bound by it. Some did end up in lawsuits." Joseph Lee argued.

"I doubt the plaintiff would win though," Pei-hua insisted.

"However I have heard of a case in which the sponsor lost," Ying Ying put in: "A mean-spirited Chinese student demanded that the sponsor support him because it was written in the letter he used to obtain his visa. When the couple refused, he took them to court. The couple feared to divulge the truth that would have made their good intention into a criminal act of conspiring to cheat America. Consequently, the court ruled against them. It was very sad." Ying Ying sighed.

"I believe that was not widespread," Joseph Lee tersely ended the subject. He did not wish this subject to be the focus of conversation. It was too heavy, too serious, and embarrassing to all Chinese.

Andrew Johnson was very interested in Meilan's story, as well as in her, an attractive woman, a movie star from China. He was among the very first American businessmen who went with President Nixon when he visited China in 1971. He gave Meilan his business card and told her to call him if she needed help.

As conversations rambled, attention turned to Li Yong.

"He is an actor. He plays Romeo in the Huntington Theatre's production of *Romeo and Juliet*." Pei-hua would not miss the opportunity to add her favorite piece of information.

"Oh, how wonderful. We should all go see the production." Herald Schmidt said with a smirk.

Li Yong thanked him gratefully.

At the end of the evening quite a few paintings were red-dotted. They were sold but the collectors had to wait till the show concluded to pick them up. Six of Meng Song's eight were reserved, including that set of four Joseph Lee loved so much. Herald Schmidt bought it. Andrew Johnson bought five others. The proceeds would support Song's tuition and living expenses for a year. Some other artists sold one or two. They were priced much lower than Meng Song's. A few artists didn't sell any.

As usual, reporters from several newspapers were present. Gallery openings were not major events by any standard. But China Society's openings were often written up in the papers and pictures of selected guests often appeared in the society sections. Meilan's pictures inevitably occupied the most eye-catching spots. Because the exhibition was a provocative one it aroused the curiosity and interests of a few TV producers who asked to interview Joseph Lee and an artist. Joseph Lee asked Meng Song to go with him. He explained to the TV audience the significance of the exhibition and discussed several samples of Song's paintings with his slides shown on the screen. This event drew quite a bit of attention fot Song from the collectors and artists communities. His two remaining pieces were sold a few days after the TV interviews were aired. The same TV shows also brought collectors to Song's studio. They also resulted in bringing collectors' attentions to other artists' works.

The day after the opening, reviews and stories appeared in newspapers in English as well as in Chinese. The largest newspaper in New England lauded the effort of China Society for mounting such a show that might be considered ground-breaking because it was the first time an important group show featured the young generation of Chinese artists from north, central and south China exploring the artistic movements, tendencies and achievements in China.

A curator from the Fine Arts Museum called to congratulate China Society and highly commended the show. He said: "I am very pleased to see that your gallery is filling the lacunae of our Museum. The museum has not only a great collection of Chinese art before the 20th century, it also has a wonderful collection of recent Chinese art but our policy prohibits showing art of living Chinese artists. Your work complements the museum's effort."

A phone call interrupted the joyous mood brought about by the success of the exhibit. Denis answered it and gave it to Ying Ying.

"You'd better answer it. The man is speaking Chinese," Denis said.

It was from the office of Taiwan government representatives in Boston. After an initial greeting the man said: "I heard that your gallery is showing communists' work." The tone was not harsh but the words sounded like a reproach. They stunned Ying Ying.

"No, sir, the artists came from the Chinese mainland but they are not communists. The exhibition is purely artistic. It has no political implications." Ying Ying politely explained though there was no need to explain. China Society was an American non-profit organization, not one backed and controlled by the Taiwan government.

"They are from the Mainland. How can you be sure that they are not communists? To exhibit them is to promote communism in China. We are very disappointed and hope you will do something about it." The man became more adamant.

"China Society's mission is to bring the arts and culture of the Chinese people to the public. It cannot exclude Mainland China. The Society is an American organization without political affinity. And I am afraid, sir, it will not be influenced politically by me or anyone else. There is nothing I can do." Ying Ying firmly stood the ground.

"Wow, what's that all about?" Denis questioned. Jennifer was befuddled by Ying Ying's remark.

"Isn't it obvious? The Taiwan officials think we are helping promote the Chinese communism."

"I suppose our show indirectly paints a positive image of the Mainland. Or at least brings China's name further to the fore. That's what Taiwan officials don't like." Denis made an accurate observation.

*   *   *   *

There were differences between the Chinese students from Taiwan and those from Mainland China. One of which was financial conditions. In the 1980s Taiwan had developed a strong economy, as one of the Four Small Dragons of Asia. The kids from that rather affluent society had no worry about money when they came to study in the States. Sometimes a parent, or both parents, would come with the child, stayed at the Ritz, the Sheraton, or one of the other high-end hotels while shopping for things he/she might need in the school year. Buying a brand new car and a house for the kid was not uncommon. Then Mom and Dad would make sure the kid was comfortably settled before they left for home. A student from China, on the other hand, would only have thirty dollars in the pocket, needed to find a job immediately, or, in rare cases, rely on the victimized sponsor's involuntary support.

A few of the artists found a good way to make money. They set up their easels, paint boxes or drawing pads in the Boston Common to do portraits for small fees. These artists had gone through vigorous training in Chinese art schools in the Soviet Socialist Realist tradition. In American art schools, since twenty some years before, training in realistic depiction had been relinquished. These Chinese artists impressed their portrait "customers" and their America colleagues. They only charged seven or eight dollars for a charcoal or pencil drawing that would take them ten minutes to do. For an oil-pastel they would charge twelve dollars. They made a nifty income just working on the Common. They did life-size or near life-size oil on canvas portraits in the subjects' homes because the artists had no studios of their own.

Some artists were content with this work. Some grunted that their true creativity was stifled.

"You cannot divide yourself into two parts. One part does this hackney commercial stuff and the other part tries to create innovative masterpieces." There were some artists, Meng Song for example, who refused to "contaminate" their mind, to work with the type of painting they despised as being trite, without artistic value.

Actors had no immediately sellable assets like the painters. The jobs they were able to get were very limited, waiting on tables was about it. For musicians the opportunities varied. A couple of exceptional opera singers won competition after competition, and were offered contracts from major opera houses. A few pianists and violinists emerged as international concert soloists. Those who did not stand out above the average, except a few who tenaciously, stubbornly hung on, gave up their long years of training and their dreams of performing on stage, bowing to enthusiastic audiences while they applauded, and standing ovations, to engage in mundane menial work such as painting houses, putting up replacement windows, living in rich people' houses as helpers, selling homes and such in order to earn a living.

"Why are we doing these things? Is there a future? Is this what we came to America for?" When they got together someone would grumble at their dismal existence.

Live-in help was not a bad job. In many cases it was the ideal job, not only room and board were free, a stipend was usually in order. The hours were short and flexible; the work was light and minimal. Meng Song had such an arrangement in Cambridge. The man of the house was a lawyer and his wife was a physician. They had their practices set up in their house. They had two large macaw parrots. The couple gave Meng Song a very large room, which he used as his bedroom/studio. He also had his own private bath and kitchenette.

His only duty was to feed the birds. The couple took off for vacation several times a year. Song often wondered how they maintain their businesses while being absent several months a year. One time when the couple went away, at a moment of whim, Song painted a mural of a jungle scene around the four walls in the bird's room and added some special lighting effects. The birds thought they were back in nature. The couple came back to see such wonder and were overjoyed. Despite Song's declination they insisted on paying him for his creative art.

One violin student also had a live-in arrangement in Weston. The couple had two dogs and a large talking parrot. Every day he took the dogs out for walks and fed the bird. When the bird spoke to him he couldn't resist the temptation of teaching it some Chinese, even a few swear words. One day the owner threw a dinner party. Among the guests was a Chinese professor. The clever bird seeing this Chinese face began to show off its linguistic talent and said:

"*cao ni ma, cao ni ma. Ta ma de.*"

The Chinese professor was dismayed and asked the host where the bird learned such language. Without understanding what the professor meant, the host proudly replied: "My live-in help, this wonderful violinist taught it. Isn't that clever?" The professor wasn't sure whether he should blow the bubble or not. He remained silent for a while. The host, expecting to hear compliments from his guest on his smart bird, was disappointed at the latter's reticence. He asked:

"Jack, what did it say? Did he make any sense?"

The professor pondered for a second and summoned his courage to tell the truth. "Ah... Harry, to tell you the truth, the bird just uttered some very vulgar, foul words. They are very offensive."

Harry drew in a deep breath, stared at the bird for a second and yelled: "Du Hang, Du Hang, would you come here?" Du Hang entered the room with a pleasant smirk and nodded to the guests. "Yes, Mr. Mason."

"What did you teach my bird to say? Why did you teach him to swear?" Harry demanded.

"No, Mr. Mason, I didn't teach him to swear. I just swore at him and he learned." Du Hang replied insouciantly.

"Why did you swear at my bird then?" Harry Mason was confused and upset.

"Oh, because he swore at me first," Du Hang answered self-righteously.

Li Yong went through many jobs. Without experience for any work he was first hired as a kitchen factotum in a Chinese restaurant. His work included sweeping the floor, cleaning the stove, cooking rice, de-shelling shrimps, scaling fish, pealing onions, chopping meat and vegetables, boning chickens and ducks and taking out the garbage. Because he was not facile enough he was fired the first day.

His friends urged him to apply for a waiter's job.

"It's easier and can make you more money," they said. But he had no experience at all.

"Lie about it. Did you think we had experience?" They advised.

So he was hired and fired on the same day. When he went to the third restaurant he could truthfully say that he was experienced. He used what he had learned from the previous restaurants to help him hold the job for a few days. When he mixed up a customer's order and begged the cook to make another one, the cook, having a stack of orders on his counter to fill, refused and cursed him. He cursed back. Loud shouting and fighting erupted. The cook chased him out with a cleaver; the owner told him to leave.

He told his friends about the incident. One friend pulled up his sleeve and showed him a big scar on the forearm and said:

"You know where this came from? A cook poured a ladle of hot oil on me." Li Yong blanched.

"These cooks, they have all the weapons to back their fury. What do we have?"

Another friend said: "Shouting and cursing is a way of life in the kitchen. You just have to ignore it if you don't want to get hurt."

Chatting about restaurant experiences went on. Beside the kitchen horrors there was sometimes humor in the dinning room. As one told:

"One time I worked in a French restaurant. Every day the maitre 'd lined the waiters up to check their fingernails and of course their uniforms, and to remind us the minutia of manners. I was the only Chinese waiter there. I knew he paid extra attention to see if I had abided to all his rules. One time I carried a tray of deserts. As I was serving them someone bumped me and a scoop of ice cream fell right into a lady's low-cut dress. In a moment of haste I stuck my hand in the lady's brazier to fish out the ice cream."

Everyone in the room roared.

"My first job was delivering food. I didn't know how to drive a car. But I couldn't tell the owner that. I rode my bicycle to deliver smaller orders to closer places. That worked out fine. But when the order was big and the location was far the owner insisted that I drove the restaurant's car. There was no excuse for me to argue so I audaciously went inside the car, started it, moved one inch and it stalled. I kept trying and trying. Finally I got about a mile. Then it stalled for the last time. I had to walk back. The owner was furious when I confessed to him. Of course that was the end of my food delivering career," another put in.

When all restaurant jobs failed Li Yong found an easy one, to stick restaurant flyers under the doors of apartments. But it wasn't really easy because all the front doors of the apartment buildings were locked. He had to wait for some occupants to enter or exit to push himself in. If there was no one coming in or out he had to keep waiting. Once inside, he felt like a thief sneaking about. One time as he was crouching down to perform his duty, the lady inside opened the door at that exact moment. He started her and embarrassed himself too. Then he was yelled at by the restaurant owner for bringing back more than half of the flyers. His friend scoffed:

"Why, are you stupid or something? Why didn't you just chuck the rest?"

Finally he had the good fortune to land a babysitting job. That was after he auditioned for a part in New York. The agent told him:

"You have potential. But you must work on you English. Come back in a few years."

He took the advice seriously and assiduously studied the language, carrying a book and a dictionary with him all the time. Whenever he had a chance he would read aloud. He even had a small mirror in his pocket for checking the correctness of his tongue's position. The two children he babysat were four and five year olds. He watched Sesame Street with them; conversed with them; told stories to them and acted for them. The children understood him despite his broken English. They liked him a great deal because he was so much fun. They corrected his pronunciation. For instance the five-year old said: "Li Yong, it's 'father' not 'farder.'" While entertaining the children Li Yong used them as a practicing tool.

He was still in his first year at Boston University when he participated in the events for the celebration of the school's anniversary. He recited Martin Luther King's "I Have a Dream" speech. Though he had to check the dictionary for meanings and pronunciations of most words, his delivery moved the audience to tears. The Boston Globe, in reviewing the daylong event, singled him out for special accolade, calling his performance "the highlight of the day."

*   *   *   *

Since the first meeting at China Society's gallery opening Pei-hua could not expunge the image of Li Yong from her mind. He was so handsome, witty, and well-mannered. Those bright and limpid eyes, that firm jaw and straight nose, that confidence and slight hint of sarcasm written on his lips, and that wonderful Beijing accent constantly drowned her. And an actor!!! What a refreshing profession, one that she dreamt of!! How many actors had she known? None. Yet bashfulness curtailed her urge to talk about him to Ying Ying. She did not have many opportunities to see him. Even chance-meetings were rare. Whenever she found out Li Yong would be attending a monthly artists gathering at China Society she would avail herself for the event too. After several such meetings she boldly asked if Li Yong would go to a concert at the Symphony Hall with her. This was a huge step, as she had never initiated a date. Before the concert they had dinner at an Italian restaurant near the Symphony. Ineluctably more personal topics entered the conversation. She told Li Yong that her grandmother on her mother's side went to school in Shanghai and her grandfather on her father's side grew up in Beijing. She also told him about her high school and college days in Taiwan, a very relaxed and easy life filled with youthful innocent mirthfulness. Li Yong told her about his life, which were a glaring contrast to hers.

He was glad that Pei-hua and Ying Ying had not reacted to him in a seemingly exalting but in reality patronizing or demoralizing way as many

'Taiwanese' did toward the Mainlanders. The former usually expected the latter to be boorish and uncouth. When noticing refinement, style, broad knowledge in someone from the Mainland, they would often make remarks that seemed insinuative, such as "You don't look like a Mainlander." A few times Li Yong countered with questions like "How should a Mainlander look?" or "Did you think we are all country bumpkins, gruff boors?"

Yes, the chasm was definitely there. Few from those two parts of the world mingle. The irony was that many of the people from Taiwan did not regard themselves as Taiwanese as they were called by the Mainlanders.

In Taiwan there were three kinds of people: The Native Taiwanese, the indigenous, and "the people from foreign provinces." The indigenous people or the autochthons were called "the mountain people" who inhabited the land for many centuries. The native Taiwanese were those whose forefathers counting back four generations had migrated to the Island from the Mainland. Those moving to Taiwan after World War II regarded themselves "Mainlanders," and were called "people of foreign provinces" by the native Taiwanese.

In the U.S. the Mainland Chinese view all people from Taiwan "Taiwanese," once their enemies, now their new acquaintances. On the one hand they treated these Taiwanese with utter politeness; on the other they didn't trust them. At the film screenings presented by the Mainland Chinese students at M.I.T., one would sometimes see the organizer getting up to announce: "Mainland schoolmates, please let our Taiwanese friends be seated first since we may not have enough seating."

One artist, Lu Wen, told Ying Ying: "Don't think you can have true friendship with a Mainland person. It is not possible. You will never understand them and they will never regard you as one of them."

It disheartened Ying Ying who regarded some of them her good friends. But then, what about Lu Wen? Was he a real friend?

Li Yong told Pei-hua a story about him and a girl, Sandy, who played *Juliet* opposite him as *Romeo*.

Sandy was the daughter of a Korean War veteran named Roy. Roy used to tell his family about one incident during the War that was etched in his memory: One night the U.S. solders encountered the North Koreans in the dark. He was lying prone by a hillock ready to shoot any approaching enemy. A sudden thunderclap and bright lightening revealed a Chinese solder standing right before him with a gun pointing at his head. Startled, horrified, gaping at the enemy, instead of firing a shot, he froze. The Chinese solder hesitated, kicked Roy's rifle away, bent over and jerked off the gold chain and pendent dangling from his neck and walked away. Roy always wandered why the Chinese solder did not kill him.

Li Yong was stunned by Sandy's story. He reached a hand to his neck from which a chain and a pendant hung. He took the chain and pendent off and showed them to her. The pendant opened to a small picture of a young American couple. On one side of the pendant words and numerals were engraved. The words read "Roy Ferguson." This pendant and the chain were given to Li Yong by his father before he left home. His father said: "If by any miracle you find this person, give it back to him."

Li Yong's father was a Chinese veteran of the Korean War. In one combat against the Americans, at one dark moonless night he moved toward an American solder lying prone on the ground. He was about to shoot him when a blast of thunder and lightening almost blinded him. He saw his enemy, a very young boy, with a frightened expression; his large eyes hooded under thick lashes, emerald green, as revealed by that flash of lightening, begged for mercy. His heart rent, soldier Li's hand softened. He couldn't kill the boy. He never wanted to kill in the first place. He jerked off from the American's neck a chain and pendant, perhaps as a souvenir?

Who would believe that the children of the two solders of opposing camps would one day meet and play opposites in *Romeo and Juliet*? Isn't it drama within a drama? Sandy brought Li Yong to meet her parents. They welcome him like a son returning from a battlefield. They often asked him and Sandy to "come home." "Without your father's compassion at the moment none of us would be here," said Mrs. Ferguson. She was the girl in that picture in the pendant. Li Yong and Sandy were destined to be together. Kismet had it so.

Then, with what was Pei-hua left? With pain, a broken heart, with no one's shoulder on which to cry. It ended before it even started. She kept these innermost feelings to herself. Li Yong had not the slightest hint. At least she did not lose face.

*   *   *   *

Struggling to keep food and shelter and go to school at the same time was tough. Even Meilan who claimed to have tens of thousands of U.S. dollars in the bank, lived meagerly and was forever in search of chances to make a buck. Ying Ying often kept an eye and ear open for performing opportunities for her. One time Meilan was overjoyed at one such opportunity and exclaimed:

"Ah, it comes just in time. I have absolutely no money and my refrigerator is completely empty. I only found two potatoes and a bag of peas. I am baking the potatoes and boiling the peas now. That's going to be my supper."

Suddenly Meilan shrieked: "Oh no, I smell something burning. Let me see what it is." She put down the phone to check her oven. When she returned she said: "Now I have nothing to eat. My potatoes are burnt like two pieces of charcoal. And the peas, they taste like ..., errrr. "

"Oh, Meilan. Let's go out to eat. I can't believe you are so destitute. What happened to your money? You said you had lots of it."

"That's true. But I put my money in a twelve-month CD account that I cannot touch without being penalized. So I had to borrow some money. Those singing engagements are pathetic. The miserable pay is far less than what I had been paid in China."

"Of course, in China you were a big star," Ying Ying said.

"True. In China I only gave concerts in huge halls to thousands of eager audiences. In Boston, I sing in Chinese restaurants, street fairs, or office parties. No one, beside the Chinese, knows who I am."

Yet she was optimistic. She talked about being invited to play the lead in a Broadway show, *The King of Chu Bidding Farewell to His Favorite Consort*.

"But my current indigence is only temporary. When my Broadway show opens everything will be different."

One of the odd jobs she got was housekeeping for an elderly lady on the Beacon Hill. The lady had many rules she had to abide. For example, the wooden furniture had to be cleaned with a damp cloth first, then with vinegar, finally wiped with a soft cotton cloth dabbed with olive oil; no commercially prepared cleaning agents were allowed; the narrow ledge of the baseboards had to be brushed and wiped with a damp cloth; the plush carpet had to be vacuumed in one direction, not haphazardly; each crystal piece dangling from the chandelier had to be taken down and washed then dried with cloth every week. Then the "maid," that's Meilan, had to stay in her quarter when all her chores were done, and not to come out unless summoned with the ring of a bell. Meilan lasted one day on the job.

The next job of hers was night-watchman for Polar Company. One day some friends were having a gathering. Meilan walked in, in her night watchman's uniform and high heels.

"I have to go to work shortly. Look at me. Do you believe I can beat off the burglar with my club?" She taunted.

"Meilan, why are you wearing high heels? You would do a little better in flats," Pei-hua commented.

"I don't have any flats," she huffed: "You should see me after work. I am limping like this." She mimicked herself. "I can hardly walk."

"How on earth could our Miss Liang be doing this type of hard work!!" Woolan cried in indignation.

"My movie star days are over. Why did I have to come here? I can't face my fans in China now! I am so ashamed," she whined dramatically. Then she brooded for a moment. An idea came to her. "Hey, I should call that Mr. Johnson. I forgot all about him. He said I should call him when I needed help."

"What do you think he can do for you?" Pei-hua asked.

"Get me a job would be a start."

With a student visa Meilan must be in school. She enrolled herself at Berkeley School of Music. She sang well. Her teacher said she was most suited for country music. But she had her mind set on opera. She told her teacher that her ambition at the moment was to sing at the Metropolitan or on Broadway. Her teacher said those were two entirely different things. Berkeley did not train opera singers. If that was what she wanted she should go to Boston University. She chose to stay at Berkeley. One pressing issue facing her was following the lectures in class. The little English she knew was far from being adequate. To remedy the situation she bought a small recorder and used it in the classroom, then asked a friend to translate it for her after class. After a while it became a big burden to her friends who began to make excuses. She asked Pei-hua and Ying Ying for help. Both were very busy people and could only help her occasionally. She struggled on. And she never ceased looking for opportunities and ways out of her straits.

Give Andrew Johnson a call, she decided.

Andrew Johnson was delighted to hear from Meilan. He could and was happy to do a lot for her. As a start he gave her a job in his company.

"You will be a valuable addition to my China-Marketing Department. There will be other things you can do. We will figure them out later," he said.

The annual salary was a hefty $100,000. Her position in the Department was only second to its Director. The company also sponsored her application for a permanent resident status from the Immigration and Naturalization Service. In less than a year she should have the enviable green card in hand. Andrew Johnson also gladly granted her time off from the office for her school. Now she could easily afford to pay for the service of translating the lectures she recorded.

Meilan possessed an extraordinary dexterity in swaying people. She was confident. And she was an eloquent, persuasive speaker. She also knew perfectly her physical attractiveness and how to use it to her advantage, to augment her other abilities. She made Andrew Johnson believe that she was not only a top movie star in China but also a very powerful and influential person as well; because her fans included important people in the government and private sectors, she could get things done easily.

"China is a country where contacts count for all. Without them you can spend an unlimited amount of money and time to accomplish nothing," she told Johnson. She also told everyone at China Society that she was good friend with the Minister of Culture, Minister of Overseas Chinese Affairs, bank presidents, university presidents, and many other leaders.

She persuaded Andrew Johnson to take a business delegation to China. It was just what he had hoped to do but did not have the right person to expedite it. With Meilan this plan would be easily carried out. At the same time the INS approved of Meilan's application. The business delegation that Johnson's company had organized consisted of presidents and department heads of major companies in trading, communication, electronics, manufacturing, and financial institutions in New England. Some of those companies had made many futile attempts to develop businesses in China. Their representatives traveled back and forth many times in vain. What looked like good prospects turned out to be wishful thinking; handshakes, and promises, but contracts were all rendered ineffective.

"Because they did not talk to the right people, or know how to negotiate. They were ignorant of the Chinese way. They can carry on and get nowhere. But I can help them achieve their goals." Meilan's promise was tantalizing. All the company representatives were enthused, hopeful, anticipating success.

Meilan wrote and called her important contacts informing them of the coming of this groundbreaking delegation. She promised that China would benefit from this visit immensely. More crucially, she promised lucrative benefits to the individuals involved. Without this incentive, she knew, no one would care. She asked them to aid her assistant, who would be in China a month prior to the delegation's arrival, to make relevant arrangements. Then she called her close friends and family members, giving each of them assignments to handle different aspects of the project.

She needed a Chinese secretary. Frankly secretarial skills were of little consequence. A good-looking man, who carried himself well, could speak convincingly to the Chinese, and acted servilely to her were the criteria. Woolan met those requirements perfectly and Meilan knew it. He had gotten his green card a short while ago making his traveling much easier. She gave him the title of "assistant" and sent him to China ahead of time to coordinate with her helpers there. They ably arranged press conferences in each city; reserved convention halls in Shenzhen, Guangzhou, Shanghai and Beijing; printed posters and flyers, and handled myriads of minutia. Then they carefully and thoroughly reviewed a long list of Chinese businesses and decided which ones to invite to the conferences in those four cities.

Meilan, a shining movie star in the minds of over a billion Chinese, was now a shining star in the business circle in China. Her celebrity status alone attracted business leaders to pay good registration fees to the conferences. Every one of them wanted to do business with the American companies, to develop business in America. They also wanted to buy American goods. Numerous orders were given to Meilan who guaranteed to fill those for them. Beside the conferences, there were many meetings with government leaders vital to the success of the delegation's goal. She used every ounce of her muscle, pulled every possible string, bribed every official that deemed necessary. She got the doors open for the companies in the delegation. What others failed to achieve in three years she achieved in three weeks. The trip was a smashing success.

As Meilan and the delegates returned to Boston Ying Ying and the other friends threw a welcome-home party for her. With her fetching stage presence and lilting voice Meilan gleefully announced:

"China is wonderful to me. After being away for three years, they still embraced me as warmly as ever. Oh, you should have seen them. People would stop me on the street and say: 'Miss Liang, you are back? We knew you would be back. You wouldn't desert us. You were just visiting America, to better your singing and acting. Then you would come back to us.' A taxi driver showed me the cassettes he listened to all day long. They were collections of my songs. He said: 'I cannot go a day without listening to your songs. When will you cut a new record?'"

"Of course your fans are loyal, Meilan. You are the best-selling platinum-record singer," Denis commented.

"That's true, Denis. Before I came to America, China loved me as a first-rate singer and movie star. That's all. Now they regard me as an accomplished business expert and a patriot who is willing to give up the material wealth of America to dedicate herself to China."

"You should be a business-ambassador," Ying Ying joked. Meilan ignored her banter and went on:

"Film producers wanted to make movies about me. Publishers wanted me to write my autobiography. Large companies fought to offer sponsorship of a music and dance show I would bring to China. It would go on tour throughout the whole country, you see. And those business deals!! They tore up the contracts signed with European and American companies to sign new ones with me because they loved and respected me to the utmost. There was a lot of money to be made from these contracts and they wanted me to make it. But little did they know I was only representing an American company. I was invited to speak at a business conference. All the big shots from every province attended. Everyone took notes. They regarded me as the highest authority on U.S.-China trade. They asked all sorts of questions. All the conferences were televised nationwide too."

She yawned after talking so much in such high spirits. "Oh, I'm so tired."

"You and your experiences will certainly make a great subject for a film. Did you have a good night sleep, Meilan?" Denis asked.

"What sleep? I'm still in jetlag. Besides, China kept calling and faxing me stuff in the middle of the night. It's their daytime. They didn't care that I should be sleeping"

Jenny asked: "Why did they keep calling you?"

"Business. They are eagerly waiting for information." She turned to speak to the others: "I already consummated one business deal for a company yesterday." She took out some papers from her handbag and handed one to Pei-hua and one to Ying Ying. "These are two of the purchasing orders. See if you can find the items for me. I will give you 3% of my commission." She turned to Denis and Jenny:

"Are you able to handle some business and make some money? If you think you can do it I have other items for you."

Peihua looked at the contract and smirked: "Smart, really smart. You have the Chinese companies' names whited out to prevent your gofers here from contacting them directly. And 3% of your commission?"

Meilan said matter-of-factly: "Of course. One has to protect oneself."

Pei-hua perused the contract further and said: "I can't find any place to buy second-hand CAT scanners."

Ying Ying read the sheet of paper and said: "Second-hand buses? automatic control? What is automatic control? Hospital beds?" She handed the paper back to Meilan and jokingly uttered: "Meilan, why not can-openers and skin lotion like you talked about before?"

Meilan replied seriously: "They have those now. Really. These things are badly needed. Try to get them for me. I don't have time to do it myself."

Denis and Jenny had no interest or ability to find those or other items. So Meilan did not give them any order forms.

*   *   *   *

It was not only fame and glory Meilan reaped from this trip, there were other personal gains as well. The company leaders in the delegation held her in awe. George Hemmingway and Robert Sinclair were founders and CEOs of large corporations. They did not have particular goals for the trip. It was an initial exploration for them. They needed to see the business environment first-hand before making specific plans. Unexpectedly, they saw the ease and grace with which Meilan operated. Awe and admiration rose in their mind, amorous emotions in their heart. They fell in love with her. So did Andrew Johnson.

She met the biggest business leaders in China who were desirous of collaborating with her in various ventures. One big company asked her to represent them in setting up headquarters in Boston. She gained substantial amount of knowledge from the trip that became indispensable assets to her when establishing her own conglomerate a few years later. As a minor gain Andrew Johnson promoted her to Director of China-Marketing. Her old boss was demoted to the position of her assistant.

She moved from her small room to a luxury apartment in the Prudential Tower Apartments. She let Woolan go because in Boston he was of no use to her. Her regular appearance at large parties thrown by Hemmingway, Johnson, Sinclair, and other notable Bostonians, and her charm and style, were the talk of the town and news in the gossip columns. She was no doubt a socialite of Boston's high society.

The three gentlemen often invited her, respectively of course, to theatre events, concerts, exclusive clubs, expensive restaurants, not only locally but also in New York or elsewhere by flying in their private planes. Meilan enjoyed the high society life style she was led into, and she also knew where to draw the line between herself and the men who treated her like a queen. After all, she had ample experience on how to preserve herself during the Cultural Revolution. Equipped with that skill, dealing with Boston's gentlemen was like "a small dish of vegetable" as she described it. She was not without her eye searching for a suitable man to marry. But her suitors were not your ordinary eligible bachelors. They all had wives. On some occasions one or two of them mentioned the words "not getting along well" with the wife and "divorce." But until then she was not going to get seriously involved.

*   *   *   *

Woolan had reached the time to divorce his titular wife. It was decent of him not to demand alimony from her. She, however, gave him $50,000 to help him get started. But the money would not last long. He had to find works to make money. Restaurants were the first logical place. He didn't qualify for a waiter's job for lack of experience. Very unwillingly, like Li Yong, he took the job of a factotum in the kitchen.

His mind was filled with plans and ideas on how to make big money like Meilan, lucky Meilan.

There are so many things I should be doing. Kitchen help is not one of them. How about selling Chinese goods in the American market? I have the suppliers' names from that China trip. But alas, Meilan had all the contact information. Chinese herbal medicine! That should be a good business. How about weapons? China needs it. United States has it. Why can't I facilitate the trade? Fish and shrimps, those are good import items. Or timber."

He still believed he could do any or all of these despite his failure in earlier tries. He blocked out the cooks' yelling. He did not care about their cursing. His mind was completely preoccupied.

He was fired after two days.

He went to see Ying Ying when he had a chance. Ying Ying asked how he was doing. He said:

"Peeling shrimps, wrapping dumplings and wantons, sweeping the floor, cleaning the stove, carrying piles of dishes and huge bags of garbage, be yelled at and threatened by the chef with a big cleaver, that's my daily encounters. But no more. I was fired."

Ying Ying smiled and tried to be lighthearted: "These are what go with the territory, a kitchen-help's professional hazards. No big deal. It's not as bad as baking bricks, I suppose." She chuckled thinking about Woolan sweating in the brick factory outside of Beijing.

"I suppose so. But I wasn't abused by the other workmen in the brick factory. Here, they always swear at me in Cantonese that I don't understand. I just shut my ears, not listening to their voices or seeing their faces. I keep thinking about my plans and I say to myself, 'never mind these stupid people. One day I'll show them.' "

"But how did you get yourself fired?"

"I completely ignored the cooks. They were angry and complained to the owner. So I was fired," Woolan said while taking out two newspaper ads and two application forms to show Ying Ying. He pointed to one ad and then to the other:

"Look, Ying Ying, this place wants an automobile mechanic and this one wants an electrician. I think those must be better jobs than kitchen help. So I picked up these application forms. Will you help me fill them out?"

Ying Ying looked at him for a second and plainly said: "Woolan, auto mechanic and electrician? These are technical jobs."

Woolan wondered why Ying Ying made that comment. *Doesn't she know I can do these works?*

"You know that I can fix cars and do all kinds of electrical work. I've done them in China."

Yes, Woolan had told Ying Ying about his building a house single-handedly, and doing all sorts of work by himself. Recently he had fixed a TV he picked up in the street.

"But they require licenses. Do you have them?" She asked tauntingly.

"No, I don't. But I can show them and convince them," Woolan persisted.

"No way. Woolan. You have to have a license in order to get the job.

Forget it."

Woolan brooded for a while. Optimistic enthusiasm returned to him. "Ying Ying, I am going to try importing goods."

Woolan's earlier attempts to import goods were still fresh in Ying Ying's memory.

"Not medicine, construction materials, woman's apparel or fresh fish, I hope."

How much had she done for him!!! She was not foolish, just being kind and unstinting in giving help to friends in need. She made appointments for him to meet with appropriate people and went with him to play interpreter for him. But none of his ideas were feasible.

"No, Just grocery items." This was a most practical idea he had. Grocery always had a market. People must buy food. "Yes, dry mushrooms, dry shrimps. The dry goods are easy."

"Right. At least that will be easier than importing fresh fish and shrimps." Ying Ying chuckled.

"If they were packed in ice properly, that still could be done." Woolan firmly believed the seafood company had made a mistake not accepting his idea.

"But Woolan I felt like a fool helping you sell the idea to that company." Ying Ying still felt embarrassed thinking about that failed negotiation. She was no businesswoman. It was ludicrous for her to be in such a position talking about something totally foreign to her.

"I often wonder why I always let myself be put in awkward situations."

"Because you are warmed-hearted and kind to people. Everyone expects you to help, and you don't have the heart to say no." Woolan spoke his heartfelt truth. "I am sorry to have put you through that."

"You make me seem like a saint. What help do you need from me this time?" Ying Ying smiled and was ready to do everything she could to help him.

"The grocery stuff I can handle. I have other plans. When it's time to carry out my other plans I will need your help."

"What? To sell high-tech equipment and weapons?" Ying Ying jeered.

"China is different from years ago. People are eager to do business, to make money. You know, the government has loosened up its control. Private industries are allowed, to some degree…. I met up with many important contacts." He took out a pile of business cards and shows them to Ying Ying. "See. I got these cards. Some of those people I have met, some I haven't. But they all have my card. It's important."

"You have the time to meet those people? Were you supposed to be by Meilan's side at all times?"

"No, not all the time. I did what I needed to do for her and then I had free time to myself."

"What do you expect to accomplish?"

"Oh, U.S.-China trade. Years ago, we could only hope to sell Chinese goods to America not vice versa. Things are changing now. China has the money and interest to buy now." Woolan had ample confidence: "This is the time for me to play a role. China is not familiar with America. They need someone like me as a bridge. I have a distinct advantage because I have a green card. I can go back and forth. Most other Chinese can't do that."

"Meilan said the same thing. Don't you know that she brought back a ton of orders from China to buy goods from America?"

"Of course, Meilan is at a greater advantage. Her relations with the high-up cadres are exceptional. Nevertheless, there is room for more than one Meilan." His confidence did not diminish.

Dreams were sweet. Ideas were grand. Realization of them was, however quite another thing. Woolan's dreams must remain dreams.

Sometime later he was hired by a Chinese home remodeling contractor to paint a three-decker in Watertown. It was not interior painting, but exterior. He had built a house, but never climbed a 50-feet-high ladder, for fear of height. Carrying a five -gallon paint in one hand, and a brush in the other he climbed upward. The ground was uneven; the ladder was rickety, he was giddy. As he was reaching the top he tried to grab hold of a piece of clapboard with his right hand that held the paintbrush. He almost lost his balance. He jolted. The paint spilled right on the head of the contractor standing by the ladder giving him instructions, the brush also fell and hit him. The contractor was furious. He pointed a figure at Woolan and shouted:

"You stupid God-dammed fool. You told me you had built a house; you could do any kind of work. Look at you, stupid."

When he was on the steep roof painting the dormers he slipped and slid fast down and off the roof. He reacted quickly and grabbed a tree branch on his way down the ground.

He quit the following day.

The struggle went on.

Chapter 2

$\mathcal{I}$n the fall of 1988 Dr. Joseph Lee was planning an expanded series of events at China Society to celebrate the Chinese New Year in February of 1989. The Trustees suggested mounting a showcase of Chinese music and dance. It would be the first such project ever presented in Boston. There were two other pioneer events: a dramatic presentation of a play by a Chinese playwright and a Lantern Festival celebration on the 15th day after the Chinese New Year.

Joseph Lee told Denis who was appointed the publicity manager for the events: "Please send a program description to the Mayor and the Governor. Herald will write a letter to the Governor proposing February as Chinese Culture Month. The Governor will make an announcement to the media."

Ying Ying suggested that they should ask Meilan to oversee the Chinese music and dance program. Meilan agreed after some persuasion.

"Is there a large enough pool of talents in Boston we can draw on?" Meilan asked.

"I am not sure how big the pool is because we have not worked with Chinese musicians and dancers," Denis replied.

"We'll know when we put out a call to artists in the Chinese newspapers," Ying Ying maintained.

"That is too iffy. What if you don't get enough qualified talents? There may not be any. You have to be prepared. Without knowing the resources such a plan is risky." Meilan had a point there. But where would they find accountable performers?

"I suppose there must be some talents in Boston, or New England for that matter." Denis was hopeful.

"There are many of them in New York. I can get them for you." Meilan volunteered.

"That'll be wonderful." Denis was happy.

"But we have a limited budget. Bringing people from out of town is expensive." Ying Ying knew what the budget for this program was.

"No, it won't cost you. They will be happy to have the chance to perform in Boston." Meilan assured Ying Ying.

"Do you really think so? Why would they do it without pay?" Ying Ying was not convinced.

"Meilan must have ways if she said she could." Denis would rather trust

Meilan.

"Why don't you believe me? Do you know them better than I?" Meilan questioned Ying Ying. "Do you know how things are done in China?"

"We cannot pay the market rate but we will pay them. Please give them our event schedule and ask them to prepare their best numbers." Denis was anxious to nail it down.

"Also ask them to give us the pertinent information about the performers and the program. We will put them in our program book." Ying Ying was more thoughtful about details. She was thankful to Meilan.

"Ha, don't be so hasty. How could you just let them decide? They will laugh at you for being so slapdash, so unprofessional. They must come to audition first, to let you people choose what numbers you want. We did those things very seriously in China." Meilan was right, of course. Denis and Ying Ying were only concerned about the budget.

"I know. But if we ask them to come and audition for us we must pay for their airfare, hotel and meals, in addition to some sort of a fee. I don't think the Society has the budget. What do you think Denis?"

"I am afraid it will be tough. I never heard Joseph mention any budget for this type of expenses." Denis replied.

"No, no, no. You don't need to pay for any of those things. They will drive up. And they can stay in somebody's house. You don't need to pay them anything." Meilan was very confident.

Denis and Ying Ying were incredulous, yet they still brought this idea to Joseph Lee's attention. The latter agreed to take on Meilan's offer and added a line item in the budget.

* * * *

At the same time Ying Ying announced a call-to-artists in the papers. Within two weeks several dancers came knocking on her office door.

The first one was Manna, a woman from Taiwan, accompanied by her Caucasian husband, Roger. Roger showed a great deal of enthusiasm. He spoke before Manna said hello to Ying Ying.

"I was happy when Manna told me about your announcement. She just came here, and is alone at home when I am at work. She has no friends here. With nothing to do, she is bored to death. She is a dancer. I would like her to meet other Chinese people."

"That is very good. Manna, would you do a segment of your dance for me?"

"Yes, but I don't have music." Manna said.

"We have a cassette player."

"I didn't bring a tape." Manna said: "But I can do it without music if you must see."

"Yes, please. This is an audition. I have to see you dance," Ying Ying smiled friendly. Manna did a short segment.

62

"I am only auditioning people. Liang Meilan will be in charge of repertoire and rehearsals. She probably will ask some dancers to learn a group dance."

"Who is Liang Meilan?" Manna inquired.

"She is in charge of this program. And she is a famous singer-dancer-movie-star from the Mainland," Ying Ying informed her.

"The Mainland? They are so backward. Why do you have her in charge? They have nothing except the revolutionary-inspired Eight Exemplary Dance-Musical-Drama," Manna scoffed scornfully.

"You know about the Eight Exemplary Dance-Musical-Drama? How did you hear about it in Taiwan?" Ying Ying was astounded.

"Not in Taiwan. I was in Japan for a year. I heard about it there. I even saw *White Haired Girl* and *Red Detachment of Women*. The movie version, of course. They are bad. They are a mixture of Chinese opera and western Ballet, plus military cadence. They Looked awful. I think they must have changed Chinese classical and folk dances so much that they are neither-east-nor-west."

"It may not be what you think. I have seen Meilan do classical dance, for example, *Flowery Spring River at a moon-lit-night*. It was very beautiful," Ying Ying argued. Then she changed the subject.

"Hey, Manna, would you be interested in joining our cultural enrichment program? We bring dancers, musicians, visual artists and speakers to area schools. The artists sign up for the service." Ying Ying thought since Manna stayed home feeling bored this program might suit her. And she would be an added resource for the program.

"Manna, I think this will be good for you to participate. You get to meet more people," Roger urged.

"It sounds good. But tell me more about it. What will I do?" Manna asked.

"Demonstrate dance at schools. We will pay you an honorarium."

"Oh, that sounds exciting. I will be happy to be part of it." Manna accepted the opportunity with joy.

"I am happy too because Manna will have something interesting to do and her talent will be put to meaningful use." Roger was obviously excited.

"Next Tuesday we are sending two dancers, one visual artist and a workshop leader to a school in Cambridge," Ying Ying said while turning the pages of her notebook. "Here it is. Can you do it next Tuesday? I was just about to call the dancers. If you can go I will only call one of them."

"Oh, that's exciting. I would love to do it," Manna said cheerfully: "But I don't have my costumes here. I left them in Taiwan. I never thought I would need them again."

"China Society has many costumes for the school program. What dance would you like to do? I'll see which costume will suit you," Ying Ying said without hesitation.

"Oh, anything, really." Manna sounded as if she knew all the dances. "How about *Lady Wang Zhao-jun*?"

"That's a good piece. We have exactly the right costume for that," Ying Ying said. "I will bring the costume to you Friday. Where do you live?"

"In Cambridge." Roger said and jotted their address down on a piece of paper for Ying Ying

"Oh, that's swell. Very convenient for you." Ying Ying also wrote down the school's name and address, as well as the time of the event and the teacher's name for Manna.

"Do you know how to get there? Do you drive?" She thought about this practical question. Since Manna just came here she might not have a driver's license.

"Yes I drive." Manna chuckled. "I was a business woman in Taiwan. How could I not drive?" She looked at the address and said again: "I have a map. I can find it."

"That settles it. I am glad you are on our team. Thank you Manna, Roger." Ying Ying extended her hand to shake with them.

On Friday, after work, Ying Ying brought the costume to Manna. Their apartment was very spacious and stylishly furnished. Manna invited Ying Ying in. Roger came home shortly. Roger was the owner of an upscale furniture company and a manufacturing company of porcelain and glassware. He often took business trips to Taiwan. There he met Manna, a sultry dance-hall girl. He quickly fell in love with her. When he returned to Boston he called her everyday and had long conversations each time.

"A few months afterwards, I went to Taiwan to ask for her hand," Roger said. He had one arm around Manna who snuggled in his bosom on the sofa and her head leaned against his chest. Her very long and thick hair cascaded over his torso. Roger picked up her hand and kissed it. Ying Ying did not want to disrupt their intimate moment. She rose to her feet to say goodbye and reconfirmed with Manna of her participation in Tuesday's program.

On Monday morning Ying Ying called Manna again to reconfirm her engagement for the next day. She did not call the other participating artists since they were old hands in these activities. Once the assignment was given no reminder was necessary. With Manna, Ying Ying was unsure.

"I am sorry, Ying Ying. I am afraid I won't be able to do it," Manna's utterance surprised and irked Ying Ying.

"What? You can't do it? But you have committed yourself to it last Wednesday. I thought you were happy to have the opportunity." Ying Ying knew these words were pointless and would mean nothing to a person without good faith, a person to whom words and promises had no value. "All right. No problem. I will call other dancers and see if someone can do it at this late notice."

*   *   *   *

Two other dancers, Sally and Susie, came to audition together. They did a Taiwanese Aboriginal folk dance and a classical ribbon dance, both in full costumes and to taped music. Ying Ying was happy to see them take the audition seriously.

"Very good. I like the two dances. Where did you study dancing?"

"We were trained by the National Taiwan Arts Institute," Sally said with pride.

"Oh, wonderful, so you are professionally trained. I think Meilan will pick these two numbers. She is in charge of our program and is a professional dancer from Mainland China. She will plan the repertoire and oversee the rehearsals. She will teach two group dances. I believe you will be asked to take part in the group dances." With Manna's negative reaction and criticism of Meilan fresh in Ying Ying's memory she added: "Meilan is very good."

"We are professional dancers too and often performed together as a team," Sally said.

"Yes, I can see that," Ying Ying said in an apologetic manner. The two women had not been in this country for long. Their hope for making it in the dance profession had all but dwindled. Both divorced, without money or marketable skills, they took any menial jobs they could find. At that time Sally was a chambermaid at a hotel; Susie was a live-in help for a handicapped old woman. How much they would be paid to perform in the showcase was an important concern to them.

The next two dancers, Linda and Ching Ju, were in completely opposite situation from that of Susie and Sally. They shared some commonalities with Manna in that they were also married to rich businessmen, had come to America only recently, and stayed home with not much to do.

Linda's husband was a Taiwanese who owned a large building material company in Watertown. She liked to dance but never had any formal training. Ching Ju's husband, Dr. Jack Morrison, was the founder of JM Bio Tech in Cambridge. The company was young, with focuses on pharmaceutical and biological research, products and supplies. Its business developed quickly and the company was very profitable. Ching Ju was a champion of Chinese folk and classic dance of China's Bi-annual National Dance competition. She had spent two years in Japan working as a bar waitress. Jack Morrison met her while vacationing in Japan. He was attracted by her beauty and charm. Within two weeks infatuation turned into love and a marriage proposal. They got a marriage certificate at Tokyo city hall so that he could bring her to the U.S. In Boston they had an elaborate wedding. That was when Ching Ju realized she had married a rich man.

Ching Ju had no friends in Boston. Jack Morrison saw China Society's announcement in the paper and thought it would be a good chance for his wife to meet some Chinese people. Ying Ying noticed Ching Ju was a gorgeous young woman, slim, well shaped, fashionably dressed and with the face of an angel. Her smile brightened up the room. Her Mandarin had a touch of a Shanghai accent. She did a Chinese classical piece with such skill and style that Ying Ying bypassed Meilan and gave her a solo part immediately.

A few days later came a saucy twenty-two-year-old girl from Beijing. She was a grand price winner of ballet and second place winner of Chinese folk and classic dance in the Bi-annual National Dance Competition four years after Chin

Ju. This girl, Chen Ailing, was equipped with beauty and sprightliness, and was ready to conquer the world. Her interpretation of a Buddhist deity in *The Apsaras Of Dun-Huang* was unusually enchanting indeed. Ying Ying unreseredly recommended to Meilan to feature that number in the dance concert.

Both Ailing's and Ching Ju's repertoire needed chorus dancers. Ying Ying asked an instructor of China Society's dance class to work with Meilan to choreograph movements for her students to take parts in the dances.

After Pei-hua saw these two dancers she couldn't refrain from marveling:

"Ching Ju and Ailing are simply captivating. And they are the same height, probably the same weight too, and have similar facial features."

Meilan proudly explained: "In China, physical features are the first and foremost requirements of performers. The government sends scouts to every corner of the country to find qualified little girls. They look at the girl's parents and grandparents to predict her height and weight when she would grow up. They also measure the girl's height and the length of her legs as an added determining factor. The facial features must meet very high standards too, you know, eyes, nose, mouth, eyebrows all must conform to the idealized, set image. In short, the face must be pretty. So, all performers, especially dancers, almost look the same. Unlike in America, anyone can be a dancer if she wants. In China, it's up to the government to decide."

"No wonder you share some commonalities with them too," Pei-hua commented.

"I was picked at age nine by the government's talent scout. Then I was taken away from my parents. China Song And Dance Company was my home ever since. It's the number-one company in the nation. It's a boarding school as well as a performing group. Every one of us girls must go through ten years of grueling training. Only once or twice a year were we allowed to go home. To tell you the truth, I was not the top dancer in the Company," Meilan stated.

"But people said that you were a main dancer in your company." Ying Ying corrected her.

"That was after I made a name as the top pop singer. After the Cultural Revolution the government sent a delegation of dancers and singers abroad as People's Friendship Ambassadors to carry out the mission of promoting mutual understanding and friendship. I was left behind, not given the honor to represent my country. I was not only disappointed, but also deeply hurt. That spurred me to explore other possibilities to earn fame, to show them who Liang Meilan really was, to let them know how wrong they were to leave me out. I took to singing pop songs. To everyone's surprise I became enormously popular before the Mission group returned. My records were sold in tens of millions. My audience were electrified watching me sing on stage. That greatly boosted my popularity as a dancer, and awarded me the ticket to movie stardom," Meilan recounted her story.

China Society's call to Chinese instrumental musicians brought a good number of responses. Dr. Joseph Lee and Ying Ying were relieved. With these local talents a wealth of programs would be guaranteed. The New York group was not crucial to the show anymore. Meilan still insisted that it was necessary to invite the New York group. She dutifully took a trip to New York. Two weeks later she went to see Ying Ying and said:

"I talked to the Plum Blossom Dance Group. The artistic director Li Ching and I go back many years in Beijing. We are good friends. I said 'Ying Ying was helping China Society organize a show. She needs your group to perform in Boston. And she wants to audition you first.' She said: 'Audition? Why does she need to audition us? Doesn't she have confidence in us? How much is she paying us for the audition? Is she paying for a first-class or economy-class flight? What about hotel and meals? Is she compensating us for our loss of wages while going to Boston?' I said 'you have to drive up and stay in people's houses. And there would be no pay for the audition.' She was all upset. She said 'What? She is not paying for these and she wants us to go to Boston for an audition? Who does she think she is? Chairman Mao?'" Meilan seemed to have totally forgotten whose idea it was to send for those dancers not only without compensation but also expected them to pay for their own expenses.

Ying Ying was irate and said: "God, Meilan. That was exactly what I predicted they would say. I told you not to ask them for a try-out. Just ask them to come and perform. We will pay them the proper performance fee. Because we don't have the budget to pay for those expenses. But you were so adamant about bringing them up here for a try-out. You said 'If you didn't, they would think of you as being slapdash. They would not respect you.' Remember?"

Meilan still insisted. "We always have to have try-outs in China. So don't blame me for suggesting it."

"Oh, forget it." Ying Ying wanted to put it behind. Joseph Lee walked in at this moment. He asked:

"Meilan, can you get one of your rich friends to underwrite this cost?" He was worried about the budget. Fundraising was a perennial challenge.

"But Joseph, this is not a personal matter. I am not in the position to ask. I think if you write them a letter asking for donations they cannot decline." She was good at extricating herself from difficult situations.

"All right, I will write them a letter. However, it doesn't mean I agree with you. Rich people ask their rich friends to contribute to charities all the time. Our Trustees always solicit donations from their personal friends for the Foundation." Joseph Lee corrected her.

Meilan easily and seamlessly changed to another subject. This was another prowess of hers.

Her friends admired her forte and overlooked her weaknesses. They were grateful to her for not forgetting or forsaking them when she *flew to a high bough*, as the Chinese phrase went. That was a remarkable quality in her character.

*   *   *   *

In January of 1989 the Governor signed a proclamation to designate

February as Chinese Culture Month. The ceremony was held at the State House.

The first Chinese Lantern Competition Call-For-Entries drew over a thousand lanterns from high school and college students, art students, professional artists, and other people. Because no one had any notion about Chinese lanterns aside from the simplest kind sold in Chinatown gift shops, the program organizer encouraged them to set their imaginations and creative energy free. The results were exceptional. A panel of five jurors spent several days carefully reviewing the entries. Difficult though it was, they selected three winners from each of the four groups—high school, college, artists, and general public. The jurors recommended that all the lanterns be shown in the galleries.

There was only one gallery available at China Society, however, because the other one was reserved for an exhibition of Chinese paintings and calligraphy during the same period. Only a couple of hundred lanterns could be displayed in that gallery. More spaces in the city had to be used. Joseph Lee called the Mayor's office and the State House. Consequently, both committed large areas in their buildings that were easily accessible to the public. Mounting the show was not a simple task. Layouts for the three exhibition spaces had to be sketched out to allow each individual lantern to get its much deserved, undivided attention while related motifs and themes were grouped together. Articles about the origin and tradition of the Chinese Lantern Festival were printed in the catalog that included photos of many of the lanterns and a list of each entry. Press releases were sent to all the media.

The hanging required many volunteers. Ying Ying suggested calling the military bases for help. The first call was to the navy base. Before she called the air force, the navy called back and said they would be happy to help. On the scheduled date thirty navy men came. They even brought their own ladders and tools. Denis bought the hooks and filament. He and Ying Ying split the duty of supervising at the City Hall and the State House. Jenny and Missy oversaw the operation at the gallery. The navy men whistled and hummed away while working. They said it was a pleasant and welcome diversion apart from their humdrum routines. There were many more signing up for the job but only the first thirty were picked. Dr. Lee thanked the navy and commended Ying Ying for her idea. At the opening of the exhibit, in front of the TV and still cameras, the Mayor spoke and gave out cash awards and medals to the winners. A large crowd of onlookers stayed for the reception. The atmosphere was effervescent. The event was duly reported in the TV evening news and the newspapers.

*   *   *   *

The theatre production was the most difficult project the Society had ever taken on. The director Mr. Yu was given full responsibility to carry out the production from the beginning to the end. No one else had the slightest idea about how to produce a play. Mr. Yu suggested three scripts for the Board's selection. The Board kicked the ball back to him. So he picked a historical piece, *Intrigues in the Manchu Imperial Court*. Immediately he was faced with several problems: The play had 26 characters. Beside Li Yong there was no Chinese actor in the whole of New England. Qing dynasty robes of any sort were nowhere to be found, not to mention the large number of robes for royalty and other denizens of the Forbidden City. The Peabody Museum had a few in its collection. Yet it would be ludicrous to even think of borrowing them. Beside, they might not be suitable for the play even if the Museum would lend them, which would never happen. Then there was the issue of designing and constructing the sets. The jobs required a designer familiar with the period and locale. Where was Mr. Yu going to find the people to do these things? He was from Taiwan and not familiar with Boston's Mainland Chinese community. It was Pei-hua who reminded Mr. Yu to use Li Yong as a resource. He must have some knowledge of what possible theatre artists there were. Yet he confessed that he knew of no other professional actors of Chinese descent in the area.

Without better alternatives Mr. Yu resorted to planning on an international cast with Caucasian actors taking on some of the bigger roles if necessary. The lesser ones would be given to dilettantes from the Japanese, Korean, Chinese, Vietnamese, Thai and Cambodian communities.

The auditions spanned several weeks in order not to miss any potential candidate. A tall and slim twenty-six-year-old physician in suit and tie walked in Yiing Ying's office. A grin lifted the corners of his mouth. His eyes glinted.

"I heard about your audition. But you did not specify the time. So I just came. I hope I have not inconvenienced you," he said.

"Oh, no, no. We didn't expect a host of actors swarming our audition. Sporadically trickling in was what we thought it might be. So we didn't set a specific time." Ying Ying answered with a smile.

The young man extended his hand and said:

"Kevin Hong. I live close by here, in the South End."

"Ying Ying Fang, or Fang Ying Ying. Pleased to meet you." Ying Ying smiled and shook his hand, then pointed to a chair. "Have a seat."

Kevin took a seat. "I am normally not dressed like this. But I thought I should be a little formal coming here," he grinned again. From a large manila envelope he pulled out his headshot and resume. "I have done quite a bit of acting in school, high school and college, I mean, even while I was in med school. And I am beginning to do professional work although my schedule does not allow me to do it full time."

Ying Ying looked at his resume:

Education: Harvard Medical School.

Employment: Internship at Brigham and Women's Hospital.

"But you are a physician?" Ying Ying chuckled incredulously.

"Yea," Kevin replied: "But my primary interest is theatre. Med school was my parents' idea. My father is an artist as well as a physician."

"I see. The arts have quite a strong pull," understandingly Ying Ying said. Then she changed the subject to the audition: "Do you want to read from the script or from the material you prepared?"

"I will do a monologue and then read something you give me. How's that?"

"Sure, that's perfect."

His monologue was selected from Hamlet. The parts Ying Ying asked him to read were those of Emperor Guangxu, Eunuch Li Lian-ying and General Yuan Shi-kai.

He was most suited for the Emperor's part. If all our actors are his caliber we will be all set. Ying Ying said to herself.

"Thank you very much, Kevin. I will call you in a few days. You are very good." Ying Ying said. Kevin shook her hand and left.

The actors coming to audition in the following days could not compete with Kevin. As such Ying Ying cast him as Emperor Guangxu. He was overwhelmingly happy to get the lead role.

Mr. Yu tried his best to cast a Chinese for the major female roles of Lady Zhen, Empress Dowager, and the Empress. But he couldn't find an actress qualified to play Lady Zhen. He asked if Jenny would do it. Jenny declined saying she wouldn't know how to play a Manchu court lady.

"But Jenny, you did Hello Dolly and other school plays. You have acting experience. Come on. You are perfect for the role." Denis tried to persuade her.

"Yea, Jenny, do it, do it." Tonia was enthused.

"Although the real Lady Zhen is in no comparison with Jenny on her looks, but who cares? The audience would love to see Lady Zhen as a knock-out beauty," Ying Ying said: "Jenny, don't decline any more. Just say yes."

"Let me think about it, okay? You keep auditioning people. I will be a back-up in case you really cannot cast that role," Jenny said. Every one felt relieved and elated. In their mind the role was already cast. They had to concentrate on casting Empress Dowager, the Empress and Lady Jin. A young woman named Hu Ning was cast as the Empress. A semi-professional actress from Beijing yet she hardly spoke English.

Tonia was given the duty of helping Hu Ning with pronunciations and enunciations and Li Yong of helping with delivering her dialogues and understanding the role.

"Don't worry, you can do it. I played Romeo without knowing English either." Li Yong encouraged her.

With ample acting experience Hu Ning quickly grasped the essential aspects of her part and learned her lines.

Li Yong coached the Caucasian male and female actors in the movements and mannerism suitable for the period and their respective characters.

Dealing with rehearsals was a daunting effort for Kevin. His internship often required him to take the evening shift. Evenings were when rehearsals were held. He traded schedules with his colleagues a couple of times each week. He never skipped one rehearsal and was always on time. He memorized his lines before others did theirs. His portrayal of the character was convincing. But he did not grasp the courtly ritualistic mannerism of the Emperor. For example when taking a seat the Emperor would lift the back panel of his robe in a certain way. Kevin simply plumped himself down. Li Yong told him:

"The way you sit yourself on a seat and the way you walk are no different from a street kid in America. This is the Manchu imperial court of the 19[tt] century. You are the Emperor. You must move and act with dignity."

Kevin nodded, blushed. The following rehearsal witnessed a true Manchu Emperor. Every one was amazed. Ying Ying asked him:

"What happened? Did the ghost of the Emperor enter into your body?"

"I got hold of some Chinese movies about the 19th century royalty." Clever and intelligent!!!

Li Yong had to drill even the smallest minutia of a court lady's proper mannerism with Jenny and the women playing the two other important royalties. The Manchu ladies' elaborate headdresses and elevated shoes were a challenge to the female actors. The palace ladies were proper and decorous in their movements in keeping with their restrictive attires. Their backs were always straight. They hardly ever ran. When they walked, they swung their arms back and forth but the body remained still, almost stiff. They turned their heads slowly and gracefully. Several weeks before opening night the director asked the female actors to wear the shoes and headdresses during rehearsals in order to practice how to walk and move.

Since there was no place in New England to rent the costumes and accessories, Mr. Yu called his friends at the TV stations in Taiwan asking to rent some from their costume collections. But nothing would be available at the time he needed them. Besides, rented costumes would not be entirely suitable because the colors, styles, even the fabric might not be what the director wanted; and the sizes might not fit the actors. The best solution would be to custom-build according to the designer's drawings and the measurements of the actors. Mr. Yu looked into costume-making companies in China. Their prices must be affordable, he thought. Yet the exorbitant quotes were appalling, much to his surprise,

"Why is it so expensive? We can never afford that. I thought things were much cheaper there," he asked.

"Sorry. They would be cheap if you were in China or from China. You are in America. And they can sense that you are not from China. They think you must be mega rich. They don't know to what extent they can gouge you," Li Yong said. "Why don't you have the costumes made here?"

"I suppose that's the last resort. But it will be very expensive too. I am not sure if China Society has the budget. And I don't know any designer or costume builder. Can you find them in your school? I don't know the theatre community in Boston."

Li Yong had just the right guy in mind. Lu Wen, a classmate of his at Shanghai Drama Institute, was a costume design major at Boston University. He accepted the job and designed the costumes with such understanding and authenticity. The construction of the costumes fell on the shoulders of a team of costume majors at the Mass college of Art. They were overwhelmed by the number and complexity of the costumes and accessories they needed to build.

"We have never seen a production with this many costumes, shoes, headdresses, hats, and paraphernalia. Why do you need to be so elaborate? Why not let the characters wear the same costume throughout?" a theatre arts professor commented.

The costume builders had three months to tackle the job. Near the end of the three-months they were still far from getting the job done and could not possibly finish the costumes on time. They were stressed out. The director and the production team were worried but did not reveal the crisis to alarm the actors who had asked about the costumes many times. When they did not see any they became worried and restless. Some asked:

"When can we see the costumes?"

"Are we going to have costumes?"

"Will they be done on time for the opening?"

That sent the costume builders to ire. They said:

"We don't tell you how to act. You don't tell us how to sew. Don't worry. You will have your costumes on opening night."

In fact the costume builders were nervous and distraught. They were not at all sure they could complete the costumes on time. They recruited more classmates to help and worked very long hours. Gladly, by the time the dress rehearsal came along, most of the costumes and accessories were ready. There were still a few with only roughed in hems and sleeves. But the audience could hardly notice it.

In addition to sewing, the costumes must be embellished with various embroidered motifs designated specifically to each character in the hierarchy of officialdom or royalty. There was no place in Boston that could do this job. Ying Ying came up with an idea: to ask Zhang Ze to paint them. Zhang Ze was a skilled painter of realistic landscape and portraiture, also trained in Chinese ink-and-color painting of the meticulous style. He accepted the assignment saying that he could definitely paint the motifs to resemble embroidery.

When each costume was roughed in, one of the seamstresses would deliver it to Ying Ying or Tonia, who in turn would call Zhang Ze to pick it up. The excellently designed motifs of dragons, phoenixes, peonies, plums, bamboos, deer, birds, water, mountains, and clouds were exquisitely painted selectively on different robes as appropriate to each character's rank and position. The costumes came out dazzling. No one in the audience could believe it was not actual embroidery when told.

Meng Song offered to design the sets, paint the backdrop and soft scenery. He had never designed stage scenery before but he was amply knowledgeable in history, familiar with the story, and had a clear vision on what the sets should look like. The director and everyone else trusted that he could do a good job.

Hou Shang from Shanghai Drama Institute, a sound and lighting designer, was a graduate student at Tufts University Theatre Department at the time. Li Yong recruited him for the production.

When Meng Song came to China Society to paint the soft scenery or oversee the construction of the sets he was always chauffeured by a girl, and a different girl each time. Denis often joked about it:

"What makes this guy so irresistible? All these girls!!! Blonde, Brunette, Red Head, he's got them all."

"It's amazing that he still finds time to do the work for our production," Ying Ying added to Denis's banter.

"I wonder who is really his girl friend. Or he just plays around with everyone equally," Jenny questioned.

"I bet he will bring the real one on opening night," Denis said. He might be right.

Meng Song also graciously volunteered to paint a 14' x 4' promotional banner. It was hung outside the theatre like a marquee. Unfortunately, because it was not bolted to the wall, someone could not resist the temptation of owning it. Before the show closed the beautiful piece of art disappeared. Thanks to the thief for not taking it before the show closed. To China Society this was a big loss because meaningful memorabilia was thus gone forever.

The carpenter who built the set, Chong Teng, was a musician trained by Beijing Conservatory and Boston Conservatory. Whether it was fate or lack of excellence, he was not able to build a career with his clarinet so he turned to building things with his hands. While a student, he was a member of the BU orchestra. His command of the English language was close to none and he often responded to the conductor's questions and comments with a single word of "yes." He also made no effort to better his language ability. An anecdote of his communication mishap had famously circulated among the Chinese students:

One time the conductor gave his rehearsal schedule verbally to the orchestra members. Chong Teng missed the first rehearsal because he did not understand what the conductor had said when he made the announcement. Another member of the orchestra, a student from Taiwan, told him about the schedule afterwards. Chong Teng missed the concert for the same reason. There were two clarinets in the orchestra. With him absent that left only one. The conductor was greatly upset but Chong Teng was nowhere to be found because he was at a party in his friend's house. In a regular practice session the conductor saw Chong Teng. He was irate and asked:

"You skipped rehearsals and were not present at the concert. What were you trying to do? Did you understand me when I announced the schedules?"

Chong Teng smiled and said: "yes."

The conduct was abraded: "You knew the rehearsal and concert schedules and did not show up?"

Chong Teng smiled and nodded again: "yes."

The conductor was enraged. "Do you want to leave the orchestra?"

"Yes." Chong Teng said

"Get out!" The conductor was furious. He thrust his baton toward the door and yelled.

Chong Teng looked around, all confused and said: "*shi ma shi ah? Ta sheng chi le*?." (What's going on? He is angry?) Then he took out his clarinet and began to play.

*   *   *   *

Denis, Ying Ying, Missy, Jenny and Tonia were responsible for tackling the production's publicity task. Their exhaustive effort coupled with the novelty of the production did draw much media attention. One TV station promised to shoot a segment before the opening. Another station asked to tape a scene at their studio. Several newspapers asked for pictures to accompany their stories about New England's first production of a Chinese historical play. Director Mr. Yu asked Ying Ying if there were enough completed costumes for one scene. At that moment most of the costumes were only half done. There was not one single finished piece. Mr. Yu was unnerved and asked:

"Are we going to miss the opportunity of a TV spot? I don't think the TV stations would tape and air segments of a play that often. What do we do now?"

The actors were frantic. Ying Ying asked the head seamstress Beth what to do. Beth was greatly peeved. She vented:

"There are still weeks before the show opens and you are asking about completed costumes?"

Ying Ying appeased her: "Don't be upset, Beth. I'm not questioning the readiness of the costumes. It's that we are going to have a TV taping and we must have some costumes. That's all. Perhaps I can take some pieces that are near completion and try to get some help to finish them."

"Just don't ruin my work," Beth grunted.

Ying Ying picked out one of each for Empress Dowager, Emperor, Empress, Lady Zhen, Lady Jin, Eunuch Li Lian-ying, and Eunuch Wang Shang. She called several volunteers to help, and asked Pei-hua, Missy and Tonia to join the work force with her.

"But Ying Ying, I can't sew," Pei-hua complained.

"I can't either. Neither can Missy and Tonia. But we must try. Not major work, just rough in with hand," Ying Ying insisted.

They roughly hand-stitched the crucial places to make the costumes passable for temporary use. After that they undid what they had done before taking them back to Beth.

Kevin was exhilarated by the TV taping though he knew it would be difficult to take off from his hospital duty in the middle of a workday. Trading schedules during the day was impossible. He did not mention it to Mr. Yu or Ying Ying, however. There was no sense getting them all wrought up. He would go even if it meant losing his internship. He pondered over how to break it to his chief physician. He had no other alternatives but telling him the truth and ask to be excused.

"Dr. Gibson, I need your permission to have tomorrow afternoon off," he said to the chief physician.

"What for? We need you here tomorrow, you know that," the Doctor inquired.

"But I... I ...cannot be here. I... I have an ...an...important thing I... I must... attend to," he stuttered.

"What's more important than your duty here?" the doctor smirked.

"I... I... have to ...be at...at the TV station."

"Doing what? The TV station?" The doctor was befuddled.

"A... a taping." Kevin couldn't help chuckling.

"An interview? What have you done to deserve an interview? Why wasn't I informed earlier?" The doctor was further perplexed.

"No, it's not that. It's this play I am in. The TV station gave it a spot, like a preview. It's a publicity stunt. You know." Kevin spelled it all out.

"You are in what??!!"

"A play," Kevin explained, "You know, a stage production."

"You mean a drama?" The doctor couldn't refrain from amazement. This was too big a surprise. "Wow, I didn't know you have been secretly plotting a career change," Dr. Gibson joshed.

"Would you give me the afternoon off?" Kevin knew he had gotten the permission already.

"Sure, sure. I can't hinder the making of a star, can I?" Dr. Gibson Jokingly remarked.

Kevin went to China Society before everyone else that afternoon. He went over his lines and reviewed the blockings to assure that he would give a perfect performance. When everyone was there he told them how he coaxed the good doctor into giving him the afternoon off.

"Wow, it's so touchy. We didn't realize that you might not be able to make it," Jenny exclaimed.

Mr. Yu had the group walk through the segment to be taped. It looked good. At the TV station, when they strode into the studio all stunningly costumed and made up, the program host, the producer and the camera crew all let out a "Wow" simultaneously.

*   *   *   *

Meilan selected a few solo- and duet pieces from the dancers' repertoire. Manna was distressed because Meilan did not choose her solo piece. She skipped many rehearsals that affected the progress of the rehearsal. That was her intention. She further complained to Ying Ying with an air of arrogance.

"Why did you let that Mainland-maid take charge of this? She is an uncouth yokel, no style, like all other Mainland-maids. They are an inferior, worthless bunch. How could you have put them on a par with us?" Manna never hesitated to blatantly voice her discriminatory and contemptuous scurrility toward the Mainlanders. Ying Ying was incensed by Manna's fatuity and bigotry. She retorted:

"Manna, I don't think the Mainlanders are inferior to us. What made your say that? Meilan is not uncouth. She

she is doing a wonderful job teaching the group dance and leading the rehearsals. Can any of the dancers do that?"

"Oh, so you think she is great. I can tell you this much. She thinks the dancers from Taiwan are amateurs. She gave all the solo parts to the Mainlanders, not even one to us. That's not partial? She is insanely selfish, I don't understand why you side with her. Well, I guess I'd better get out of your program before you kick me out." She stormed out of Ying Ying's office.

After Manna walked out Meilan re-choreographed the group dance. As the rehearsals went on, Linda began to skip and complained about things too. Susie and Sally grunted about the honorarium not being commensurate to their effort and time spent. Meilan was annoyed by their attitude.

"What is it with these Taiwan girls? Why are they complaining all the time? If they were better trained dancers we wouldn't need to rehearse this much. How much do they expect to be paid? They are not professionals. They should be grateful to have the chance to learn from me for free. I have had enough with them. If they don't shape up I will quit."

Meilan's criticism of the Taiwan girls embarrassed Ying Ying. But she had nothing to say because Meilan was right.

"Meilan, I apologize for the Taiwan girls. I will speak to them. You have experienced all kinds of situations. If anyone can manage this situation, it would be you," she mollified Meilan. "Dr. Lee is counting on you. You know that. You can't let him down."

"I am doing the best I can to help you. But you must speak with the girls," Meilan softened.

Linda was the weakest among all the dancers since she had no formal training at all. A chance to show herself off on stage was more than a dream to her. Learning new dances was also a valuable opportunity. She was more enthusiastic than the others in the beginning. But Manna's vicious vilification of Ying Ying swayed her. They often chatted on the phone.

"Ying Ying is so damn partial to those Mainland-maids. She thinks they are superior to us. Can you stand that? We all know that those boorish bumpkins are uncouth, not presentable. Yet Ying Ying treats them like stars and put us down as supernumeraries. I couldn't take that, so I quit. Why are you still there to endure the humiliation?"

"Well, I... I "

"You know, China Society and their bunch of useless people are exploiting us. They are using us to make money. You know how much ticket proceeds they will reap? What are they paying us? Peanuts. Only enough for toilet paper. Susie and Sally need that money. You don't. You should not be used by those exploiters. They treat you the worst. You'd better keep away from them." Linda was riled. Before Ying Ying had a chance to speak to her she provoked Meilan to an argument at the rehearsal. It was planned. Meilan was livid and said:

"Your dance is already marginal. Don't make trouble and cause us to lose time."

"You think only the stupid Mainland-maids can dance? What do you know? You have not seen what good dance is. You take your Mainland bumpkins and go to hell," Linda shouted and tore out of the rehearsal hall.

Rage swept through Meilan. "I have never seen anyone so incredibly scurrilous. She is not even good enough to be a back-up and she thinks she is a star?" Meilan stopped the rehearsal and dismissed the dancers.

Manna's diabolical scheme to take the project down for her vengeance worked. Sally and Susie wavered and thought about quitting. Ying Ying knew it would be unproductive to appease Manna. Doing so would only give her a taste of victory and to press on for more. The only thing to do was to contain the damage by talking to Sally and Susie so that they would not desert. Ying Ying took the two women and Meilan to a small restaurant for a quick supper before the rehearsal. She worked out a congenial atmosphere. Then she began to test their feelings about the project.

"I was sorry that Manna and Linda were upset and dropped out. This is a community event. And it is to celebrate our New Year. I didn't expect anything unpleasant to happen. But it's all right. I believe they will put aside their grudge even though they have left the show. I am glad you are not deserting. I want to thank you for it."

"You are professional dancers. You not only have the skill but also the right attitude. You do well." Meilan gave them an uplifting pep talk.

"Well, we have the professional morale. Once committed, we must go through with it. This is professionalism." Susie said in a righteous tone.

Ying Ying was very pleased and said: "I know your talent and time are worth a lot more than what we are paying you. I will try and find some money to pay you more." She was thinking about dividing the money saved from not paying Manna and Linda to pay the main dancers more.

Publicity, or the lack of it, often made or broke an event. China Society did not hire professional publicists at all. But the job was well done by Denis, Ying Ying, Jenny and Tonia. Jenny carried out her daytime work during the day and handled her rehearsal in the evenings to perfection. But then, all the other actors also had to manage their day-time jobs.

On opening night a large crowd packed the house. The Chinese community was astonished to see such a large-scale main stage production of a Chinese play. The audience was impressed and pleased. Kevin's colleagues from the hospital were amazed at his performance. The audience commented on Jenny's beauty. The reviews were mostly good. They lauded the Society's audacious experimentation; extolled the leading actors for their performances; and described the costumes as "elaborate and gorgeous." One reporter wrote: "The Emperor's Favorite Consort was the most beautiful Asian woman I have even seen." But they criticized the choice of the play as "irrelevant to our time and society."

Mr. Yu felt the criticism on his choice of script was unfair.

"Historical pieces rarely have relevance to the current society and time. How many Shakespearian plays are relevant to our society and time? We study history and try to make it relevant to us," he said.

All in all, the whole project was a smashing success.

Chapter 3

After celebrating the success of the series of events, the excitement simmered down. In April, good news about several musicians aroused interest among China Society's people again. Baritone Han Tu won first place in the Metropolitan Opera Competition. Immediately he was given a contract by the Met and moved to New York. Soprano Zhi-an won second place in the same competition. But she did not get a contract with any one company. Instead she was engaged by a number of opera houses on a non-contractual basis the year following the competition. An agent signed her up and earnestly worked to arrange auditions for her. She had a small baby that would have made her constant going out of town difficult if not for a most loving and understanding husband who gave up his own career as a baritone singer to take care of the baby. Eighteen-year old violinist Ma Ya won first place in an international violin competition in Europe and became an active soloist in concerts nationally and internationally. The success of these musicians was heartwarming to Joseph Lee who regarded them as friends and protégés of the Society and was always very proud of them.

Cambridge Museum mounted a solo show for Meng Song who was highly recommended to the Museum by Joseph Lee. Every one at the Society was happy for Song because this was a new step for the advancement of his career. If he were excited, he certainly didn't show it. Denis, Ying Ying, Jenny, Missy and Tonia helped move his paintings to the museum and watched the museum staff hang them on the wall. Those people must have hung hundreds of shows before. They were fast and accurate. The whole show was hung in a few hours.

It was sulky and drizzling on the day of the opening. Meng Song's friends arrived before most other guests. Meilan did not come. The roomful of people were eagerly anticipating Meng song's arrival. When he finally entered, with such easy composure, dressed in black, he had a dark-haired, light-skinned, beauty spa made-up girl in a white gown by his side. All heads turned toward them. Some began to clap, others followed as if a pair of celebrities just came from Hollywood. Pei-hua whispered to Ying Ying:

"Look at them!!!"

Denis said, "wow, a pair of movie stars."

At the height of the reception when the room was crowded, people's chatting was droning incessantly, food and wine were consumed, some people,

Denis among them, spilled into the hallway. A few minutes later, Ying Ying saw Denis return to the gallery, and scoot toward Song. He whispered in his ear, grabbed his arm and pulled him out into the hallway.

"What's going on?" Ying Ying wandered. Then she and the other three young women grew curious. They made their way to the door. Denis returned to the gallery door trying to hold back a titter. He said to the girls, while his eyes were staring in Song's direction.

"Let's Just see how he is going to handle this."

The four followed his gaze and saw a Chinese young girl with spiked, variegated hair, lashes heavy with mascara, purple eye-shadow, glitters on one side of her temple, large gold dangling earrings and bright red lips. She wore a fashionably loose white shirt, the left shoulder-line of which came off her shoulder by four inches; the top four buttons were left undone revealing her cleavage and part of her bare breasts; a golden belt tied around her waist; a pair of black silk pants that were too long for her, the extra inches gathered at the bottom over her red high heel slides. Ying Ying had seen this woman before, the only Chinese woman ever seen with Meng Song. The girl had her arms around Song's neck, her face almost touching Song's. Naughty Jenny wended her way unnoticeably to a poster board near Song and the girl, pretending she was looking at the poster. In fact she was eavesdropping on them, trying to see how Song would extricate himself from the tightening net.

"I am sorry that I am late. I had a hard time finding this place. I also had no clue what time the reception was." The young woman spoke in heavily Taiwanese-accented Mandarin.

"Oh, it's all right. It's not an important event. I wasn't going to come, but..." Song said. Jenny suppressed her chuckle. He had apparently not told this woman about his opening reception because he was taking that dark-haired Caucasian beauty. And this spike-haired Chinese girl had no idea that she was only one of his numerous women, and one that he would probably never take to anywhere because she was not presentable, lacking in class, only good enough as a playing thing when he had the interest.

The woman's amorous feelings were uncontainable. She ran her hands over his arms, traced a finger along his profile, squeezed his hands, and cupped his face in her hands and kissed him. Then she tried to wipe the lipstick marks from his mouth with her fingers. Song was painfully aware of the staring eyes of Jenny behind him and Denis and the three other girls at a distance. But the most anxiety he suffered was the worry of being seen by the white-gowned woman, his date of the evening.

"Shin-shin, I will come to your place after the reception for as long as you want. I promise. But I cannot spend time with you here because there are many people inside waiting to talk to me. .."

"Can I go inside with you? To meet those people?" The girl asked.

"No, no. Those are boring people. You don't need to meet them. Just be a good girl, go home and wait for me. I will be there soon. You just go along home now. Okay?"

80

"I want to go inside with you." This girl wouldn't give up. She pulled out all the tricks from the bag to tempt the man she wanted. She held Song's arm in her bosom and softly rub against it while kissing his face.

"It's too crowded in there. The air is stuffy. Don't go in." Song gently pushed her away, did all he could to rid of her.

"I just came. Can I wait for you here?" The girl backed up one step but still kept a thread of hope.

"Be a good girl and do what I say. Go home and wait for me. I promise I will be quick. Okay, mmmm?" He continued to coax her into obeying him. To add to the strength of his word, he kissed her lightly on her lips.

"Oooookay," the woman agreed. "Be quick. Don't let me wait too long." She wiped off the lipstick mark from his face with one hand and held onto his hand with the other. He shot a glance at the gallery door and quickly walked her out of the hallway to the elevator. When he strode by Denis and the four giggling girls, he said: "Guys, don't laugh at my awkward predicament."

The reviews came out in the following days, nothing short of accolades and predicting brilliance of an artistic career in the years to come. The artist's photos prominently occupied the top of the arts sections. Collectors fell in love with his work; art investors saw it as a good investment opportunity. Within ten days most of his paintings were red-dotted. Galleries on Newberry Street fought to represent him. Overnight his name became a hot topic in the art circle. His roguish behavior also became known.

One day there came a girl to China Society to ask if anyone knew where Meng Song was. She had chauffeured Song a few times before and became more or less familiar to the people there.

"He grew to be distant and indifferent to me. I didn't see him for weeks at a time. I don't know where he is. I thought he might be here sometimes. This morning I saw him hugging and kissing a blonde girl in a bookstore. I avoided being seen by them and snuck out." The heart broken girl said.

"He doesn't come here unless there is a specific reason." Denis said with sympathy.

"We are lovers. At least I think we still are," the girl said. "We were classmates at the art school. When I first saw him I thought he was eighteen years old. He looked so young and so gorgeous. But he was not eighteen. He was twenty-six. I was immediately enthralled by him. I always tried to speak to him. He rarely replied. Just smiled. That unforgettable smile!! We became intimately involved shortly after." Tears filled her eyes as she reminisced. "He is the personification of an artist with that special trait and aura throughout, I always think. He is a man of fine tastes. He loves classical music, ballet, good theatre and is very knowledgeable about them. He listens to music when he paints and even when he sleeps." She talked as if to herself.

Ying Ying found no words to comfort her. Denis said: "You should not have been too serious with this guy."

"But we were in love," the girl said. Denis made no more comment on that playboy who changed girls like people changed shirts. Getting women to fall for him was such an easy game. More than once Meng Song said to Ying Ying and sighed:

"I am so tired of these girls. They stick to me like flour to a wet hand. I can't shake them off. It's most nettlesome." It was beyond Ying Ying why those girls would behave that way.

"Perhaps if you don't put your wet hand in the flour jar in the first place you wouldn't have that problem." She taunted. Meng Song only smiled.

*   *   *   *

China Society's various program committees often recommended events and projects to the Board of Trustees. The Board would decide if a project was feasible. The implementation duty always fell on the staff. A program might prove to be unfeasible sometimes at the implementation stage.

The Performing Arts Committee chair Louisa Kingston, recommended a classical music concert at the Board meeting.

"We have not explored classical music talents locally. I am sure there are many exceptional ones, for example, Yang Dan is one."

"What does he play?" One Trustee asked.

"Piano. Different composers' work." Louisa replied.

"Not Chinese music?"

"No. Although western music does not fall within the realm of Chinese culture but he is of Chinese descent. I think it is justifiable for us to present him," Louisa said.

"Yes, of course. The visual artists we presented did not work in the Chinese media and styles either. Many Chinese pianists are exceptional. Of course they play Western composers' work," another Trustee added.

The Board voted unanimously to accept Louisa's recommendation.

Ying Ying knew how much Louisa admired Yang Dan. One afternoon Louisa scooted into Ying Ying's office, breathless and excited, she said:

"Yang Dan, ... Yang Dan. You got to meet this pianist. He is a young lad, but a great pianist."

Ying Ying had never seen Louisa so enthused. She asked:

"Louisa, where is he? How do we get to meet him? I will tell Dr. Lee about him." Ying Ying noticed Louisa was breathing heavily. "Why are you so out of breath?"

"I double parked. I ran in. Can't stay. I will get a ticket. I just wanted to tell you about this kid. He is great. You must meet him. He is at NEC." Before Ying Ying had a chance to say another word, Louisa ran out.

NEC, that was the New England Conservatory. It shouldn't be difficult to find him.

Two days later, a lanky young boy walked in with a small piece of paper in his hand. He said his teacher told him to come and see Dr. Lee. That piece of paper in his hand had Dr. Joseph Lee's name and China Society's address on it.

"Dr. Lee is not here right now. Do you want to wait? Or do you want me to

82

tell him that you are looking for him? What's your name?" Tonia asked.

"Yang Dan," the boy said.

"Oh, you are Yang Dan, the pianist. Our Trustee Louisa Kingston raved about you." Ying Ying cast a quick glance at him. He was thin and tall, with red streaks in his hair. *He had colored his hair!* Ying Ying thought.

"You study at NEC?"

"Yes. I gave a recital at my teacher Mr. Malone's house. Louisa Kingston was there."

"You must be so wonderful to have impressed her that much."

"I am new here. I Just started this semester." He did not address Ying Ying's comment.

Yang Dan was seventeen-years old, just graduated from a music high school in the Midwest. A child prodigy, he was sent to the States at age eleven. Jason Malone saw this extraordinary talent and thought he should bring as much attention as he could to this student of his. He presented him in a small recital at his house to which Louisa was invited.

One day Dr. Lee and Ying Ying each got an invitation from Yang Dan to a concert at Jordan Hall. Joseph Lee decided to attend the concert to give the kid some support and encouragement. Denis, Pei-hua, Jennifer and Missy also went and got tickets at the door. It was an unforgettable evening. The NEC Orchestra played Chopin's Concerto #2 with Yang Dan as the soloist. He walked on the stage wearing a black tuxedo. A white handkerchief showed its corners from the breast pocket. A touch of a smile and ample confidence arched across his face. He swept a scan around the audience making everyone believe that he was acknowledging his attendance, then he gave a deep bow before stepping toward his bench, unbuttoned his jacket and sat down. He adjusted the bench to his comfort, wiped across the keyboard with a handkerchief, then sat in silence for a few seconds. The conductor waited for his signal to start.

"Such a young kid! He moved, acted, performed like an old pro." Dr. Lee told Ying Ying and the others that it was one of the best performances he had ever heard.

As the concert ended, Dr. Lee and his company went to the green room to congratulate him. Yang Dan was joyful when seeing them and said: "Oh, Dr. Lee, thank you all for coming." He shook everyone's hand. Ying Ying introduced the other girls to him:

"Jenny and Missy are also work-study students at China Society, like me. Pei-hua is from BU."

"I am Ying Ying's good friend. Your performance was phenomenal," Pei-hua said. Jenny and Missy also lauded him.

There were other musicians from China associated with China Society. A few were winners of international competitions, discovered and brought over by Boston University's music professors. The head of BU School of Music was often invited as a judge in vocal competitions worldwide. She had the best chance to discover new talents and Boston University amassed the largest number of outstanding Chinese vocalists and instrumentalists. Harvard and the

New England Conservatory also had a few.

Joseph Lee was most impressed with the four vocalists--two sopranos, a baritone, and a bass--who had won Metropolitan Opera competitions, and caught much attention from the critics. A young pianist from Taiwan, Samantha, a freshman at Harvard University and a winner of the International Chopin Piano Competition in Warsaw, stood out as a critic's favorite Ma Ya, a young violinist from Beijing and a freshman at the NEC reached the audience's soul with her music. Even the ushers at Symphony Hall said: "She is the best soloist here I have heard for a long time." Her looks were just as arresting. When she shopped in women's boutique stores, a few times the owner or manager walked up to her and asked if she would model for them.

Joseph Lee invited Yang Dan, Samantha and Ma Ya to join China Society's Education Outreach Program to perform and conduct panel discussions in public schools. They happily accepted.

The Education Outreach Program was designed for different grade levels of the public schools to enrich the students' cultural experiences and to elevate their appreciation for the arts. Furthermore, the young musicians and artists served as examples of how kids could excel when they tried.

"You will be role models for the kids, to inspire them to set goals in life and to strive for high achievements," Joseph said to the program artists.

The program was the only one in the state offered to inner-city public schools free of charge. China Society raised funds from private sources to pay the participating artists and musicians. Tonia was given the responsibility to set up schedules with the schools for the presentations of the program.

No musicians comparable to Yang Dan, Ma Ya and Samantha were ever introduced to those schools. After Yang Dan played Rachmaninoff Sonata no. 2 some kids said, "It is so neat. I have never heard anything like that." The music teacher came, brushed his hand over the piano, and said: "This piano has never been touched by a pair of hands like that. You have made its day."

Yang Dan and Ma Ya had never played together before. For their first assignment they planned to play Carmen Fantasy by Sarasate. They had one rehearsal together. Ying-Ying was there to observe and was awestruck seeing how the two musicians easily understood each other without even speaking a word, just a point at the score, a nod, a smile sufficed. They played perfectly and beautifully together. *They look like a perfect couple. Would they have a future of togetherness?*

*   *   *   *

Fate treated people with injustice. For example, Ailing and Meilan, both beautiful, both entertainers, why did one have the world wrapped around her little finger and the other could hardly even put food on the table? Why did all the girls swarm around Meng Song like flies around honey while Old Huang could not even hold onto his wife?

Old Huang from Hong Kong was International Foundation's bookkeeper, an honest and hard-working man approaching sixty. His wife was a petite woman, fortyish, always with a coy smile and leering eyes. She was attractive, and she knew it. They had a college-age daughter still living at home. Mother and daughter often dressed alike and competed for attention. Mrs. Huang worked in a flower shop. There was a twenty-five-year-old Jewish man that often came to the shop and ordered flowers to be sent to his house. Shortly after, Mrs. Huang began to get bouquets of flowers sent to her from another florist. Each time there was a card that said "From your admirer, Ross." She finally figured out Ross was that Jewish young man. She never said a word about the bouquets but treated him with unreserved attention, always filled his orders with special care.

Then one day he said to her, "I would like you to arrange flowers for all the rooms in my house. Could you come to my house to take a look before you design the arrangements?"

She hesitated for a moment not sure if she should agree. After all she only knew him as a customer. Would it be all right to go to his house with him? Ross realized it was unthoughtful of him to make that request.

"I apologize. It was an unreasonable request. I hope I have not put you on the spot."

Intuition relieved her of her concern. "I suppose it's all right," she smiled and said softly.

As his car approached an estate, a wide expanse of green grass, trees and flowers spread behind a wrought-iron fence; a large gate opened to reveal a long driveway leading to a majestic mansion. She was astonished by the scene. *This is his house,* she wondered?

Did he really need her to design flower arrangements or was it a pretext to bring her to the house to impress her? Only he knew. Mrs. Huang carefully studied and noted down each room's furniture and décor. She wanted to do the best job she could for this house. It was a rare opportunity, one that might never repeat itself, for her to show her talent, to satisfy herself, and to please him. The plan she came up was exceptional. There were different sets of designs appropriate for different occasions. Motifs and colors might be changed every so often to bring fresh looks to the rooms.

Ross threw a large party for over a hundred guests just to present the first round of installation. He invited Mrs. Huang and her husband to come. He sent her a gift. It was a designer evening dress that fitted her as if custom made.

Mrs. Huang had never worn such an expensive, classy gown before. She could not believe the reflection in the mirror was her. Now she needed a pair of nice shoes and some jewelry to complete her attire. She bought a pair of expensive high heels. Real jewelry was out of the question. Only custume jewelry was possible. She had no other choice.

Old Huang was dumbfounded to see his wife transformed to an elegant, classy lady preparing to attend a high-class party. He told her that he was not going to go because he always felt uneasy among strangers; he wouldn't know what to say or to do. Beside, he didn't have a nice suit for the occasion. Mrs.

Huang made no attempt to persuade him.

Ross sent a limousine to pick up Mrs. Huang. He greeted her at the entrance of the main hall and introduced her to his guests. He said:

"This is the lady we are honoring tonight. Her flowers brightened up my rooms, as well as my heart and soul."

That was some introduction. His guests began to whisper, was this woman writing a new chapter in his life? Mrs. Huang felt a little awkward. She was not used to mingling with socialites like those in the party. She looked shy and timid. Ross found that particularly alluring. He never left her alone for a second, but stood by her side at all times, tending to every little need she had. She completely forgot that she was a woman over forty, married and with a grown daughter. She felt like a young girl out on her first date with a boy. She appeared so in his eyes too.

The two quickly fell in love. Ross proposed marriage. She said: "My daughter is twenty-one, only three or four years younger than you. I am afraid I am too old."

"Nonsense. You are the first woman I have truly loved. You are not a day older than I am in my eyes. Beside, what does age matter?" The young man was seriously enamored.

It was not without a struggle within Mrs. Huang. Her reason and emotion clashed time and again before she asked Old Huang for a divorce. The old guy was stupefied.

"Why? Just because he paid you to arrange flowers?"

"No, I love him," Mrs. Huang replied plainly.

"You love him? What about me? What about our daughter? The boy should have asked to marry our daughter, not you. You are mad. He is only a boy. He is almost twenty years younger than you. Why do you want to marry him?" Old Huang had a hundred reasons for objection.

"I want to marry him because he is young, he is handsome, he is rich and he loves me. I am almost twenty years older than him? You are almost twenty years older than me. So there." She had all the reasons to defeat Old Huang.

Old Huang was defeated.

Mrs. Huang married the rich handsome young guy who loved her.

When Old Huang recounted his ill-fated situation, tears streamed down his cheeks.

*   *   *   *

Contrary to Old Huang's fate, Meng Song had never tasted the loss of a woman. The only woman who had ever rejected him was perhaps Jenny. As a habit of his, Song asked every decent-looking girl, even some not so decent looking, for dates regardless of race, creed, single or married. God forbid, he had to be rejected by a young and innocent American-born who hadn't had any experience in dating men from China. Jenny would not risk being toyed with and tossed around by this Casanova no matter how enthralling he was. She had seen other women snagged in that dreadful destiny. Song was baffled. For a while he lost interests in all his numerous trophies. Perhaps it was the ultimate truth: "That which comes too easily holds no value; the harder it is to reach the more tantalizing it becomes."

He felt anxious.

Languidly Meng Song wandered around. He bumped into his spike-haired China-doll from Taiwan except this time her hair was not spiked or streaked with golden color. It was half shaved and dyed purple. He had avoided seeing her or answering her calls for months. As there was no answering machine in his room, by choice, he never knew who had called him. He never picked up the phone when it rang. His phone was only for out-going calls.

"I don't want girls to want me. I will take them when I want them." This was his adage. He scorned those who were "flour sticking on his wet hand."

The China-doll was inflamed to see him and said: "Song, you still have not picked up the jacket you left in my apartment. You'd better come with me to get it." This was a snare she set to get him. Even as they climbed up the four flights of stairs and entered her room, she wasted no time but to strip. No sooner did Song realize the beguile than he uttered a stern demand:

"Wait! Stop!! What are you doing? I am not in the mood." He turned around and left.

As he left China-doll's apartment Meng Song mindlessly got on the subway to go to China Society. At the front door he bumped into Hu Ning, the girl who played the Empress in *Intrigues in the Manchu Imperial Court*, whose sensuous, voluptuous body had long tantalized the artist. They were both happy to see each other again.

Hu Ning was first trained as a gymnast. When the prospect for success in gymnastics became foggy she turned to acting. Though without a diploma from the esteemed Beijing Drama Institute, she apprenticed at the People's Theatre and was trained by some first-rate directors and acting coaches who were impressed by her appearance and intelligence. She began her acting career on the stage. Two years later America tickled her fancy as it did many Chinese men and women. She fled China by swimming from Shenzhen to Hong Kong. It was not an easy task. She and her fellow skulkers were caught several times and punished for their flight. The luring power of freedom, however, as attested by those who had experienced it, fired Hu Ning's desire to try again and again until she succeeded too. In Hong Kong she was introduced to a man named An Kai who had also escaped China the same way but many years earlier. He had settled in Boston, worked in restaurants, and saved up some money. He was going to Guangzhou to find a bride. At his stop in Hong Kong his luck struck. He met Hu Ning. He enticed her with generous gifts of money, jewelry and clothing. She had no idea what he did for a living but thought he must be rich. She married him.

In Boston Hu Ning was often left home alone because An Kai was busy working. She took an English-as-a-Second-Language course at Bunker Hill Community College where she met many other Chinese. It was there she heard about China Society's audition announcement.

"Hi, how are you?" Meng Song greeted with a wide grin.

"Oh," Hu Ning smiled radiantly, "how are you?"

"You came to see Ying Ying?" Meng Song was making conversation.

"Yea, are you here to see her too?" Hu Ning gave him another smile.

"No, I came to see Dr. Lee. But it's not important. I am glad to see you here."

"Hmmm."

"Do you mind if I ask you to have coffee with me?" It was so easy and natural for Meng Song to ask a girl out. Hu Ning had no excuse to decline his invitation. She liked to have coffee with him too. After having coffee lunchtime was near. Song very effortlessly asked to take Hu Ning to lunch. She happily went with him. When they left the restaurant Meng Song casually put his arm around Hu Ning's waist. Hu Ning was self-conscious about that, her mind fought with her feelings and told her to pull away. Song was so irresistible. Yet she was married. She should not lose her head over him.

"When did you get married? After the play production?" Meng Song was shocked to hear that she was married.

"No, long before that. I was married before I came here."

"Oh? You came here alone?" Meng Song couldn't restrain his curiosity. There were married people from China coming to the States without their spouses.

"No. We married in Hong Kong," Hu Ning clarified her situation.

"He is an American? Where did you hide him? Why haven't I met him?"

"No, he is a Chinese, but an American citizen. He's busy working all the time." Hu Ning was a little shy about her constant solo appearance.

"So, he works all the time to make money for his beautiful wife to spend and to play around?" He was flirting with her, aptly.

"I don't play around," she blushed, smiling coyly.

"Mmm, Okay, okay. That's good. You don't play around." The flirtation continued, not so much in the words, but in what was behind those words and in his repressed chuckle, in his eyes. A wave of pleasure washed over Hu Ning. For a moment she completely forgot that she was married.

She joyously accepted his date to have dinner the next day and dance at a nightclub after that. Being alone most of the time, Hu Ning felt good to have a handsome man by her side going to restaurants and nightclubs. After dating Caucasian women almost exclusively, except for that dissolute debauchee from Taiwan, Hu Ning was a fresh change for Meng Song. And she was more sensually appealing than all the girls he had been with.

Meng Song took Hu Ning to L'Espalier, a classy French restaurant on Gloucester Street. The presence of this handsome couple drew many gazes as they entered. Hu Ning smiled proudly while casting a swift glance around the restaurant and its customers. She had never been to a restaurant like this or had a companion as handsome as Meng Song.

She enjoyed the dinner immensely although, frankly, she didn't know what was on her plate. She would have preferred Chinese food so much more. Meng Song felt very much at home with his food and wine, and with the restaurant. It was the father of one of his girlfriends who took him to this restaurant the first time and many subsequent times. He was living in the same house with the girl and her parents then, in an old mansion on Brattle Street in Cambridge, as sort of a houseguest. The old attorney was very found of this young artist and was pleased to see his daughter having such an exceptional boy-friend. He might have secretly hoped that the two youngsters would tie the wedding knot, only to have his dream shattered when Meng Song decisively moved out leaving much of his personal belongings in their house.

He took Hu Ning to a nightclub on one of the Boston harbor islands. They danced like lovers, with such intimacy.

"You inflame me, Hu Ning," Meng Song whispered in her ear during the slow fox trot music.

"You are holding me too closely," Hu Ning murmured. She felt his hand on her back pressing her amply endowed breasts to his chest. Her heartbeat fastened. An unfamiliar sensation started her.

"Not close enough. There are two layers of clothing between us. They should be off," he boldly flirted. If the lights were not so dim he would have seen her face flushed.

"Meng Song, you ..."

He kissed her. She swooned.

*   *   *   *

As the taxi turned into her street, she said to Meng Song.

"I should get off here."

"Why? Your husband is waiting up for you?"

"He may be asleep by now. But I don't want to take the chance." A tinge of embarrassment and shyness flashed across her face.

"All right," Meng Song said and told the driver not to go any farther.

The taxi pulled to a stop. Meng Song paid the driver and they both got out. She bid him good night and began to walk down the street to her house. He stepped up, grabbed her arm and pulled her into his bosom and pressed his lips over hers.

Meng Song added a new entry in his little black book in bold black Chinese characters of Hu Ning's name and phone number, underscored in red.

Meng Song's image swelled in Hu Ning day and night. Their tryst at the nightclub replayed in her mind endlessly. She was intoxicated. For several days she couldn't eat or sleep; couldn't hear her husband when he spoke to her. She attended a banquet one day. There were hundreds of guests in the restaurant. She saw Meng Song in everyone. She felt dizzy and almost fainted. Most of the time, she did not leave her house but waited for a call from Meng Song. Every time the phone rang her heart skipped several beats.

Yet he did not call. She became despondent and doleful. But her reason told her not to be silly; after all she was a married woman; one evening of rendezvous was all she could hope for; Meng Song must have cautioned himself not to make further moves.

Then he called. It was a week after that evening.

Hu Ning was ravished. But that ravishment was tinged with sadness, and exasperation. "I thought you would never call me again. You have had your fun with me." An accusative tone mixed with heartbreaks.

"Oh, no. I was working on my paintings. I have not stepped out of my apartment since our date." The easy explanation was couched in a soothing voice.

"You could have given me a short ring. Just to let me know you had not abandoned me." Hu Ning could not but pour her heart out. She wanted to tell him how much she had missed him day and night, stayed home to wait for his call. She paused for a second waiting to hear Meng Song's sweet comforting words. When they did not come, she asked: "Why are you calling me now?"

"I want to show you what I have been working on. Do you want me to pick you up at your house?" He ignored her question and asked her a question instead. Those powerful words coupled with his pleasant voice all but elated Hu Ning and swept away all the feeling of melancholy that had consumed her for a week. She did not give any thought about the sincerity and truthfulness, or lack of them, in Meng Song's utterance.

"No, I will meet you at China Society." She felt very gingerly about letting him into her house. What if at that very moment her husband happened to pop in?

Half an hour later she met Meng Song at China Society's front door. Without entering the building they quickly made their way to the subway station.

Meng Song's apartment was on Harvard Avenue off Harvard Street in Brookline. It was on the third floor of a brick building, a very large place that he shared with 3 other people. He had a spacious bedroom/study. There was a dining room which he used as his studio wherein paintings were spread out on the floor and on a large table. A water pitcher, ink slab, color palate, brushes in a porcelain cylindrical holder were lying at one end of the table. He let Hu Ning browse through his work for a moment but made no attempt to talk to her about it. Then he steered her to his bedroom. It was simply but tastefully furnished, a tangible statement of the artist.

"Very nice room," Hu Ning commented.

Without any opening ritual, Meng Song wasted no time but casually strode up to her, wrapped his arms around her waist and murmured in her ear:

"What is your room like? Will you let me see your room?" Hu Ning knew it was a flirt that needed no reply. It was such a simple, innocuous few words yet it exuded enormous sensual arousal in her. She melted in his embrace and kisses. A whole week of thirst had finally been quenched.

She did not know if she had hoped for this, anticipated this, or prepared for this. She betrayed her husband completely when she united with Meng Song.

In the following weeks and months Hu Ning was completely beside herself. Her head reeled, her emotions awry. When she was intimate with her husband, Meng Song's image occupied her mind.

One day after being together in his apartment, Meng Song said to her: "I will be away for sometime. I will call you when I come back."

"Where are you going?" A natural and reasonable question.

"Out of town. I don't like nosy women. Don't ask me questions. I will tell you if I think you need to know." Not a very gentle answer but Hu Ning accepted it. Nothing Meng Song said or did would bother her. She snuggled against his chest, quietly, her arm draped over his waist.

"It's late. You'd better get going." The voice was gentle but there was no warmth in it. Hu Ning raised her head to gaze at him. He still had that enticing smile on his face.

"Get dressed, okay?" The voice was more gentle, the smile more enchanting. Hu Ning summoned her will to pull herself up and off the bed. She put her clothes on like an obedient little girl. She bent down to kiss him before she left. Passively accepting her kiss, he didn't get up to see her to the door. She quietly opened the door and closed it behind her.

The frigidity in Meng Song contrasted glaringly with the steaming heat that used to radiate from him whenever he held her in his bosom. What was the cause of this sudden change? It baffled Hu Ning. Little did she know, Meng Song had met another woman, a blonde from Finland, and he was consumed by his searing lust for her.

Hu Ning desperately counted every minute waiting for Meng Song's call. One month had lapsed and there was no call from him. Like a sleepwalker, she wondered to Meng Song's apartment. She stood outside for a minute. Her mind was blank. Then she subconsciously knocked on the door, not expecting to find Meng Song inside. After a short while, the door opened to reveal Meng Song, a towel wrapped around the waist of his otherwise naked body.

"You are back?" Reality did not hit Hu Ning at first. She was thrilled to see him. Before Meng Song could utter a word Hu Ning pushed her way inside the door and into his bedroom where she saw a blond girl reclining in his bed. A sheet covered half of her nudity. A sudden thunderbolt blasted over Hu Ning. She turned around to face Meng Song whose nonchalance impaled her heart. She darted out of the room. Meng Song did not stop her or say a word to her.

She could not go home. She needed someone to lean on. China Society, that's where she wanted to go.

Denis, Ying Ying, Tonia, Missy and Jenny were sitting in the office discussing their new project. They were surprised to see Hu Ning apparently in distress and tears. After Hu Ning recapitulated her story Denis could not repress his ire.

"This God damn Meng Song. I don't care how good an artist he is, he is a fucking bastard. How could he have treated women like this, especially one he was associated with at work?!"

"Huh, he was trying to do that to me before. I mean, he asked me out, but I refused," Jenny said peevishly.

"Hu Ning, didn't you know Meng Song was like that? He only fools around with women. He has no love for anyone, only lust. Why did you fall in that trap?" Ying Ying sympathized with Hu Ning but at the same time she couldn't help scolding her.

"He has some nefarious magic over women. That's why, except for our strong little Jenny," Denis said: "Try to forget the whole thing. It's not worth your tears." The three girls also tried to console her.

"But Hu Ning, I must say that you were playing with fire. It was a dangerous game. What if your husband had found out?" Denis was feeling badly for her husband, a hard-working, wife-loving man, to be cheated like that.

Shame and desperation enveloped Hu Ning. Yet she still could not shrug off the spell cast on her by Meng Song. She wished that Meng Song would let her share him with that blond.

*　　　*　　　*　　　*

Among Jenny's admirers, Kevin Hong, the twenty-six-year-old physician-actor, was the one having the courage to approach her. They shared common interests in theatre beyond their acting in *Intrigue in the Manchu Imperial Palace*. He aspired to become a professional actor. Jenny had planned to study stage design at the Royal Academy of Dramatic Art after Tufts. Kevin imagined that one day he would be in a production designed by Jenny. He optimistically believed that he and Jenny would make a good pair. A few times he invited Jenny to productions at the American Repertory Theatre or the Huntington Theatre. Jenny declined without giving an excuse. Kevin was disappointed, frustrated, but still hopeful. He was patient and confident. *I will defeat Michael and Sean and win her over in the end,* he believed.

Kevin was wrong.

Jenny did see a lot of good qualities in Kevin and liked him. He was entirely different from the playboy Meng Song. But there was a great barrier standing between them. She never disclosed to anyone the feelings hidden in a dark corner of her mind: The fact was that she would not date a Chinese. She would not keep Chinese friends. Missy was an exception. Their work-study program at China Society brought them close together.

Missy came to the States with her parents at age thirteen. Unlike most Chinese from Taiwan, her parents were not foreign students, but immigrants. They operated a tea store in San Francisco. Both she and her brother were obligated to help in the store after school. A few years later they finished high school and were admitted to MIT, over 3000 miles away. But the parents did not mind. They were proud of the kids being accepted by one of the nation's most prestigious schools. To most Chinese parents Harvard and MIT were the best schools.

In her junior year Missy did her work-study program at China Society and befriended Jenny. Now she had finished her school, her mother called her back to California to help with the tea business. A strong sense of duty and a habitual obedience to the parents left Missy with no choice but to go home. That decision disrupted her relationship with her boy-friend Eric. They were so deeply in love that if they were a few years older or had a reliable income they would have been married. Missy's homebound decision broke Eric's heart. The two cried every day like helpless little children.

"Don't be so sad. It's only a few hours of flight from Boston. Eric and you can visit each other easily," Jenny said.

"No, it won't be that easy." Missy muttered.

"Why doesn't Eric go to California with you? Why must he stay in Boston? He can find a job there." Jenny asked.

"That would be too big a move for him. He just got a job offer here."

"Well then maybe you can come back and marry him after a while. I don't suppose your mother wants to keep you home forever," Jenny tried to console Missy.

"My mother may want me to marry a Chinese in San Francisco. I don't know. Even if she doesn't, the future is unpredictable. Once we separate I am afraid that's it," Missy wept.

"Why do you have to listen to your mother?" Jenny truly did not understand how a mother could dictate a grown daughter's life like that especially when this action might destroy the daughter's happiness. "You are an adult now. You have the right to live your own life."

"I have the responsibility to my family." Missy and her brother always felt that parents came first, family before one's own well being. It was a tradition so opposite to the American way yet they were brought up in that tradition.

It was inconceivable to Jenny. Her parents never taught her Chinese tradition and value although they venerated that tradition and lived their lives under those guiding principles within it. They were extremely sensitive to their daughter's feelings and needs. They were reluctant to impose a value that was foreign to America in which Jenny was born and grew up.

"That is so backward. Parents should be thinking of the well being of their children, not the other way around. Children do not cater to the parents' needs at the expense of their own happiness. Your parents, excuse me for saying so, are too selfish," Jenny said in exasperation.

"That's the American way of thinking," Missy said.

"Don't you hate them, your selfish parents I mean?" Jenny bluntly asked.

"No, I don't hate them," Missy replied in surprise. "I love them. They are my parents. How could I hate them?"

"To tell you the truth, I hate my parents," Jenny confessed.

"Why?" Missy was appalled. "I haven't heard you talk like that. Why do you hate your parents? Did they treat you badly?"

"Oh no, they were good to me. They are always good to me because they must be the best in everything, best parents, model parents. I cannot find faults in them. Do you know what it's like living under the shadow of perfect people? That's why I hate them."

"Jenny, you are not making any sense. How could you hate people because you cannot find faults in them?" Missy was puzzled. "You should be grateful to your parents who are good to you."

"Please, I don't want to talk about it," Jenny ended the conversation abruptly.

Missy was mystified. One time Jenny got a call from her father telling her that her mother was very ill. Jenny did not go home to see her. Missy couldn't understand why.

It was apparent that the two girls had come from two entirely different worlds. Missy wondered if all American youth, and Chinese American youth were indifferent, even hostile to their parents.

Missy had always adored Jenny for her looks, envied her for her family background, and jealous of her for the admirations guys had bestowed upon her. But now she felt sorry that her friend was so cold and resentful toward her parents.

*　　　*　　　*　　　*

This was the year 1991. Pei-hua graduated from BU School of Law, Li Yong from BU School for the Arts with a master's degree in theatre arts, and Jenny from Tufts with a bachelor's degree in theatre arts.

Pei-hua's parents flew in to attend her commencement. They asked if she would go home with them for a vacation. It sounded tempting but she had just started working at Swanson, Williams and Murphy in downtown Boston and should not take time off so soon. She promised that she would visit home the first chance she got.

She moved to Tremont On The Common, a nice apartment building conveniently located on Tremont Street, facing the Boston Common and within walking distance to her office. Her friends threw a party to celebrate her new job and her new home. Li Yong did not attend it.

Li Yong's assiduity in learning English had paid off. He called the agent in New York that had told him to come back when his English was better. As soon as the man picked up the phone Li Yong did a monologue for him. The agent was so impressed that he asked to see him. The date clashed with Pei-hua's party. He was regretful to miss the party, but his career preempted all concerns. No one could blame him.

Ying Ying made a toast to Pei-hua:

"Pei-hua, congratulations to you for joining the class of sperms."

"What?" Pei-hua did not get it.

"Haven't you heard? Lawyers are sperms. Only one in millions may be human," Ying Ying bantered.

"Oh, come on!!!" Pei-hua whined.

"Do you know why sharks don't bite lawyers?" Denis asked.

"Why?" Jenny asked.

"Because of professional courtesy." Denis chortled gleefully, then turned serious: "Sorry, Pei-hua, we are all very happy for you so let's have some fun.

Okay? You are not mad, are you?"

"Mad at the bunch of you guys? Not worth it," Pei-hua retorted.

Li Yong went to New York and signed the contract. Soon after that he was cast as Song Liling in *M Butterfly*. He invited his good friends to his place for an intimate and casual gathering. Everyone congratulated him for his success – a budding acting career promised to fully bloom on Broadway.

Pei-hua found a chance when Li Yong was not surrounded by his guests to toast to him. Wistfully she said:

"Li Yong, wish you all the success. We will see you on stage." Her eyes dampened, a soft smile lifted the corners of her mouth.

"Thank you, Pei-hua, not only on stage. I am sure I will see you off stage, often." His searing gaze impaled through Pei-hua's eyes. Blushed, she lowered them. A touch of self-consciousness scalded her face.

"Really, Pei-hua, I will come back to see you every chance I get. And I hope you will come to New York too."

Pei-hua regarded him, a question in her mind. *What did he mean?* Li Yong understood it. But he only said: "I wish to be a special friend, a close friend of yours. Will you allow me?"

"But, what about ... what about Sandy, ... your girl-friend?" Pei-hua asked wistfully.

"That was over, some time ago. Pei-hua, I hope you don't mind..."

Pei-hua's feelings were mixed. She had secretly loved Li Yong for three years. But Li Yong was in love with someone else. Now that he had broken up with his girl-friend, or was it that his girl-friend had broken up with him, he came to her. Did she mind? Of course she did. She was not his first choice. However, Li Yong and Sandy were dating before he met Pei-hua. So the question of choice was impertinent. She did not answer Li Yong's question. She was silent.

With Sandy, Li Yong felt obligated. They dated for two years, partly because of that special tie, the story of their fathers in the Korean War, partly because Sandy's parents treated him so well, always invited him to their home. But the feelings between the two were never very strong. He did not feel that he had found the love of his life. When they decided to split up both felt liberated. It didn't take long for Sandy to go out with another man. Li Yong liked Pei-hua from the start. But he was not free to pursue her at first. Then he was embroiled in his struggle for making a living, his study and career, that he had no time or desire to start a romance.

He saw through Pei-hua's mind in her reticence. He couldn't blame her.

"May I call you or write you, Pei-hua?"

How could she refuse that? She lifted her eyes, softly and tenderly. "Yes. I'd like that."

*   *   *   *

The Boston Common with its throngs of people engaging in different activities was in plain view from Pei-hua's new apartment window. She liked to look out the window to see children playing, seniors sitting on benches reading, chatting, or just watching others, young people playing balls, riding bicycles, skateboarding, jogging, ... In the summer evenings there were entertainment programs sponsored by the City and presented by various organizations. She and her old chums sometimes went to watch the performances. On Saturdays and Sundays she walked in the Common for her weekly exercise.

That Saturday while taking her walk, she saw an elderly Chinese couple sitting on the bench. They looked weary and dejected, not speaking much to each other, nor enjoying the scene. They were just there, waiting. But what were they waiting for? She wandered yet did not ask. The next morning she went to the Common for a walk again. She saw the same old couple still sitting on the same bench. The old woman was sniveling, the old man looked distraught. They incited Pei-hua's curiosity and concern. She went over to ask how they were doing and whether she could be of help. Upon hearing her caring words the old woman burst out crying. The old man also wiped tears from his eyes.

"Our son and daughter-in-law left us here yesterday. They said they would come back in an hour."

"They haven't come. I am afraid they are not coming," the old woman cried harder. She wiped her tears and nose with her hand and sleeve. Pei-hua took some tissues from her bag and handed it to the woman.

"We don't know what happened. Did they have an accident? Did they forget us?" the old man said.

"They don't want us anymore. We are a burden. We are useless," the old woman complained.

Pei-hua was mortified by their situation. She had once heard of a story about an elderly man in wheelchair being abandoned in a park. What kind of animals would do such a thing?

"Where do they live? Do you have their address and phone number? I will call them to pick you up." Pei-hua wanted to see the heartless couple and give them a lecture.

"We don't know their address or phone number. We don't speak English and we are helpless without them. We never suspected that they would leave us in the park," the old man said.

"Do they live far or close by?"

"Far, very far," the old woman replied. Their plight singed Pei-hua.

"Don't worry. I will help you," Pei-hua reassured them. "Come with me to my apartment and then we'll see what to do." Pei-hua bought some take-out from the near-by Chinese restaurant for the old couple who must have had no food or water since the day before.

The old man related their situation to Pei-hua: "There are many mothers brought over here by their sons or daughters to baby-sit the grandchildren. Or go out to work as housekeepers or babysitters for people."

"They are younger and stronger than we are. We cannot do those works.

Our daughter-in-law often quarrels with our son about us. She said that we took up a room, ate too much food and were useless," the old woman cut in. "She told our son, one time I heard, that he should put us on the street for the government to take care of. She got money from the government on our behalf but we have not seen the money."

Pei-hua was indignant. She called Ying Ying.

"Ying Ying, can you come over? We have a situation here. An older couple was abandoned by their son. They need help. You know better about how to get help for them. Would you come immediately?"

Ying YIng came shortly and called the senior service agency in Chinatown. Mrs. Ku came to the rescue. She sighed in exasperation.

"Why didn't they call us instead of just abandon the elders in the park? I don't know how these young people grew to be so diabolically cruel-hearted."

Mrs. Ku told a disheartening story of an elderly Chinese lady from Singapore:

"This poor woman!! Well. She was a rich old woman until her son wheedled her into giving it all to him, over ten million dollars. He said that she didn't need all that money as long as he, her son, took care of her, and he needed it to start his business. After he opened his business with the mother's millions, the son claimed that the mother was poor and must rely on welfare. He applied for welfare on her behalf and sent her to us. You think this is atrocious? It is perfectly legal. This is our law, our system!! Children are not responsible for their parents, every other taxpayer is. The mother thus became a charge of the society. The son never even came to visit her. Last year the old woman, so disgusted with her fate, so tired of her life, killed herself by jumping from the top floor window." Ying Ying couldn't believe the story. She shook her head and sighed.

"Why does America have such a stupid law!" Pei-hua muttered to herself.

Mrs. Ku immediately put the old couple in a senior housing project. Normally there was an application process and a waiting period; various papers were needed too. But this exceptional situation was an emergency case. The couple told Mrs. Ku that their passports were not on them; they had no papers. Ying Ying was indignant and wrote a story about the incident, to castigate the inhumane behavior of the son and daughter-in-law, and to waken people's conscience. The article was printed in a Chinese newspaper.

Once the old couple was in the senior service agency, Pei-hua and Ying Ying needed not to worry. Mrs. Ku had her ways to resolve any paperwork and identity issues there might be.

*   *   *   *

Meilan had not been seen or heard from for a while. What was she doing? Where was she? Ying Ying and Pei-hua were wondering. Meilan and the two girls, especially Ying Ying, had developed a good friendship. While being with her two friends, Meilan was a natural, honest, unpretentious, unassuming woman without any of the pomposity she often displayed in public. She had so many interesting stories to tell, stories about her life in China, particularly those during the Cultural Revolution, the ordeals she went through in her childhood under the grimmest disciplines of her dance training, and her rise to fame as China's most beloved singer and movie star. She told them in such color and flavor that she brought every detail to vivacity making her listeners feel as if experienced first-hand. For example she told Pei-hua and Ying Ying:

"At three o'clock in the morning, I sneaked out of my bed, very surreptitiously, in complete darkness. I stealthily slinked out of my dorm room. In the predawn grayness, shadowy figures might faintly be visible in the hallway. I darted furtive glances around. When assured that no one was there to detect my rule breaking, I snuck into the studio to strenuously drill what had been taught in class during the day. I wanted to excel, to surpass all the other girls. Like my dorm room, the studio was pitch-black. I felt my way to the exercise bar, gripped on it. It was dead silent. I began to bend my body toward the bar, then lift my left leg straight up." She re-enacted it, right hand gripping on an imaginary bar. "These were warm-ups, you see. Then I stretched my left leg backward. Oh! I kicked something, and brought out a sound of "Ou." I was startled. It was a girl!! She was there doing the same thing as I was. You see how competitive we were? We each wanted to outdo the others."

In 1975, at the height of the Cultural Revolution Meilan was fourteen years old. Even at that tender age she was sent to the countryside to do hard labor.

"I was sent to the farm to till the field, plant the seeds, pluck the weeds, and harvest the grains among other things. My daily chores included carrying buckets of water from the well to our quarters. They were a few thatched roofed, mud walled huts. The well was several *lis* away. Three *lis* equal a mile, you see. In order to fill the huge water jar I had to go back and forth many trips to trudge those *lis* with two large water-buckets hanging from a shoulder pole. They weighed me down, literally. When I got to the huts, I swear, I was a few inches shorter." Pei-hua and Ying Ying burst into a convulsion at her dramatization.

"In the fall, after the harvest, hay was piled and tied up. I had to carry the humongous piles one by one from the field to another location, again many *lis* away. The pile was so large that one person could not handle it. Two people picked it up and put it on my back as if I were a donkey. ... " At this point Pei-hua's and Ying Ying's stomachs hurt from guffawing. Pei-hua couldn't restrain herself from commenting:

"Meilan, come on, it couldn't be true. You are fooling us."

"But it was dead true. You don't believe me? Just ask any of the guys from China. They will have stories ten times more incredible to you than mine." Her seriousness convinced the two girls from Taiwan.

"With that huge pile of hay on my back-- they were huge, but the weight was still manageable, I bent forward at ninety degrees, trudging slowly and laboriously." She was re-enacting it. "If you walk toward me you would only see the big pile moving forward." The scene was played vividly in front of her audience's eyes.

"Meilan, you are an amazing actress. No wonder you are the top dancer, singer and movie star," Ying Ying praised.

"I have told you that I was not the best dancer in our company. It was my singing that brought me fame. But at first no voice teacher would take me because I had no talent."

"Meilan, what is it? You were not the best dancer? And you had no talent in singing?" Pei-hua questioned, not believing what she had heard.

"But it's true. I persistently pursued those music teachers. Finally one teacher took me on, though he still didn't think I could get anywhere because of the poor quality of my natural voice."

"Your natural voice was poor? I can hardly believe it." Ying Ying always admired Meilan's voice and enjoyed listening to her cassette tapes. "Isn't the quality of one's natural voice innate? Training only improved the techniques."

"Well, my teacher thought I didn't have it. If the good singers were in the country he would not have taken me. Since they were on tour abroad, and our country needed new singers, my teacher thought I might have a small chance. But I worked very hard, learnt everything he taught me. Shortly thereafter I began to perform for the workers, farmers, and solders. I also emulated the stage presence of Taiwan and Hong Kong singers, I danced around the stage; smiled and talked to the audience, made flirtatious eye contacts, and gestures with them, asked if they liked my singing; were they well entertained by me. They were thrilled. They had never seen anything like it. They loved it. I was the only entertainer that interacted with the audience like that. The Hong Kong and Taiwan singers had not appeared in China yet at that time. I only had a few chances to watch their videotapes. Those were eye-opening experiences for me. I thought, good heavens, that's how they perform? Our singers stood on the stage with both hands folded in front of the stomach; the body never moved; the eyes stared straight over the audience head. There was not the slightest connection between them and the audience."

Meilan cracked a few more watermelon seeds, took a sip of her tea, and continued. "So, when our famous singers returned they were petrified by my newly found popularity. I became the top singer over-night. The Central Film Production Company signed me up for a few films. Riding on the success of my singing career, my films were destined to be well-received too. In fact, they were door busters. I received the Golden Rooster Award for best acting. It was equivalent to the Oscar Award of Hollywood."

Ying Ying and Pei-hua were often amused by Meilan's heart-warming stories. They laughed and cried with her.

"We don't have too much to share with you," Pei-hua conceded. "Our lives in Taiwan were comparatively simply and bland, not colorful like yours. All we can tell you are how strict our parents were, how hard we had to study for the college entrance exam, how girls avoided boys, and so on."

The two girls missed Meilan when they didn't know where she was. Yet they had nothing to worry about since she had all the financial stability and enviable social status. Mapping out her grandiose expedition to conquer the world must be what she was doing.

It was early evening on Friday, Pei-hua and Ying Ying were having dinner together in Pei-hua's apartment.   At this moment, they were sitting by the window taking in the scenes of Boston Common, drinking tea and chatting. Dusk gradually descended on the Common's ground. The strollers, cyclers, roller-bladders, and skateboarders were woven into a lively tapestry of genre called leisure in the park. The bench on which sat the old couple abandoned by their son and daughter-in-law was now empty.

The phone rang. It was Meilan.

"Meilan?? Where have you been? What have you been doing? We almost hired a private investigator to find you," Pei-hua exclaimed. Meilan said she was out of town.

"Would you come over? Ying Ying is here." Pei-hua urged.

"I knew she was there. I called her first. When there was no answer I knew she must be with you."

"Tell her to come. She must come" Ying Ying urged.

"Ying Ying said you must come."

Half an hour later Meilan was at the door. She came in, threw her purse on the table and plumped herself on the couch. A story was written on her face waiting to be told.

"There is one thing I have never told you. It was a love story that took place in Beijing."

Pei-hua poured a cup of tea for Meilan and put two plates of nuts and watermelon seeds on the table. This was to prepare an atmosphere for a good story. Immediately both Meilan and Ying Ying dug their hands in watermelon seeds. Pei-hua put the kettle on the burner to boil more water.

"I met a man in Beijing, a Taiwanese man, Wang Kai-de. He worked for an American high-tech company that sent him to Beijing. One evening he came to see my show at the People's auditorium. The next day he sent me a bouquet of flowers with a note saying that he enjoyed my songs and admired my singing. He said he would like to come again, to see me in the back-stage. The following evening he came to my dressing room after the show. He was a soft-spoken, polite gentleman, very different from all the men I had met. He had an accent that sounded so good. I liked it a lot." Meilan began telling her story.

"That must have been a Taiwanese accent. You like the Taiwanese accent?" Ying Ying asked curiously. To her, Beijing dialect was far more pleasing. She was proud of her Beijing accent that she worked hard to acquire.

"Oh, yes, it is soft and musical, very pleasing to the ear, very suitable for the man. We quickly fell in love. I accompanied him to visit all the great scenic spots and historical sites in different provinces. He took tons of pictures. We spent many quiet evenings in my house listening to music, talking, cuddling. I enjoyed cooking for him. You see, when you love a man you like doing things for him. When he took trips back to his company headquarters in the U.S. I missed him every minute. He called me everyday and we talked for a long time.

He spent thousands of dollars on the phone with me each time he went back to the States. And he always brought me nice gifts. We talked about marriage. And he sponsored me to come here." Meilan was lost in reminiscence.

"What happened after that? Why haven't you married him yet?" Pei-hua wondered.

"That's the tragic part. While in Beijing, he lived in a dream world, so far removed from reality. America is another story. This is where his reality resides. Where his wife resides. That reality prevented him from marrying me."

"What a bastard!! A duper!!" Pei-hua exclaimed wrathfully.

"A classic story from cheap novels." Ying Ying was dumbfounded.

"But not completely," Meilan said ruefully. "He said his wife was very ill for a long time. For years they had no conjugal relations. Of course that did not appease me. I almost lost my sanity. I hit him and bit him."

Pei-hua and Ying Ying couldn't help their chuckle at the image of Meilan biting the man.

"Ill for years? What kind of illness? What monster of a man that guy is! If the wife is sick he should take care of her instead of leaving her alone to have an affair with someone else." Pei-hua found no excuse for the man's behavior.

"Mental illness," Meilan slowly dragged out the words. "He said her condition was severe. Most of the time she did not recognize him. She was violent sometimes. She screamed, yelled, cried, or laughed. She threw things around and broke things. It was hard for him to deal with. He didn't know what to do. So he jumped at the chance when his company asked him to manage their Beijing branch."

"Could he put her in an institution?" Ying Ying asked.

"He could have. But he didn't. He was a kind man. He hired a nurse and a housekeeper to take care of her. At first I did not believe him. I was furious. I screamed, cried my heart out, threw things at him, broke my vase, scratched him, hit him, bit him. I was no different from the mentally crazed wife of his." She painted an even more vivid picture for Pei-hua and Ying Ying.

"Poor Meilan," Ying Ying said gently.

"Then what happened?" Pei-hua couldn't wait to hear more.

"A few weeks ago I went to Los Angeles, to his house. I knew he was away for a few days. I took the opportunity to see his wife. I wanted to prove that he was lying, that he had changed his mind on me. His housekeeper asked who I was. I said I was a relative from China to visit them. She told me the Mr. was not home. I said I came to see the Mrs. She stared at me and said the Mrs. could not see me because she was very ill. I said that was why I was there. I came just to see her; I brought some special remedy from China that would help her. The housekeeper was skeptical and hesitant. Suddenly a loud and shrieking voice broke out inside followed by noises of banging and things breaking. The housekeeper hurried in. I followed. A woman in bare feet, disheveled hair, terrified eyes, and a twisted mouth, held a pillow in her hand and ran out from a room. She threw the pillow in my direction. The housekeeper went and grabbed her, pulled her back into her room. The man did not lie to me," she sighed. Pei-hua and Ying Ying also sighed.

"I didn't see him on that trip. I just stayed in the hotel for weeks before coming back here."

"What are you going to do now?"

"I don't know. If I didn't love him things would be simple."

Love is bondage, and the kind most difficult from which to extricate. There might be many good options awaiting to be explored. Yet to the person in love, there was only one option no matter how impossible it might be.

Chapter 4

*I*n the fall of that year International Foundation organized a three-week cultural study tour to China for its members. Eighty people registered. The tour coordinator offered Ying Ying and Pei-hua half price to join. They were not required to perform specific duties in exchange. There were already two tour leaders responsible for logistics and assistance to the tourists. Having Ying Ying and Pei-hua was reassuring to the all Caucasian group, quite understandably.

The journey took 23 hours from Boston to Shanghai with one stop at Los Angeles to change flight. It was dusk when they landed at Shanghai airport. Receiving them were a team of four tour guides waving small American and Chinese flags and holding a banner inscribed with "Welcome Boston-Culture-and-Arts-Tour to Shanghai." A female-guide walked up and shook hands with the leader of the Boston group and spoke in English: "You are Mr. Stevenson, I suppose. I am Bi-hua, your chief tour guide. I will make sure that your stay in Shanghai is a very pleasant and rewarding one." She led the group to two large buses that took them to Hua-ting Sheridan, a very luxurious five-star hotel. There the doormen and the clerks behind the counter wore nicely designed uniforms. The female clerks were beautiful. They were all about the same height and same weight.

China has this thing about uniformity. All their dancers are from one cookie cutter. Now their hotel clerks are from a similar cookie cutter, Pei-hua thought.

The clerks spoke English and greeted the guests with smiles. The presence of Ying Ying and Pei-hua in an all-Caucasian group attracted more attention than expected. The clerks seemed to be deciding whether the two were guests or tour guides; and whether they should speak English or Chinese to them. Pei-hua smiled and spoke in Chinese: "We are members of this group. It's our first visit to Shanghai."

Their rooms were large and nicely appointed. In the bathroom, the cups were wrapped in white tissue paper, towels were new, small cakes of soap and small bottles of shampoo were neatly arranged at their proper places. A card on the bathroom counter marked, "The water is potable." It must have been a big deal to have potable water coming out from the faucet. In the room a bouquet of flowers and a large crystal bowl filled with a variety of fruits sat on a table. In the small refrigerator, small bottles of juice and wines were chilled. *Of course, this is the Sheridan*, Ying Ying thought.

After they showered and changed Ying Ying and Pei-hua went to the restaurant on the first floor to have a late supper with their fellow tourists. They saw a group of Asians at a near-by table talking and laughing. They spoke Japanese. The Japanese were world travelers.

There were no scheduled activities after supper. Some went to their rooms to rest. Ying Ying and Pei-hua decided to go out for a stroll and to explore.

"You wait here for me. I am going to my room to fetch my purse," Ying Ying said to Pei-hua.

As she stepped out of the elevator a young men followed her to her door. She turned around to face him. The young man grinned at her and said:

"Miss, you are from America, aren't you?"

"Yes, I am a tourist," Ying Ying replied.

"I envy you from the bottom of my heart. You and I are about the same age. You have the good fortune to be in America, taking a trip to see China. You must have a lot of money. Yet I am stuck here with nothing. I am intelligent. I have ambitions. But I don't have your luck," the young man spieled. Ying Ying didn't know what to say. She did feel some sympathy toward him. But there were tens of millions of young people like him. What could she do? She did not want to be rude by ignoring him, by letting herself in the room and closing the door. She just stood there letting him speak one more minute or two.

He glared at her intently for a moment and said: "Do you think Heaven is fair?" Then he answered his own question: "No, the Old Heaven is never fair." He paused a second and continued: "Do you find in you heart a little sympathy for a young man like me?"

I sympathize with all those who cannot fulfill their wishes, their ambitions and dreams. But how many dreams, ambitions, and wishes become reality? The thought quickly flitted through Ying Ying's mind.

"I think everyone deserves to have a chance,"
She replied.

"That's right. I hope you will help me get that chance."

"Me? How?" Ying Ying was baffled. What could she do to give him that chance?

"For a start, you can help me get to America." The young man sounded as if he was asking his girl-friend to go out for a dinner.

Many stories and images instantly rushed to Ying Ying in a montage: Woolan's entrance to the U.S. through marriage to an older woman tourist he met by chance; twenty-three-year-old artist Gong Heng persuaded Joanne, an American artist traveling in China, to get him to Boston. ...

"I was happy to be able to help him. He is a terrific artist," Joanne had told Ying Ying a few weeks after Gong Heng's arrival at Boston. "But I expected him to be on his own once he was here. Yet he is still staying in my father's house because I have no place to put him. Everyday he sits in my father's chair, drinks beer and watches TV. My father is sort of fretted."

Girls crossing the Pacific by way of marrying U.S. citizens were common. Then there were those who fled China by swimming from Shen-zhen to Hong

Kong. Hu Ning was captured several times before she succeeded. Her husband did the same a few years prior to her exodus. She had made a poignant remark about the eagerness of many people in China:

"We would eat shit if that's what it takes to get out of China and to go to America."

And Woolan's words, "as long as I could leave China to come to America I would be willing to sell my body and soul."

All these still resounded in Ying Ying's ears.

"I don't have the ability to do that for you," Ying Ying gently broke the disappointing news to the young man. He was not thwarted, however.

"You do if you want to. Look at me. I am a good-looking man. And I am intelligent and capable. You won't regret it if you get me to America."

What is he thinking? Is this a prevalent tactic, to entice a female traveler with his physical attractiveness into slaving over the difficult task of getting him to the States? Woolan was a very handsome man, so were the others I have heard about. Did their success stories give inspirations to their fellow countrymen? These men were prostituting themselves. A feeling of disgust and chill spiraled through her.

"I am sorry. But I am only a student. There is nothing I can do to get you to America." Though her voice was gentle as usual, there is an undeniable coldness that blocked the man from further pursuit.

"It's too bad. I had hoped you would have had a farther sight and compassion, and the eye to recognize an opportunity. I will go to America, sooner or later. Maybe I will see you there. Boston, isn't it?" The man's voice was calm and cold.

"I am sure you will. Yes, I am from Boston."

The man turned to leave, raised his hand to gesture a good bye and walked away. Ying Ying's eyes followed him for a second, shook her head slightly, before she opened the door.

*   *   *   *

As she entered the room the phone rang. She picked it up. A gentle female voice asked:

"Miss Fang?" it said in English with a Chinese accent.

"Yes." Ying Ying answered while wondering who that might be.

"This is the front counter clerk. You have a call from Wen Yan or Mrs. Meng."

Wen Yan or Mrs. Meng? Oh, it's Meng Song's mother. Meng Song must have told her about my trip, Ying Ying pondered.

"Song gave me your itinerary. That's how I knew you had arrived," Mrs. Meng said. "It's still early. Let me come to see you." Ying Ying thanked her, then hurried to the lobby to tell Pei-hua that they must not go out for a walk but to expect Mrs. Meng.

Mrs. Meng came with two packages of presents for Ying Ying and Pei-hua.

She was a lady of fifty, genteel, suave and urbane. Ying Ying and Pei-hua expressed their gratitude and apologized for not having brought gifts for her.

"No, don't mention it. You are traveling. The lighter the luggage the better it is. You must not think of bringing presents for people. Song told me all about the two of you. I am forever indebted to you for giving him so much help," she continued: "You only have three days in Shanghai? Not much time. And there is so much to see. I can show you around."

"Thank you Mrs. Meng. But our tour package includes quite a few sites already. We shouldn't trouble you to do that," Pei-hua said.

"Well, then, I will come pick you up after your scheduled activities. I will prepare a few flavorful dishes for you," Mrs. Meng said graciously.

The next morning while the group was having breakfast in the hotel's restaurant Ying Ying and Pei-hua went out to scout for food that local people ate. They saw an open-front store swarmed with a large throng. Curiosity propelled them to scoot over to see what was in there. By pushing through the throng, they were thrilled to find a small breakfast take-out place with items they had not seen since they left Taiwan. There was a big wok filled with oil, and a clay oven. A man was making dough cakes covered with sesame and small strips of plain dough. When dropped in the wok full of frying oil the strips immediately puffed up to ten times their original sizes. The sesame covered dough cakes were baked in the oven. These were *you-tiao and shao-bing*, breakfast favorites of most Chinese. The two girls couldn't wait to have some. But they had to wait for their turn. The mess of people shuffled one another and fought for attention from the two guys tending the wok and oven.

"Hay, hurry up. His mother's ass, I have waited too long," a customer cursed. 'His-mother's' was a swear word, no doubt. 'His mother's ass' was worse. Yet they were used indiscriminately to express an emotion or simply as a meaningless expletive.

"You dog fucked, don't try to get before me." One began to jostle the other person aside. The two almost got into a fist fight.

"Hay, Let me tell you. Hurry up. Why are you shit so slow?" one was shouting at the cooks.

...

...

"His mother's. Stop his mother's barking." The man behind the clay oven huffed through gritted teeth.

"You, his mother's, go away if you can't wait," Yelled the irate man deep-frying *you-tiao* by the wok.

Ying Ying and Pei-hua were taken aback by the profanity these people used and amused by their brazen manners and wretched behaviors at the same time. They smiled pleasantly while giving the guys an once-over. One of the cooks noticed the two smiling young women. A question flitted through his eyes. He pointed at the girls and asked:

"How many do you want?" Pei-hua and Ying Ying quickly glanced at each other in disbelieve. Ying Ying answered politely:

106

"Thank you. We would like to have two *shao-bing* and two *you-tiao*, please."

"Thank you?" "please?" Where did that come from? Those were words long disappeared in the local people's language. *Where did these two girls come from?*

Without a word the men wrapped two *shao-bing* and two *you-tiao* in a torn piece of old newspaper and handed them to Ying Ying.

"Twenty cents," the man said. That was about six cents in U.S. currency. Ying Ying paid and thanked him again. The man nodded.

This little interlude stupefied all the customers. They gaped speechlessly.

Ying Ying and Pei-hua returned to the hotel and ate their most favorite breakfast--*you tiao* and *shao bing*, in Pei-hua's room. They each opened a bottle of juice from the refrigerator. As they finished eating, it was time to join the group for the day's sightseeing.

It was a full and tiring day riding in their chartered bus to see places and to shop. They noticed that Shanghai was under reconstruction. Everywhere houses were torn down; roads were dug up. The whole city was a construction site. But the progress was slower than snail crawling. The workmen had no proper equipment such as backhoe to dig and remove dirt. They used shovels. It was as if they were scooping the dirt with a spoon one at a time and moved slowly step by step. It took forever to move only a small pile of dirt. The two spectators wondered how long it would take them to build one house. They also saw broken glass bottles strewed over the crowded streets.

They visited a number of the "official" tourist attractions such as the Bund, Yu Gardens, Shanghai Museum, and Jade-Buddha Temple. The members in this group were more interested in shopping. They eagerly grabbed the lowly priced but well-made clothing and crafts items. The Friendship Stores were major shopping sites catering to tourists. The merchandize was priced higher than elsewhere. The qualities of the goods were presumably higher too. Strangely, the store was very dark, almost black, as if no lights were on. In fact there were a couple of very dim twenty- watts bulbs hanging from the ceiling of this large store. To examine the design on the fabric, for example, was virtually impossible. The sales clerks were impatient and inexpressive. When asked to show an item the clerk would ask in a testy voice: "are you buying it? If you are not sure, don't ask to see it."

Why were the clerks in the Friendship Store so unfriendly? The customers soon understood. It was a state-owned store; the manager and clerks were paid a meager wage. Whether they sold anything or not made no difference. Whether the store made a profit or lost money was nobody's concern because no one but the government had a stake in it. It was the same in all other Friendship Stores throughout China.

The group returned to the hotel to freshen up and put their purchases in the rooms before going out for dinner. Very timely, Mrs. Meng knocked on Ying Ying's door. The two girls did not have time to take a bath. They followed Mrs. Meng out of the hotel. A car was waiting there.

They entered it. Mrs. Meng told the driver to go home.

"The car was borrowed from old Meng's *dan-wei*," she said to the girls. They understood *dan-wei* meant "unit," an office, or work place. Few people owned personal vehicles.

Mrs. Meng's home was an apartment in a large, solid, old brick building. They plunged into darkness as they entered it. After a few seconds their visions were adjusted. A 20-watt bare bulb dimly lit the foyer. A stairway ran upward along the right wall. The walls around the foyer were damp, covered with beaded- or strings of water. Shanghai's high humidity began in late spring. The balustrade, though it looked old, was built with high-quality hard wood and was finely carved. The apartment was spacious and scantily furnished. A hanging light fixture, a chandelier of sort, with five lamps, gave out dim and cold light. Mr. Meng's rolled-up paintings were piled on a table. On another table laid his ink well, brushes, mineral colors in rock and powder forms, a small water bottle, and several small bowls for mixing colors.

"This apartment was vied for by several very high-ranking cadres. But because of Old Meng's respected status in the art circle we beat every one else," Mrs. Meng smiled proudly. "It is the best apartment in Shanghai. You see, it's very large. There are three rooms beside this living-dining room. One room is reserved for Song. When he comes home he will have his private world."

Mr. Meng was a gentleman in his early 50s, refined in demeanor and soft in speech. He asked about Song's life in Boston, whether he had shown any achievement in the arts; did he study well, etc. In a short while another middle-aged lady, Mrs. Yang, came. She was a good friend of the Mengs. Pei-hua was instrumental in helping Mrs. Yang's son Yang Hui to study in America.

Yang Hui was ten years old when the Cultural Revolution started. His schooling was disrupted. A few years later he was old enough to be sent to a labor camp in the countryside. Because his father was a military officer of the Nationalist army who missed the boat for fleeing to Taiwan, Yang Hui was more severely dealt with than other kids of his age. When the father was ill and eventually died in the prison he was not allowed to see him.

He only had the opportunity to finish a third-grade education. Ravenous for knowledge, he got hold of high school textbooks and other kinds of books, and assiduously studied whenever he had some spare time after the grueling work in the labor camp. As the Cultural Revolution ended and schools resumed, colleges were accepting students. The opportunities, however, were of no avail to him. He was still detained by his labor unit and not allowed to take the examination. The opportunity was reserved only for the classes of workmen, peasants, and soldiers. Finally, after a few years, he was permitted to take the college examination. He passed it and entered Shanghai Medical School. In the last year of college he wrote Song expressing his desire to further his study in America and the urgency of leaving the country before graduation. According to Chinese regulation, a medical school graduate was obligated to render ten years of service to the community before having the freedom to do something else. He had no resources or contacts in the U.S. except his childhood chum Meng

Song. Meng Song mentioned this to Ying Ying asking if she could help. Ying Ying discussed it with Pei-hua at length. Pei-hua came up with an idea:

"My uncle is a professor at UCLA. I will beg him to sponsor Yang Hui. See if he would be willing to write to the immigration office to guarantee sponsorship for Yang Hui."

"Do you think that would be possible, to sponsor a total stranger?"

"I don't know. But I will try to persuade him. He may do it for my sake."

Professor Liu agreed to write that letter. That was how Yang Hui came to America.

Yang Hui attended Harvard Medical School. He did very well. But his thick Shanghai accent made his oral reports impossible to understand. Ying Ying told him how to pronounce the interdental sound of th, which posed difficulty to many Chinese; how to differentiate r and l, some Chinese often mixed them up; where to accent the syllable and where to place the intonation in a sentence. The latter two issues were common to most non-English speakers, not just Chinese. Yang Hui diligently practiced. A few months later he thanked Ying Ying for teaching him those things.

"My classmates were amazed at my improvement. They can understand my speech and carry on discussions with me about my report now," he said.

Mrs. Meng was a superb gourmet cook. Every dish was exquisite. The turtle dish was exotic to Ying Ying and Pei-hua. Mrs. Meng served them the soft jelly-like part of the turtle and said that was the best part. The Da-zha crabs were extraordinary. It was an expensive delicacy. The dinnerware was of fine porcelain from jin-de-zhen. The polished bamboo chopsticks were finely embellished with exquisite carvings at one end. Mrs. Meng used a different pair as serving chopsticks. The etiquette and her manners spoke of a cultivated background and a genteel society wherein she was brought up. That background and society were demolished during Mao Zedong's time. People with that background were severely denounced, humiliated and punished. Mr. Meng was imprisoned for two years. All the while he slept on a damp cement floor in the jail without a blanket or a sheet. Consequently he developed rheumatism from that.

On their way back to the hotel Ying Ying and Pei-hua noticed an unusual thing. The cars were running in darkness with the headlights off. Only occasionally the headlights would flash a second. After the flash the street seemed even darker. Their curiosity propelled them to ask the driver why the headlights were not on. The driver explained:

"Lights waste electricity."

"But isn't it dangerous to drive in the dark?" Ying Ying asked.

"We flash the light once in a while," the driver explained matter-of-factly. To him the girl's question was superfluous.

"But after you flash it the street looks darker. You can't see a thing."

"But I already saw the street when the light flashed. That is enough." The driver wondered why the girls couldn't understand such an obvious thing.

On the second day the group visited more famous sites and shopping places. In the evening Ying Ying and Pei-hua had dinner at the Mengs again.

On the third day two buses carried the group to Suzhou. The tour guide introduced the city saying it was China's Venice because of the many canals and houses built along the water. Of course Ying Ying and Pei-hua had read about that famous scenic city and longed to see it since years ago. But the city was far from what they had envisioned. It was old and dirty. The glory of yester-years had all but faded. The water smelled fetid; the houses looked dilapidated. Suzhou was famous for its private gardens built for the enjoyment of the scholars during the Ming and Qing dynasties. Some older ones in Suzhou dated back to the third century.

The group only had time to visit two famous gardens—*Zhuozheng Yuan* (Humble Minster's Garden) and *Liu Yuan* (Lingering Garden) among about 200 of them. These gardens, an epitome of the cosmos, reflected the scholar-gentlemen's longings for a life of leisure and communion with nature, away from the hustle and bustle of the city and the intrigues of officialdom.

The next stop was Beijing. Ying Ying looked out from the plane's window as it took off and hovered over Shanghai. The view impressed her as a mess of shattered crockery. Shanghai used to be called "a city without nights" and "a brilliant jewel of the East" because of the bright neon lights that never went off. Now cars ran in darkness at night. It was also called "the largest cosmopolitan city in the East." The glory had broken to pieces like the aerial view of the city. A wisp of melancholy lodged in her eyes.

*   *   *   *

Ying Ying had a special mission in Beijing. Her professor at Harvard asked her to bring a scroll to his old friend Mr. Yang, now a powerful official in the Chinese government. Ying Ying called his office, asking for an appointment to see the old gentleman. The bureaucrat said she could not see the deputy minister. She explained that she had brought a valuable gift from the deputy minister's old friend in America. She had to present it to him. After a moment of silence the voice on the other end said that she could drop off the gift at their building.

"May I be assured that Mr. Yang would get this gift?" Ying Ying asked.

"I only told you to come here and leave it with the guard. I did not tell you that it would definitely get to the deputy minister. You decide what to do." The man hung up.

It would be better to risk losing the scroll then bringing it back to Boston because there might be a slight chance that Mr. Yang would get it. With that in mind Ying Ying and Pei-hua called a taxi and made their way to Mr. Yang's office. They were stopped at the entrance. After they repeatedly explained to different people and begged them to help, one man took the scroll and said:

"All right I will accept this on the Minister's behalf." He was ready to turn around and leave. Pei-hua quickly asked:

"Mr., should we be getting a receipt or a note to prove that we did deliver the scroll to the right place?"

"No. If you don't trust me, take it back," the man said irascibly. Not knowing what to do, Ying Ying smiled and said:

"It's not that we don't trust you, sir. It's that we need to show the professor that we did deliver his gift to Mr. Yang. But if it's not convenient we will not ask for a receipt."

That was their first and only interaction with a Chinese authority. When they told this story to their Chinese friends in Boston, the latter laughed and called the two girls naive.

"I can bet my life that the guy who took it from you never had the intention of giving it to the Deputy Minister. Who is going to find out? You might as well throw it in the garbage than handing it over to that guy."

Several tourists in the group were under the weather. Fever and cough kept them in the hotel the whole time while the others rushed through the Forbidden City, the Summer Palace, Temple of Heaven, Ming Tombs, Mao Zedong's mausoleum, Tiananmen Square, the Great Wall, Beihai Park, Rong-Bao-Zai, and Tian-Qiao Bridge in three days.

Ying Ying knew Beijing as if she had gown up there. Her knowledge of the city came from the novels and other books she read. She had visited the streets and *hu-tongs*, the historical sites in her dreams and reveries. The people of Beijing, in the past, moved and talked vividly in her imagination. She loved their accent, their mannerism. Her grandfather had a *si-he-yuan* (quadrangle-courtyard-house) on Wang-Fu-Jin Boulevard that used to be home of a Manchu Prince. She wished that she had asked her parents for the house number so that she could go and see how it was now.

At one area in the Forbidden City a stream of soft music wafted in the air. Ying Ying and Pei-hua immediately recognized the familiar tune and looked at each other in elation. It was "Xiang-Fei Lei," (Tears of Lady Fragrance, the Imperial Consort.) The music was used in their production of *Intrigues in the Manchu Imperial Court* in *1989*. The final climax of the play was when Emperor Guangxu's Most-Favorite-Consort, Lady Zhen, was being put to death by her mother-in-law, the powerful Empress Dowager, Cexi, who ordered her to be thrown into a well. Lady Fragrance was a sobriquet of Lady Zhen. The well now stood as one of the points of interest to tourists. Ying Ying and Pei-hua lingered before the well in silence; condoled the fate of that poor woman and many others in history.

In Yi-Ho-Yuan (Garden of Harmony and Peace), Summer Palace of Dowager Cixi, the group was led to walk through the more than 700-meter long corridor whose beams and posts were meticulously decorated with scenery and figures of historical and legendary significance. On the long arched bridge they saw the temple on Wan-Shou-Shan (Mountain of longevity) that was destroyed by the English and French armies in 1860 and restored by Empress Dowager in the 1880s.

The famous and infamous Marble Ship was an attraction that no tourist would omit. Ying Ying and Pei-hua talked about an episode in *Intrigues in the*

Manchu Imperial Court in which the extravagant Empress Dowager used the funds for building a modern navy to build this marble ship.

Despite abundant postcards, books with numerous nice pictures of the historical and scenic sites in Beijing, Ying Ying and Pei-hua were still clicking away on their cameras. For sure, pictures with views and angles chosen and snapped by oneself were infinitely more memorable than those published works from professional photographers.

There were local Beijing people enjoying their day in the Summer Palace. They saw Ying Ying and Pei-hua walking with a group of foreigners and naturally assumed that they were tour guides. They asked the two girls:

"Are you *di-pei* or *quan-pei*?" The two had never heard of those terms. But they figured they must have meant "guides for the local city" and "guides for the whole tour." Ying Ying smiled and said:

"We are..." before she completed her sentence Pei-hua playfully said:

"*Quan-pei* (guides for the whole tour). We took these people here from America," she chuckled. One of the Beijing guys said:

"Oh, you are from America too!!!"

Another guy said: "Yea, look at their cameras. What makes and models are they?" Ying Ying and Pei-hua showed the men their semi-professional Nikon and Cannon. The first man acclaimed:

"Ah, nice cameras. They must be very expensive. You people in America are rich."

The second man said: "I hope some day I can go to America too. Then I will be rich."

"Go away! You? Don't dream. How would you get to go to America?" The first man scoffed scornfully. Then he turned around and asked Ying Ying and Pei-hua:

"Were you born in America? But you speak Chinese."

The second man was exasperated by the first man and muttered: "Don't you slight me like that. You wait and see."

"No, we went there from Taiwan," Pei-hua replied to the second man's question.

"Taiwan?" The men acclaimed. "That horrible place?"

This remark brought back to memory what artist Lu Wen had told Ying Ying a number of years ago:

"We were led to believe that Taiwan was a horrible place where people were suffering from starvation and oppression. They were in deep water and burning fire."

Upon that Ying Ying had retorted: "That was what we believed the Chinese Mainland was like."

*   *   *   *

Pei-hua had written her aunt in Xi'an. She looked forward to the chance to meet this aunt for the first time. The evening of their arrival, her uncle came to the Golden Flower Hotel to see her. The geologist was awestricken when he saw the luxury of the hotel; marveled while taking in every sight. As expected he invited Pei-hua and Ying Ying to dinner at his house the next day. Their apartment was in no comparison with Mr. and Mrs. Meng's in Shanghai. It was very small and without a kitchen. The aunt cooked on a tiny coal burner in the narrow, enclosed cement balcony. There was a faucet on the wall in the balcony to give her water for cooking and washing dishes. Despite the limited facilities the food she prepared was sumptuous. There were sixteen varieties made of pork, beef, chicken, duck, fish, shrimps, scallops, crabs and vegetables. The ambrosia was fitted for the nobilities of the past era. Ying Ying thought this meal must have cost them an arm and a leg. The people in China were living in meagerness yet they were so warm and hospitable to their guests. Ying Ying wanted to give them some money but decided not to for fear of hurting their pride. Pei-hua met her two teenage cousins. The youngsters and their parents expressed strong interests in America. Studying in an American university was their goal. Pei-hua promised that she would help in anyway she could.

Xi'an, called Chang-an in history, was an ancient capital of twelve dynasties beginning in Western Zhou (1046-771 BC). The city's cultural and archeological wealth and the number of historical sites were incomparable by other cities. The amazing terra-cotta warriors and horses from a site near the tomb of Qin Shi-huang, the First Emperor of China, standing imposingly in battle formation in a protected pit, were the first sight of wonder the group took in.

These were among the burial objects of the First Emperor. Ying Ying had read about the accidental discovery of the figures by peasants and subsequent excavation in archeological journals. Western scholars were skeptical in the beginning about the authenticity of these awe-inspiring, lifelike and over life-size sculptures dating back to the third century B.C.. They didn't seem to be the precursors of Chinese sculptural tradition of later ages. As more and more were unearthed, however, their shear numbers and the historical and literary evidences silenced all suspicion and confirmed the fact that the tomb and all the burial objects were ordered by the First Emperor himself, shortly after he was enthroned, to be constructed for his burial. These took thirty-nine years to complete. Most visitors bought one or two pieces of minuscule replica sold at the souvenir stores.

Other sites they visited included the Forest of Stone Steles, The Great Wild Goose Pagoda and the Small Wild Goose Pagoda, Ban Po Neolithic village, and Hua-qing Spring. Renowned Tang dynasty poet Bai Ju-yi wrote a long epic poem, "The Song of Eternal Sorrow," that told the story of Emperor Tang Ming Huang and his Favorite-Consort Yang Yu-huan, better known as Yang Gui-fei. It alluded to Hua-qing Spring as where Yang Gui-fei had bathed. Now seeing the spring, a romantic image was invoked in Ying Ying's mind. Like Lady Zhen of over two millennia later, Yang Gui-fei was also put to death, not by her mother-in-law but by the demands of the angry soldiers escorting the Emperor in his flight to the south after the fall of the capital, Chang-an, the present day Xi'an. The Emperor's indulgence in his love for Yang Gui-fei caused him to neglect the wellbeing and security of the empire leading to the dynasty's near downfall.

Xi'an also mounted a large-scale dance drama in the imagined dance style of the Tang dynasty for the entertainment of foreign visitors.

Ying Ying had long loved the Neolithic potteries unearthed from Yang Shao and Ban Po. She had a few pieces of replica in reduced scale that she valued.

As they arrived at Guilin Pei-hua and Ying Ying were both sick. They empathized with those few members who were ill since arriving in Beijing and missed all the sightseeing. Pei-hua and Ying Ying were not willing to give in to their indisposition. Guilin was famous for its natural beauty. 'The mountains and streams of Guilin surpass all under Heaven' was its well-deserved laudation. The boat-ride along the Lijiang River was memorable. The Seven Star Cavern with fantastic stalagmites and stalactites, and watercourses, was fascinating and breathtaking. Guilin was home of a number of ethnic minority nationalities. Ying Ying and Pei-hua were most interested in the attires of the people of *Miao* and *Zhuang* tribes. The *Miao* women's dresses were elaborately constructed and embroidered, and adorned with silver ornaments. Ying Ying and Pei-hua each bought a set. The large and flamboyant silver headdress, ornate silver bangles and anklets posed a problem for packing. None of those fit in their luggage.

"Can we just wear the headdresses?" Ying Ying joked. In the end they resorted to carrying the headdresses by hand.

The last stop before Hong Kong was Guangzhou. White Swan was again the top five-star luxury hotel in that southern city. Guangzhou was famous for its juicy sweet lychee fruit. It was better than those grown in Taiwan. Ying Ying and Pei-hua had it as breakfast and as desert after lunch and dinner. That was all they enjoyed in Guangzhou because they still had a fever, feeling limp and languorous, not interested in sightseeing. Besides seeing the Sun Yat-sen Memorial Hall they stayed in the hotel the whole time.

In Hong Kong everybody had a great time shopping. Ying Ying and Pei-hua were still not well. They only managed to meet up with a few old classmates from Taiwan University who returned to Hong Kong after graduation. A reunion always brought back fond memories.

The students from Hong Kong and other parts of the world in Taiwan were called "overseas Chinese students" who were admitted to college with lower test scores. It was a political strategy to win overseas Chinese's moral support. Local students resented this policy because the competition for entering a good college was fierce. Each admission to an overseas Chinese meant one less chance for the locals. In the schools, local students in general only rarely mingled with the overseas Chinese students.

*   *   *   *

The second day after returning to Boston Ying Ying went to work. An assignment was already waiting for her. Denis had planned to hold a monthly soiree for all the artists, musicians and theatre people who were associated with China Society's programs at one time or another. He assigned Ying Ying to send each person an invitation.

It was going to be a regular event. After the first round of invitations it would only be announced in the monthly calendar in the Society's newsletter. Keeping all those artists connected and bringing them up to date with the Society's activities was the purpose of the soiree.

None of the dancers responded. Chen Ailing's invitation was undeliverable. Ying Ying was a little curious because of Ailing's close tie with China Society's Education Program. Denis was a bit concerned. He went to the restaurant where Ailing used to work to ask if they knew where she might be. He got her address in Dorchester. He suggested to Ying Ying that they pay Ailing a visit.

Ailing was surprised to see them when she opened the door. She did not invite them in, instead she whispered:

"Thank you for coming to see me but I cannot talk to you now." She looked over her shoulder to see if there was anyone behind her, and spoke softly:

"I will try to come to your office when I can."

At the same time a woman's raucous voice rapped in Mandarin with a thick Taiwanese accent from inside the house.

"Who is out there? Whom are you talking to?" Ying Ying couldn't figure out who that might be.

Ailing replied timidly in Chinese:

"Two old friends I haven't seen for a long time. They dropped by to say hello." The voice inside shouted some more. Ying Ying and Denis were disconcerted but had no time to ask because Ailing hastily closed the door on them and said:

"I cannot talk anymore."

"What's that all about?" Denis asked Ying Ying who shrugged and said:

"Who knows? She seemed to be in some sort of wretched predicament. We'll see when she comes."

Ailing did not come until weeks later. She appeared tired and haggard. The radiance that used to glow on her face had vanished. Her eyes were slightly swollen. Her long hair, that once flowed freely and naturally was tied behind her head. As soon as she sat down Denis brought her a cup of tea and asked what had happened to her.

Chen Ailing, the beautiful dancer, similar to Meilan in her ambition and physical attributes, was a far cry from the latter in destiny.

After winning First Place in China's Bi-annual National Dance Competition she joined Beijing Central Dance Company, with a promisingly brilliant career ahead of her. America's becking was too tempting to resist. She cajoled the organizer of a commerce delegation to falsify their staff list to include her as a clerk of their company so that she could go with them to America. She believed that her talent and beauty would open all doors for her in that land of opportunities. Soon, however, she was disillusioned. Her appearance at China Society's showcase of Chinese music and dance in 1989 was the only chance she had to perform on stage in Boston. She could not find any job except for teaching dance at the Society's Arts Education Program. Even that part-time job was due to Dr. Joseph Lee's goodhearted help. The income from it was too small to support her livelihood. She was anxious to find other more lucrative opportunities. Her visa expired. Her status became that of a "blacked out." "Blacked out" was a term used among the Chinese people who came to American legally as visitors at first but overstayed their visas and became illegal. This was no small matter. She couldn't get a student visa because she was not qualified to attend college, or had the money to pay. The only way for her to change her status was to marry an American citizen, ideally a wealthy American citizen.

Like a ravenous man not picky about food, she looked at all U.S. citizens as her savior, and readily gave herself to them, as bait in the hope of catching one fish. Strangely, she failed that too. Fate was not kind to her. On several occasions Ying Ying was tempted to ask Denis why he was not interested in Ailing. Soon she realized that he was seeing another Chinese woman.

Steven was a volunteer of China Society's Arts Education Program. A thirty-year-old Caucasian, Steven had met Ailing on several occasions. Ailing showed ample interest in him, but it was unrequited. She expressed her discomfiture to Ying Ying and asked if she could pry into the affair for her. When the opportunity came Ying Ying chatted with Steven and eased in the subject on Ailing. She intrepidly plunged into this personal question:

"Steven, why don't you ask Ailing out? She's quite lovely, isn't she?"

"Yes, she is very pretty, but I am seeing someone, besides ..." the words trailed off.

"Oh, I see." Ying Ying was sort of disappointed. "You should bring her here some time. We'd like to make her acquaintance."

"It's not a her, Ying Ying. It's Cecil. He came to an exhibit with me one time. You don't remember him."

"Oh—" Ying Ying tried to hold back her surprise.

"Yes, Cecil and I have been together for four years."

In desperation, Ailing took a waitress job. All hope lost, she became quiet and reserved. She rarely talked, hardly smiled, never reacted when yelled by the cook and kitchen help.

Then the cook Ah Tu noticed her. *This girl is good looking; why didn't I notice her earlier?*' He thought. He began to treat her nicely. In a month or so he asked her to marry him. He was a U.S. citizen. So she married him to legalize her stay in America. It was her last resort, a marriage of convenience. That was okay with her if she could live a more or less normal life. But the old Chinese tradition required them to live with his mother. That would be all right too if the older woman was not an exceptionally abusive mother-in-law. The mother and son were both uneducated, boorish, uncouth peasants from the countryside outside of Taipei. The land reform in Taiwan in the 1950s made all peasants landowners. The dramatic increase in land value in the 1970s made Ah Tu's family multimillionaires. In the '80s they sold the land and moved to America, thanks to Ah Tu's sister who was a bargirl married to an American GI in

116

the later 1970s and was eligible to apply for her family members to immigrate.

Hitting, cursing, starving and other forms of maltreatment to a daughter-in-law were a most shameful, ugly tradition among these people. Ah Tu's mother had a great deal of unwarranted hatred toward her daughter-in-law. Ailing, being frightened constantly, always tried her best to please the older woman.

After washing the dishes in cold water in that winter day--because she was not allowed to run up the utility bill by using warm water, she brought a bowl of grapes to her mother-in-law. The old woman slapped her when her hands trembled from fear. She spilled the grapes.

"You clumsy pig, useless cheap whore. Other than selling your ass can you do anything right?" The old woman kicked her down and knelt on her stomach, slapped her face repeatedly, pulled her hair and banged her head on the floor. Ailing dared not do so much as shield her face with her arms.

Ailing's past behavior, giving herself to many men, had been gossiped to the old woman's ears and caused her wrath and always called the younger woman a cheap whore.

"You shameless whore. You soiled our name and bring bad luck to us. I am going to kill you," she screamed and began to choke Ailing. Ailing coughed and struggled. The old woman banged her head on the floor more forcefully. Then she pinched her face. Ailing cried from pain.

Another time her mother-in-law pushed her from behind and she fell down the stairs. She lost her baby as a result. Being ordered to kneel on the floor or be locked up in the bathroom without food for days was not an infrequent occurrence.

In fact Ailing never sold herself for money. On the other hand, Ah Tu's sister, a bargirl, a euphemism of prostitute in Taiwan, did sell herself to the American GIs. This sister-in-law also abused Ailing verbally as well as physically. When the sister-in-law called Ailing a whore, Ailing retorted:

"I was a professional dancer selected by the government. It's a respected profession. I did not sell my body for money." This remark infuriated the sister-in-law who jumped on Ailing, grabbed her hair and hit her with a pan. The mother-in-law slapped her repeatedly, chased her out of the house and threw her things out from the window. When Ar Tu came home at night and saw her on the street with no place to go he quietly entered the house without saying a word to her.

Ailing huddled by the wall all night. She was too ashamed to ask for help from her acquaintances. The next day Ah Tu begged his mother to allow Ailing to come back in. The mother finally agreed under the conditions that Ailing kao-tao to her and his sister; vowed to obey and serve her and the sister like a slave, always; and never defy their orders and demands. Ailing accepted and abided by those conditions.

While in private, Ar Tu said of his mother to Ailing: "She is my mother. She has the authority to do anything she wants. You married into this family, you must obey her."

Ying Ying and Denis were both appalled and outraged at Ailing's misery. Denis even questioned why she did not stand up to her abusers.

"You could have fought back. Why did you just let them do that to you? They hit you, hit back."

Ying YIng urged her to extricate herself from that torture chamber. Ailing was a completely broken woman. She had lost her confidence and self esteem.

"I don't have any power or any means. I have no place to hide either. How can I fight back? I cannot even get away from them. To these people once a woman enters their door she is their property. She will never escape their iron clamp until she is tortured to death by them. If I flee from them they will find me and bring me back. Beside, I have no money. How do I survive? It will cost money to get a divorce too."

"Don't be silly. Pei-hua will help you with the legal proceedings. You can move in with me immediately while Pei-hua handles your case. We will help you to get some training for the job market." Ying Ying assured Ailing. Denis encouraged her to be strong.

Ying Ying called Pei-hua. She put down her work to come and talked to Ailing. She promised that nothing untoward would happen if she left her husband. Pei-hua promised to handle it all for her.

"You don't need to go back to your husband's house anymore. Forget about your personal belongings. I don't think they are that important. Just stay with Ying Ying." Denis suggested.

"Should I tell them that I am going to leave?" Ailing timidly asked.

"Why? You don't owe it to them. I will send them a letter to tell them that I represent you in your divorce," Pei-hua said.

Ailing stayed with Ying Ying for a while. During that time Pei-hua and Ying Ying drilled in her the importance of self-alliance, self-confidence, self-esteem and perseverance; the future was in her own hands; only she could build it.

She took their advice; diligently tried to find a job. Finally she found a cleaning job at Dancing Star Ball Room Studio.

Denis got the permission from Joseph Lee to allow Ailing to open ballet and Chinese folk-and-classic dance classes at China Society's studio without charging her a fee, and paid her to teach a class for the Society's Youth program, the incomes from which plus the income from her cleaning job would support her simple livelihood. She moved out of Ying Ying's apartment to live in a small rented room. Her life was gradually back on track.

At Dancing Star she secretly observed instructor Sidney's private lessons. She practiced the steps by herself. Being a professional and award-winning dancer learning new dances was easy for her.

After several months, Ailing found an opportunity and casually brought up her dance background to the studio owner:

"Michelle, I didn't mention anything about winning top prize in national dance competitions in China, did I?"

"No, you didn't. You are a dancer?"

"Yes, I won first place in the bi-annual dance competition in China. I won a gold medal in the ballet category, and second prize in the Chinese classic and folk dance category. I also do ballroom. But I didn't compete in the ballroom category." She stretched the truth about ballroom dance.

"Really? Hmm, that's interesting. Why didn't you use your skill instead of doing house cleaning?"

"It's not easy to make a living with dancing. I do teach Chinese dance at China Society."

"Uh huh!"

Ailing hoped in vain for an offer from Michele to assist Sidney or another instructor.

"Michelle, would you think, if I offer a class in Chinese dance at the Studio, there will be students? Will it help the Studio in anyway?" Ailing was testing the water. "I will only ask for a small fee, if you agree."

Michelle thought about it for a while and said: "We can give it a try. If there are too few students we don't open. Since the studio space is not used a hundred percent, there will be slots that you can use. Who knows? It may grow the studio's business." The risk of losing money was Michelle's worry. She agreed, however, to experiment with the idea.

Once she became an instructor Ailing felt her standing in the studio had moved up. She could speak to other instructors as equals. She was happy. The color and radiance returned to her face. She was as attractive as ever. And with those trying experiences she grew to be more mature, not taking things for granted, not flaunting her looks, not expecting gains without working hard.

Sidney asked to collaborate with her in teaching large classes. They choreographed steps and movements together with refreshing results. After a while they decided to enter the New England Professional Ball Room Dance Competition. They practiced every day for months. Ailing had to buy a costume for the competition. The cost of it was almost too prohibitive. But she had to have one at any expense.

They won the grand prize!!

When the gold medal was handed to them, all the sweat, soreness, and money spent paid off. They became highly sought after instructors. The fees for both the group lessons and private lessons hiked accordingly. They appeared in dance events and competitions as guest stars. The remunerations were high.

Sidney had a good business mind. He asked Ailing to partner with him to open their own studio; Ailing would still teach ballet and Chinese dance in addition to ballroom. Ailing agreed. They rented a large enough space in the South End and named their studio "DanceArt." She continued to teach one day a week at Dancing Star Studio to repay the kindness of her old boss.

Denis offered to increase her fee from the Youth program.

"I understand that your fees are high now. How should we adjust your pay?"

"No, Denis, I can never ask for more pay from you. In fact I should donate my service now that I am making much more money than before. But I will close my own classes here." The students from her own classes followed her to

DanceArt Studio.

She was grateful to this wonderful country called America, for giving her the opportunities to fulfill her dreams. To repay the beneficence of the society she designed and conducted dance workshops at a number of area schools free of charge.

Despite her full schedule she worked hard to improve herself by taking courses at Bunker Hill Community College. She was determined to be fluent in English, speaking as well as writing. She had always admired Ying Ying for her mastery in this foreign language.

*   *   *   *

Like Ailing, the woman whom Denis secretly admired was also a waitress and a 'blacked out.' Unlike Ailing, this woman did not have stunning looks. She was over forty years old and had a teenage son in China. There must have been something about her that enchanted Denis. Yet he never asked to date her. He just frequented the restaurant where she worked everyday to see her and have conversations with her. Pei-hua was surprised to see an American man being so reserved. "I thought they were all very forward."

Without action or emotional expression, Denis's intention was vague to the woman. One day she said to him:

"I am going to get married."

"Get married? To whom?" He was dumbfounded and solicitous.

"Oh, it's not a real marriage. I have 'blacked out.' Only marriage to a U.S. citizen can save me from that. It will cost me $40,000, and the man two years of freedom. But I will get a green card," the woman said dryly.

"Don't be silly. It is too risky to marry someone for a green card. You don't know what the guy is like," Denis adamantly objected. Ailing's ordeal was still fresh in his mind. He was sincerely concerned.

"It's nothing. It's being done all the time. There is no risk. After getting the marriage certificate we go our different ways. We don't live together."

"I don't think that's a good idea. If you needed that sort of help why didn't you tell me? I would marry you. We don't need to consummate the marriage if you prefer. And it won't cost you a penny." Denis earnestly persuaded the woman to give up her plan. The marriage would be real if the woman would not object.

The woman was fifteen years older than him. Some people pointed out the big gap in their ages. He argued:

"It doesn't matter. Older men marry younger women all the time."

"But, Denis, you are letting the woman exploit you to attain her goal. How could you enter a marriage so lightly?" Ying Ying saw a re-run of Woolan's story only this time the roles of man and woman were reversed.

"No, Ying Ying, only if she had manipulated me into it, then I would be exploited. But she didn't. She is a nice woman. I am happy to marry her. She is not exploiting me," Denis retorted. Ying Ying had nothing more to say.

I hope you are doing this because of true love, Denis, not because of sympathy, Ying Ying thought.

Chapter 5

Roger and Manna moved to Lexington. Manna gave birth to a son. She liked ma-jiang and often invited Linda and the other dancers to her house for dinner and to played that game. And to show off her house, of course.

"Oh, my god, this is such a large and luxurious house," Susie exclaimed as Manna was giving her guests a tour.

"Oh, it's nothing. You should see Ching Ju's house. I heard it was a twenty-million-dollar estate in Weston," Manna said enviously.

"Twenty-million dollars? You are not kidding us, are you?" Linda's eyes were wide with disbelieve.

"Nothing unusual. Ching Ju's husband is filthy rich. He owns this big company, called JM Bio Tech or something. It's in Cambridge. Makes ton of money. What's twenty millions to him?" Meilan put in.

Meilan and Ailing did not know how to play ma-jiang because it was not a popular game in China at that time. They just sat by the table and watched.

Ching Ju did not come to Manna's party. After her initial acquaintance with those Chinese she met at China Society, she moved away from that circle altogether.

The twenty-million dollar estate people talked about was designed and built specifically for them. Beside the main mansion, there was a separate building containing a theatre, a dance studio, a large ballroom, two art studios and servants quarters. There was also an independent guesthouse.

Her regular activities included planning large parties to entertain her new friends in the affluent and fashionable society, selecting entertainers to garnish those parties, shopping for clothing and accessories in the most expensive boutique shops or fly to fashion capitals around the world to shop, going to the spa, gym, and beauty salon, frequenting the most upscale restaurants of different styles. Her husband was very pleased with her ability to transform herself from a waitress to a high-class society lady with elegance and social poise in such a short time. He said to her:

"Darling I am very proud of you. You add class and taste to my life. Before you, I had no time and no one to spend my money on. Your extravagance and style are worth every dime. Money well spent. I am happy."

At Manna's ma-jiang parties Roger patiently watched their little boy and served the ma-jiang players tea, fruit, preserved plum, confectionaries, and watermelon seeds, the kind of snacks women in Taiwan always had at the ma-jiang table.

"Your husband is a very nice man. He waits on your guests while you have all the fun," Susie stated in admiration.

"Yes, he is a wonderful guy, very considerate, very loving, and very kind to people," Manna agreed and emphatically praised Roger.

"Everyone's fate is so different," Ailing said thinking about her own wretched misfortune. "You are so fortunate to have married such a good man."

Though Manna had eased her grudge against Meilan, she could not bring herself to excuse Ying Ying. She resented Ying Ying for discrediting her contempt toward the Mainlanders. She never invited Ying Ying to her home. At these ma-jiang parties she showered caustic, brutally acrimonious attacks on Ying Ying and China Society. Meilan felt uneasy and extracted herself from further association. Besides, her tight schedule for Boston's elite social events did not allow her to lavish her time sitting and watching people playing ma-jiang.

Ching Ju and Meilan often appeared in the same parties, functions and fundraising events. But the two were hardly close or on each other's guest list. Could it be jealousy or competitiveness that had put a barrier between them? Or because of Meilan's low opinion on Ching Ju's background? She had openly expressed her disdain of Ching Ju to Ying Ying:

"A nobody-knew-who-she-was kind of performer in China, a bar waitress in Japan, that is no higher than a call girl. She happened to be married to a rich American man. How could she be put on a par with a big movie star and platinum record singer who was illustrious throughout China, loved and admired by the whole of Chinese population, and had made it in America through her own ability? There was no comparison. I feel it's an insult being mentioned in the same breath with Ching-Ju. I had better separate myself from that worthless, parasite sort of a woman."

After venting her displeasure, however, she was afraid Ying Ying might repeat her sentiment to others. She warned Ying YIng:

"This is between you and me. I told you what I felt because I trust you. Don't quote what I've said."

"Meilan, You know me better than that. When did I ever gossip?" Ying Ying was apparently offended.

Ching Ju and Manna shared some commonalities--infamous, unrespectable backgrounds, being a bar waitress or a dance hall girl; and they both married rich American businessmen. But the two women took different paths to lead their lives.

The dance-hall girl in Manna was not put to rest. It often shouted to come out. Motherhood did not agree with her although she had a second son barely a year after her first one. When Roger went on his business trips to Taiwan, Manna often left the babies to the care of a nanny to frequent bars and nightclubs. She dressed in flimsy, revealing outfits; danced seductively; often drank till tipsy; and went out with men she met in the bar. It became her life style that even when Roger was home she would go out at night by herself.

Many nights she did not go home. When Roger questioned her, she lied and said she was spending the night at Linda's house. Roger was suspicious and upset. He warned her to behave herself. She only ignored him.

When Roger accidentally found a pack of condoms in Manna's purse his suspicion escalated.

"Why do you have condoms in your purse? They are not mine," he demanded.

Manna had a fit. She shouted: "What are you doing in my purse? Don't you have any respect for my privacy?"

"Don't evade the issue. I am asking you. What are those condoms doing in your purse?" Roger's voice was raised.

"They are Linda's," she screamed. "How dare you search my purse? How dare you shout at me?" Manna shrieked.

"Why would Linda put condoms in your purse?" Roger shouted. "Don't you lie to me anymore."

"I didn't lie to you. Linda is sleeping with other men. She hid her condoms in my purse from her husband." She realized how preposterous the lie was. But it was too late.

"Don't take me for a fool. You are talking about yourself. How many men did you sleep with? I know the youe kind. You loose, wanton woman." Roger had never spoken in such a surly tone before.

Manna burst out in rage. She swore in scurrility and threw a glass on the floor. Then she stormed out of the house. Roger went after her, grabbed her arm and pulled her back. She pushed his hand away and ran to the kitchen screaming hysterically. In a fury she pull out the cleaver from the drawer and brandished it at Roger.

"I am going to kill you. I swear I will," she shrilled.

Shocked and frightened, Roger ran to the bedroom, locked the door and called the police.

Is this the sultry, coy little Chinese woman that made me swoon? What happened? Did I fail her? He could not find an answer.

Ah, the Bumblebee King Extract she made me take!! She said it would enhance my …. That's it. She is not satisfied in the bedroom.

When the policemen came she was crying like an abused child. She prevailed to the cop: "Do you think I can harm him? You believe him? A big hunk of a man, was I able to threaten him? He was the one threaten to kill me. I need your protection," she whimpered.

The policemen did not know whom to believe. To play it safe, one of them said either the husband or the wife must move to a hotel for the night. They should ask the judge to issue restraining orders against each other. Roger fled to a hotel. The following day he asked a lawyer to file for divorce.

Manna was stunned at this development. *The Americans are absurd. What is a little quarrel between a married couple? So I said I was going to kill him. They took it for real? Ridiculous. Totally ridiculous. Their men are cowards.*

I didn't know that Chinese women were termagants, evil bitches, Roger was

124

thinking, *They bewitch you with their alluring surface then turn into demons after you marry them.* He could not find one single reason to reconcile with Manna.

The divorce process was a seesaw battle for several months with exorbitant legal fees. In the end the judge gave Manna custody right of the children and Roger visitation right, alimony and child support responsibilities.

Manna's friend, a caseworker at the welfare department, helped her cheat the government. Because the left hand did not talk to the right hand, her friend was able to hide her income and declare her as a single mother of two without means for support. As such the government gave her a nice subsidized apartment for which she paid nothing due to her 'no-income, single-mother of two" status, free health care, food stamps, monthly stipend for three, and more.

Like many other parasites of the society, she took those unwarranted government handouts from the defective welfare system unabashedly, as if they were her birth right. Those handouts would have guaranteed her a worry-free life till she died if she did not ruin it. She continued a life of debauchery, often left the kids home without a babysitter and did not come home until two or three in the morning. One such time Roger came and found the kids home alone. He was enraged and appealed to the court for custody of the boys.

Manna knew that she might lose this time. She could not let the court take away her child support money and alimony. She prevailed to Pei-hua for help although she and Pei-hua had no previous contact.

"Pei-hua, you must help me. The court and the judge are discriminating against me because I am a Chinese. They are partial to Roger because he is a white man. They will give my boys to Roger. How brutal it is!!! How could they take the kids away from their mother just because the mother is not a white woman?"

"No such thing, Manna." Pei-hua would not hear any more of Manna's wild accusations. "The law does not, and will not discriminate against you because you are a Chinese. The judge gave you the boys at first. You violated his trust and judgment. So he wants to re-examine the case. The law is fair."

"But Pei-hua, you must think of some way to help me. You can't just see them taking my kids away," Manna pleaded. "We are Chinese. Don't you want to help your compatriot and to fight discrimination?"

"How can I help you? You should not have left the kids without care when you went out. I am sure you know that. It has nothing to do with discrimination. Don't let that notion torture you."

"I went out just that once for an emergency. Roger happened to come to my apartment that day," she lied through her teeth.

"But your boys told Roger that you often left them home alone."

"Oh, kids. How can you trust the kids? They lie a lot."

"I think you have lied about not having left them home alone except for that one time." Pei-hua did not back off.

"What kind of a lawyer are you? Lawyers are supposed to get the clients out of predicaments, not to cross-examine them. You sound as if you were representing Roger." Manna was enraged. "All right, Pei-hua, if you are not willing to help a compatriot, I won't beg you." She hung up the phone.

She solicited different people to be her character witnesses, to testify in court for her. She vowed that she had only left the kids alone once due to an emergency; she was a good mother; the kids would be miserable with Roger, and so forth. These people knew what kind of a woman Manna was. They knew she was lying about not having left the kids home alone more than once. They refused to lie in court for her. In the end Roger won the case.

Manna lost the boys, and of course the child support money. But she still had the alimony.

*   *   *   *

What's up with those artists?

Meng Song was urged by Joseph Lee to enter the regional artist fellowship competition sponsored by the arts councils of the six New England states. It was an important event for visual artists. Winning the competition would definitely boost an artist's career. And there was a cash award. Meng Song talked with Ying Ying about it. Ying Ying said:

"Dr. Lee thinks you have a definite chance of winning for two reasons. One is the excellence of your work, of course, the other is your ethnic background. Being an Asian you are definitely at an advantage."

"Why is that?" Meng Song did not know the government policies in America.

"Minorities would get preferential treatments in government-sponsored activities."

"What preferential treatments?" Meng Song was lost.

"Have you heard of Affirmative Action or Equal Employment Opportunity Act?"

"No, I never pay attention to those things."

"Well, under Affirmative Action, businesses, fire department, police force, and other government agencies must reserve, guarantee quotas for minorities. Even if the minority does not qualify for the job, the employer must give it to him rather than a well-qualified white person. That's the law. Let me give you an example." A story she heard before came to her mind and made her chuckle. "Some years ago, at the height of Affirmative Action policy, a Chinese guy went to interview for a job in California. This guy hardly studied while in college. He flunked many courses and almost didn't graduate. He believed that no one would hire him but went to the job fair to try his luck anyway. He got the job! He told people that as soon as he entered the room the interviewer asked 'Are you a Chinese?' He said 'Yes.' The man said, 'you are hired.'" Ying Ying couldn't refrain herself from laughing.

"That is called equal employment opportunity? It sounds like unequal employment opportunity to me." Meng Song was confused.

126

"You are right," Ying Ying smiled. "Pei-hua and I often discuss this issue. We both think it is unfair and condescending. Fair competition must be based on true equality. Preferential treatment is condescending and clearly puts the 'minorities' in an inferior rank. But that's the policy. And it is embraced by many minority people. Colleges must fill the quotas too whether the minority student qualifies or not. By extension, any state-sponsored competition must reserve winning spaces for minorities, no matter whether this person deserves to win or not. This is to follow the policy, not to be 'discriminatory.' This is also called 'political correctness.' I am sure you can see why many minorities are pleased by it." Ying Ying had long been disgusted with this policy.

Meng Song became livid. He said: "This is absurd. I have never heard of such a humiliating policy."

"But the intention of the policy is not to humiliate minorities. It is intended to protect them, to give them the opportunities regardless of whether they deserve them or not."

"This is blatantly contemptuous, skewed, biased, unequal and unjust. Any self-respecting person would abominate it," Meng Song passionately criticized.

"In Taiwan there is a similar practice. The government stipulates lower the college admission bar considerably for minority students of Mongolian and Tibetan ancestry, and overseas students from Hong Kong, Singapore, Malaysia and elsewhere. The excuse is, according to the government, 'because these students can't compete with local students for admissions.'"

"There are students from Mongolia and Tibet going to Taiwan?" Meng Song found it surprising.

"No, not directly from Mongolia and Tibet. They are descendants of Mongolian and Tibetan ancestry. Their parents moved to Taiwan after 1949. They went through elementary- and high schools just like the other kids. But they were given preferential treatment."

"Why?"

"Well, for political reasons. In America, the government was apologetic to the minorities for their unfair treatment in history. This policy is to make-up for its past mistakes and warrant a fair practice in the present. The idea is good. But the practice has gone too far."

"Well they should correct it," Meng Song commented.

"For sure. But our voice and opinion will not be heard. It's useless to trouble ourselves with these societal issues. There are just too many policies that make no sense and situations unacceptable to me but what can I do? For example if your parents are old, poor and ill, you are not morally, much less legally, obligated to take care of them. No law will punish you if you put them on the street. On the other hand, if you discipline your child by giving him a spanking you may end up in jail and lose that child."

"That is total madness," Meng Song huffed.

"Listen to this. If a young girl, as young as eleven-years old, gets pregnant, she can go to the welfare department asking for help. You know what help she will get?"

"I can't imagine."

"The welfare department will provide her with free housing, food stamps, free medical care, a monthly stipend and all the rest of a full package of benefits. The child will immediately be emancipated from her parents and declare independence."

"This is completely insane. What is the rational behind it? I think this is to encourage little girls to debauch. What is the point to this? And how could an eleven year old live by herself? What kind of a society will it eventually come to?" Meng Song, a loose man himself, being so passionate about this subject was not what Ying Ying expected. But it was not about promiscuity among adults. It was about little kids who still had a long way to go before reaching adulthood. What did they know about life? Why did the system not try to guide them to the right direction, teach them about moral behavior and responsibility, instead of encouraging them to indulge in kiddy sex and helping them to stray into a dark dead-end?

"I don't know," Ying Ying shrugged helplessly. She changed the subject:

"Let's return to the question on hand. About the arts competition..."

"I'll not be part of it. I don't want to be awarded a prize if I don't deserve it. It's too insulting that way. And I would never know what my chances were without the minority factor," Meng Song insisted.

"I think you should still enter. Perhaps you can ask them to disregard your ethnicity and only look at your work." Ying Ying's suggestion was reasonable. Meng Song took her advice. In his artist's statement he stressed his desire for the jurors to disregard his ethnicity; if ethnicity must come into play he would rather withdraw.

Meng Song did win the competition. He felt good and proud knowing it was his art, and his art alone, that brought about this honor. The director at the New England Arts Foundation was very interested in his work and asked to send his solo show on national tour. Meng Song accepted this enviable offer and began to create new works. The Foundation mapped out twenty cities for the show to tour in two years.

During that time Meng Song entered other national and international arts competitions and often won top honor. His name became well known and his works avidly collected. The galleries asked him for more. Collectors reserved all the pieces in the touring show waiting to receive them after the show closed. Some museums in California, Massachusetts, New York, and Illinois invited him to mount solo shows. His success was remarkable.

The old gang was happy for Meng Song, no doubt. At the same time they wondered what success would do to the man.

"Do you think he will change a lot now that he is a nationally renowned and much sought-after artist? Will he spend most of his time cranking out paintings or will he continue his dandy life style?" Denis posed the question.

"Have you heard that old habits never die? When have you seen him working diligently? With this new-found success I bet he will dally even more." Jenny made an insightful assessment.

Jenny was partially right. However, while Meng Song made no effort to refrain his dalliance, he did put in more effort in making art to fulfill the galleries' demands.

Yang Dan and Ma Ya, now in their early twenties, continued to be active in concert halls internationally. Raving reviews followed one after another wherever they performed. Though no longer in school they still maintained their student status in order to be legal residents. BU and NEC agreed to issue them Form I-20 respectively. They signed up for a course each semester with tuition waived. As highly accomplished musicians they could have easily applied for green cards. But they dreaded the amount of time and effort the process would entail. They were occupied by busy concert schedules. However, the inconveniences at U.S. Customs when reentering the country could be overwhelming at times.

They had fond memories of their involvement with China Society's program. They kept the connection intact. Whenever possible they would appear at the Society's events. People thought the two were an ideal couple. But they were not romantically attracted to each other; they only worked together occasionally. After some time, Ma Ya went to Europe and Yang Dan moved to New York.

Lu Wan was married and had a son. He had established himself as a renowned mural artist and a designer of special visual effects. Museums, theme parks, and movie production companies often hired him to create works of monumental scale. His own production and consulting company flourished quickly. He had to hire artists to assist him in carrying out the large number of commissions waiting to be delivered.

Li Yong's lead role in a Broadway show kept hem very busy. He only had Mondays off when the theatre was dark. On Saturdays he had two shows. Occasionally he let the understudy take over a Tuesday show so that he had two free days to see Pei-hua in Boston. Pei-hua often visited him in New York on weekends.

In New York, many Asian American actors clamored about forming a union. They protested against the 'unfair treatment' of Asian actors by the film, TV, and theatre industries.

"There are so few roles for us. They could have written more for us or easily changed some secondary roles into Asian characters. There are roles where ethnicity is not an issue. We should have been given those, but weren't. The industry is just very inequitable." They complained, and they persuaded Li Yong to join them. Li Yong, however, had a different outlook. He expressed his view to Pei-hua:

"I am not interested in protesting and demonstrating. What little time I have I use it to improve my acting skill, taking classes in singing, dancing and speech. I believe I will have opportunities if I am good. I wouldn't want a role just because they are obligated to give it to an Asian. It's bad enough that government and publicly supported establishments have to abide to the unfair law that forces them to hand out jobs to minorities regardless of their qualifications. The entertainment industry is a cluster of private businesses. Their main concern, like all commercial ventures, is to earn profits. No one has the right to dictate how they run their business or stipulate who they should hire. If I am good, I will have a job. I want them to hire me because I am the best choice. The writers and producers should be allowed to have the freedom to do their jobs without fear. The last thing we want is for the government to reach its claw into the entertainment industry. If we allow that to happen, the next thing would be to control what a novelist should write, to demand every novel to have certain number of Asian characters in it."

"Pei-hua couldn't agree more with Li Yong. Meng Song had said similar things when he was entering the New England regional artists fellowship competition. These were proud individuals, to whom "equal opportunity" meant the most qualified people got the jobs; preferential treatment directly contradicted equal opportunity. Pei-hua had immense respect toward these two men for their integrity and dignity.

*   *   *   *

As a liberal Denis often engaged in intensely emotional, sympathetic discussions on the "oppressed minorities" and such related issues. He was one of those white Americans who felt a gripping sense of guilt toward minorities, especially the blacks, and harbored an urge to make it up to them in as many ways as possible.

Ying Ying and Pei-hua, on the other hand, thought that the functionality of history was to enable people to see the past like a reflection in a mirror. It taught people to avoid repeating the mistakes of their forefathers. That was enough of an apology. If we insisted that only monetary compensation was acceptable as a tangible form of apology, then we must decide where would be the cut off line? The beginning of the first European setting foot in the new world? The beginning of conflicts between the Europeans and the Indians? The beginning of the first African man brought to this land as a slave? Or the first Chinese peasant brought to develop the American West?

The two women held strongly their views on true equality. Affirmative action, equal opportunity employment and preferential treatment were inequality, they asserted,

Pei-hua, Ying Ying, Tonia and Missy each received a meeting notice from a group called Asian Women In Power. Tonia and Missy were indifferent about it. Ying Ying and Pei-hua saw it as another narrow-minded small clique banding together to vent their grudges. They did not embrace separatism. These groups excluded other gender and ethnicities. They were blatant separatists and not fitting to the two young women's interests. Denis criticized the two for being apathetic.

"I think you should have been more sympathetic toward their causes rather than taking a pococurante stand. You are Asian Women, why would you not support them?" he questioned. With hot blood pumping in him Denis went to the meeting. The next day Ying Ying asked him how it went. He was reluctant and embarrassed. Finally he said:

"I only heard them complain about social injustice. There were no productive discussions. I wanted to join in but they told me that white men were not welcome and asked me to leave."

"Why am I not surprised?" Ying Ying smiled and said. "Will you criticize me for being apathetic again?"

At this moment, a man wearing a wide grin on his face knocked on the door as he let himself into the room.

"Hi, Sun Sang, how are you? What have you been doing?" Ying Ying greeted him. Denis said hello and strode out of the room.

This man was introduced to Ying Ying a year ago when he first arrived in Boston from China. He had little formal education but was a very intelligent and industrious man with an entrepreneurial spirit. Like many who came under the false pretense of a company employee sent to the U.S. on business, he over stayed his visa and became an illegal alien. Unlike those "blacked out" girls each of whom hastily grabbed hold of a U.S. citizen as a life savor, he had a wife in Beijing that precluded him from taking that route although his physical appearance could have easily captured a woman to rescue him.

"I am doing import from China. It's not easy. The competition is too stiff."

"What kinds of goods do you plan to import? Have you learned all the requirements and procedures in the import business?"

"Right now it's automobile disc-breaks. The procedures I have already learned while in China. I was doing import and export with Soviet Russia. I also tried to bring in other kinds of merchandise such as women's apparels, purses, hair ornaments, custom jewelry, garden benches, crafts items, etc.. No success so far. I have the suppliers lined up. Prices are very good. But the buyers tried to crush us. They are brutal."

"Garden benches and hair ornaments? Such a wide array of different things!! Have you formed a company?"

"Yes, I have a partner. My immigration status ... you know. So I need to have a partner who is legal. My wife's cousin is a permanent resident. We jointly incorporated the company. He is a lab technician who knows nothing about international trade nor has any interest in it. I am doing it all."

"Yours is a legal business entity and minority owned. I wonder if you would be eligible for government assistance. I'm not sure if international trade would qualify. But the Federal Government has a program that helps minority-owned businesses."

"What minority? Ours is not owned by a minority." He was completely confused by Ying Ying.

"You and your partner are a minority," Ying-ying explained softly. But it came as a shock to Sun Sang:

"What? We? The Great Han people? How could we be a minority?" He was seriously confused.

"In America we are a minority," Ying Ying grinned

"We are the majority in the world," Sun Sang insisted confidently and unwaveringly.

"But we are still a minority in America," Ying Ying chuckled. "You need to legalize your stay. A 'blacked-out' is not the way to be."

"I know. But there is no particular loophole in the immigration law that suits my situation. I need to spend huge legal fee to legalized my status. I must earn money first."

Ying Ying was distressed by the so-called illegal immigration problem. In her opinion it was pestiferous to a lawful society. Just within a small circle of Chinese she knew quite a number of them who over stayed their visas and became "blacked-out." She knew there was a substantial number of people from different countries who chose illegal shortcuts to enter the country and stayed.

She wondered why a country whose citizens and legal residents were bound by so many laws would allow such widespread illegal practices by foreigners.

Equally puzzling to her was how the government and the legal system had blindly allowed people to openly break the law. For example she had seen wealthy new immigrants hiding their money in order to claim welfare benefits including subsidized housing, SSI, free health care, food stamps, deeply discounted heating and other utilities, free milk, baby food, and clothing. She was at someone's apartment in the deep winter. The temperature in the room was above eighty degrees. The windows were wide open.

"Why do you keep the windows open?" she asked.

"I need fresh air."

"But you are letting all the heat leak out.."

"I don't pay for the heat. The government does. Why worry about it? Only a fool would not take full advantage of the free stuff." The man's answer irritated Ying Ying. He and his family lived in a government-subsidized townhouse in an upscale neighborhood with convenient access to everything. Their spacious and well-equipped apartment was newly refurbished. It was no different from an expensive plush apartment rented for thousands of dollars a month. Their neighbor across the street paid three thousand a month for a townhouse exactly like theirs. Yet they only paid less than three hundred. Their ground was landscaped by a professional landscaper in the spring, summer and fall seasons. In the winter their driveway was cleaned by a snow-plowing service at no cost. Sometimes they claimed that they had no income. The small rent was thus exempt. Several other occupants in other units paid nothing for years. The housing authorities used taxpayers' money to pay regular rents for them.

"It's easy to get sick this way," Ying Ying said again.

"The hospital and medication are free. It's my right to use them. Only a stupid fool would waste that right."

In another couple's apartment Ying Ying saw an abundance of baby food and juices piling in a room. She asked why they bought so much more than they needed. The husband said:

"We didn't buy them. They are all free. Why not take them?"

The wife laughed and said: "Our welfare caseworker asked me if there was anything else that we might need. What a stupid question? Although we are well provided for. There really isn't anything more we need. But no one is content 100% all the time. Of course there are a lot of other things I wish to have. But I didn't say a new Jaguar or a mink coat. Ha ha ha. I just said, as a joke, that I wish my family could eat lobsters and fillet mignon more often. You know what? The caseworker wrote me a note and said take this to this place. They will give you lobsters and fillet mignon at no charge.'"

The woman chuckled. The husband added:

"The Americans are so stupid." They laughed heartily.

These two exploiters worked under the table and made decent incomes. Yet they did not report them to the IRS. Their friend, another rapacious weevil preying on the welfare system, advised them to report a small portion of their income and pay a little tax. He said:

"This way you will get social security payments when you reach 62. All you need to do is to pay income tax, no matter how small it is, for ten years, to qualify for a life-long benefit."

One professor sponsored his fifty-year-old relative's immigration. The relative refused to find work and relied completely on welfare. The professor asked him:

"Why don't you try to get a job? Working in the grocery store or anywhere is better than not doing anything."

The man said: "I have housing, food, money, medical care; everything I need is given to me for free. Why should I get a job? My medical care is better than yours because yours is paid by an insurance company that dictates what and how much you will get. And you have a co-payment on top of your premium. Mine is paid for by the government. It's a blank check. There is no limit. And there is no co-payment for anything. Your doctor prescribes generic medicine for you and mine gives me name brands for free. If I had worked I would lose all the benefits and when I retire I would not qualify for any free benefit. So why should I get a job?"

The eloquent argument irritated the professor. He shook his head and sighed when telling the story to friends: "I regret that I have brought a parasite to this country."

Parasite!!! What a perfect word to describe these people. But can one blame these people? It was the poorly designed welfare system, or a good system poorly managed, that left so many deplorable loopholes of which those people could easily take advantage.

But then, was this situation not comparable to the bilingual education program? The welfare agencies and the inner city public schools needed head counts for government funding.

The professor came from Taiwan in the early 1960s. Immigration laws were stringent at that time. Foreign students had to obtain working permits in order to work two or three months in the summer to earn tuition money for the next school year. Working without a permit, even for a day, if caught, would mean being deported. It was grim. But it was the law to which all foreign students abided without question.

Some people criticized Ying Ying for her righteousness, her insistence on ethical conducts, her intolerance for societal exploiters, law circumventors and other pernicious elements. She was brought up to be an upright, law-biding person. Her father's precept was etched in her mind:

"Rather sacrifice yourself for the benefit of others than sacrifice others for the benefit of your own."

It had been a guiding principle all her life.

But this idea was scoffed at by some of her associates. One even said:

"Is your father delirious? Why did he give you this ridiculously detrimental idea? Remember. 'those who are not selfish will be condemned by heaven and destroyed by earth.' This is everyone's guiding principle."

Chapter 6

$\mathcal{T}$he news media outfits tried to fulfill their civic duties as responsible citizens, to pay-back the community that had made their businesses successful. Sometimes they would organize conferences or panel discussions on pressing issues often reported in the news, such as race, drugs, alcohol, teen pregnancy, dropping out from school, suicide, destructive behaviors, violence, threat to the society, and others. The so-called leaders of different communities were invited as speakers and panelists.

During a panel discussion Ying Ying spoke about racism. Her views riled the other Chinese representatives at the discussion. She said:

"Racism is not an endemically American issue. Nor is it worse in this society than elsewhere. As much as it is a social ailment and we all wish to cure it, it is a part of our existence and nearly impossible to eradicate. It is in the human nature to dislike, to look askance at those who are different from us. Discrimination exists in every place and at every period of human history. You can impose a law to prohibit it; you can teach people to change their attitude; you can even punish those who infract the law. But you cannot alter people's way of thinking without brainwashing them.

"The American government has already done a great deal to change it by enforcing many rules and regulations. Most white Americans feel a floating sense of guilt about what blacks have suffered historically, thus an urge to make it up to them. In other parts of the world, no such effort is evident. In China, for example, discrimination is blatant. It was reported some years ago, that a black foreign student was severely beaten by a number of male college students because the man had dated a female student of that college. Those Chinese young men, patriotic and nationally/racially solipsistic, were enraged. They openly announced: 'How dare a black guy date our female schoolmate? It is humiliating to us.'" A stir arose from the audience. Ying Ying ignored it and continued:

"The beating almost caused an international incident as reported in the newspapers. Doesn't this incident poignantly illustrate the non-monopoly nature of racial discrimination in this country? Few people see that.

"Ethnocentricity as we know it is another common phenomenon. Didn't the Germans claim their race to be superior to all others? Japan regarded so highly of herself that they ventured to conquer the world. China has displayed such a strong Sinocentric view as reflected in her name, the Middle Kingdom, the center of human civilization and superior to all. Emperor Qian Long of the Manchu dynasty treated the British envoy, the Earl of MaCartney, as a tribute bearer from an inferior nation. He wrote to King George The Third in a highly patronizing tone."

Her views and candid statement were far beyond the expectation of the event organizer, the people from the newspaper. They had heard more than enough complaints from different ethnic communities about social injustice, and demands for compensations from the society. They had never heard a single one with Ying Ying's view.

The other representatives from the Chinese community were peeved to hear someone amongst themselves voice an contradicting view that upset their intention to emphasize the severity of racial discrimination in America. They interrupted Ying Ying several times during her speech. But Ying Ying was determined to present her point. After the meeting the representatives confronted her with harsh protest and criticism. They even questioned why she was anti the Chinese-community.

In another panel discussion sponsored by the same newspaper the subject was to explore the phenomenon of Chinese youth's performance in school. They invited Ying Ying to join the panel and said:

"We think you provide a valid view although the Chinese community was strongly against us inviting you to this discussion."

According to statistics, Chinese youth had very low dropout rates; they generally did better scholastically than others in school and had higher average SAT scores; they had a much lower rate on most of the common problems. The number of students admitted to the top-notch universities in the country was disproportionate to the Chinese population.

Ying Ying offered her opinion:

"I believe it is due to the Chinese parents who stress the importance of their children's education and conduct. The children are instilled with the idea since they are very young that they must study hard; do well in school, avoid the wry-behaviors of their peers; respect their parents at home and teachers in school.

"The parents may be poor but they want the children to have the best education and extra-curriculum cultural activities, such as taking lessons in music, dance, painting and drawing. If the children are guided in the right direction during their formative years they are less likely to do the wrong things when they grow up."

Ying Ying's statement was based on her observations and a commonly held perception of many Chinese. She was not a sociologist quoting figures and numbers to support her point. Again her utterance irritated the other Chinese representatives. One glowered at her and said:

"That is a myth, a prevalent myth costing the Chinese community dearly. We have been called the model minority. We are silent. We don't disclose our problems. We don't ask for handouts. But government money is not a handout.

It's our right to claim it. Like other minority communities, we have problems. The same problems of kids doing drugs, abusing alcohol, committing suicide, dropping out of school, just like other kids. Why don't we get help?"

Ying Ying was squelched into silence.

As the meeting adjourned, that representative shot a resentful look at Ying Ying and said:

"Hey, we should have a talk. You know how destructive your statement is? If you don't know what to say, don't say it. If you don't know what we stand for you shouldn't have come to the meeting." The brusque utterance stunned Ying Ying. She brooded over the reason behind that surliness. It was not difficult to figure it out. It was money, government subsidies that these people were after, like welfare agencies and bilingual programs. They were willing to distort the facts in order to obtain government funding.

Another incident that perturbed Ying Ying was the Chinese community's fight for a lower entrance threshold to Latin School, a special examination-based secondary school in Boston. As the statistics showed, Chinese students were represented in disproportionate numbers already. Other minority groups, because their kids could not pass the examinations, had only very few in that school. As such, affirmative Action forced the school to set aside quotas and low admission scores for all minority children except for the Chinese.

At a community meeting the claimer stated: "Chinese *is* a minority just like any other. Our kids should enjoy the same preferential treatment. We demand that our kids be admitted at that low score just like the blacks and Latinos. We should take action."

Ying Ying was very disturbed. She felt it was fair that the school treated Chinese and white children equally. She voiced her comment:

"Chinese children's scholastic records are high nationwide. They are represented in schools at much higher ratios in relation to the Chinese population already. I don't think the school needs to lower the entrance requirements for them."

She was silenced by resentful eyes and harsh voices. One senior member chastised her:

"Fang Ying Ying, you have done enough damage at the conference already. Please keep your opinions to yourself. Don't harm our community any further."

More severe criticism on Ying Ying's position on social issues came from Chinatown. She received a letter condemning her for her ignorance and misrepresentation of the community.

"... Who do you think you are? What gives you the right to speak on behalf of the community? You are an outsider, not one of us. You know nothing about the community. You have not gone through the things as we have. You have no understanding or sympathy to the Chinese of America. You are a detriment to our community. "

Ying Ying felt hurt and dejected because of the letter at first. After much pondering, she became humbled by how little she knew about the Chinese Americans. She was truly an outsider who had just been here for only a few years. She thought she had learned enough about America. She might be very wrong. *There must be good reasons for their inequitable claims and demands,* she thought. *I should try to learn more about what the Chinese Americans have experienced and how they feel.*

*   *   *   *

One day at a function she sat next to a man who grew up in Chinatown. Like many young people who moved away from Chinatown after finishing school and finding jobs elsewhere, this man, Peter Si, lived in the dorm while in college and found a teaching position in the history department at Boston University after finishing his Ph.D.

"Ms. Fang, I am aware of the controversies surrounding your position in regard to the community's needs." After some polite, casual conversations Peter Si opened this serious topic. "I totally understand your points. But I have to say that the community has its reasons for objection."

"I appreciate your candidness, Peter. I regret that I have offended the community. I didn't know enough about the Chinese-Americans' experiences. I shouldn't have voiced my opinions." Ying Ying honestly admitted her mistake.

"Oh, no. Don't apologize. What you have said is correct. But there are a lot of unbalanced emotions, too much feeling of injustice from generations of prejudice and discrimination inflicted on the Chinese-Americans. Their reaction is understandable."

"Peter, I wish you would enlighten me on that. May I prevail on you for a meeting to talk about it?"

"I will be happy to. Shall we meet at China Society or have a lunch somewhere?"

"I think a restaurant is not a good place for a serious discussion. How about you come to China Society? In fact, if you don't mind, may I ask a couple of other American-born Chinese to come too? We can have an interesting panel discussion from a few different angles perhaps. I will get takeouts for lunch."

"I don't suppose there are dramatically different views among us the American-born Chinese. I believe we all went through pretty much the same experiences." Peter remarked.

Ying Ying contemplated whom she should ask to speak. Jenny was the first coming to her mind. Jenny was in graduate school then and only worked ten hours per week at China Society.

Ying Ying was surprised as well as puzzled by Jenny's reaction when she approached her.

"Ying Ying, I wish you had not asked me. It is an issue I have avoided. It is too difficult to reflect on the experiences of being a Chinese-American."

The usually charming, happy, positive, easy-going Jenny suddenly became reserved and uptight. Her tone of voice was weight-laden and serious. It surprised and perplexed Ying Ying. She would never have expected any unhappiness in Jenny's childhood and youth. She seemed so well adjusted and balanced.

"Why, it was that bad? I can't imagine. Do you care to share it with me?" Ying Ying did not mean to pry but her curiosity got the better of her. "Since coming here as a foreign student my experiences have been nothing but positive. And I thought I knew the society and the people very well. But I must have been wrong because my views and stand have made people in the Chinatown community angry. I should really understand the community better. What people have gone through? What makes them think and act the way they do? What is their perception of themselves in the context of the society at large? As a start, I need to know what American-born Chinese is. Do they identify with other Americans? Are they treated the same way as other Americans are by their peers? Do they value their ethnic origin? Do they cherish the culture of their ancestors? There are so many questions I wish to find answers. I need your help. I will invite three others to our discussion It's going to be informal, mostly for my benefit, to tell you the truth. There will only be a few of our close friends. Jenny, I hope you will not decline my request."

Jenny had never declined Ying Ying's requests before. She felt uneasy to say no this time too. She hesitated for a while then decided to compromise.

"All right, I will try. It's going to be difficult. I cannot be sure whether I will be open and frank about it."

"Once you open up, to talk about it, face it head on, you may think it's not so difficult after all."

"Maybe."

The other two people were Winston, a software developer in his early thirties, and Marilyn a law professor of about forty. They gladly agreed to come and give their candid expositions. Ying Ying asked Pei-hua, Denis, Tonia, Missy and other staff members to attend as audience.

*   *   *   *

On Tuesday, Tonia ordered lunch for the group from a Chinese restaurant and made a large pot of green tea. Ying Ying opened the discussion by asking a series of questions as a guideline but the speakers did not need to answer them one by one.

Basically she was interested in knowing what was it like when they were growing up? Were there other Chinese-Americans or Asian-Americans in their schools? Were they treated the same as other American kids by their teachers and peers? What were their family backgrounds, the parents' education, professions and financial status? Did those factors affect their status among the other kids? Did they identify themselves with other Americans? How did they feel about their Chinese heritage? Was ethnicity an issue? Was racial discrimination and prejudice a dark cloud circling over their heads?

Winston volunteered to speak first, followed by Jenny, then Marilyn. Peter would make his presentation last.

Winston's characterization of his experiences was lighthearted and humorous. He mostly talked about his childhood. Since college, the issue of being a Chinese-American hardly existed.

"Apart from my looks, I am no different from other kids. Nobody cared. No one treated me differently. During elementary school my family lived in an upper middle class neighborhood. There was another Chinese family with two kids on my street. And there were two other Chinese kids in my class. We all had similar backgrounds. The other Chinese whom my parents socialized with also had similar backgrounds. They were from Taiwan or Hong Kong, a few from China. They came as graduate students; settled around Boston afterwards. They all had professional jobs and financial stability, lived in upscale areas, choice neighborhoods with good schools for their kids. Chinese people were exceptional 'education junkies.' They couldn't give enough to their children.

"The teacher treated all the kids the same way. I couldn't tell if anything was different," Winston recalled. He smiled. "There was one instance in third grade art class where we were doing Chinese characters as an art project. There was a Chinese girl named Emily Tang, but since I had gone to Chinese school and knew how to write some characters, and even knew such a thing as stroke-order, I was suddenly the class expert and got praises from the teacher."

"For the most part, being an ABC was not a big deal." Winston continued. "There was one instance though. In first or second grade, a few kids called me a 'Chinese pig.' I don't think they really knew what it meant or what they were saying. Nevertheless, I got upset. Actually I really didn't care, but I felt like I should have cared. So I cried and told the teachers. My parents got involved somehow because my mom was neurotic and probably freaked out about it. She complained to the principal. The principal, the teacher and the kids apologied to my mom and me. After a while it all blew over and was forgotten." Winston chuckled. The others in the room smiled and made mild remarks. Peter Si's expression, however, was grim. He muttered something to himself:

"It's not funny. I don't think the kids were innocent." But no one paid attention to his words.

"There was another occasion in third grade when I first went to the Weston school. I had just gotten my haircut by my dad. It looked really bad. The next day I felt terribly embarrassed. I started crying because my haircut was so funny looking. All the other kids got normal haircuts from hairstylists or barbers. This was much more serious than my ethnicity. It was devastating to me," he laughed.

Winston talked about the kids' feelings about their Chinese heritage. "We were not overly aware of our Chinese heritage. Children don't care about those things. But our parents insisted that we must go to Chinese school to learn the language and culture. I can't think of any kid who wanted to go. I can't speak for all kids, but my focus during Chinese school was (a) devising ways to annoy the teachers, (b) devising ways to get out of doing homework. It included

140

tearing out a page of the homework and saying that I never got it. (c) devising ways to entertain myself. I accomplished it by writing in my books and drawing pictures all over the existing artwork. Our graffiti inevitably included poop, pee, penises, scars and blood." Everyone in the room, even Peter, laughed with him.

"Chinese school wasn't really that bad. The bad thing about it was that it was on a Sunday afternoon from two to four or something like that. And any activity that eats up free time is looked upon as an annoyance, not to mention a school-related activity not of my own choosing that takes up time. None of the students, except for the nerdy ones, really tried at Chinese school and I don't think we really learned much there. We didn't see the practicality of it other than to avoid punishment from our parents. I think if learning Chinese reading and writing were put into a more practical application, kids would be much more enthusiastic about it. Instead of reading about Wang Da-zhong and his *xin yi fu* I'd teach all the "winds" and all the numbers so we could play mahjong or maybe order off a Chinese menu." More laughs in the room.

Ying Ying wondered, beside Pei-hua and herself, who else would know what he meant by "winds" and "numbers." The mahjong tiles had four pieces of "Winds," those of Eastern, Western, Northern, and Southern. And there were two sets of tiles carrying numbers from one to nine.

"Some proactive Chinese parents also organized Family Camp in the summer." Winston gave another side of his childhood experience. "It was pretty fun. Most kids wanted to go and ended up making their parents go. Family Camp was different because you didn't have homework. All we did was hang out with our friends." He added: "It's a kid-oriented activity: no classes, only sports time and free time. It was then that kids got to even up the score a little bit because usually the parents didn't like to go a week without a real toilet or hot shower. They had to suffer in sleeping bags without heat at night and other real amenities. Kids can manage that sort of thing without much fuss. The kids like it because it's pretty lawless. The parents don't mind as much because a kid is not going to get seriously lost or in trouble in that environment. So I think parents felt a little less compelled to constantly keep an eye on their kids."

Someone asked Winston about his dating experience. Before giving a reply he chuckled.

"I was kind of a flirt even as early as first grade. I really liked this Chinese girl in my class, Sophie Lin. I already had a few different 'girlfriends' at that time. Sophie was one of them. I remember asking one of her friends to tell her that I "liked her liked her," but only if she admitted that she "liked me liked me" first and not just liked me. Otherwise, I would just like her. I remember thinking that I would marry her, even. In high school and college I dated different girls, Asian as well as non-Asian. Race didn't matter to me as long as I liked the girl. I don't think my ethnicity mattered to the girls either."

After some questions and comments after Winston's talk Jenny began her talk. Her heart was heavy, her look was despondent.

"I envy Winston for having such a fun-filled childhood. I am afraid I don't have any interesting incident to report. My parents came from Taiwan too. My father is a well-known scientist. My mother is a successful writer. They both teach at Dartmouth College. We lived in a small town. I went to a private school where kids were all white."

"So you were seriously discriminated against," Peter cut in.

"No. Discrimination was foreign to me. Throughout elementary and secondary school I didn't have any sense of that. I was a member of the choral group, the speech team and swimming team. I was an editor of the school newspaper, and was cast in three stage productions. In *Hello Dolly* I was cast as Dolly. It did not even cross my mind that Dolly should have been played by a Caucasian girl. In *Babes in Toyland* I improvised a gymnastics suite on stage, that brought me loud applause from the audience. Many people said that I was stunning. My teachers were partial to me. And I got along with other kids beautifully. My parents did not impose any Chinese value on me or insist that I learn Chinese. I could speak that language before I went to school. Since first grade, I resented it because no one else in the school spoke it and I didn't want to be different. My parents bribed me into speaking it. If I didn't speak one word of English in a conversation they would give me a quarter. If I spoke one word of English I would be fined a nickel. It only worked for a short while. Then I would not give them any nickel anymore. And they finally gave up. Other than that they did not make me do anything or prohibit me from doing anything. They never tried to steer me one direction or the other. They gave me complete freedom to make my own decisions and develop to my potentials. They were perfect parents. I couldn't find any fault in them and had nothing to complain." Jenny paused. Her remarks befuddled everyone in the room.

"It sounded like you had a perfect childhood. Why are you unhappy?" Pei-hua couldn't help but asking.

"You don't understand. My parents were the source of my unhappiness. Don't you hate people who are perfect? My parents are incredibly perfect. They are highly educated, highly accomplished. And they are model parents. They typify the elite Chinese, the Chinese snobs who excel in everything they do and are superior in every aspect to others. I felt inadequate and unworthy next to them. I couldn't bear the insurmountable weight crushing on me. My mother kept telling me that I need not use them as role models; I should just do my best. That's all. You see, this is an example of her being a perfect mother. My friends all have things to complain about their parents. They have good reasons to hate their parents. I had nothing to contribute. I couldn't find a single reason to hate them. No one would understand why I hated them. I hate being their child. I hate being a child of that special elite class of Chinese. I just want to be an average American kid." She paused a second and continued:

"More and more I want to dissociate from anything that is Chinese which might remind me of my background. I chose to forget my Chinese language. I don't keep Chinese friends. I never agreed to go out with Chinese guys. I know this sounds irrational and awful to you. It is a dark secret of mine. Maybe it's an ailment. I didn't intend to reveal it but Ying Ying asked me to speak and I couldn't camouflage it in my talk."

"Oh, Jenny, I am sorry to have made you face the sore spot in you. I hope you will forgive me. I also hope that this sore would heal now that you have confronted it." Ying Ying apologized.

Marilyn offered yet another angle of an ABC's outlook.

"I grew up in a Jewish neighborhood In New York City. There were no other Chinese-American kids in my elementary school, and only one in my junior high. She had moved to my neighborhood from Chinatown. She was shocked to find me so different from her. I was just another American girl. I went to a high school near Chinatown. There I had many Chinese schoolmates. My dad is a pastor of a Chinese church in Queens. While I was growing up in the 1970's, many of our church members lived in the suburbs. They came to the States originally as foreign students from Taiwan and Hong Kong. They all had professional jobs and pretty good incomes. We had two worship services, one in Mandarin and one in English. Aside from my family, I only saw other Chinese people on Sundays, until I went to high school. Most of the ABC kids that I knew understood the Chinese language but rarely spoke it.

"I dropped out of Chinese school because it conflicted with the cartoon program on Saturday mornings. My parents did not insist that I go. I remember I couldn't handle chopsticks before age fourteen. My parents spoke English to us, so I did not understand or speak Chinese until I studied it in college. Learning Mandarin Chinese in college was a huge turning point for me. Living in Hong Kong for one year after college was another huge turning point. Before that I had very little China-consciousness. So had not other ABC kids. Learning Cantonese helped me immensely in communicating with my mother and my relatives. My mother and I developed a sweet friendship after we began to converse in Cantonese together." In high school and college, the Chinese and other Asian-American students started to hang out together. In college, many of us met each other through the Chinese classes. Most of my close friends were Asian-Americans."

"Why? Do you feel closer to them because of your common ethnicity?" Pei-hua asked.

"I don't know. It was not a conscious choice. But we naturally gravitated toward one another. And we shared commonalities in many aspects. When you have things in common it is easier to build friendships." Marilyn replied. Then she continued to recount her younger years.

"At that time, ABCs sometimes felt embarrassed by parents and relatives who did not speak English well. By the time I got to high school, I knew I was an ABC and I wanted to marry an ABC. But I ended up marrying a Swiss. I hope to learn and embrace his heritage as well. I want to be a world citizen.

"The past four years I have spent summers in Xiamen co-directing a program for American law students. I love being a "bridge" between the US and Chinese cultures. Two years ago, I also spent one semester teaching at Xiamen University. After spending more time in China, I am now fluent in Chinese and feel most comfortable in bilingual situations with folks from overseas. I admire all immigrants in the US. I embrace my bicultural heritage. I am so thankful that

God has given me Chinese parents.

"I guess I've evolved from a cartoon-watching-skipping-Chinese-school-not-able-to-use-chop-sticks American to wanting-to-marry-another-ABC, to lived-overseas-Chinese-American to world-citizen-wannabe." Marilyn ended her talk with a satisfied grin. Her audience applauded.

It was Peter's turn. His presentation became a real discussion session instead of a speech or a report. People asked many questions because Peter's exposition was diametrically opposed to the other three and so mind-boggling.

"I have friends and colleagues from Taiwan and China. From our regular and constant association I see the difference in our respective outlooks. That's because our backgrounds and experiences are completely opposite." Peter started his talk.

Pei-hua interjected her observation: "Yes, the Chinese Americans are no different from other Americans. The only difference is their appearance. On the other hand they had nothing in common with the Chinese or other Asians except outward appearance. I even doubt if they feel like Chinese at all." Pei-hua glanced at Peter and posed a blunt question: "Do you feel you are a Chinese?"

"That's where you are wrong, Pei-hua." Peter chided mildly and smiled. "The local-born Chinese-Americans have little commonality with the native Chinese, as you have said. But they are very different from other Americans aside from being born on the same land and perhaps went to the same schools."

"This I don't understand. You were born here, brought up here, educated here. Then what else made you different from the others beside looks," Denis asked.

"We are not really Chinese. We don't think of ourselves as Chinese." Peter did not answer Denis's question directly. Instead he looked at Ying Ying and Pei-hua and said: "Most of us know little about China. Your culture, your traditions and values are so remote to us. Some of us, only a small number of us, vaguely know why and how our ancestors came here and how much hardship and persecution they had endured. Yes, there are those whose parents or grand parents came after World War II. But the discrimination they suffered may not be less than those of us who go back four generations."

Ying Ying made a comment: "I realize that some form of discrimination existed. I heard about black people having to sit in the back of the bus."

Peter glared at Ying Ying for a second and said: "Is that all you've heard?"

"That's not bad enough?" Ying Ying answered his question with a question.

Peter sneered: "That was the most innocuous," he replied. "I won't blame you for not being familiar with that part of American history. I suppose the history of racial issues in this country is not a subject that people in China pay a lot of attention to." Peter used gentle language instead of calling Ying Ying ignorant. He went on in saying: "Ying Ying I suggest that you read some books on this subject. There are many of them."

"You are right. It is not a subject that we know anything about. Do all minorities share a similar fate? From what I hear now, it appears that even Chinese Americans don't have similar experience."

"The blacks were brought here as slaves in the beginning. And they were kept as slaves until Lincoln liberated them" Peter did not answer the question. He wanted to give Ying Ying some basic information.

"This much we know. We studied American history, as part of our World History course in high school."

"The Chinese were hired from Canton to build the American west. They worked in the gold mines, farms, light industries; they built houses and roads, reclaimed swamplands, and most of all, they built the transcontinental railway. Their contributions are numerous and significant. They were paid much less than other workmen and their contributions were only scarcely recognized. Instead they were persecuted; their children were not allowed to go to school. Then, in 1882 the congress passed a Chinese Exclusion Act to ban Chinese from coming," Peter recounted.

Most Chinese-Americans were not familiar with that part of the history. It was not taught in classes and there was no reason for them to discover it. It certainly was not something that Ying Ying and Pei-hua were cognizant.

"That is disheartening," Ying Ying sighed: "Chinese Exclusion Act!! Is it still in force?"

"No." Peter glared at Ying Ying wryly as if saying, *You are more ignorant than I had thought*. "It was repealed in 1943 because China was a staunch ally of America in WWII."

"Then Chinese people in this country have been treated fairly since then. I suppose," Pei-hua maintained.

Peter did not respond to that remark.

"The fact is that since the mid-19th century the disdainful attitude toward the Chinese unfailingly passed on from generation to generation. People are taught from early on that Asians are subhuman to whites. Some people never get beyond that attitude. The notion is so deep-rooted that it is ineradicable. The memory of WWII was replaced by that left from the Korean War and Vietnam War in both of which Chinese fought against Americans. They were enemies. That further entrenched the hatred and contempt toward the Chinese. They were demonized as silly awkward animals. It allowed whites to kill them easily, and their women to hate Asian men." Both Ying Ying and Pei-hua were disturbed and enraged. They felt an insult too immense to bear.

All the while they saw Peter inflamed with anger. Peter's voice trembled. A deeply wounded heart had skewed his views. He had lost his emotional equilibrium. His words grew to be more inordinate.

"My uncle and his wife were a highly educated and physically attractive couple when they were young. My uncle was a space engineer and my aunt was a physician. But even with that, they were execrated and ridiculed, mocked and made fun of by their white neighbors who rallied and petitioned for the couple to move out. Some threw garbage on their lawn because they were 'slant eyed,' because they were 'chinks.'" Peter's face was veiled in pain and wrath, tears brimmed his eyes.

Winston, Marilyn and jenny just said that they were not aware of any discrimination. Why was Peter's story so opposite to theirs?

Ying Ying tried to console Peter. "Peter, don't let the past distraught you."

"They called Chinese all sorts of ugly names." Peter ignored her: "nips, chinks, coolie, gooks. The adults passed on their hatred to the children. These ideas were rarely challenged by the younger generation of which I belonged," Peter went on.

"These were in the past. I think it's different now." Pei-hua tried to convince Peter as well as herself. "Otherwise all Chinese in this country would be suffering, not just the native-born. Yet honestly, Peter, I have not felt or heard of any unfairness from the people I know."

"Winston, Marilyn and Jenny had different experiences than yours. I think each situation is different," Denis said.

"I do believe that America is a place of equality, fairness, liberty and equal opportunity. Some of those recently coming from China said they were overwhelmed by the abundance of freedom and opportunities. They didn't know what to do with all those." Ying Ying remembered clearly who had said that to her. She chuckled in that somber atmosphere.

"You don't have the background to sense it," Peter rebuked. "Do you know that white women decry Asian men, considering Asian's facial and physical features as 'deformities' or deviations from the aesthetic tastes of the whites and therefore not acceptable? It would be a violation of human value and repulsive for a white woman to date an Asian man." Peter's wrath expanded, his raised voice glacial.

Winston glared at Peter in disbelieve. *Those were very ugly words he used, 'deformities?' 'deviations from the aesthetic ideal?' 'violation of human value?' 'repulsive?' What monsters had this man encountered?* Winston and his friends gave no thoughts regarding the girls' racial backgrounds when asking for dates, nor had they been rejected by Caucasian girls due to their ethnicity. He had mentioned it in his speech earlier. Now he wished to reiterate it but decided not to because this was Peter's presentation. He should not contradict him.

"What?!!" Ying Ying was perturbed. She lost her equanimity for a moment. Indignation rushed through her head.

"Women have different experiences. White men love Asian women as trophies, but often not as equals. I don't doubt there are many white men pursuing you. But make no mistake about it. They want you because you're exotic. They've had their white women. You are something new to be tried, an exotic delicacy to be had. That is the mind of the dominant race in the hierarchy of people," Peter added in a despiteful tone.

Denis thought that was a very skewed opinion. He could not refrain himself from making a comment:

"Peter, do you really think you are being fair in your analysis of white men's psyche? I can say that either I or any white male I know has that attitude toward an Asian woman."

146

Peter and Denis carried on a debate. Each would not give in to the other's argument.

For the first time Ying Ying felt her ethnic pride was seriously injured. Her people, 'the Great Han people,' as Sun Sang called it, were being trashed by another race. *This was outrageous, utterly insufferable*. Racial sensitivity erupted like a volcano in her.

Then, for a moment, Winston's and the other two women's statements went through her head. She re-evaluated them and regained her equanimity. Was Peter's story true? Or was it a one-man's emotionally charged biased account? She knew of many Chinese men who married Caucasian American women. It never appeared to be less than usual. Furthermore, there were numerous instances, even among her friends, when Chinese males stood out. For example, Meng Song was relentlessly pursued by Caucasian American girls. And pianist Yang Dan told her one time:

"The kids in school look up to me. I've always been featured as a soloist in the school' s concerts. I have won many competitions. So they sort of regard me as a celebrity or something in the school. I believe it's the same with Ma Ya." Ma Ya, the violinist, smiled and nodded.

Denis once maintained: "Yang Dan and Ma Ya were not your average minority. Being exceptionally talented, highly accomplished, certainly set them apart. And their good looks are a caviar "

These words resounded in Ying Ying's ears. It was hard for her to believe that Chinese men as a whole were rejected by Caucasian American women as "inferior." Then why would Peter make up such a story?

"Peter, not that I doubt your words, but it is hard for me to take in."

"You want me to tell you more? I don't have such imagination as to concoct so many stories," Peter countered.

"I think I have heard enough. It's too disturbing to me," Ying Ying said.

They concluded the discussion. Peter promised to keep in touch and keep Ying Ying up to speed on current Chinese-American issues. Ying Ying thanked him and promised that she would try to keep herself informed.

*   *   *   *

The business trip to China reaffirmed Meilan's confidence: *China is mine*. She always believed that. Now was the time to leave Andrew Johnson's company. She had learned all that she needed from that company. and acquired all the useful information and contacts in the business. Working at Johnson's company would hinder her advancement in building her own business. With that in her head, Meilan avoided discussing her business ambition with Johnson. Instead she told George Hemmingway about her plan to take a music and dance group to perform in China.

While having dinner with George Hemmingway one evening, with a glass of wine in hand, she said:

"The Chinese public loves me. If I go back to perform now my audience will

147

be as enthusiastic as ever."

"I have no doubt. And I think you should do what you think is best," George Hemmingway responded.

"I plan to take a group of American singers and dancers there. Now is the time, before China sees performances from abroad. When more foreign shows appear in China, it will not be as easy for me to make money."

"I hope you will allow me to support your venture," George Hemmingway offered. This was exactly what Meilan wished to hear. But she did not want Hemmingway to think that she was accepting a favor from him. She must let him know it was a mutually beneficial partnership. It would sound much more palatable.

"How about let's collaborate? We both invest in this venture and we will split the profit."

Hemmingway smiled. Join venture was not what he had in mind. He was hoping to marry her. He planned to propose for her hand this evening.

"Meilan," Hemmingway covered Meilan's hand with his own and said in a sincere tone: "please don't put a gulf between us. You know how much I love you. I want you to be my wife."

This was an old story. He wanted her to be his wife. But he already had a wife.

"George, I appreciate that. But you know it is not possible. You are still married," Meilan replied.

"This is what I want to tell you tonight. My wife has agreed to a divorce. Our attorneys are working on the proceedings. The settlement is where the crux lies. How much money her lawyer will advise her to demand and how much my lawyer will advise me to give. Her lawyer doesn't know it but I am willing to give her as much as it takes. I don't anticipate too much difficulty."

Meilan was surprised. She thought those rich men only fooled around behind their wives back, to have a little extramarital affair. Divorcing the wife to marry a mistress would be far from their mind. Meilan had too much self-respect and dignity to allow herself be so involved. Her association with these gentlemen stopped at dinner, theatre, concert and similar events. Physical intimacy was off limits. Whether this unreachable moon was an irresistible impetus urging Hemmingway to divorce his wife in order to marry Meilan, one would never know. Should Meilan be grateful and accept his proposal?

"Oh, George. I don't know what to say. I know how much you love me. I should feel very happy and honored. But I cannot marry you just yet. Because I have this dream, to form a music and dance troupe to tour the world, to build schools of international performing arts, from elementary school to college, and to found a TV and film production company among other things. My name will be the eponym of all these establishments. I must do this first."

"I admire a woman with vision and ambition. You certainly have the ability to do them by yourself, my darling. But please let me be your partner, or just let me give you my support. Don't push me away. Marrying me will not hinder your plans. It may help you achieve your goals faster."

148

"You are right, dear George. With your money, everything will be easier. But that's not the same as if I do it all by myself. I hope you will understand."

Hemmingway recognized the impossibility of persuading Meilan. That tenacity, that obstinacy was rare among the women he knew. This quality of Meilan's fascinated him.

"I respect your wish and admire your pertinacity. I will not pressure you to do what is not right for you. But I hope you will accept this as a gift." He took out the diamond ring prepared for the engagement he wished to take place that evening. Now he just wanted her to have it as a gift from a friend.

"It's a friendship ring. Please don't refuse it." He took Meilan's right hand and put it on her fourth finger.

Meilan looked at the ring. The glittering stone must have been three carat in size. *It will hurt him too much if I don't accept it.*

"It's lovely. Thank you George. I accept it as a symbol of our everlasting friendship." She lifted her glass to clink with George's then took a sip.

"I hope one day soon, after you fulfill all your dreams, you will allow me to enter your life," Hemmingway said ever so gently after taking a sip from his glass. It was a proposal. Meilan understood it.

"Of course, George," Meilan answered with sincerity. This time she covered George's hand with her own. George turned his hand to pick up Meilan's and kissed it.

"You will need seed money for your current project. Let me underwrite the cost of your venture. Please. don't decline it," George felt that the distance between Meilan and him had been considerably shortened this evening. He was in a position to offer financial support to Meilan.

"Thank you George. I know I should just say yes. But I need to see if I can do it without your financial backing. Would you agree to a business joint venture? I have calculated the cost of the project. It will be around $300,000. You put in that amount as your investment. My investment is my name that will be a big draw to the audience, and my part in the performances, and of course my effort to carry this project out. We each own 50% of the venture and will share 50% of the profit. What do you think?" Meilan proposed.

"Whatever you say, dear. Your part is worth 100%. But if you say 50% it will be 50%. But $300,000 is too small an amount for such a big project. I will lay out half a million as my 50%," Hemmingway said. He was satisfied that Meilan would accept his money. Profit from the investment couldn't be farther from his mind.

"Okay. We are equal partners. In China, my audience base is broad, but ticket prices are low. Our profit will show only after the breakeven point of one million US dollars. That will take a lot of tickets," Meilan was thinking aloud.

What if they didn't make money? She would not lose a dime because Hemmingway's half million would be more than enough to cover all costs including costumes, travel and subsistence, performers' fees, staff salaries, her compensation and all other expenses. If the project did not sell over one million dollars worth of tickets, Hemmingway would be the one to lose some cash.

"I understand. I am not worried about the return. There are many arts ventures losing money. And there are people who are willing and able to support the arts without thinking of making the money back. Hemmingway was honest and forthright about it, not just to please Meilan. "Don't try to be frugal on the budget."

Once the plan was on the drawing board she began to make arrangements in China and auditioned singers and dancers in Boston.

"Meilan, we thought you were bringing dancers from China to tour the U.S. That was what you told us so many times. Why do you need Boston dancers?" Pei-hua was confused.

"No, no, this is something else." She clarified it for Pei-hua. "I will do that later. Now I am taking American musicians and dancers to tour China. I have lined up all the big cities. My sister has signed the contracts on my behalf. China has not seen foreign music and dance shows. My idea excited them. The market is definitely good. This is the right time. In a few years, China's door will be wide open and other shows will go there. It won't be as easy to make money anymore then."

Meilan did have a far-sighted and an acute business mind, Pei-hua thought.

"Gosh, Meilan, you certainly have the eye to recognize opportunities in advance." Pei-hua made this remark that seemed half jeering and half praising: Meilan took it as an honest and sincere accolade. She proudly replied:

"I do have a good brain for business. I will be very busy auditioning performers and shopping for costumes in the next couple of weeks. There are lots of things to do. You can't imagine how complex it is. This is a group of 30 some people, plus instruments and costumes. Oh, I already feel dizzy just thinking about it."

"Do you have a manager?" Ying Ying asked.

"Yes, thank God. This is a very experienced stage manager. And he is not going to charge me much. Because, he was all elated about the opportunity to see the places in China. I have told the performers that this trip would give them a chance that is hundred times better than a commercial tour would be in regard to sightseeing in China. They will see what normal tourists don't get to see. They are happy. The free trip is counted as a large portion of their pay."

"Why aren't you taking Woolan along?" Pei-hua asked. "He went with you on your last trip with the business delegation."

"I am not sure whether he would be useful this time. He doesn't speak English. He can't communicate with the other members. That's a big drawback." Meilan expressed her concern.

"You have an English-speaking manager who cannot speak Chinese. I think you have to have a Chinese guy to handle those minutiae in China. I can imagine how tiring that can be if you have to do it all by yourself," Pei-hua stressed.

"I suppose you are right. This time there will be a lot more detail work than last time. I do need a gofer. Yes, may be I should take Woolan along."

Woolan was happy that Meilan would take him along. He had reached the end of his rope in Boston and needed to explore China again. He served Meilan well during the three months of rehearsal, costume shopping and other pre-production work. Meilan was pleased with his performance.

They were in China for two and a half months. Meilan's extraordinary self-promoting skill resulted in media hype and large sums of advertisement money. Newspapers and television interviewed her and gave extensive coverage of her events. Banners that read "Patriotic Super Star Returns," and her pictures were seen everywhere. Several large companies endorsed her and paid dearly for advertisement spots in the lavishly printed program books, and on posters hung in the performance halls and auditoriums. Some took full-page ads in the newspapers celebrating her homecoming and the excellent shows she was to put on.

Each time before the curtain rose names of the major supporters were announced. Meilan, without the help of a publicity expert, came up with these tactics herself to build the momentum and attract sponsorship and advertisements. They toured seventeen cities and brought in more than two million U.S. dollars. The singers and dancers, thirty in all, were paid $50 each for each show. The total pay was $25,500, a very small amount. The whole project cost her less than $200,000. At $5 per ticket, that was what the Chinese market would bear at that time. The proceeds totaled $300,000. The bottom line would be a profit of $100,000 as her own pay. A pretty good, money-making project already. Beside that, there were large sums of revenue from sponsors and advertisers, plus the $500,000 cash investment from Hemingway. Those were the project's profit. Yet she was not going to split that with Hemmingway. She figured the major income was not a regular result of the show, only the ticket proceeds were. The extra income was a garland for her fame and special talent. It rightfully belonged to her and only her. As such, with a clear conscience, she kept the $1,500,000.

The money she made was deposited in the Bank of Hong Kong in order to avoid paying the IRS.

The tour was exhausting as she described to her friends in Boston:

"Two or three days at each city. The kids, I mean my performers, some of them got sick. They were not used to the food. They liked Chinese food, the kind they got in Boston. But when they had to eat bean sprouts and tofu every day, they couldn't take it. Toward the end every one lost weight. Their clothes were tattered. They looked like beggars." She often subconsciously exaggerated to entertain her listeners who unfailingly laughed every time.

The success of this project enticed her to do a reprise, or a similar one each year without involving Hemmingway. Some of the performers from the first trip stayed with her. Some left. She auditioned and selected new ones to replace those. She said the new ones were even better. There were jazz singers and instrumental musicians, tap dancers, and country singers. These were more representative of American culture than other genres, thus a sharper edge for hyping and more powerful magnetism to Chinese audience.

Woolan went with her again.

Although the reprise lost some of the original's novelty, she got the same level of sponsorship and media splash nevertheless. She toured 19 cities some of which were repeats some were new.

In this second trip she reaped more than fame, glory, and a lot of cash. In addition to those, the Beijing government gave her one hundred acres of land bordering a park for her to build an international arts institute that she had often talked about. The Ministry of Culture promised to help her form a first-class dance company to tour the world. These were once laughed at by many people as wild dreams of hers.

"I will hire the best musicians, artists, dancers and dramatists from all over the world to teach at my institute." Meilan boasted. "Ying Ying and Pei-hua, I will invite you to teach too."

"We are not the world's best musicians, artists, dancers or dramatists. How do we qualify to teach?" Pei-hua taunted as she often did.

Meilan felt discomfited. "Ai, there are other things you can teach." Then she diverted to other subjects: "I have laid the ground work for a TV program, a production company, a record company, a dance troupe, a high-class fashion boutique chain and a fashion manufactory. These are all connected to the art institute. Everything will be named Meilan."

"Meilan, you are going to be a big conglomerate," Pei-hua jeered again.

"Yes. Seriously." Meilan sensed the sarcasm in Pei-hua's tone this time:

"My name will make a good brand-name. Every one in China knows me. It will sell products. It will get attention." Confidently she continued:

"I will hire Elisa, my old boss at Andrew Johnson's company, to be my assistant. She is a shrewd businesswoman."

Pei-hua tauntingly warned her: "Make sure you can trust her."

"Of course." Pei-hua's insinuation of Meilan's betrayal of Johnson's trust completely escaped her. She simply replied: "But she will be loyal if she can make more than she deserves. I won't let her know my China contacts anyway. So what can she do?"

"You certainly know how to avoid pitfalls," Pei-hua subtly jeered.

"Is Hemmingway going to invest in your ventures?" Ying Ying asked.

"I am not going to accept his investment. I met two big businessmen in Hong Kong. One is an American in the movie industry in Hollywood. The other is a Japanese. They were very interested in my ideas and wanted to join me in forming a corporation called Meilan Development, Incorporated. We are pure business partners, unlike George Hemmingway who is interested in me personally."

"I understand." Ying Ying could see clearly that Meilan would not want to feel beholden to anyone. "He is waiting for your success and fulfillment, remember?" Ying Ying was referring to Hemmingway's marriage proposal.

"Yes. But I cannot think about that now." Meilan was fully focusing on building her empire.

*　　　*　　　*　　　*

Meng Song's sister Lingzhen came from Shanghai in the summer of 1990. It was a surprise to everybody because he had never mentioned anything about having a sister; and how was she able to come so easily while U.S. visas were very difficult to get in China.

But no one asked about it, not even Ying Ying when Meng Song asked her to put his sister up for a few days. Lingzhen was staying with her brother and his two Caucasian housemates in a South End apartment temporarily until she found her own place,

"Why do you need to send her to my place for a few days?" Ying Ying asked absently.

"Ah—mmmm, because," Song reluctantly smiled: "I ...I ... have a visitor."

"An out-of-town visitor who will stay with you?" Ying Ying asked innocently.

"No, she is in Boston. But she will go back to her home country in a week." Song grinned with a little blush. It dawned on Ying Ying instantly. He didn't have to say more. The girl must need to stay with him for those days. His sister would be in their way. *This is Meng Song. Always intimately involve with girls,* she thought.

"Oh, I see." She blushed.

Lingzhen apologized when Ying Ying picked her up: "I am sorry to bother you. But my brother said it was okay. I hope it's not too much trouble."

"Of course not. I am happy to have you for a few days. We can get to know each other more quickly this way."

Lingzhen was a very refined young lady. And she was much more open than Song. The two girls became friends quickly. In those few days she told Ying Ying a lot about herself and her family, and what they had gone through during the Cultural Revolution. Near the end of that destructive period, she was fifteen and was sent to do hard labor in the countryside. One time she fell to the bottom of a hill and broke her back. The pain from the injury stayed with her till this day. When her father was imprisoned, their house was ransacked, and everything confiscated, they were given ten *yuan* of RMB (*Ren-ming bi*, Chinese currency) a month to live on. She and her brother dared not step out of their home for fear of being stoned.

"Why was your father imprisoned?" Ying Ying inquired.

"Because they interpreted his painting erroneously and accused him of being a counter-revolutionary," Lingzhen said matter-of-factly. "Many artists didn't escape that fate. They were beaten, humiliated, and jailed. My father was lucky. He was spared from the beating."

She was a graphic designer intending to study computer graphics at the Massachusetts College of Art. The subject was new at the college. She thought it would be a highly marketable skill to acquire. Ying Ying was impressed by how well informed this young woman was about the American job market, much more so than Ying Ying herself who paid little attention to the practical side of life.

Lingzhen only brought a few pieces of clothing with her from Shanghai.

She knew the styles would be unsuitable. She asked if Ying Ying could take her shopping for clothes. They started from some moderately priced stores. She looked around with disinterest, and made no comment. Then they went to Bloomingdales and a few higher-priced stores in Chestnut Hill Mall. She was somewhat pleased.

"This is okay." She picked up a shirt. Ying Ying looked at the price tag and let out a breath. She said:

"Too expensive. I can't afford it."

"That's the problem. The good things are too expensive. The cheap things are just that, cheap," Lingzhen said.

Lingzhen returned to her brother's apartment four days later. Seeing the questions in Ying Ying's eyes Meng Song volunteered his story. This was unusual because he normally would not divulge his private matters.

"She returned to France yesterday," he said.

"How will you maintain your long distance romance?" Ying Ying jested.

"There is no more romance. Yesterday was the end," he said plainly.

It was simply beyond Ying Ying that one could so easily put a period at the end of a steaming love affair instantly.

"When and how did you two meet?" she asked, with a smile and casually.

"Over a week ago in a restaurant. She was a tourist about to complete her visit to the States. A very beautiful woman," Meng Song honestly confessed.

"But how did you get to date her?" Ying Ying was truly curious.

"Oh, I asked the waiter to send her a drink on my behalf. When the waiter pointed at me to her, she smiled at me. I walked over to sit at her table."

How trite!!! He learned his tact from some romance movies or TV shows. Ying Ying tittered.

"She was alone?"

"At the moment she was. In fact she was waiting for someone. But I had enough time to exchange phone numbers with her."

"So you just called her for a date?" Ying Ying held back a laugh.

"Yes. I called the following day. She said she already had a date that afternoon. I said 'call him and tell him you cannot make it,'" Meng Song chuckled. "We spent the afternoon and evening going to a movie, then dinner, and dancing at a nightclub." Meng Song grinned.

"Wow, she actually canceled her date with the other person." Ying Ying remarked with amazement.

"Yes. I took her to her hotel late that night. I was going to kiss her and say goodnight. There would be more days to come. But she invited me to her room."

"Wow." That was all Ying Ying could say.

"I thought since we would spend the rest of her days here together why not save her hotel expenses? I suggested that she move to my apartment. She was very happy."

"Did you tour Boston with her?" Ying Ying thought about the French girl and her purpose in Boston.

"No, seeing my room was enough for her," Song smirked naughtily.

"I see. So she traveled all the way from France to the great city of Boston so that she could spend a few days in your room. And you are not going to keep in touch with her."

"No, not likely," Meng Song replied nonchalantly.

That was Meng Song's romance. A few days of burning, consuming, lustful, cloy sexual entanglement with a stranger left with a vacuity, without a trace in his heart. Did he ever have any feeling while with a girl or just purely carnal desire, sexual satisfaction? What difference is that from a lower animal? There were a few instances when strange females called Ying Ying at work, in anxious voices, asking about Meng Song's whereabouts.

"He was supposed to visit with me last night. But there was no sign of him. I don't know whether he is in town or not? I waited for him the whole night. Oh, he is free as a bird," the woman said.

"I have no idea where he is. This is my office you are calling, in case you didn't know." Ying Ying was annoyed at those women calling Meng Song on her office phone. She wanted to tell the women not to do that again.

Another time a girl with a thick Italian accent asked for Meng Song. She met him on the airplane traveling to India. The woman said, she would like to stay with him for a day or two if he were in town.

"Are you his girlfriend?" After explaining herself the girl paused a second and asked:

"No, I am not his girlfriend. If I were, would he have given you my phone number?" Ying Ying questioned, feeling slighted: "I don't know where he is. And I don't know when he will drop by. But if I see him I will tell him that a girl he met on the plane has called."

When Meng Song went to see Ying Ying in her office she demanded:

"Meng Song why do you give my office number to those girls? They keep calling here to disturb my work. A girl you met on the plane thinks this is your girlfriend's number. Can you not give people my number? I am not your answering service."

"Sorry," Meng Song smiled shyly. "They asked for my number. I didn't want to give it to them."

"So you gave them mine?"

"I thought if they called in the evening no one would be here."

"Then my answering machine would record their messages. Please tell the girls that the number is no longer yours."

"Okay," Meng Song grinned. "Ying Ying, Lingzhen is trying to find a room. Can you help?" He handed over a newspaper.

"There is an extra room in your apartment. Why can't she rent that?"

"No, I use that room as my studio. Beside, I don't want her in the same apartment. Not convenient."

"Uh huh." Ying Ying peered at him knowingly.

After Meng Song left, Ying Ying called a few places advertised on the paper. In one call she said:

"Hi, I saw your ad for a roommate. I am calling on behalf of a girl who just came from Shanghai."

"She is the sister of an artist, isn't she?" The woman on the other end demanded. Ying Ying was puzzled. *How did she know?*

"Yes". Then she asked: "How did you know that?"

"The artist is my boyfriend." The woman said. "Or at least I think he still is. But I haven't seen him for a long while. He called, out of the blue, yesterday asking if I would let his sister share my apartment," the woman said, in a pettish voice. "I said no. He can't treat me like this. He comes whenever he feels like it and disappears without a trace. And as if it is not enough that he is avoiding me he has to put his sister in my apartment to let me know that he is not ever going to spend the night here again. I can't take that crap." Ire turned to sobbing. Resolutely she said: "I am not going to have his sister sharing my apartment."

"I understand. And I am sorry. But please don't feel too bad. Meng Song is like that. Not only with you." What else could Ying Ying have said?

Ying Ying finally found a room for Lingzhen, in an apartment with three other Caucasian-American girls.

A few weeks later Meng Song and Lingzhen attended an event at China Society. They both dressed sharply. Lingzhen looked like a fashion model. Instantly she caught the attention of a reporter from a major newspaper. He snapped many pictures of her and followed her around all evening long and said:

"You are so gorgeous. I wish to marry you." This was American humor. But it did not sit well with Meng Song when he overheard Denis telling it to Ying Ying. He was enraged and made some very profane remarks.

"I want to kill that fucking bastard." Meng Song said.

Ying Ying was shocked to hear him using such vulgar language as he was always urbane in his speech.

"Why?" Denis was puzzled. "It was only meant to be a compliment even if it could have been couched in finer words. There was no harm."

"Such a joke is intolerable to a Chinese. He should have known that," Meng Song retorted.

"But he didn't know that," Ying Ying said, and followed with a joke. "He is only a crude American. He doesn't know any better."

Song's strong reaction stunned Ying Ying. She couldn't believe that a man with his untrammeled, unscrupulous attitude and behavior in regard to man-woman relationships could not tolerate the reporter's lighthearted joke. Ying Ying's disbelief was further intensified when Meng Song called her one day to tell her his worries about Lingzhen.

"Ying Ying, should I be worried? Last night I called Lingzhen at 2am. She was not home." His voice was filled with anxiousness and anguish.

"Where did she go?" Ying Ying asked innocently and absently.

"She was with Jason." His uneasiness was apparent.

"Then, she is in good hands. What's there to worry about?" Ying Ying was thinking about a woman's safety in the city at night.

"You ... you don't think I ... I need to worry about her being with Jason? What are they doing at this hour?" Meng Song was till perturbed.

"Oh, I see." It dawned on Ying Ying what Meng Song was worrying about. She chuckled and said:

"Nothing to worry about. They might be watching a late night movie."

"You really don't think there is anything to worry about?"

"Yes, nothing to worry about. They are in love. It's natural that they like to spend more time together."

"I just don't want her to be hurt. If Jason is serious about her I don't need to worry. Should I give Jason a warning?"

"I see." Ying Ying smiled. Meng Song was worried because he always treated girls as playthings to be tossed away after the novelty wore off. And girls would not let go of him like flour sticking on a wet hand. He couldn't shake them off. He hated to think that his sister was a plaything to Jason whom one day would want to shake her off.

"Just leave them alone. Don't do anything. They will be fine." Ying Ying tried to ease his mind. And she added jocularly: "Don't worry. Jason is not you."

Meng Song laughed. His worry was somewhat eased: "Okay, I trust your judgment."

Jason, a journalist, was a son of a wealthy Bostonian Brahmin whose forefathers came on the Mayflower. In the 19th century the family amassed great wealth from the US-China trade. Their company was based in Salem while their huge mansion was built in Newport.

*   *   *   *

The tea business of Missy's parents grew steadily. They hired a couple of hands and Missy was freed from her duty. She went back to Boston. Jenny was happy for her because she and Adam would be reunited. But it did not happen. Adam was already married. Their love was too fragile to pass the test of time and space.

Jenny graduated from Tufts with a master,s degree in Theatre Arts. She was accepted by the Royal Academy of Dramatic Art in London to pursue further training in stage design. Both Michael and Sean felt dejected having to part with her. Kevin asked her to keep in touch. She made no promise to any of the guys as the future was vague. It would not be fair to expect any of them to wait for her. And she was not sure whether she would come back to them either. This was not her grandparents' time when a promise of love was a life-long commitment.

Ying Ying and the China Society crowd gave her a farewell party wishing her success and a speedy return. Her parents came to Boston to see her off and give her their best wishes. And of course they were paying for all her expenses in Europe. She did not refuse their money.

*　　　*　　　*　　　*

In 1994 Ying Ying graduated. It had been seven years since she left home. She had promised to go home as soon as she finished school. She must fulfill that promise now.

She received a letter from her father. It revealed a kind and loving father's inner conflict when hearing the daughter's homebound news.

"Ying my dear daughter: Your mother and I have waited seven long years for your return. Our longing gaze has bored through the autumn water. The day has come. Yet we should not be so selfish as to drag you back home and keep you here so that we can be happy. Your future and happiness are more important than making us happy. Your earnest concerns now are your career and the 'major event in life.' We will be content if you only come back for a visit."

"Longing gaze has bored through the autumn water!" Such intensity of emotion! Such undivided mental focus and fixed vision while wishing for the daughter's return! So powerful that they impaled through water! Father's words touched her tender heart and brought tears to her eyes.

"Major event in life" was a reference to marriage. Twenty-eight years old! She had passed the proper age for marriage, according to the tradition of her parents' generation. She should get married now. Everything must take place at its proper time.

"Being proper and upright" was imperative in a person's conduct and behavior, father had taught her. They became the principles of her life in years to come. While a teenager she instinctively knew that she was not supposed to have boys in her orbit before finishing college although father did not tell her so in so many words. She willingly abided to that unspoken rule, and even developed a self-protecting bulwark: She would feel harassed and offended when pursued by a guy. She coldly turned her back to those showing romantic emotions. The guys called her "Princess of Iceland" behind her back. She knew it too. Her attitude did not stop the guys from pursuing her, however.

When she was twelve-years old her family moved to Zhong Shan North Road in Taipei. Directly across the street from their house was the house of General Liang and his family. General Liang had several children. One was a nineteen-year-old boy, a student of the Air Force Academy. Ying Ying's father took precautions to avoid the meeting of Ying Ying and this young man. He kept a great distance from this colleague and his family; declined their invitations to dinners and gatherings.

One Day Ying Ying was riding her bicycle and the young man was riding his from the opposite direction. They both stopped at the same time near her house. Ying Ying rang the bell and waited for the servant to open the door. The young man gazed at her for a moment before ringing the doorbell across the street. He must have been a member of that household.

Two days later Ying Ying's mother gave her a letter and said::

"Someone from across the street sent you this letter? Who is it?"

158

"I don't know. Let me see." Ying Ying looked at the envelope. The sender's street address was one digit smaller than hers. It was General Liang's house. She opened and read it. It was from the young man she bumped into the other day.

"I was immediately captivated by your beauty. Your lovely image surrounds my consciousness every moment since that day. ... Would you accept me as a special friend? (signed) Your admirer, Liang Ken."

She tossed it on the floor as if it were poisonous, and shouted: "What is this? Mom, you read it. This old, grown-up man said some awful things to me." To a twelve-year old, nineteen certainly was old.

He wrote, and wrote and wrote. She did not read any of them. Her mother sometimes opened one out of curiosity. She said: "This boy is mad. He is seriously infatuated. If father read these letters he would kill him."

"Ma, don't tell me about his guy. I feel so ashamed." Ying Ying's reaction was exceptionally strong.

"But Ying Ying dear, there's nothing to be ashamed of. It's normal for a young man to like a young girl." Mrs. Fang was not as obstinate as General Fang.

"I hate it. Look how old he is and how young I am. And even if I am old enough I still don't want to be bothered." Ying Ying spoke with resolve.

One time a lady came to see Ying Ying in her school. She told Ying Ying that she was General Liang's daughter-in-law, Liang Ken's sister-in-law. She came to beg her to show some compassion toward Liang Ken. Ying Ying felt annoyed and disgusted. She turned to stride toward her classroom. The lady stopped her.

"Young miss, have some manners. I just came here to speak to you. I am not here to bother you."

Ying Ying was aware of her rudeness. She stopped: "I have manners. But I don't like to hear what you have to say."

"I will be brief. Whether you like him or not, he is seriously in love with you. "

"In love? Lady, I am not even thirteen. Tell your brother-in-law to stop his lunacy," Ying Ying shouted in a huff. The lady ignored her obstreperousness and continued to say:

"He is going to fly the plane with a broken heart caused by your heartless rejection. Why not have a little compassion? Acknowledge his letters; show some willingness to accept his friendship."

" What friendship?" Ying Ying cut the woman's words short. "Didn't you hear me? Your brother-in-law is mad. Why is he doing this to me? Can't you see he is hurting me?" Ying Ying ran to her classroom.

The young man persisted. Sometimes two or three letters a day. Ying Ying became moody and irritable. General Fang finally found out and was enraged. He wanted to go across the street to reproach the father and beat up the son. Mrs. Fang stopped him:

"Think about it. All he did was write letters. It is not a crime. If you do that, people will think he has done something serious to our daughter." That reasoning calmed him down. But he insisted on moving away from that street. So they sold the house and moved.

It didn't take long for the man to find Ying Ying's new address, however. Letters poured in. General Fang was indignant and began to blame Ying Ying. She was already irate with the situation; to be blamed for something that had nothing to do with her was unbearable. She was distraught. A year later they moved again despite the trouble of selling and buying large mansions. General Fang did not mind.

Of course it did not stop Liang Ken. He found out Ying Ying's new address again and continued to write for years. All the letters were burned, chucked in the garbage, or flushed in the toilet. She never read any.

In her senior year in high school, one day the postman handed her a bunch of mail. The one on the very top was from him. A wicked idea came to her mind. He was a full-fledged Air Force man by then. The Air Force had very strict rules governing the men's behaviors. She did not have a way to deal with this guy before. Now she could easily punish him. She wrote a powerful and threatening letter of complaint to the Air Force and enclosed his letter with it. She cited her father's position, a Four-Star-Army General, and said that he was going to take action if the Air Force did not; "my father's action would be damaging to the Air Force," and so forth. Two weeks later a letter from an Air Force General came apologizing to her and her father, and stated that the person in question would be punished. However, Ying Ying knew he would not be severely punished on the account of his father being a General as well.

Two months later, one sunny afternoon Ying Ying was playing in the garden and heard the bronze knocker tapped on the front gate. Someone must have seen her from the decorative see-through-patterns on the wall to decide knocking instead of ringing the bell. She strode to open the door. It was him!! In a reflex, she pushed the door to close it only it was blocked by him. Astonished at his boldness, she raised her gaze at him for the first time apart from that time four years ago when he rode his bicycle toward her.

Her gaze was cold and livid. She did not utter a word. He, on the other hand, had a warm smile on his face. He said:

"I was imprisoned for two weeks because of your letter to the Air Force General. I was not allowed to spend the New Year with my family. But I was glad because you knew I existed." *She is seventeen now, a young lady, no longer a little girl. She is more beautiful than before.* His eyes feasted on her from head to toe.

"Huh, I can't believe it. Will you stop bothering me?" She pushed the door to close it in his face. He did not resist.

That was the last time she saw him. He never attempted to see her again. But he continued to write. When she was in college he sent letters to her departmental office. When the secretary complained., Ying Ying said:

"They are not my mail. I have nothing to do with them. Just throw them away or whatever." The secretary was curious and would occasionally peek at one.

160

Before her graduation, sometime near the commencement, one day the secretary said to her:

"Ying Ying, may I tell you something?" Without waiting for an answer she continued: "This guy who writes you everyday..."

Ying Ying interrupted her and said: "Don't tell me about him."

She ignored Ying Ying.

"Hear me out. This is interesting. He said you would go to America after you graduate. He would never have a chance to see you again. But he would never stop loving you and you would be in his dream forever. In a few days he will bid farewell to you during the commencement by circling the sky over our campus three times."

"He is really mad!" Ying Ying said.

During her graduation ceremony a plane flew low and circled three times over their heads.

Ying Ying left Taiwan and never heard from this Liang Ken again.

*   *   *   *

There were many others unwanted pursuits that aggravated her. Shortly after she bumped into Liang Ken, she bumped into another guy. This time it was in the living room of her own house. A young man named Huang Han brought a package from his parents to give to Mrs. Fang. When Ying Ying strode into the living room Mrs. Fang introduced them out of courtesy. He was an overseas Chinese student, a freshman at Qing Hua University.

Who would think such an accidental meeting would end up in so much botheration!

After he left her house, like Liang Ken, he began to send her letters. At first she could not figure out who had authored the letter. She opened it and realized it was from this eighteen-year-old college student from Hong Kong.

"I want to thank my parents for giving me the package to deliver to your house. I want to thank the good old Heaven for arranging our seemingly fortuitous meeting. Fate has extended his hand to bless us. He guided me to Taiwan instead of London so that I could meet you. Now, I have found meaning in my life."

Another one!! Angrily she threw the letter on the floor, feeling harassed again. The letters kept coming. Instead of from one guy now they were from two. In wrath, she complained to her mother.

"What's wrong with these guys? Are they all out of their minds?" she shouted. "How do I stop them? Ma, can you tell them to stop bothering me?"

"Just ignore them." Mrs. Fang had heard her daughter's complaints too often. This was her only advice.

Huang Han showed up at her school one morning. He asked a girl where he could find Ying Ying. The girl scooted to her classroom with a stupefied look in her eyes and said:

"Ying Ying, there is a man outside looking for you. Why?" Girls were not supposed to have male visitors in the school.

"What man?" She was alarmed. She charged to the window and looked through it. For sure, it was as she had suspected. She quickly backed up from the window as if being pushed. She told her classmates:

"Hurry up. Close the windows. Ling, go tell him to go away. Doesn't he know this is a girls' school and men are not allowed here? Tell him I will be punished because of him."

After that episode Huang Han never tried to see Ying Ying again. But he kept writing for a year.

In her sophomore year in high school, there was a boy from Jian-Guo School who was the talk of the town. Wherever she went she would hear girls mentioning this name, Lin Ching-de. She had never met him. So hadn't many of the girls. But that did not stop them from talking about this "legendary" young man.

That summer there was a large-scale inter-high-school performing arts exhibition. The students gathered at the Presidential Square for the opening ceremony. When the event's chairman stepped up to the podium a drone arose among the girls. They were enthusiastically talking about him. Some suppressed giggling pierced the monotonous drone from time to time. Ying Ying glanced at the podium. An impression of this boy imperceptibly etched in her mind. He was exceptionally handsome and had a deep silky voice. His stage presence was striking.

The following day her school's folk dance program was to be staged at the Chung Shan Auditorium. She strolled across the hall holding her costume and accessories in her arms. One piece of gauzy scarf flowed from her arm onto the floor unnoticed. A deep silky male voice called her attention from behind:

"Miss, you dropped this." She turned around. It was that event's chairman. He bent over to pick up Ying Ying's scarf and smiled:

"Lin Ching-de," he announced his name.

"Thank you." She took the scarf, but did not give him her name.

A few days later, in the evening, the young man came calling upon her. Her reaction was different from what it was to the two letter writers. She was older now. And this young man was about her age. So she let him in the garden. Strangely, her father, who happened to be strolling in the garden at the moment, was not angry. He even spoke to the boy, asked if he would like to have tea. He politely said:

"Thank you, uncle. I am not thirsty. But may I ask for your permission to take a walk on the street with Ying Ying?"

What an audacious request!!! How dare you??? You haven't asked me yet, she gaped. But her father said:

"All right, don't be long." It gave her no excuse to refuse him. She had to take this walk with him. *How slimy!*

"Why didn't you ask me first? How do you know that I would agree to take this walk with you?" she demanded as they closed the gate behind them.

He grinned. "I didn't. That's why I asked uncle first."

How cunning!

That was the only time they met.

The first year in college, while walking to class, Ying Ying occasionally heard some guys yelling: " Lin Ching-de, hurry, hurry, she's here."

Another voice, deep and silky, followed: "Hey, guys, don't yell. You are embarrassing her."

What did he tell those guys? Ying Ying wondered

His attempt to win her favor, like all the others, and ended futile like the others.

In her last year in high school Ying Ying entered an inter-high-school writing competition. One of the judges, an old professor from Taiwan University, read her writing and gave her a very high score. This professor liked to surround himself with fine literary young minds. He had a circle of such young people picked out from several colleges. He predicted these people would be future scholars and writers. Ying Ying was picked to be included in that group as an exception.

A high school kid, barely sixteen, Ying Ying was humbled by these mature, sophisticated students from reputable colleges. She attended the frequent gatherings; listened intently to their conversations; spoke when she had something meaningful to say. They thought she was intelligent, well spoken, and well mannered.

One evening the gatherings lasted till quite late. As they were leaving the professor asked his teaching assistant, Chen Yin, to walk Ying Ying home. Ying Ying told herself not to worry about this guy. He was a graduate student, a teaching assistant of the professor. He was respectable. He would not act like the other fools.

The walk lasted about 20 minutes. She had a bag full of books and other things. He insisted on carrying it for her. She thanked him. They had some nice conversations on the way.

Two days later she got a letter from him. " ... I had the most delightful evening walking and talking with you. ... I wish that I would always have the honor and pleasure to carry your bag. ... Please allow me to see you again. ..."

Him too? Will there be one exception? Her heart became heavy since handling the situation with Chen Yin would not be easy. She should not be too brash to him on account of the professor. She must let him keep his face. She decided to be as gentle as possible while letting him know what she was thinking. She wrote him:

> Respected Mr. Chen: I respected you as a teacher and was surprised by your letter. I wish you would treat me as a student and give me guidance. Please do not write me any more. And please retract what you have said....

She wished that without hurting his pride she had put him in his place. Chen Yin realized that he had done something foolish and never bothered her again.

The worst and most frightening thing a guy did to her, or because of her, was trying to take his own life in his dorm at the Normal University. Ying Ying had never really met this man. He came to Church one Sunday and saw Ying Ying singing in the choir. He came to talk to her after the service. She didn't spend more than two minutes with him and had little recollection of him afterwards. But he began to write letters too. By this time, Ying Ying was very used to such behavior. She simply ignored him.

One day she heard this chilling story. This guy left a note on his desk saying that he had nothing to live for because the girl he loved did not give him any hope. "And that girl is Fang Ying Ying." His roommates found him in time and brought him to the hospital. Ying Ying was deeply troubled by this incident.

Why do I meet all these lunatics? What is wrong with me?

"Ma, do I look coltish? Giddy? Profligate? Is that why these men think they can approach me?"

"No, you are nothing like that. You are a well-bred young lady. You are pretty and graceful. That's why young men are attracted to you. You should learn to accept it and ignore it instead of being vexed by it," Mrs. Fang reasoned to her daughter.

*   *   *   *

In the summer before her senior year in college a schoolmate came to visit her. It was different this time.

Kang Wei was a Chemical Engineering major. She had never met him before that day when he boldly asked her for a date. She was well known to the guys in her school as an unapproachable "Princess of Iceland" because she had declined everyone's date. *Why is this one not dismayed? Doesn't he know that I do not accept any dates?*

Kang Wei had his mind made up on Ying Ying since he first saw her in freshman year. However he was very cautious about making any move after witnessing other people's failing attempts. *Don't be hasty. Wait for a good opportunity. In the mean time watch how she turns away the others.*

Ying Ying thought he was somehow different from the other young men. But she could not put her finger on what made him different. She only knew that she was not overcome by an adverse feeling when he asked her out. She accepted his request and went to a movie with him. After that they had dinner together. Her very first date!! She couldn't believe it. In the following weeks and months they went on short excursions to the scenic areas near Taipei, and rambled in the evenings. They lived in separate dorms. It gave Ying Ying the freedom to go out with him without her parent's knowledge. Their friendship became big news on campus. Many guys were jealous of Kang Wei, some plotted to traduce him in front of Ying Ying but without success.

On her twentieth birthday, Kang Wei threw a large surprise dance party and invited over a hundred schoolmates. No student in the school had ever thrown Such a party before. He spent a lot of time planning it. He rented a large hall and hired a decorator to make sure every detail was perfect. Small flower arrangements and candles adorned the lace-covered ice-cream tables; lighting was soft and romantic; exquisitely made hors d'oeuvres on silver platters were served by uniformed waiters. It was not only a surprise to Ying Ying but to all the guests as well, as few of them had ever seen a party like that. Everyone fully enjoyed it. Some asked: "Where did Kang Wei learn how to do this?"

Once Kang Wei confessed to Ying Ying:

"Someone like you. I mean you are not just a beautiful girl, you are special. From the first time I saw you sing solo in the choir with that special aura, I knew the chance of meeting you would be slim. Everyone in our dorm was talking about you. They all wanted to meet you. I knew that if I were to abruptly try, I would only be rejected. Then I wouldn't have another chance. So I waited for three years. During that time I saw those guys try and fail. But this is our last year in college. My last chance."

After graduation Ying Ying passed the study-abroad-examination. Kang Wei had to fulfill his military service for a year. They had three months left before she would leave. He went to see Ying Ying at her house everyday. Ying Ying's mother liked him. Even her father tolerated his visits provided he did not stay too long. And he knew, without being told by anybody, how long was appropriate for him to stay, and when he should leave. Sometimes he would ask for permission to take Ying Ying out.

One Saturday afternoon he took Ying Ying to a movie. When they return home Ying Ying's number-three aunt was just leaving. They greeted her. After she left Ying Ying noticed that her mother's expression was grim. Kang Wei thought it was not a good time for him to stay so he said goodbye to Mrs. Fang and left.

Ying Ying tried to find out why her mother was dour. But Mrs. Fang wouldn't speak to her. Ying Ying felt uneasy knowing something must be very wrong and it had to do with her.

"Ma, what is it? Please tell me," she begged her. "Please, I am worried when you are not talking. Did I do anything wrong that made you unhappy? Please tell me. I apologize. I will never do that again." She begged her again and again. Mother still did not speak.

"Did Third Aunt say anything that made you feel bad?" This was the right question to ask because mother responded.

"Yes. She said something about you. And I think she is right. It's all for your own good."

This was serious. Whenever Third Aunt criticized her, mother's mood would be sullen for days and it would take Ying Ying so much effort to turn her around.

What could Third Aunt have said this time?

"Ma, what did Third Aunt say? I haven't done anything wrong or offended her in anyway, did I?"

"It's not that. She just thought that you should not have let Kang Wei tie you down. She said Kang Wei was not good enough for you," her mother finally spoke up.

"What?" Ying Ying was astonished. "I am not being tied down by Kang Wei. We are just friends. Beside, Kang Wei is every bit as worthy of me as anyone. What did she mean he was not good enough for me? You and Dad like him. Why did she think that he was not good enough?" Ying Ying was riled by her aunt's insidious opinion.

"She is only thinking of your well-being. She thinks so highly of you, like Dad and I do. We all wish you to have the best. She said you were such an outstanding girl. The whole world is out there waiting for you. All kinds of deserving men are there for you to choose. Why settle with a schoolmate who has nothing to offer? As the saying goes, there are mountains beyond the mountain, skies beyond the sky. Why stop at the first mountain?"

Are my feelings not important? The quality of the man is not important? What is the other sky or mountain? Is a girl like a precious merchandize waiting for the highest bidder? Ma would not have had such notion on her own. Why is she always swayed by Third Aunt? Ying Ying's defiance was aroused. But she couldn't show it because the woman was her mother.

"Ma, Third Aunt over worries about me. You know I am a sensible girl. I will not be so easy as to commit myself to a guy at this time. Please not to worry, I will put my whole mind on nothing else but study. I won't disappoint you." Ying Ying's mollification soothed mother's mood gradually.

The worry of losing Ying Ying haunted Kang Wei constantly. Once she left Taiwan chances were she would be surrounded by many high-calibre men in that foreign land. He would not even have a fair chance to compete because of geographical distance. He must think of how to keep her. *An engagement. Yes, I should propose for an engagement. That would ward off the other men.*

But his proposal was not accepted.

"Our relationship is above such hackney," she declared. "Marriage is so mundane. We should not be bound by it."

"Ying Ying, my dear, marriage is not mundane. It is the ultimate statement of love, a sacred relationship that brings union between a man and a woman. It is the only way that can keep us together forever. I love you. I want to spend the rest of my life with you. And I am so afraid of losing you. Please don't reject me," he persisted.

"No, I think what we have is romantic. There is no bound, no obligation. We are together because we want to be, not because we have to. Isn't that romantic? Let's not spoil it." A life-long platonic love! What a free spirit and otherworldly fantasy!

That fall after graduation, Ying Ying left for the United States. Kang Wei was in a military base for basic training, a national service required of every male college graduate. During those four months, a reserve was not permitted to leave the base for any reason, except for, perhaps, the death of a parent. So, Kang Wei was not able to see Ying Ying off. He was sitting on his bunk at the moment Ying Ying's plane took off. In melancholy, he sent his blessings, and prayed for a future of togetherness. There was nothing more he wanted or wished for.

In the following months, he wrote many letters, but only received occasional brief replies talking about her school and work. He could hardly detect any emotion or feeling in them. Was she too busy to write? Or had she relinquished all they had so soon? There were rumors about Ying Ying dating someone else in Boston. He had lost her; the thing he dreaded most had become real, he thought. Separated by thousands of miles and blocked by his inability to go to her while the other man was right there next to her. What could he do? His hope was snuffed out. In dejection, he accepted his defeat, his fate.

A year later he completed his military service, passed the examination for studying abroad and enrolled at UC Berkeley. He heard about Ying Ying getting married. His last glimmer of hope was extinguished. *I should not disturb her now. I should let her live a peaceful married life.*

In her years in Boston Ying Ying wondered why Kang Wei did not write anymore? *Did he meet someone else and fall in love?* A deep-rooted pride prevented her from trying to find out or writing to him. Subconsciously she was hoping Kang Wei would write her again. She built a wall of coldness and aloofness to block those men in Boston who had revealed romantic yearnings toward her. It was hard even for Pei-hua to understand why she avoided romantic involvement. She could not reveal the real reason.

*   *   *   *

Dad, I will disappoint you this time. I can't get married just because it is the right time. The thought went across Ying Ying's mind as she read her father's letter.

Taiwan at last, after seven years!! Stepping out of the walkway in the airport, Ying Ying's parents rushed over to embrace her. They cried. They looked much older and had turned a little grizzly. Ying Ying's heart was wrenched. *I must have changed a lot too*, she thought.

There was so much to talk about. Mother asked whether she had anyone in mind for marriage. When Ying Ying said she had decided not to get married her mother was flabbergasted and said:

"How can that be? School and marriage are equally important. How can you have one and forgo the other? You must not be foolish."

"Ma, you and dad told me not to be foolish to have boyfriends before. Now you want me not to be foolish to stay single?"

"Of course, dear. There is a proper time for everything. Marriage is a necessary step in the journey of life. One must have it to complete that journey."

Mother took her to visit Third Aunt's family. Cousin Hui was married and lived in another part of the city. She came to join the reunion. Third Aunt's husband, Uncle Chao, said Ying Ying had changed too much, he almost couldn't recognize her. Cousin Hui sensed that comment was demoralizing for a woman. She hastened to salvage the situation.

"Cousin Ying is always beautiful. She is more beautiful than ever with that touch of maturity."

"Little Ying, have you selected a *dragon-riding husband* yet," Third Aunt asked?

"No, there is no *dragon-riding prince* there for me to find. I was too busy studying."

"Oh, yes, you have your doctorate now. Wonderful. But you see, a girl of your age should be married. This is your most important thing now. Don't wait too long before you become an old maid. How old are you now?" Third Aunt enthusiastically offered her opinion.

"Third Aunt, have I been away so long that you have forgotten my age?" Ying Ying's incisive remark was mixed with a broad smile.

"Oh, how can I forget anything about you? It's just that I am old now. My memory is not like what it used to be. If I don't try, I remember nothing. You are the one I love most, more than your cousins. I held you all the time when you were a baby. Do you remember that? Of course you don't. How could a baby know who is holding her?"

"But Third Aunt, I remember it perfectly because you keep reminding me. I must thank you for that."

A few days later, Third Aunt came to see Mrs. Fang. The two sisters talked in a locked room.

"Number Four Sister, I am very worried about Ying Ying's major-event-in-life. She is what? Twenty-seven? Twenty eight now? Before you know it she will be thirty. My Heavens, an unmarried girl of thirty. An old maid!!! That is dreadful. We don't want her to be an old maid for life." Third Aunt showed her deepest concerns.

"Third Sister, this is something only Ying Ying will decide. We cannot do anything." Mrs. Fang didn't have a good answer for her older sister.

"Nonsense. What are we here for if we cannot do anything for our kids? I have been thinking about this for days. And I talked to a few friends about it."

"What? You talked to your friends about Ying Ying's major-event-in-life?" Mrs. Fang was not pleased about this. It was denigrating to Ying Ying.

"I didn't talk to just anybody. You know me better than that. I have a large circle of friends, some with unmarried sons. I only considered the topnotch bachelors, General Li's son, for example. He was also America educated. He is now Vice president of the Bank of Taipei. Mrs. Li is most enthused about bringing the two youngsters together considering the two families' comparable elite social standing and Ying Ying's accomplishments and looks." Third Aunt made her points emphatically.

"But Ying Ying and her father will not accept match making. You know them." Mrs. Fang knew her husband and daughter only too well. She was smart to block her sister from taking further actions.

Ying Ying stayed home for three months. Then the heartbreaking scene at her departure seven years ago was replayed. She told her parents that she would come home every year from then on.

*   *   *   *

Upon returning to Boston, Ying Ying faced with another serious decision, a career choice. Should she work for an architectural firm downtown, or the city government, or find a teaching job that might take her out of Boston? If she wanted plenty of free time, a decent pay with superb fringe benefits, and an unbeatable retirement package, all without doing much work, a government job would be ideal. But she had no desire to trash her talent that way. She didn't care much about salary and benefits. Retirement was the remotest thing that had not even entered her mind.

This architectural firm had a certain attraction because she had always admired its founder, Mr. Qian De, a Fellow of the American Institute of Architecture, who had built numerous major edifices in different parts of the country and abroad.

Then there was also the possibility of going back to China Society. The Board of International Foundation had offered her directorship of China Society. Joseph Lee preferred to step down from that position and just be the Curator. Though not well paid the job would afford her opportunities to do more than a single line of work such as designing buildings. She could shape her job and re-design the programs, and develop new programs as she saw fit.

The exciting potentials propelled her to choose China Society over the others. No sooner did she report to work than she laid out her task priorities. Fundraising was a pressing issue, one she must carry on whether she liked it or not. New programming needed to be developed. She had a number of ideas in mind.

She knew how much time Joseph Lee spent on fundraising and how much he disliked that part of his job. The Trustees were usually involved in various capacities in fundraising events. In regard to programming, the Trustees could bring Ideas to be discussed at board meetings and an ad hoc event's committee would be formed to work with the CEO and staff to carry out the ideas.

Louisa proposed a documentary exhibit summarizing China Society's accomplishments over the past ten years plus an art show, a performing arts project, and a symposium. A formal dinner at $500 a plate would inaugurate the series.

Brigitte, another Trustee, did not like that idea.

"We need to have something new. Something we haven't done before. Those exhibitions, music and dance performances are so trite. We can't draw big gifts with those. A fashion show. I can get you the most famous designer from New York to do a show here. Or we can do an antique-show-and-sale. If you want a big celebrity I can get whoever you want." But she did not say what to do with the celebrity, as a guest of honor at the benefit dinner? How much would it cost to have this celebrity? Would the money raised be enough for paying the celebrity?

A fashion show? How much would it cost to pay the designer and the models? How much would it cost to design and set up the show room? An antique show? Is Brigitte going to take on the responsibility of arranging the event? No one else has the resources for or experience in mounting such a show. Would these projects be profitable enough to be called fundraisers? What if it would create a deficit instead? Many questions rose to Ying Ying's mind but she did not bring them to the table. Brigitte would not take it well.

After many discussions the Board chose the old rut—a performing arts presentation, visual arts exhibition and symposium. Louisa was voted to chair the event's committee. To placate Brigitte, Andrew Johnson, the Chairman of International Foundation's Board, suggested taking on either a fashion show or an antique show in the following year. Brigitte would chair the event and appoint members to her committee. They should begin to make contacts and preliminary arrangements under Brigitte's direction. Brigitte was appeased.

"Oh, I didn't mean to do it this year. Oh, no, no, it's much too soon. I need at least a year. After all, this will be the largest and most important event China Society will ever have," Brigitte said.

Louisa told Ying Ying not to worry a bit about the fundraising project.

"You just concentrate on your job. Although you have been with China Society for years but to be CEO and director is a big job and it is new to you. We have very broad programming too. You will be overwhelmed." Ying Ying thanked her for her thoughtfulness and began to concentrate on proposal writing in addition to laying out programs.

*   *   *   *

She reviewed China Society's past grant sources and sent for their current guidelines. A few strong ones had just changed funding interests in response to urgent societal needs. Arts and humanities were scratched. In their stead were teen pregnancy and drug abuse rampant in schools and on the streets. Ying Ying had to try cultivating and developing new sources. She would not reshape a program for the sake of chasing grants. She only tried to research the grant-making community to find any possible matches of their interests with China Society's programs. The application deadlines were close one to the other.

Some people thought proposals could be one-size-fits-all. That was a myth. Yes, one could send the same proposal to different places with only a change of the grant-makers' addresses if he didn't mind the waste of energy, paper and stamps, and invariable rejection letters. The fact was that rewriting and rearranging the information of the same proposal to suit each grant-maker's guideline would take a considerable amount of time. Ying Ying's multiple duties left her only a limited amount of time for this task. She hoped the application could be simplified to actually to be one-size-fits-all. One uniformed guideline for the applicant to write one proposal that would be accepted by all grant makers.

Denis, now Ying Ying's staff, offered his assistance in proposal writing. Ying Ying gave him an easy one to do since he had not done a proposal before. It was for a small city grant. The application was simple. Ying Ying had done it twice, while still a work-study student, when Joseph Lee was too busy.

Ying Ying's old schoolmate, Sharon Hays from Harvard, came to see her one day while she was in the middle of writing a proposal. Sharon asked how many she had to write and offered to write one for her. Sharon was an English major and a staff writer of a magazine. There was no doubt that she could write.

"Let me do one for you. It's ridiculous that you have to be swamped by proposal writing. Come on you have better things to do."

"Okay, Sharon, thanks. I am going to give you the Mass Council one. It's due in two weeks. You think you will have time to do it?" The deadline was actually twenty-days later. She gave Sharon an earlier date just in case the latter missed the deadline. Ying Ying gave her a copy of a previous application as reference.

"Look at you, a new director, laden with all sorts of responsibility. You need more help. Let me take the graphic design work off of your hands too. I will get it done for you. Don't worry. I know some good graphic designers." The graphic work was for the big project Louisa was chairing. The graphic work fell on Ying Ying's shoulder. Sharon's offer was another much-needed help.

A week later Ying Ying called Sharon to ask whether she needed any more information for writing the proposal. It was a pretext. Her real intention was to remind Sharon about the application. Sharon said she had enough materials and guaranteed that she would have it on Ying Ying's desk in a few days. Before the two-week drew to a close Ying Ying called her two more times. Sharon was roiled by her persistent bother. Finally it was the day of the deadline. Sharon was nowhere to be found. Ying Ying was seriously distressed. She called and called until she reached Sharon.

"Sharon, would you please return the application form and the materials to me?" She did not ask why Sharon would pull such a destructive stunt on her, nor question whether she knew the severity of losing the Mass Council grant. She wished Sharon would apologize for what damage she had done. But she did not apologize. As for the application form and materials, she never brought the back to Ying Ying. With only four days left, Ying Ying rushed to the Mass Council to pick up another application form and put other things aside to write this proposal. She learned a painful lesson.

Denis did finish his assignment and turned in the application to the city on time. But disappointingly his application failed to be funded. Ying Ying was more surprised than angry. How could he have failed? This one was a guaranteed grant. What did he write? What did he miss? Ying Ying read the copy of the proposal in which Denis put in much unnecessary information and did not address the crucial questions.

Ying Ying's success rate in proposal writing was quite high. The failed ones were because the proposed programs were outside of the grant-makers' funding scopes although from their guidelines it seemed to fit.

Grant proposals, interim reports, and final reports were revolving, never-ending tasks. Ying Ying just treated it as an inescapable routine chore. She must do it but not allow it to interfere with her real work.

*　　　*　　　*　　　*

Over a year after the grant-makers' decisions were announced, there came a letter from a foundation demanding China Society to explain why no acknowledgement of a grant awarded, or a progress and final report hadn't been submitted. Ying Ying was perplexed by it because that foundation had not made a grant to China Society. She called to inquire the mixed-up. In the end the mystery was solved. The foundation did award China Society a grant. A letter and a check were sent to China Society over a year ago. But the mail never reached Ying Ying or anyone else.

"I don't recall ever having received your letter and check. But I may be wrong. Please allow me to double check with our accounting department and call you. The mail might have been lost," Ying Ying told the Foundation. She had no doubt that the mail had strayed. But public relations tactics required her to never state the fact so candidly. The following day the Foundation called her again and said the check was never cashed. Needless to say, the check was lost in the mail.

"That explains it, ma'am. The post office has lost our mail too often and carelessly delivered other people's mail to us almost on a regular basis. We have had people's passports delivered to us, I have called and written the Postmaster General numerous times." Ying Ying vented her dissatisfaction with the postal service.

She wrote a letter to the Foundation apologizing for the mishap and submitted a program report, though technically the program was not supported by funding from the Foundation. She hoped that this incident would not negatively affect China Society's future funding opportunities.

The post office's negligence was too numerous and inexcusable. Ying Ying was particularly upset when many checks were lost. There were times when contributions from their benefactors and Trustees were lost. She would never have found out if the donors had not asked whether she had gotten their checks. There were ticket agencies selling tickets for China Society's events. One time a bunch of checks from an agency were scattered on the street, with the envelope torn. A few times strangers came in with checks endorsed to China Society they found on the street. The stories were too numerous to recount.

Ying Ying called the branch office repeatedly to lodge her complaints but with no result. She wrote to te Boston Post Master General and appended a log of such incidents. The Post Master General apologized and promised to correct the situation. He went so far as sending a postman from the branch office to Ying Ting's office to assure her China Society's mail would be handled with special care. Despite all that mistakes continued to happen. Ying Ying began to wonder if those wrongly delivered mail that she underlined the correct addressed and put notes on the envelopes alerting the postman to re-deliver were ever actually re-delivered. She saw it on national news on the TV about bags of mail being dumped by mailmen.

She gave up the never-ending and hopeless battle eventually.

*   *   *   *

As she contemplated the Society's mission and functionality, and its existing programs Ying Ying saw one vital component, that of theatre arts, being missing. Theatre arts was no less an important part of any given culture than music or dance, visual arts or literary arts. It should be presented along with other forms of arts and humanities programs for promoting understanding and appreciation of a culture. *How could Chinas Society leave out theatre arts?*

Her love for the theatre, her fond memory of her high school and college days when she was cast as leads in school productions, swelled in her heart. This personal reason coupled with a strong sense of duty propelled her to propose a theatre program—to form a repertory theatre group--to the Board.

"Chinese theatre works were not produced anywhere In New England. We should found a theatre arts program in order to fully realize our mandate and obligation, to fill the lacunae, so to speak." She justified her proposal.

The Trustees vigorously debated the validity and viability of Ying Ying's recommendation at Board meetings and in private conversations.

"Theatre program was not specifically written in our charter. In fact it was not even mentioned. I think our founding Trustees never intended to include it in our programming. Should we amend our bylaws in order to add this program?" One Trustee brought up a legal issue.

"A theatre program certainly has its place in our organization. But we must carefully weigh the gains and losses, and our capability to carry it out without breaking our bank. How much would this subsidiary cost? How are we going to fund it?" Another Trustee brought up a financial issue.

"Yes, will public funding and box office proceeds be enough to support it," the third Trustee asked?

"We cannot count on any public funding until the program is established and successfully operated. That will take two or three years. Ours won't be a large commercial operation. Box office proceeds won't be very significant. Our previous productions have lost money despite their success, meaning good reviews, audience accolades and so on," the fourth Trustee commented.

"Because the production costs were too high. We spent too much on costumes. Some friends of mine said the costumes are comparable to those of Broadway productions."

"Maybe we should not be so extravagant next time."

"The issue here is, are we the Trustees willing to underwrite the deficits? It is our responsibility to keep the books balanced."

"And don't forget the more serious issue: human resources. I suppose we are not going to do Shakespeare or Bernard Shaw. We will only put on Chinese plays and we need Chinese actors. Where do we find them? They don't exist in New England. It was a daunting task casting for the last two productions and we had to use non-Asian actors."

"Scripts are another important issue. Ying Ying, didn't you have a lot of trouble finding good translated Chinese plays? As I understand, there are very few theatre pieces that have been translated into English."

These were legitimate concerns. They were debated, discussed at length. The proposal was tabled and re-studied. There were a few Trustees giving their unfailing support because they had unreserved confidence in Ying Ying. They had supported every proposal presented by her. Ying Ying defended the proposal under discussion convincingly from issue to issue. Her conclusion was:

"Although there is no guarantee of financial self-sufficiency for the theatre company in the next couple of years, this groundbreaking pioneer work will put China Society on the map. I will do my best to seek grant money and outside support. In the event of a deficit, I will be the first to contribute. The proposed program will be a new and unique addition to New England's cultural scene, a major contribution of our organization. For this reason I think it is well worth whatever effort is required to establish this program. Human resources and scripts are hurdles that we can work hard to overcome. They are long-term needs and we should make long-term plans. I propose to establish two other subprograms to address these needs."

"More new programs? What are they? You are sure we can handle them?" One trustee questioned.

"One is a drama workshop. This is an answer to the human resource issue. The workshop will offer training in acting, directing, stage- and lighting designs, costume design and stage management. Instructors will be faculty members we invite from various university theatre departments. We will recruit students from the Asian community. The workshop will produce one show each year as a practical training for its members, and assist with the theatre company's professional productions. These members will eventually be our resources."

"It may work. But it's a long-range plan that requires funding," another Trustee commented.

"Let's discuss it in detail after we hear what is the other new program."

"The other is a playwright's platform. Each year we invite a few Chinese playwrights from different places to take residency here. Like visual artists colonies, we provide the playwrights with meal and lodging. They will work for three or four months writing scripts, discussing and critiquing each other's work; and translating selected existing work for productions. This way we will build a collection of theatre works to enrich dramatic literature."

"Three or four months may be too short for most playwrights to write a complete script."

"We will only invite those who already have a concrete idea of a piece. It is possible to write it in such a short time. If it is not complete the playwright can

174

continue after the residency."

After more discussions at subsequent meetings, the Trustees agreed that these programs would be beneficial to the community and inspire young Asians to pursue a career in the theatre. The project might interest some funders to lend a helping hand. The Board voted in favor of establishing China Stage Repertory Theatre Company as a wholly owned subsidiary of China Society. A few of the Trustees pledged support right there and then, to make up the deficit in the event the project was in the red.

The Board appointed Ying Ying Artistic Director of China Stage until they found another qualified candidate. She accepted the appointment though it meant added responsibility without additional pay. It was an opportunity for her to do something in the field of her strong interest, and to learn about theatre production first-hand. But first of all, she must equip herself with sufficient knowledge. She quickly filled her bookshelves with titles on theatre arts and began diligently to study them. It was as if she had gone back to school again, reading eagerly whenever she could find a free moment. This new challenge was exciting and invigorating to her.

She engaged instructors for China Stage Drama Workshops; publicized the playwright's platform; and planned China Stage's inaugural production. She hired a seasoned director originally from Russia, and an award-winning stage and lighting designer and a costume designer from China.

The Russian director, Vladimir, held long discussions with Ying Ying about what play to produce. They decided on *Yuan Ye (The Wild Land)*. Written in the 1930s by a renowned Chinese playwright, Cao Yu, *Yuan Ye* had been held as a modern classic in Chinese dramatic literature. It was the third of a trilogy, the first two being *The Thunderstorm* and *Sunrise*. In the trilogy Cao expressed his indignation against such social ills as oppressions and hypocrisy. He called for revolts against traditions. He claimed that only by doing so could one be the master of his/her own fate and social changes might be brought about. The young playwright was ahead of his time.

The life-like and colorful dialogues were written in the Beijing dialect. The playwright was not afraid of loquacity and repetition because they reflected how the Beijing people spoke. The characters were so real that they seemed to be jumping out of the pages. But a literal translation would not be fitting for the American audience. For one, the production would be too long. Then the arresting quality of the Beijing dialect would be lost in the translation, no doubt. Many slang and cursing words, if translated directly, would render meaningless and be confusing to the audience. The engaging quality of the characters' verbosity that made them so much like the real Beijing folks would not work in an English-language production. Furthermore, the stage was different from real life. A play was not a slice of life.

After those considerations Ying Ying decided that an adaptation rather than a direct translation would be more suitable. She sent out notices calling for dramatists who might be interested in the job. Regretfully there was no response. It left Ying Ying a challenging and exciting prospect of taking it on herself. But she had never written a play. She pondered on how to approach the task.

Confined by the three walls and the space contained by those walls, and the limited possibilities of scenes, a stage play did not have the fluidity of a film. It must be more compact. The dialogues must be purposeful in order to keep the tension of the plot from slacking. She thought about these issues. The original plot and the characters must be kept intact while the dialogues were rewritten.

In the final product, she successfully instilled a flavor in the dialogues to reflect the period and place, and the specific location of a small town in China.

A small miracle: A good cast came together after many call-to-the-actors announcements and auditions. It was, however, only the beginning of a saga. The play only had six characters, making it more manageable than the previous ones. Of the six actors, Alan and Mike were professionally trained and well experienced in acting. Joe was a science major at M.I.T, active in acting since junior high. Fran, a forty-two-year-old woman originally from Taiwan, working as an executive in a large corporation, played the role of the blind mother. She had good experiences and acted in China Society's previous productions. Betty, a young woman from Boston College, and Larry, a graphic designer, had only interest but no acting experience. The four young actors, Alan, Mike, Joe and Betty happened to be Eurasians. It would take some coaching to attune them to their characters.

From books and films, and from her grandmother's stories, Ying Ying had a firm grasp of the culture, people's mannerism and behavior of early 20th century China. She shared that with Vladimir and suggested that the acting should appropriately reflect the period and the locale. It was not Vladimir's philosophy. But he agreed to go along for this production.

*   *   *   *

The rehearsal did not move smoothly. Three weeks into it Larry asked to be dismissed because he found that acting was too difficult for him. He'd rather be a stagehand. Ying Ying scrambled to find a replacement and failed. Finally, a Trustee, Professor Deng, who used to act in college in Taiwan stepped up to fill in. The team spirit so important in sports was also important in a theatre project. But it was lacking here. Ying Ying keenly realized it was the semi-voluntary nature of the jobs that led each person to think he was not bound by the project. If the set designer were well paid he would not have walked off to do other jobs leaving this one dragging; the actors would be more on time for rehearsals and more willing to do what was demanded of them.

Acting was magic. An actor, male or female, professional or dilettante, once cast in a show automatically felt special and exuded an air of a star. He or she instantaneously developed a temperament, an ego. Ying Ying understood it because she was there before, during her years in high school and college. She remembered what headaches she had inflicted on the production crew and the director when she was playing the lead in *Autumn Begonia*. She told them that she had no time to do it. She skipped rehearsals for the slightest reasons. The director did not dare to censure her but pleaded with her; the production crew pampered her as if she were a big starsaying that without her there would be no production.

Oh, I was so bad. With that understanding, Ying Ying tolerated the time when Joe came late for rehearsals and made up false excuses. A few times he openly challenged the director's knowledge on China of the early 20th century. Allan objected to having his picture in the newspaper; grunted when asked to be present at a TV studio for a taping; refused to take his shirt off in a scene that called for it. Ying Ying only placated them.

"Is the guy an actor or not? What actor would not want to have his picture in the paper or be seen on TV?" Denis was bewildered.

"Allan, if you were to play Song Liling in M Butterfly, would you not take off your pants for the scene?" the director asked him.

"That one is necessary. This one is not," Allan retorted.

"But it is necessary, Allan. Tiger is a rough guy. The playwright made it very clear that he drank wine, and had his shirt off. It's only the shirt, not the pants, why is it so hard for you?" Ying Ying asked.

When in private, Joe made a crude comment on that: "Allan must not have a good male physique to show off. That's it. He is ashamed of letting people see his body." Even if that were the case it still would not have been a good enough reason for an actor to refuse doing a scene properly.

He was a six foot and two inches, handsome and well-built young guy. He looked very good in his shirt. It would be hard to believe that he was ashamed of his body. He insisted on keeping his shirt on for the scene. As a compromise he gave in on the TV taping and publicity photos.

Despite her sedulous effort Betty could not develop an empathy with her character, Jinzi, a complex personality, through her the playwright, Cao Yu, voiced his social comment on a society in which women's fate was in the hands of her parents, in-laws and husband, never in her own. Jinzi was not such a woman. On the contrary, she was a model modern woman, in the mind of the playwright, who defied tradition and broke all the rules. She violated her mother-in-law's authority, betrayed and deserted her loving husband, and allowed her lover to kill her husband before running away with her. She was a woman unacceptable by any standard and at any period of time. Yet it was the young playwright's fulmination on women's unequal social position at the time around mid 1930s. He wanted China to wake up to the fact that women too might choose to be who she wanted--independent, bold, unbound by tradition, daring to do what she chose to do.

On the other hand, as a character in the play, her mannerism must be in keeping with the time and locality where she lived. It was a challenging role for Betty to play. The director and others tried to help her understand the character and how to play it. The success was minimal. Joe and Allan, her husband and lover in the play, thought Betty was too pure and innocent, too uptight to play such a complex woman. They suggested to "corrupt" her by taking her out to bars and nightclubs, to loosen her up, so to speak. That would be an activity outside the rehearsal. Whether they did or not, the rest of the cast and crew didn't know.

An even more serious situation was that the director's artistic vision conflicted with that of Ying Ying's. A well-experienced, seasoned director, Vladimir liked to experiment with untested innovative ideas. For example when Larry dropped out of the cast Vladimir wanted to replace him with a young black female to play the senior male character. He said even without making her up the acting would let the audience believe the character was an elderly man. Ying Ying did not agree with him. She said: "Your idea is fine. But for this production we are going to do it with the traditional, naturalistic style. We talked about it in the beginning. This is not an experimental piece. I'd like the audience to see it as it should be, a Chinese play depicting a story in the early 20th century. The old man should be played by a Chinese man."

There was also a disagreement about the stage design. Vladimir did not discuss his idea with Tan Jin, an award-winning scenery designer and set builder from China. When Tan's design was presented to him a month before the show opened he vehemently criticized it to Ying Ying:

"This is too realistic and traditional. We don't have a revolving stage like Broadway. And the ceiling is only sixteen feet high. The opening is twelve feet high. There is no possibility to fly the trees up after the first scene. How do you change this elaborate scene without taking a lot of time? I want the scene change to take less than a minute. He has to redesign the set," Vladimir argued.

"I think it is a very good set of designs, period appropriate, close to what the original playwright had described, and three changes of sets were not too many. The wilderness scene does pose some problem." Ying Ying looked at the woods, the hills, and the railroad tracks. Tan Jin painted a huge backdrop depicting the woods and the railroad; mounted large boulders and tall trees on stage for the first scene. The same set was to be put up for the final scene. The tall trees were painted soft scenery hanging from pipes. If the ceiling were high, they would be flown up and off the stage opening.

"But we can think of a solution." Ying Ying did not give up.

"Ying Ying, please. Forego those trees. The audience has imaginations. They know there are trees, only invisible. We are not doing a film. And we don't have a Broadway stage. Why insist on the impossible and the unimportant?" Vladimir was already exasperated but tried to reason. Ying Ying refused to budge.

"I will find a way to change the scenery."

She asked a dozen of her friends to help with scene change and practiced at the tech- and dress rehearsals. As the first scene ended, three stagehands were positioned to lower the pipes. Several others quickly wrapped the painted trees on the pipes. Then the pipes were hoisted up. The boulders, made of lightweight materials, were easily moved away. For the final scene the trees were let down from the pipes.

Vladimir shook his head in disapproval and said irately: "I have never seen an army of stagehands for a play with six characters." He was not exaggerating. There were twenty stagehands.

Vladimir's interpretation of the characters' conflicts was also different from what Ying Ying had in mind that was to adhere to the original playwright's intention. When this was brought up Vladimir was exacerbated.

"Ying Ying, I am the director who should have authority over the whole production. You are opposed to everything I do, against every idea I have. Why don't you direct it yourself? I quit."

He threw the script on her desk and stormed out. Ying Ying was determined to face the difficult situation with equanimity. She walked into the rehearsal room and announced to the actors that the director was absent; she would sit in for him and oversee the rehearsal. At this time better than half of the play had been blocked. The actors still had not fully memorized the lines. They just went over some scenes that Vladimir had blocked. Ying Ying had no intention to assume the role of the director or do anything new until she was certain that Vladimir was indeed gone, not just threatening her at a moment of rage.

Two days later Vladimir came back and apologized to the cast about his absence and thanked Ying Ying for overseeing the rehearsal. He never said a word about his resignation.

*   *   *   *

Another stumbling block was the management of the Tower Theatre. The manager denied every reasonable written request Ying Ying presented. He only allowed access to the theatre one day before the show opened for stage setup, dress rehearsal and tech rehearsals. That was very unreasonable. Other companies often took as much as a week to set up the stage, plus three days for rehearsals.

Ying Ying pleaded with him for one more day because it would be virtually impossible to do all those on one day. The man said:

"You need to pay one more week's rent to have one more day." Not having the budget, the production team was pressed to work in frenzy, not daring to waste one minute. They arrived at 8:45am to wait for the door to open at 9:00am. The manager would not let the stage designer borrow his scissors, pen, straight pins or duck tape, much less a couple small pieces of color gel.

The manager yelled: "You people should have known that you only rent the theatre. I am not your supply store. People always take things from here and did't return them. You know how annoying that is? And color gels cost money. You should get your own. And you have to remember, don't come in earlier or leave later than what's laid out in the contract. No one is going to open the door or lock up if you don't adhere to your schedule. And don't move anything around in the back stage and the wings. If you must move anything, be sure to put it back exactly where it was."

Ying Ying reacted to his bluntness impassively.

"I understand all your frustrations. We will abide by all your rules. We will move things back to where they were before we came in; keep your theatre in good order, not borrow anything from your office, and promptly strike and load out after the last show. I promise you."

"You need to put that in writing," the manager demanded.

"No problem." Ying Ying complied and immediately wrote down what she promised.

She apologized to Tan Jin: "I am so sorry for the inconvenience. I should have gotten all the color gels you need and brought scissors and tapes, and other small items, if I had known."

Fran, the actress playing the mother, was irked by the manager's ill-manner and irascible temper. She vented to Ying Ying:

"This wretched guy is not fit for the job. How could he be so abrasive to a customer? And you, Ying-ying, how and from where in the world did you acquire that patience? I would never be able to take that crap."

Ying Ying only smiled and said mildly: "Fran, he was not aiming his vexation or impertinence at me. He was just fed up with the different groups using his theatre. So I don't take his abrasiveness personally. Confrontation will only further rile him. I have a play to produce. What would be the consequence if I lost my temper and caused more intense conflict? We might lose the use of the theatre. At least we would have had some very unpleasant time. So, it's better to look at the big picture and ignore the fuzzy details."

The stage scenery was loaded in and set up, lighting was laid out, color gels were mounted before 4:00pm, followed by a tight tech rehearsal and two dress rehearsals. The dozen stagehands clothed in black to maneuver the trees, walked on and off stage like a row of soldiers. Other stagehands also walked like cats. The rehearsal went without break, no mealtime for anyone. And Ying Ying closed her ears to grumbles.

Finally, it was opening night. Everyone was fired by anticipation. Betty suddenly showed extraordinary improvement beyond anyone's expectation. All the props were neatly laid out on a table in the back stage. Stagehands were familiar with their tasks. No costume mistress was needed backstage this time because the changes were easier. The actors could manage to do them themselves. The make-up artist had convinced Allan to let her make him look the part. The last obstacle was overcome.

But another worrisome problem arose. No one had seen Joe or knew where he was. Curtain time was drawing near. The director and stage manager got increasingly worried. The actors became fidgety. Ying Ying, on the other hand, was surprisingly calm not because she had a solution but because she was keenly aware that having a nervous breakdown would not change the situation. She talked with the director trying to find a solution. The director summoned the stage manager and said:

"You take it on. There is no one except you who knows a single damn line.

It's either you or Ying Ying must do it."

"No, no, I don't know the lines. Da-xing is a lead role. I don't know how to act at all. Even if I knew the lines you don't want to have someone who does not know how to act to fake it. And who is going to stage-manage?" Sam protested.

"I always thought it was too risky not to have understudies. I know. No money. Can't afford to pay for understudies," Allan muttered.

"I can play Da-xing. But who is going to play *The Idiot*?" Mike was an exceptional actor. He would do well playing Da-xing even without rehearsing that part. He had watched and understood every role in the play. But the character of The Idiot is just as important a role and there was no one to substitute him.

"We can't do it. I guess we will just have to apologize to the audience and cancel today's show." Fran was giving up.

"We can't do that. That is so unprofessional. Have you ever heard of a cancellation because one actor failed to show up?" Vladimir was exasperated.

"We can, if an actor died," Allan said casually.

"Yea, the audience will understand. We can tell them that Joe just died in an accident," Mark jested.

"Right, an accident of being killed by us." Allan's remark brought laughter from the rest of the cast.

"Let's wait a few more minutes before getting panicky." Ying Ying ignored Allen and said: "But Sam, if Joe doesn't show up there is no other choice but you. You can fake it. And I will manage the stage." She cleared her throat and said. "Don't even imagine using me. Can you envision me playing Da-xing? I'd rather close the show."

"Forget that." Vladimir reiterated his objection.

The actors grunted and muttered as Vladimir told them to warm-up. Sam kept checking nervously to see if Joe would emerge from the curtain. Even as the make-up artist tried to persuade Sam to fill in for Joe, Joe suddenly appeared. The members of the cast let out a breath of relieve and ire at the same time.

"Where the hell were you? What shit were you trying to pull?" Betty was the first to explode before Vladimir had a chance.

"It's a wretched damn irresponsible thing you did," Allan huffed.

"You are more unbelievable than I had thought." Fran gave him a glower and spoke through her teeth.

Guilt veiled Joe's visage as he began to explain. Ying Ying stopped him.

"All right, no more time to waste. Just hurry up and get into your costume," Vladimir commanded.

Despite the scare the curtain rose on time and the show went brilliantly. Not a cue for lighting change or for sound effect was missed. The complex scenery was changed swiftly and quietly. The row of 'soldiers' marched in stealth on and off the stage putting the trees up and down without a flaw. Not a word in the dialogues was forgotten. The acting was better than during dress rehearsals. Betty blossomed. She was the star commending the audience,s full appreciation. Fran added some small businesses to accentuate her character as a blind old woman. Joe's acting moved the audience to tears. Mike, playing a retarded country folk, brought shining moments and comic relieve to the play. Professor Deng's "Uncle Chang-wu" was a perfect portrayal of a wise old country gentleman of early 20th century China. And Allan's "Tiger" with his rugged masculinity, wicked revengeful heart, violent and merciless action, and deep regret in the aftermath, realized the playwright's vision of such a man.

The success was overwhelming. The audience raved over the show. A Hollywood movie star, a Chinese descend, happened to be in town and came to see the play. She congratulated Ying Ying, exalted the production and lauded the adaptation.

"I knew the play well. I have seen different productions of it. This is the first time I saw it in English though. The adaptation was wonderfully done. The acting and stage design were excellent," she said.

A newspaper reporter said that he enjoyed every line of the powerful dialogues to the fullest aside from his appreciation of the acting and scenery. A producer of a local TV station told Ying Ying that he rarely attended dramatic performances because they did not interest him; yet he really liked this one. He marveled at the small details that only seasoned theatre goers and critics would pick up; for example he noticed the way the blind mother gazed into nothingness, and the way she touched the edge of the table. "I was really convinced that she was blind," he extolled. Many character-building details were introduced by the actors during the opening night, without the director's instructions. It was when an actor completely identified with the character he was playing.

The show ran for three weeks from Thursdays through Sundays. At the curtain call of the final show, the audience gave a standing ovation. Flowers were presented to the actors and director. The curtain closed and opened three times.

Soon, all the actors changed in into their plain clothes and took off except for Professor Deng who stayed to give a hand on dismantling the set, packing the props, costumes and make-up. Vladimir and the production crew also hurried away. Only Ying Ying and the stage manager were left to strike. Of course her friends Pei-hua, Denis, and Tonia were there to help.

"Where did everyone go? Why isn't the stage crew here to take down the sets?" Pei-hua was baffled and irked.

"Oh, I am lucky that they didn't drop out before today. I already owed them so much," Ying Ying conceded.

"It's not your personal business. You are doing a project for China Stage," Denis said.

"Well, to my friends, it's a personal favor they did for me."

"That's true. If not for Ying Ying, who would bother volunteering for these works for three weeks?" Pei-hua said.

"Without Ying Ying no one would ever have taken on such a challenging project." Professor Deng made a poignant remark.

Denis drove the rented U-haul van. Ying Ying, Pei-hua and Professor Deng drove their own cars filled with costumes and props. Tonia and Jenny rode with Ying Ying and Pei-hua respectively. It was after 1:00am when they unloaded things from the cars and put them inside China Society's building. When they came out of the building and walked to their cars they saw parking tickets on their windshields

.   "What the hell..,.?" Denis swore irefully. "This is Sunday night. What are those morons doing?"

"You should all go to the city hall to protest," Jenny said naively.

"Protest against Boston City Hall? Yea, maybe this time we will win. Four tickets!! Sunday night!!! That's just great. After all the exhausting work the whole day we don't need this." Ying Ying was livid.

"Do you really think you can win?" Pei-hua questioned. "Don't you remember all the ridiculous tickets you and I have gotten in Boston and what happened when we protested?"

"How can I forget those?" Ying Ying replied in exasperation. "One time I got a ticket issued at 9:27pm on a Monday. I protested it in writing and was told to see the parking clerk. I did. The parking clerk recorded the first part of my report, then he turned off the recorder and said: 'Who told you that you didn't have to feed the meter after 6:00pm? The meters have to be paid around the clock. Don't you know that?' I said I didn't know. I was sort of skeptical about his remarks. But I had no evidence against his claim. So I had to pay not only the regular fine but an additional late fee as well, because while waiting for that appeal the ticket was over twenty-one days old. Some time later I found out that he was a bloody liar. People laughed at me for being fooled by a Boston parking clerk."

"They should not have charged you more during the time you were waiting for their response. But who can reason with them?" Denis huffed." Those damn vermin, every one of them, just cheat and rob, and squeeze every drop of blood from the public."

"And how about that time you got a ticket accusing you for parking somewhere in Dorchester while your car was in front of the Majestic Theatre, remember?" Pei-hua reminded Ying Ying.

"Yea, that was so ridiculous. My car was in the garage all day. I stopped at the Majestic to pick up my tickets. I fed a quarter to the meter. I came out before fifteen minutes. I already got a parking ticket. And it showed the location as some street in Dorchester. I didn't even know where Dorchester was at that time. But what could I have done except to pay? You can never fight Boston City Hall. They will add more charges to you if you appeal."

"You think that was bad? Wait until you hear what I had to pay for a ticket I'd never got," Tonia said.

"What?" Denis was confused.

"Last month I got a notice from the Boston Parking Clerk's office saying that I owe $100. I was completely puzzled. When I finally got through to the

Parking Clerk's office by phone and questioned what the ticket was for, the woman said $75 was for a ticket and $25 was for a late charge. I asked her again what was the ticket for? She said for not obeying the ticket officer who told me not to park on Commonwealth Avenue. I said I never parked on Comm Ave. That day I drove on Beacon Street and stopped by the curb to reach for a box of tissues in the back seat. A policeman told me I couldn't stop there. I drove away immediately. That was all. I never got a ticket. The woman said in absolute certainty that the ticket had been blown away. How could it get blown away since there was never a ticket? The woman said, 'I don't have time to argue with you. You just have to pay the fine.' Then she hung up. Of course I just paid. I think that policeman must have quickly jotted down my license plate number as soon as I stopped. I drove away so fast he would not have had a chance to give me the ticket. He must have given it to the parking clerk's office. Is there any justice?"

"They can do anything to the motorists. People have no recourse," Pei-hua said

"Last year I got one at 2:35am when I came to the office to get something. There were many horrendous cases but I don't want to bore you with them," Ying Ying said.

"I know. Our trustees dreaded to even stop by for a minute. Parking space is impossible to find. Putting the car in the garage for a few minutes is senseless. Mrs. Sounders was ticketed many times when she double-parked in front of our building for less than a minute to drop off something at our front desk," Denis added.

"One time Ying Ying and I stopped at Tower Records. She sat in the car while I scooted in to pick up a CD I ordered. Within two minutes the ticket maid snuck by her car and quickly put a ticket on the windshield and ran off. Wasn't she supposed to warn the driver, order her to move before writing a ticket?" Pei-hua demanded.

"The City of Boston is ravenous for any revenue it can lay its hands on. It is known to be the motorists' hell," Jennifer added her comment.

Knowing the dismal situation at the Boston Parking Clerk Office they decided not to waste the effort to appeal. Just pay the fine!!

Ying Ying and Denis had planned a cast party for Monday evening. It started with a dinner at Golden Palace Restaurant. The production team, planning committee, stage crew and actors, forty-five people in all were present. A sumptuous seafood dinner with the best lobsters, shrimp and fish was specially prepared by the chef. A dance party was held at China Society's function room after the dinner. Ai-ling and Sidney came with a few of their ballroom students at Ying Ying's invitation. They demonstrated a rumba and an Argentina Tango. Since not many of those in the room knew how to ballroom dance the music was mostly disco and Salsa. Everyone had a good time in the effervescent evening.

The actors and the production crew declared that they were all exhausted and needed many days of sleep and a long vacation. Ying Ying did

184

not feel that way. She said: "I am not tired. I can do it all over again." No one understood where she got her over-abundant energy.

Chapter 7

For years China Society was a place of congregation for those artistic people from China. Not too many from Taiwan were seen. One day Dong Fei-yan, a guitarist from Taiwan, dropped by to inquire about the Society's program schedules. Ying Ying talked with her.

"You are from Taiwan? So am I. What can we do for you?"

"I am looking for a venue to do a concert. If you would help me with it I would be obliged," Dong Fei-yan replied.

"Uh huh. What kind of instrument do you play? What kind of music?" Ying Ying asked.

"I am a guitarist. Three other musicians and I have formed a chamber group. We are all very good. I am looking to have regular concerts locally and go on national tours. Your location is quite nice. It suits my purpose well. How much do you charge for a concert?" Dong Fei-yan directly entered business talk.

"What do the other three play?"

"Violin, flute and drum," Dong Fei-yan said.

"I see." Ying Ying was not familiar with chamber groups of those four kinds of instrument. "Our facilities are not for rent," she conceded. "If a program fits our requirements we present it without charging. We will print and mail out announcements; publicize the event; give a reception and so on. These are all standard."

"What about ticket proceeds?" Dong Fei-yan brought out a practical issue that Ying Ying did not think of.

"Oh, that. Usually we don't sell tickets, unless it's a formal concert for which we have to rent a large auditorium. Small concerts we present at our own facilities are free to the public. We do send out announcements and hold receptions."

"I see. That's fine. When will I know if my project is suitable for your presentation? And how soon can you schedule it? I am planning to have this first concert here and take the group to New York afterwards immediately, then several other cities. I am still networking. But I must nail down the date of the first concert as soon as possible."

"I will bring it up at our Trustees meeting next week. Do you have a tape or something that I can give him? Our Board would want to hear it. It is an important supporting material all musicians applying for concert spots must submit."

"Yes, I do have it." Dong Fei-yan opened her bag and fished for her tape. "Here you are."

"I will give you a call next week." Ying Ying put the tape in her drawer.

That evening Ying Ying listened to the tape. It was not classical music as she had expected. It was improvised contemporary music on assorted instruments—guitar, flute, drum, and violin. She had little experience and ability in judging the quality of this type of music. She wondered if any of the Trustees would be knowledgeable in it. However, she felt that she should not disregard it simply because it was an unfamiliar form to her and perhaps to a large segment of the public. On the contrary, that very fact should be reason enough for China Society to present it.

The following week Ying Ying spoke with Joseph Lee before bringing it up at the Trustees meeting. She expressed her opinion.

"I think we will be doing the community a service by bringing this type of music to them. Give them a new listening experience."

Joseph Lee, as former Director of China Society, also attended Trustees meetings. He supported Ying Ying's position and said: "I am sure a large segment of the audience is not familiar with it either and may not accept it readily. Presenting it would fulfill an educational goal of ours."

"I suppose the idea is plausible," one Trustee stated: "But it is more appropriate for International Foundation to present it. We should bring it to Herald."

The same afternoon Joseph Lee and Ying Ying went to see Dr. Herald Schmidt, President of the Foundation.

The older man was always very fond of Ying Ying ever since her work-study days. He stood up from his chair to shake Ying Ying's hand.

"Hello, Ying Ying, how are you?"

"I am fine. Thank you," Ying Ying replied.

"What's up, Joseph?" Herald asked Dr. Lee.

"Ying Ying met this Taiwanese guitarist who has a chamber group and is looking to give a concert at our facility. Their music is not traditional. It's contemporary. Our Board has decided to present it but we think it may be more appropriate for the Foundation to do it. Do you think it's possible," Joseph said handing the tape to Herald? "This is their tape if you have a minute to listen to it."

"I respect your taste. If you think it's good enough I am sure it's good enough." Herald said sincerely and with a broad smile.

"That's just it," Joseph Lee smirked: "It's new music and beyond our ability to judge how good it is. We trust the musician's claim. She was very confident in their quality. This is a new group. They wish to have their first concert here and then go on a national tour starting from New York. We admire their courage and determination. I suppose their music is not easily appreciated. But they will work on building a following, if we can we should give them some support."

"Sure, I agree," Dr. Schmidt said without hesitation. "Ying Ying, what do you think?" This question was only a show of courtesy. He knew the group must have been recommended by Ying Ying. "Either the Foundation or the Society would be fine, I suppose. It's the same organization."

"True. But neither the music nor the musicians have affinity with Chinese culture, except, of course, that the guitarist is from Taiwan. So we thought it might be more suitable for the International Foundation to present it." Ying Ying uttered her opinion.

Finally they decided that the International Foundation would be the presenter and China Society would be the executor handling all logistics. The facility would be China Society's auditorium.

Ying Ying happily told Dong Fei-yan about the arrangement. Fei-yan was pleased.

The date was set for a Saturday evening three months later when the auditorium would be available. The project was immediately set in motion. There was just enough time for designing, printing and processing the announcements, sending press releases to the media and following up with phone calls. During this period Dong Fei-yan often went to talk with Denis and Ying Ying. Her enthusiasm about contemporary music, her perseverance, and her forthrightness quickly won Ying Ying's favor. A friendship quickly developed from Ying Ying's side. She introduced Fei-yan to Pei-hua. The three often got together. Although Dong Fei-yan was married with a young child, she was not bound by motherhood or domestic duties. She chose to go places, and do things as she pleased, always by herself, never with her husband. She insisted that independence was a sign of a person's strong character.

*   *   *   *

Dong Fei-yan met her husband, Brandon Jones, while studying at Brandeis University. He was a professor of Classics. She took one course from him and immediately had a crush on him. At the time she was dating a fellow student in her school. But Chuck's dillydally, noncommittal insouciance had irked her. She saw Brandon as a convenient weapon to be used against Chuck. She wanted either Brandon or Chuck to fall in her snare. She began by creating a smoke screen. She broke dates with Chuck at the last minute and said:

"I'm sorry, Chuck, but I cannot see you tonight. I got to go to Professor Jones's to talk about the topic of my paper." Of course she made this up and intentionally left clues for Chuck to discover the lie.

"Oh, that sock. Why didn't you tell me earlier? I could have planned something else for myself. Why must you see him in the evening anyway? Couldn't you have talked to him during his office hour?" Chuck was annoyed by the lateness of the cancellation, not by losing the date with her. It was this sort of attitude that roiled her. *You just wait*, she thought.

"It's not my fault. I went to see him this afternoon but he was busy. He told me to see him this evening." She tried to pin it on the Professor. To her disappointment Chuck did not pursue it any further. Some days later she pulled the same trick.

"Hey, it's okay if you don't want to go out with me. Just please tell me sooner." Chuck was apparently very fretted.

"Be reasonable, Chuck. It's not me who has asked to see him in the evening, you know." Dong Fei-yan pretended to be peeved.

"All right then. Go see him. See if I care," Chuck said in a testy tone.

"Don't say that, Chuck. You are making me feel awful. You do care, don't you?" The sudden change to a placating tone and words was a calculated manipulation. Chuck did not argue any more.

She must work on Brandon Jones to make the triangle look real. She knew she could harness the professor, a prudish and rigid man who probably had no experience with women. Such a man would be easy to seduce. She picked a time when the professor's schedule was filled with appointments. She waited by his office door. As soon as the door opened and a student came out she popped her head in his office. When Jones saw her and looked at his appointment book she apologized:

"I am sorry professor Jones. I didn't make an appointment. I thought you might have a few minutes."

"But I have two more appointments." He looked at his watch: "One is about to be here. I'm afraid there won't be any free time," he said.

"That's okay. But I must talk to you about my topic today. I don't mind coming in the evening. I can go to your place if that's more convenient for you." She said it in such an innocent tone that it did not betray the slightest sign of her machinations.

"Uh...well, if you must do it today perhaps I can wait here in the office for you. When would you like to come?" Jones disposed of the idea of having her come to his house.

"Oh, I hate to inconvenience you like that. I can't come before 8 o'clock. I figure if I go to your house you won't have to wait specifically for me here."

"It's not a problem. I live close by. A few minutes walk." Dong Fei-yan's intention was the farthest from Jones's mind. She couldn't push it any more. *This is only the first time*, she said to herself.

"All right then, I'll come at eight." She gave him a luring smile, turned around and strode away.

She made up more deceptive stories to lead Chuck into thinking that she and Brandon Jones had been involved beyond a teacher-student relationship.

"What's going on between you and Jones," finally Chuck questioned?

"Nothing really. But he has this thing about me. I don't know. I think it's kinda one-sided, unrequited love."

She was the one being infatuated. She managed to get Brandon Jones to meet with her a number of times and eventually she did persuade him to allow her to go to his place. When she revealed her feelings to him he was greatly alarmed. The straight-laced British gentleman warned her:

"It is unethical for a student and professor to be involved romantically. It is also against the school's code of behavior. I appreciate your fond feelings but please don't let people know about it," Brandon said.

"After this semester I won't be your student anymore. All right, I won't tell anyone. But I can see you secretly, in private, can't I?" When Brandon hesitated she continued:

"We didn't do anything wrong. I don't suppose two-people-in-love is against the law. Brandon I love you." She threw herself onto the professor's bosom.

Gradually she won him over. Chuck, on the other hand, shucked her like a dirty shirt without as much as a frown and moved on to other girls.

After she finished school she married Brandon. A year later she had a son. Marriage and motherhood did not damper her career or hamper her outside activities. The kid was under Brandon's or the babysitter's care when she was out.

"Brandon is a very good man. He cares about me, and our son. But he is not romantic. He lacks passion," Dong Fei-yan told her friends.

Ying Ying liked Fei-yan's openness and bubbly personality. Pei-hua, on the other hand, had little interest in Fei-yan as a musician or as a person. However, she was broad-minded enough to be unaffected by Ying Ying's fondness of this new friend.

Dong Fei-yan had a large plan to develop her music. She envisioned a major ensemble playing contemporary music on worldwide tours. She spoke about establishing a non-profit organization and acquiring a headquarters with facilities for rehearsals, recording music and giving small concerts. At the moment she needed to incorporate her organization and line up presenters in a dozen cities for her tours. She asked Ying Ying for help. She believed the latter's experience at China Society must be useful.

"A lawyer would charge $5,000 to incorporate the organization and apply for non-profit status. That's like highway robbery. How much work will it entail? Just some paperwork that a lawyer must be familiar with and can easily do. Ying Ying can you think of any cheaper way to do it?"

"Mmmm, do it yourself," Ying Ying replied.

"I haven't the slightest idea about how to do it. It will take a lawyer to do it. I wish I knew some pro bono lawyer." She was implying Pei-hua, hoping Ying Ying would ask Pei-hua on her behalf. Yet she did not say it aloud. She was waiting for Ying Ying to offer the help.

"I will ask Pei-hua how this can be done," reading Fei-yan's mind, Ying Ying volunteered.

Before going to Pei-hua Ying Ying looked up International Foundation's Article of Incorporation, by-laws, and legal documents for tax exemption. She asked Pei-hua whether those documents were all that were needed. Pei-hua confirmed it but did not offer her service. Ying Ying called Fei-yan:

"It doesn't seem very complicated. I think you can do it without involving a lawyer," Ying Ying said.

"If so, will you do it for me? I don't have the time and my mind is not on it," Fei-yan demanded.

190

Ying Ying hesitated for a moment and chuckled: "Fei-yan, you don't have the time. Do I have the time? You don't know how much work I am doing everyday? Beside, I have not done it before either. And I don't know exactly what are your mission and goals are. it's your business. It's your responsibility to get it done."

"You are much more experienced in these things. You are working for China Society. That helps. I am not sure of my mission and goal just yet. If you do it we can talk about that. I can help you." Dong Fei-yan sounded as if she was doing Ying Ying a great favor.

Ying Ying eventually agreed to do it for her.

She laid out the organization's structure; it's mission statement, goals, objectives, and programs. She drew up a by-law and a tentative budget for the first three years. She discussed each item with Fei-yan. Then she got the application from the Office of the Secretary of State and pertinent papers from the IRS. She spent quite some time on it. After she completed it she made a copy for Fei-yan.

As the scheduled date for Dong Fei-yan's concert was approaching she withdrew her plan; "I have not lined up the hosting institutions in other cities yet. So it's too soon to have the inaugural concert," she said.

Ying Ying was stupefied by Fei-yan's sudden change of plan. She was left in a quandary. *What would Joseph Lee and Herald Schmidt say? How would it look to the public that a project was canceled for no apparent reason? How could Fei-yan be so inconsiderate of others and so selfish?* These thoughts rushed through Ying Ying's mind.

She faced the blow without voicing her plight to Fei-yan. *It wouldn't change the situation anyway. Why make her feel bad,* she thought. She went to apologize to the Board and to Joseph Lee and Herald Schmidt. She was prepared to be censured. The two men were very displeased but they did not impute the adversity to Ying Ying.

"You couldn't have foreseen this. It's not your fault. But we must take some measure against such incidents from happening again."

"I should have asked her to sign an agreement. It was my carelessness," Ying Ying conceded.

"An agreement alone would not serve the purpose unless there is a penalty for breaching it. How do we punish an artist for changing her mind," Joseph said.

"That's true. Let's discuss it at the Board meeting," Herald suggested. In fact there was already a policy in place that required visual artists to sign an agreement that detailed the responsibilities of the artist(s) and the gallery respectively. The Board resolved that the regulation must extend to the musicians, dancers and humanists. To ensure firm commitment a deposit must be paid by the individuals upon signing the agreement. When the project was mounted the deposit would be refunded in full.

Ying Ying felt it to be a shame that the organization had to adopt such a policy. If everyone were honest, responsible and reliable there wouldn't be a need to establish any preventive measure

A few months later Dong Fei-yan asked Ying Ying to arrange her concert again. Ying Ying said:

"It won't be that easy anymore. The Board has reinforced the policy. Only four times a year the curator and program committee will review artists' applications. And a deposit against breach of contract is required. The same will apply to musicians," Ying Ying declared.

"That's so awful. Why do they have to do that," Dong Fei-yan grunted. It amazed Ying Ying that Fei-yan had not realized it was her behavior that brought about the reinforcement of policy.

"Fei-yan, isn't it clear to you? You breached the agreement, leaving us in the lurch. A reputable organization cannot be damaged like that ever again."

"I didn't think it would be such a big deal. Plans do get changed, you know." Fei-yan argued.

*   *   *   *

Ying Ying's application on Fei-yan's behalf for forming Contemporary Music New England succeeded. The new non-profit organization was legally born when the Secretary of State mailed back the approved Article of Organization and the IRS assigned a Federal ID number to it. Dong Fei-yan was pleased. She forgave Ying Ying for bearing the news of International Foundation's tightened policy.

"Good. Now I can solicit private donations and apply for public support. You have to help me with grant writing," Fei-yan said blithely.

"No, Fei-yan. You can't yet. Unless you are tax-exempt you don't qualify for donations or grant support. A tax-exempt application is a separate step. The IRS will review every application and grant a preliminary determination to those deserving organizations. A final determination will be granted a few years later If the organization's performance fulfills the self-proclaimed mission and goals. So not every non-profit organization is tax-exempt."

She asked Ying Ying about how to promote the organization, how to find opportunities to perform, and how to raise funds.

"When you have a good program you naturally will send out press releases and other promotional materials. We never hire public-relations-firms to hype our events. It's very costly and the results may not be commensurate. For a young organization like yours exposure is the best publicity. Participating in a series of cultural activities at the Boston Common during the summer, for example, would let people know about your organization. That Series including music, dance, theatre productions, and so on. They are presented by the city free to the public. Newspapers will write about them. If you can get in, you will get some free publicity."

"How do I get into this summer Series?" Dong Fei-yan anxiously asked.

"The City is still accepting proposals. Prepare a good description of your program. You told me that audience and performers interaction was a strong aspect of your music. It should be emphasized in your proposal. You will need to submit support materials such as a cassette tape, photographs, and reviews if you have them. I can write a recommendation letter on your behalf."

"Can you write the proposal for me? It's a piece of cake for you. But for me? I haven't done a proposal yet," Dong Fei-yan demanded.

"Fei-yan, it may not be a big deal but it still takes time. You know how busy I am." Ying Ying pleaded for her understanding.

"Oh, Ying Ying, it won't take that much time. It's not a funding proposal. Come on." She fixed her gaze in Ying Ying's eyes demanding the latter to go along.

"All right." After a second of hesitation Ying Ying said resignedly.

"That's my girl," Dong Fei-yan chortled.

A well-written proposal, and a strong recommendation must have been the reason for Dong Fei-yan's program to be accepted by the Park and Recreation Department of Boston.

The summer-long activities took place in several other parks around the city in addition to the Boston Common. The Arts In The Park committee, of which Ying Ying was a member, agreed that Fei-yan's music was untraditional and unfamiliar to the public. That was all the more reason to put it in the program. Where would it be better than the parks? The Committee felt a sense of mission in presenting it. It was educational, not only entertaining. Ying Ying disqualified herself from evaluating Fei-yan's proposal and abstained from casting her vote since she had written a recommendation letter to support it.

From mid-June to the end of August a rich assortment of music, dance, drama, martial arts demos, juggling, storytelling, art exhibits and other activities filled the evening hours daily. Dong Fei-yan's group was to appear on the Common every other week and in two other parks twice a month. Not only was she getting publicity but also being paid. Gleefully she signed the contract with the Park and Recreation Department.

The spot assigned to Fei-yan on the Common was near the jugglers' and the monkey's stands. The audience was more interested in watching the monkey and the jugglers. Some did pay attention to the music and talked with the musicians.

The newspapers did mention Contemporary Music New England and said some encouraging words about it.

"This kind of thing builds your track record although it's only a short mentioning. You should keep it on file," Ying Ying suggested to Fei-yan.

Toward the middle of July Dong Fei-yan called Ying Ying and said:

"Ying Ying, I have to go out of town. I cannot do the park program now. Can you cancel the contract with the City for me?"

Ying Ying was flabbergasted at Fei-yan's sudden whim to breach her contract. She said:

"No, Fei-yan. I cannot do that. And you should not take the contract so lightly. This is very damaging to you even if you don't care about the Arts In The Parks program."

"We need to go to Chicago. I have made some contacts there. I am going to meet with them about the tour." Ying Ying's advice hit deaf ears.

"But Fei-yan, you are in the middle of a contract. This Series is important for your group too. Breaching a contract will have serious consequences. Not only will you not get another opportunity from the city again but you will also lose your credibility. You will be known as a person without good faith. Don't you care about this?" Ying Ying emphatically stressed her exhortation.

"Well, the national and international touring is the most important at the moment. I will worry about the other things later," Dong Fei-yan rebuffed.

"I have nothing to say if that's how you see it. But sorry, I cannot ask the Park Department to abrogate the contract. "

"You sound upset. You are not going to help a friend?" Fei-yan was disappointed and tetchy.

"Anything within my power I will do for you. But this is not," Ying Ying was truthful.

"All right then. I'll just take off without notice." Dong Fei-yan's ire was apparent.

"Fei-yan, don't be so irrational. Think it over. Okay?" Ying Ying pleaded with her, but in vain.

After she abruptly left the Boston Park Summer program without notice Dong Fei-yan did not reappear until a year later. She went to Ying Ying's office. There she met Meng Song. Ying introduced them to teach other.

"Oh, you are Meng Song!! Pleasure to meet you. I have heard so much about you. And I also saw your work at the Globe Foundation." Dong Fei-yan had undisguised zeal. *What a gorgeous man,* she thought.

Meng Song remained in his seat, nodded slightly and smiled, the usual aloofness enveloped his countenance.

"It's been a long time, Fei-yan. Have a seat." Ying pointed to the empty chair at one side of her desk. "Where have you been? What have you been doing?"

"I went to Chicago, as you know." She took the seat. "Then I spent some time in LA, then, Russia and other East European countries, after that Taiwan. In Taiwan I was involved in a production of *Midsummer Nights Dream.*"

Meng Song was apparently not interested in the conversation. He rose to his feet and said:

"I have to get going, Ying Ying." He turned to Dong Fei-yan and nodded: "Nice to have met you."

"Okay, we'll talk again soon." Ying Ying lifted herself up from her seat and said.

"Oh, I interrupted your meeting with Ying Ying? I'm sorry." Dong Fei-yan raised her eyes to meet Meng Song's and remarked casually. Meng Song just smiled and excused himself. Dong Fei-yan's eyes followed Meng Song till he disappeared beyond the office door and said:

"I didn't know he was so gorgeous. Just delicious!!" .

Ying Ying returned to her seat, smiled and jeered: "What? Puck smeared

194

love juice on your eyelids?"

"Ha ha ha." Dong Fei-yan chuckled admittedly. "I am in Midsummer Nights Dream. But even without Puck's work I never let a good looking man slip through my fingers."

"I know, you inherited the trait from your lecherous father." Dong Fei-yan had told Ying Ying about her father's amorous liaisons that distressed her mother. She admitted that her licentious impulses were inherited from her father.

"But don't play with fire. You may get hurt." Ying Ying thought how Hu Ning was hurt by Meng Song.

"Me? Get hurt?" Dong Fei-yan scoffed. "No such thing. I have a short interest span. Before the guy wakes up from his romantic dream I am already palled." She paused and chortled. "I will ask this scrumptious hunk out and see what happens."

"You wouldn't," Ying Ying argued. "How is Brandon?" Asking about Fei yan's husband was to remind her that she was married.

"Ying Ying, I know you," Dong Fei-yan laughed. "I know I have a husband. He doesn't mind, why should you?"

He doesn't mind? A husband does not mind a wife playing around like that? But Ying Ying did not voice her thought.

Fei-yan could not understand why Meng Song was non-responsive to her allurement after several attempts. She had no idea what kind of man Meng Song was. Only if she had known what Meng Song's principle was: "I don't want girls to want me. I will take them when I want them."

*   *   *   *

It was 1991. Meng Lingzhen finished her study of computer graphics at Mass College of Art. Unlike other foreign students, her visa belonged to the J category, instead of F1. It required her to leave the country as soon as she finished school. There was no possibility to have it changed to anything else except by marriage. She could not explain why the U.S. consulate in Shanghai gave her such a visa.

She had too much pride and dignity to allow herself falling into the infamous "blacked-out" category, nor would she desecrate the sacred commitment of marriage by using it to obtain a green card. She was left with no choice but to go back to Shanghai.

Jason proposed for her hand, but she declined.

"I will not marry you for the sake of a green card. That is denigrating to my character as well as to the sacred nature of marriage," she said sternly.

"But you are not marrying me for a green card. You know that, and I know that. We have been in love for three years. Where else should we go except to the altar? I was waiting for you to finish school before bringing it up."

She brooded over it, struggled over it, and talked to Ying Ying about it. Jason further persuaded:

"If you go back to Shanghai I will definitely go after you. But the Chinese government will not allow me to have an extended stay. So I will have to keep going back and forth. What for? What's there to stop us from getting married now? Why must we go through all that?"

Lingzhen finally gave in. The news put her brother's mind at ease.

"This is good. Now I don't have to worry about her anymore." Meng Song let out a breath of relief when Ying Ying asked him about what gift to buy.

"I told you they were in love. What's there to worry about?" Ying Ying reiterated her opinion.

Lingzhen decided to have the wedding ceremony in Shanghai in November. They applied for a marriage certificate from Boston's City Hall before flying to Shanghai. After the wedding they spent two weeks in Yunnan, then two more weeks in Rome.

Upon returning to Boston the newly weds got together with some friends to share their impressions of Shanghai.

"We arrived in the evening. I looked out of my window from the plane and couldn't find Shanghai because it was shielded in total darkness," Jason said.

"Shanghai was like a stretch of broken crockery." Ying Ying remembered her impression of the city. The taxi drove in darkness and the Friendly Shops with their twenty-watt bulbs were fresh in Pei-hua's memory. But she did not share her sentiment. Jenny couldn't believe what she had heard. She snorted:

"Come on you guys. Stop pulling our legs. How could the plane land if the city was in total darkness?"

"It's true. If you don't believe him go check it out yourself," Lingzhen put in.

"You never mentioned it before. Was it always that way," Jenny asked?

"Yes. But we were so used to it and didn't pay any attention to the fact," Lingzhen explained.

Jason added: "People were dissatisfied with Deng Xiao-ping. They tossed little bottles on the ground to break them as a vent to their ire."

"Why did they break bottles," Jenny was baffled.

Lingzhen chuckled and said: "Xiao-ping and little bottle are homonyms in Chinese."

"Clever!!" Jenny chuckled too.

Jason and Lingzhen settled in the townhouse they bought on Beacon Hill. They also had a "country home" in Weston and a "city place" on Park Avenue in New York. Lingzhen was heavily involved in charitable and volunteer work like all those rich and leisurely ladies. What she learned at Mass College of Art was put to rest. She enjoyed fine music and art and often flew to Europe to attend art exhibitions and opera performances. Of course she conveniently shopped in Paris during her trips.

Lingzhen and Jason frequently visited her parents in Shanghai too. They never stayed for long, just a couple of weeks at most. They were awestricken by China's giant leaps toward prosperity since the decisive metamorphosis in

1993. Not only was Shanghai bathed in glorious neon lights, China as a whole had become a haven for money-hungery opportunists. People were obsessed with the dream of striking gold.

*   *   *   *

Meilan reorganized her performing group and toured China the third time. Then she decided to relinquish this project. She said:

"The advantage I had over the other Chinese was that I had the green card two years before any of them did. As such I was able to go back there and take advantage of all the good opportunities. The music and dance I brought there were new and refreshing to the Chinese audience. So I made lots of money. Now there are topnotch performers from all over the world. The novelty has worn off. It makes no sense for me to do it anymore."

The information about China Meilan brought to her friends in Boston was diametrically opposed to what Jason and Lingzhen had brought. The difference grew in only a matter of two years. Meilan had nothing but extolment over China. As for Boston, she only had disparagement.

"Boston is like an old shabby ghost town, jejune, vapid, lifeless, whereas in China, ha, you see only prosperity, joyousness, excitement, and booming business. People are lively, excited, eagerly and diligently trying to make money. There is a popular saying: *"among the billion people, ninety nine hundred million are merchants."*

"I suppose you are not going to stay in this ghost town for long." Pei-hua taunted as usual.

"No, I cannot stay here anymore. I am moving back to China for good. Permanently."

"There is nothing permanent in life," Pei-hua said pointedly.

No large farewell party was thrown in Meilan's honor since she did not announce her leaving to her society circle. Only a few close friends gathered at Ying Ying's apartment.

"We don't like to give you a large party to mark your going away because we want you to be back," Ying Ying toasted to Meilan.

"Yes, Meilan, you have to come back. Boston is not such a bad place," Denis said.

Meilan was not alone in her sentiment about Boston and China. Other Chinese also emphatically vaunted over the exciting changes taking place in China.

"The hotels are more extravagant than any I have ever seen," Artist Zhang Ze said: "The services are out of this world. You won't believe it. But listen to this. For example, I was in the gent's room. Before I even finished doing my thing a hand reached from behind to press on the knob of the urinal to flush the bowl. No sooner than I turned around, at a start, a hot towel was thrust to me. While I was wiping my hand with that fragrant hot towel, a man was brushing off the invisible lint from my suit...." His reenactment of the service guy's actions brought laughter in the room.

"Beijing has changed so much that I couldn't recognize the streets or find my hotel. The taxi drove in circles to confuse me into thinking I was far away from my hotel. In fact I was no more than five or six blocks away. Of course, that's how he made extra money," Singer Zhi An added.

Stories about China were abundant. They portrayed a society that was slipping into decadence. Prostitution and theft that were extinct uander Mao Zedong's rule has returned and spread like uncontrollable diseases, they said.

"Without exception, in any hotel, the clerk would send a girl to your room," another one said.

'You mean it's like room service? You must take it?" Tonia and Ying Ying were both appalled.

"No, you don't have to keep her. But you have to give her some money and beg her to leave."

"Thieves, pocket pickers and muggers are rampant and highly skillful. In Shanghai there are 'head knockers.' That is a mugger who knocks your head with a rock or a bat before robbing you. You may get killed that way. And all for peanuts," Another reported.

"Swindlers and cheaters are everywhere. Do you know the popular saying that goes, 'Everything is fake. Only fake is real,'" said Old Zhang who just came back from Beijing.

"Ha ha, 'Only fake is real.' That's a great line," Denis chuckled.

"They counterfeit everything. Not just Cartier watches or Levy Jeans, and such. They even make fake eggs," Zhang Ze further reported.

"Fake eggs?" Tonia acclaimed. "How is it possible to make a fake egg? Would a fake-egg cost more to make than having a hen lay a real one?" Every one else had the same question. But no one gave an answer.

"The worst thing is that hospitals refuse to admit patients, even trauma patients, without being paid first. Without money, and a lot of people have no money, the patient just have to die outside the hospital's door. So many patients' families were desperate and without recourse. Some leave their sick family members in the hospital's waiting room and run away hoping the hospitals would have some mercy. But the hospitals just move the patients out and leave them on the street to die."

"Imagine that!! The family just abandons the sick. And the hospital just throws them out. What heartless beasts are these people? The little I learned about China in history books was opposite to what I am hearing here. What kind of society is that? Is there any sense of humanity left?" Jenny was outraged.

"How ironic. We thought a socialist country would treat each individual equally and take care of the old and ill indiscriminately, and without charge. Ours is a capitalist country. Yet we take care of the sick regardless of whether they can pay or not," Denis sighed in disgust.

"Doctors and hospitals here often give medical care to patients from other countries free of charge." Tonia was thinking of many cases she knew first hand or heard in the news reports. "How could they leave their own patients on the street simply because they don't have the money to pay?"

Ying Ying and Pei-hua were most upset when Zhi An told them about the schools in China.

"The public schools charge the kids fees for things you cannot even imagine. Things like light bulbs, chalks, blackboard wipers, brooms, dustpans, and so on. Even building repairs and ground maintenance are fee items, not to mention books, note pads and pencils. One high school student with good marks, was not allowed to graduate because his family could not afford the 50 *yuan* for his textbooks. His chances for a college education were thus exterminated."

*   *   *   *

Because of her position as President of China Society, Ying Ying had chances to know many different people from China. In the mid-90s people in China were obsessed with making money. Pure artistic pursuit waned. Dollar signs obliterated artists' sense of value. Marketability and commercialization were the only concerns of the artists. They also lost interest in leaving the country for America because China's art market was vibrant. Their work could fetch more money there.

Post mid-90s brought different Chinese visitors to China Society. Artists and musicians diminished. Literary intellectuals—writers, journalists, and teachers began to appear. People in these professions had not been rewarded with good money-making opportunities in their home country as visual artists and musicians had. America still was a land of dreams. They tried various ways to chase those dreams. For example:

Fung Yun-sen was a high school teacher in Chongqing. He and his wife had a son with a degenerative disease of the intestine. The boy had more than one surgery in China that worsened his condition. The couple learned that the Children's Hospital in Boston would be able to treat the boy. Most importantly, they learned that the hospital would not charge them. American hospitals would treat patients of unusual diseases or conditions from around the world. And the doctors usually provided the services for free. The hospitals also waived the charges. As much as it sounded like a tale from *One Thousand and One Nights,* Mr. and Mrs. Fung truly believed it because it was America, the land of dreams and opportunities.

They paid someone to write a letter to the hospital describing the son's condition. Children's Hospital indeed agreed to treat the boy. The Fungs easily obtained passports and U.S. visas. Off they went to Boston. For sure, the surgery was successful. And the hospital was committed to regular check ups of the patient indefinitely, treatments if necessary and everything else. The cost exceeded $300,000 and counting. But not a cent was tagged onto Mr. and Mrs. Fung. As if it were their birthright, their bills should be paid by American taxpayers. Since the boy needed extended medical care the parents' visas were automatically extended indefinitely, thanks to the generosity and hospitality of America. They settled in Boston. Mrs. Feng got a job as a sales clerk at a supermarket despite her inability to speak English. Mr. Fung who also knew little English was hired by an antique furniture store to restore the decorative paintings on the furniture and to make fake antiques. His art training happened to be in the right alley.

One time Mrs. Fung while riding in a friend's car was hit by a drunk driver. She was advised by a friend to seek emergency care and make a case with a lawyer, "so that you can claim insurance payment, and other things, " the friend said. So she did.

"You have to quite your job to claim that you are disabled, even if temporarily, so you can claim loss of wages," her lawyer advised. She did that too. But she was not willing to forgo an income. So she found a job as a caretaker for an elderly lady with Parkinson disease.

"I have to be paid in cash, not check," she told the new employer through a translator. The elderly lady's husband asked why she would not accept check payments. She said: "I don't trust the bank." In fact it was because she had claimed disability from the insurance company. She must not leave any possible trace for the insurance company to discover that she was working.

Her accident settlement netted her $50,000. Judiciously, she and her husband invested it in a small two-family house. They rented the larger unit the income from which paid for the mortgage, interest and tax with extra money left. Thus their housing expense was nil. It was a time when real estate appreciated rapidly. In a year the equity grew considerably. They used it to invest in another multi-family house and did the same with a third house, then a fourth house and so on. In a short period of a few years they owned several multi-family houses and moved to a nice single-family in Lincoln to live comfortably on a six-figure net rental income. This was the America they expected, a land of dreams.

Xu ling was a clerk of the city government of Nanking. She used her connection to get herself attached to a company that was sending a business team to the U.S.. Needless to say it was a good strategy to emigrate from China to this land of gold and dreams. But her visa soon expired and she turned "black." One day at a Laundromat a Caucasian American man noticed her and immediately found her attractive. He tried to make conversation with her only to get a smile in response because she hardly knew any English. The following week she bumped into that man again at the Laundromat. It happened again and again. It was not hard for the man to figure out, after the second time, that this woman's laundry day was Thursday evening. He tried to speak to her every time. Even though they couldn't communicate verbally they seemed to understand each other in some way. He began to buy a cup of coffee for her. Then a small box of chocolates, a large box of Godiva, long-stem roses, then finally he asked her to dinner in a nice restaurant. Before long he proposed and they got married.

Xu Ling was a tall and slender woman with an amiable personality. About her marriage she said to friends:

"There is no love to speak of on my part. But he is a good man and he apparently loves me. The marriage delivered me from the dead-end of 'black-out'. That was my goal. In a year or so, after I get the green card I will divorce him." But that didn't happen. Xu Ling was genuinely moved by the man's complete, selfless love. Eventually she grew to love him too. Like a fairytale they lived happily ever after.

Ming Gu, a novelist from Hunan province applied and was accepted by a Chinese language writers' symposium in Boston. Her visa was good for a month and she over-stayed. Yet due to the lapse or looseness of the U.S. immigration law she was able to illegally get a job at a large phone company selling telephone service to the Chinese community. She was even able to bring her husband and daughter over. Her husband was a high school math teacher in China. Not qualified for a white-collar job and unwilling to wait on tables he just stayed home tutoring a few high school kids of Chinese descent.

There was a woman named Huang Chin. She was hired to teach Chinese language at the University of Massachusetts. Her husband Chen Zi, a journalism professor at Beijing University, came as her dependent. He knew no English and had no marketable skills to avail him for a job anywhere except perhaps menial work like painting houses or helping in the kitchen. But both he and his wife disregarded these as too demeaning.

One might believe that Chairman Mao had extirpated the 'feudalistic' concept of class; under the proletarian dictatorship political system people would hail labor as sacred. However, it was contrary to the fact. People from China had a much stronger sense of class than those from Taiwan, a capitalist society. While even the sons and daughters of the highest-ranking officials in Taiwan washed dishes and stood guard as night-watchmen during their graduate school years in the States, their counterparts from Mainland China despised labor. When they were forced by financial circumstances to take a menial job they would forever whine and constantly vaunt their special social classes in China.

To avoid feeling useless, Professor Chen Zi decided to produce a book about America for readers in China who were curious about this country, eager and voracious to devour any information. Such a book would be a sure moneymaker, he said. But he was not equipped to tackle the subject. Just like America was to him, the subject was too new, he had no knowledge of it. After brooding over it for some time, he discussed it with his wife. They both thought Fang Ying Ying would be a good resource. He asked Ying Ying to author the book and he would publish it.

Ying Ying liked the idea. It was a good project, no doubt. She had long pondered about writing a book or a series of books to present an unbiased picture of America to Chinese readers. The topics would include the people, the society, the history and culture of America. The Chinese might very well be interested in learning everything about America--it's history, traditions and customs, education system, public and private schools, social service system, healthcare system, family relations, race and ethnicity issues and many more. The book would definitely benefit America too since it would project an objective image to a foreign people. Chen Zhi's proposal offered an impetus for Ying Ying to realize her plan.

She was confident in her knowledge and ability for this undertaking. She had been in the U.S. long enough, finished graduate school, had many years of working experience that put her in touch with people of all walks of life. Her work also enabled her to enter various levels of the society. In addition to that she planned to do a significant amount of research in all areas covered by the book.

To Ying Ying's disappointment, unfortunately, Chen Zhi had reservations about the topics she presented to him. He uttered his opinion in a diplomatic way:

"Your topics are valuable, and your ideas are lofty. It is what the Chinese readers ought to read. But people are not interested in such serious topics. Or the way you would like to present it. They like to know about America's popular culture, American people's lifestyle, fashion, dating behaviors, that type of thing. They also like to read about the dark and ugly side of the American society so that they can feel better about their own society and not regret not being able to come here. They will think: 'Oh, America is not such a great place after all. I am better off to stay put. I should not envy those people who have gone there.' You see, in order to sell the book, we have to cater to the readers' taste."

"In that case I am afraid that I am not the right person to write this book. Pleasing a readership with preconceived wry views just doesn't interest me. I will not write about teen sex and pregnancy, or wife-swapping, drug abuse or any other depraved societal ills, to give the Chinese readers a distorted image of this country. My interest is to bring people together through cultural understanding, not to feed their appetite for the absurd and grotesque."

Of course Ying Ying did not write that book.

*　　　*　　　*　　　*

After China Stage, Drama Workshop, and Playwrights Platform, Ying Ying created a fourth new program. That was a weekly thirty-minute cable TV talk show named *Culture Discourse.* She hosted it in the beginning. Each week a guest would be invited to discuss a specific subject of his/her field. Li Yong was a guest one time while he was researching for materials on a historical figure, Lue Gim Gong, a young Chinese farmer who came to American in thr late 19th century. With his experiences and knowledge in farming and fruit planting Lue experimented with improving the orange and grapefruit in North Adams, Massachusetts. In the 1880's he moved to Florida. He created what was later called the Lue Gim Gong Orange and an improved grapefruit that could withstand a much lower temperature. He was recognized as an accomplished horticulturist in 1904 when a statue of him and his favorite house was unveiled in the Florida Pavilion of the World's Fair held in New York. His contribution was further lauded in 1911 when the American Phonological Society awarded him the Wilder Medal.

Li Yong talked about writing a film script about that man and play the protagonist in his script.

"I always feel uncomfortable seeing Chinese people being portrayed in Hollywood films. I wish to project an accurate image of a Chinese man through my characterization of this role," Li Yong maintained.

To portray people who were different from oneself fairly and objectively took broadmindedness and knowledge, and a dedicated effort to do so. More often than not, the characterizations of foreign people or land were distorted deliberately, sometime with malicious intention.

There was a Chinese TV production team sent to New York to make a documentary of the city for their avid audience in China. *The True Picture of the United States of America* was the title of the film. Instead of presenting an objective, well-rounded and balanced journalistic documentary, the group chose to show the slums, the bums laying on dirty street corners, the violence in some ghetto communities, the drug users, the nude bars, the obstreperous behavior of public school students, etc. The narrative that accompanied the pictures was in a condescending tone, and described America as a depraved place. The documentary was meant to alter the old myth of America being a land of gold and opportunities resided by people in opulence, living in big mansions, driving beautiful cars, and dancing in luxurious grand ballrooms in flowing gowns and tuxedos.

Like people in many countries the Chinese people were envious and jealous of America. They all desired to go and get a share of that wealth and luxury. But not everyone's dream could be realized. For the majority who could not even afford to dream, a bitterness and sour taste were left in their mouths. They relish an image of depravity on this unreachable land, as the Chinese adage went: "When one has no grapes to eat, one disregards them as being too sour."

What satisfaction does such an attitude brin, Ying Ying wondered. *Would denigrating others elevate one's own image and esteem?*

Taiwan had remained friendly with the U.S. since the Second World War. And they had signed a mutual defense agreement. People there held no animosity toward America. Yet misunderstanding by people about America existed nevertheless. Criticizing America seemed to be fashionable. One time Taiwan's Minister of Oversea-Chinese-Affairs, Mr. Cheng, visited Boston on official business. His wife took it upon herself as an unofficial education delegate. Her self-appointed job was to observe and study the public schools system in Boston and make recommendations to the authorities in Taiwan. Her report would be printed in Taiwan's newspapers.

At a banquet in Mr. and Mrs. Cheng's honor, Ying Ying sat next to Mrs. Cheng who would embark on her tours of Boston schools the following day. To collect some background information Mrs. Cheng asked the women at her table to speak up.

"I heard the American schools are not so good. They cannot compare with ours." Mrs. Cheng made her opening remark.

"Oh, you are so right. You won't believe how bad American schools are." One woman emphatically offered her "well-informed" opinion. "The students learn nothing. And the teachers are ignorant. They are unionized. They only care about how much they are paid, not how well they teach. They band up and strike if they are not satisfied with their raise. They can never be fired no matter how bad they are. How can kids learn from those teachers?"

"The kids behave badly. The teachers don't dare to discipline them. How can you learn anything in that environment," another woman added.

"And their materials are so watered down, so much simpler than ours. Our fourth grade materials are at a higher level than their junior highschool's. Their kids, some cannot even read after graduating from highschool," the third woman chimed in.

"They fight in the classroom. They even beat up their teachers and the school does not punish them," one more voice added.

"Even their college is very mediocre. You cannot learn anything there," still another commented.

Ying Ying saw the discussion was getting out of hand. These women derived the notion from news reports or hearsay. She felt that she had to put in a different voice, to present a fair view.

"Mrs. Cheng is going to make official visits to the schools and write reports for the newspapers. I think she should get a more balanced, unbiased view on the issue. What you ladies have said is true in some isolated instances but does not represent the whole picture of American schools. I think my remark is based on my observation and experiences with a large number of Boston-area schools. Discipline in the inner city schools is a problem. Some teachers may not be highly qualified and some students have not learned much. These were reported in our national evening news. Why were they reported? Because it were unusual, not typical. Anything that's usual is not newsworthy. But despite these isolated cases, the schools as a whole are not that bad. Public schools in the suburbs are very good, in fact. Then there are many parochial schools and private schools. Those are exceptionally good. I have first-hand experience with both the bad and the good schools because I send programs to twenty-five or thirty schools each year. Many times I give talks at the schools. In the private schools, students asked intelligent and appropriate questions after my lectures. They were quiet and attentive. I think they are very smart, and well-behaved. We also cannot condemn the colleges here. If they were all bad where did the great scientists, and scholars come from?"

"Those talents came from other countries," one woman retorted. "All the good ones are from other countries. Without those brains America would have nothing. All the achievements in science America claimed credit for were actually made by foreigners who came to this country with knowledge already in their brains. America only reaped the glory."

It's useless to try changing these people's opinions. Prejudice and bigotry are deep rooted in these people. Perhaps those are am inherent part of human nature. They are the seeds of feuds among people, wars between nations. Peter Si's story of discrimination often haunted Ying Ying.

What can we do to make a difference? Would it even be possible? Why don't people open their eyes and minds? These questions troubled Ying Ying. *Education. People should be better educated to address these issues.*

*   *   *   *

"People's eyes and ears were inundated with constant news reporting violence and crime in the streets, disturbances, unrest, racial hostilities and other atrocities. Those impressionable and malleable young minds were polluted by intrusions of TV images and printed words. They became callused and accepted those atrocities as facts of life. Youth need guidance, good examples and constructive ideas to make a positive and indelible impression on them and to mold their behaviors." This was Ying Ying's unwavering conviction. She expressed her point at a Board meeting.

"Educating the young people is imperative and urgent. If we can help a few kids I think it's a worthy contribution. May I propose a new program for the Board to consider? This is a program for the elementary and secondary schools, a program named *Cultural Understanding and Racial Harmony*. Although one program may not accomplish very much in battling those issues, yet a spark might spread into a fire that consumes a mountain," Ying Ying exerted.

The Trustees embraced the idea. The *Cultural Understanding and Racial Harmony* program was thus born. It constituted a major theme in the Education Outreach Program that had already served over twenty-five public schools each year.

Beginning with a speech addressing the topic, 'Cultural understanding is the foundation for racial harmony,' the series of activities proceeded to include talks by students about their views on the subject, and writing essays as a homework assignment. Each school was to put their students' essays in a volume. In the art class, an artist would guide the students to develop ideas and create works of their own designs to address the issue.

They were given a month to finish the project. All writings and art works from participating schools would be accepted for exhibition at China Society's gallery I. Awards would be given to the best essays and art pieces.

This event was so warmly responded to by the kids and well received by the gallery audience that the program was deemed worthy to continue in subsequent years. Ying Ying planned to recommend it to cultural organizations in cities like New York and San Francisco.

*   *   *   *

Simultaneous with the kids' Harmony exhibition, gallery II had a show curate by Joseph Lee featuring work by professional artists from Germany. At the reception, in additional to the regular local visitors and the Trustees, were visitors from out of state and abroad. The staff was busy speaking with the guests. Wine and hors d'oeuvres were passing around by uniformed waiters.

There was one guest who intently viewed each piece on the wall, not speaking to anyone in the gallery. Ying Ying noticed this man but paid little attention to him.

After the guests left Ying Ying went to gather her things in her office. A knock lightly on the half opened door drew her attention. She lifted her head from her desk; a surprised expression frozen on her face.

"Ying, it's been so long. How are you?" The man had a grin on his face, a twinkle in his eyes. Before the surprise-stricken Ying Ying could react, he added: "Didn't expect to see me here, did you?"

"Kang... Wei.... " She searched for words and failed.

"Yes, Ying. It's me." He strode across the room toward her desk.

Ying Ying was completely befuddled. Her mind was blank. No words could come out. In silence they looked at each other for a second.

"Ying Ying, are you leaving? I am ... ." Denis stuck his head in the room. When he saw that she had a guest he added: "Oh, sorry."

"Yes, you go ahead, I am leaving too," Ying Ying said to Denis. Then she began to think what she should do with Kang Wei. She couldn't just tell him that she must go home and leave him there.

"Ying, shall we go have some tea or something," gently Kang Wei asked. That voice, that manner brought all the memories back to Ying Ying.

"Oh, yes. That's fine."

They went to a coffee shop on Tremont Street across from the Boston Common.

"Are you visiting here?" Ying Ying was making conversation.

"No, I came here for an interview at MIT." Kang Wei said.

"Oh I see."

"Two years after you left I left too. I attended graduate school at UC Berkley to continue studying in bio-medical science. I just received my Ph. D. and am looking for a teaching job." Kang Wei said.

"You applied to MIT."

"And a few other colleges. There are already a couple of offers. Assistant professorship. The opening at MIT is for an instructor. But I wish to come to Boston." He intently gazed at Ying Ying. "I want to move here to be near you. Ying, you are not married, are you? Don't shut me out this time." Without hesitation he candidly revealed his heart. Ying Ying had no room to retreat. She was thrust into the situation head on.

"I... I didn't shut you out. Of course I am not married." There was never any reason for her to shut him out. They were in love. If not separated by time and space they might have been married a long time ago. *Why did he stop writing? Why did he not come to me when he came to the States?*

She had many questions but asked none. Kang Wei seemed to know what she was thinking. He said:

"There were rumors about you falling in love with someone else."

"And you just believed them without trying to find out whether that was true or not?" There was a little hint of censure.

"I anxiously waited to get a few words from you but you didn't write. I struggled with myself about whether to continue writing and find out why you completely tossed me away. But I thought that was not an honorable thing to do. You don't owe me an explanation. I should be a gentleman, to bow out gracefully. When I heard that you were married all the more I could not disturb your peaceful life. I lived with a broken heart. Only a year ago I found out that I had been fooled by whomever started and spread those rumors. It was inexcusably stupid of me to have believed them. I should have known those guys were insanely jealous of me and would do anything to hurt me. And I fell into their trap." He sighed: "I fantasized that we would have a chance to meet each other sometime, somewhere. I just wished to be able to see you again. When some people told me that you were still single I could not believe it. The exhilaration was overwhelming. It was as if I was brought back to life after being dead for years. ... Ying, how have you been?"

"Just busy, with school, with work." She looked at Kang Wei ruefully. Many thoughts rushed through her mind. This was the man she loved and lost. It was all her fault. Now he was back, still loved her as before. She must cherish him, not to let her childish pride stand in the way again.

"I apologize for my tardiness in replying. Being in a strange place, school, work, everything was demanding. But that was no excuse. Then your letters stopped coming. I thought someone else had entered your life. I could not imagine that some people were creating those malicious and ugly rumors to hurt me."

"They were meant to hurt me, Ying, not you. I am so sorry. It's my fault. I was foolish." Regret was written all over Kang Wei's face. The seriousness in his expression brought a smile to Ying Ying's face.

"Do you have someone in your life," she asked, half jestingly.

"No, no, how could I? I am in love with you," he said in such sincerity.

"And yet you allowed rumors to dictate your mind," Ying Ying said softly as if to herself.

He ignored that comment, took a deep breath, and said: "Ying, let's pick up where we have left off." It's that same determination and confidence Ying Ying was familiar with.

Kang Wei accompanied Ying Ying back to her apartment and bid her good night. He repressed his urge to embrace her. They stood by her door in silence. Then he took her hand and kissed it. They both felt a surge of emotion. The memory of their love flashed through their minds and hearts. Kang Wei pulled Ying Ying close and kissed her. They were brought back to their senior year in college, the time of their intimate courtship. The time lost between them was found.

"I will pick you up at your office after work tomorrow," he said when he finally lifted his lips from hers. It sounded so much like the first time he asked Ying Ying for a date: *I will pick you up Saturday at noon time in the parlor of your dorm.* It was a statement, not a question, leaving less room for a negative answer. Ying Ying who had rejected every young suitor to that point seemed to be hypnotized by this young man. From that moment on they shared one wonderful, sweet year of courtship.

It seemed a dream. All this time in America, she kept herself away from her new suitors as she did in her teenage years. Subconsciously she was waiting for Kang Wei.

Marriage was a logical and natural step for Ying Ying and Kang Wei. They must make up for the years they had lost. There was no time to waste. Their engagement was announced so suddenly it surprised all their friends. Beside Pei-hua no one knew Ying Ying and Kang Wei were in love in college. Every-one gave them their best wishes. The wedding could not be but a major event. All of their friends and those associated with China Society were eagerly waiting to attend it. Preparing for a wedding was laborious and time-consuming. Ying Ying had no time for it. Fortunately so many came to help. Old Huang's wife promised to design the flower arrangements although she had been out of the florist business after marrying the rich Jewish man. Missy, Tonia, and Pei-hua picked out several gowns for Ying Ying to make the final choice. And of course they bought themselves the bridesmaids' gowns. Kang Wei bought the rings and ordered the cake. Denis and Sam reserved the church, coordinated the dinner, and the dance. Yang Dan was to play Wagner's *Bridal Chorus* and Mendelssohn's *The Bridal March,* Zhi-an would sing *Because* at the ceremony. Ying Ying felt very pampered. For the first time other people were doing the work for her instead of her doing the work for other people

General and Mrs. Fang flew to Boston to attend their daughter's wedding. They only stayed for a week. When the newly-weds went to Barbados for a weeklong honeymoon, the older couple flew back to Taiwan to prepare for another wedding banquet. The banquet was large and sumptuous. All the relatives, General Fang's subordinates, Mrs. Fang's church friends, Ying Ying and Kang Wei's school chums were all there. The day after the banquet their college schoolmates invited them to a dinner at a luxury restaurant. It was like a class reunion. Many of them had children as old as ten. They cheered at the newly-weds, congratulated them, blessed them, also made fun of them as they toasted:

"Kang Wei, we would like to give you this award, for your determination, perseverance, persistence, and your final victory."

"Ying Ying, we thank you for your magnanimity and kindness for keeping Kang Wei's heart unbroken."

"Fourteen years!! Wow, from our freshman year when Kang Wei dedicated his heart to Ying Ying till now, when Ying Ying reciprocated."

"Ying Ying is as beautiful as when we first saw her. We have changed so much. Old Heaven is partial to her."

"Kang Wei has not changed either."

"I think during the years when they were apart, time froze for them. Thus their reunion is a seamless continuation from the past."

They wished to have more time in Taiwan but they, especially Ying Ying, had to rush back to work that included searching for a replacement for Denis who had left China Society to further his graduate study in Chinese history. He wished to get a Ph.D. then teach in a college.

*   *   *   *

Ying Ying's wedding incited Pei-hua to think about her own marriage. She had heard too much from her mother. And it was true that she had passed a bride's age, according to the common notion of her mother's generation. Her parents were not pleased with her entangling with an actor from China. They thought she was throwing her youthful years away. More than urging her to get married they urged her to find a good man with a normal, respectable profession. "Someone who is on a par with you and deserves you" they said.

As for herself, she only wished Li Yong would bring up the issue of marriage. They had been courting for years. But separated by geographical distance their closeness remained spiritual; their connection was held by a telephone line. She would much prefer a long letter that revealed the inner feelings and emotions of his, that she could keep forever, to read over and over again. But Li Yong had no the time to write. She even had to wait for days for a short call sometimes. When she called, it always caught him at a bad time. She understood. But it did not ease her frustration. It appeared to her that if she did not take the initiative their wedding date would be indefinite. Yet it would be too difficult for her to bring it up. A marriage proposal should come from the man, not her. She hesitated, brooded over it. A dreaded thought forayed her mind. In fact it was not the first time such a thought had roiled her. She ignored it, or perhaps "repressed it" would be a more accurate description.

Does Li Yong love me anymore? Do I still hold a place in his heart? Or has it become a meaningless habit for him to see me and have me visit him? If he loves me why doesn't he propose marriage? If he doesn't care why should I marry him?

She wished to open her heart to Ying Ying. But she felt that her position in Ying Ying's mind had shifted after Ying Ying married Kang Wei. She was a little hurt but buried the thought deep inside her. For weeks she avoided Ying Ying. One evening Ying Ying knocked on her best friend's door. Pei-hua opened the door, without a word she let Ying Ying in. Ying Ying felt a twinge by the desolate look on Pei-hua.

"Pei-hua, why didn't you return my calls?" Ying Ying's complaint was mixed with loving friendship and concern. "Don't keep me away, please."

"I didn't." Pei-hua forced the words from her mouth. She glanced at Ying Ying and spoke again: "I haven't been well."

"You were not well? Why didn't you let me know? Are you all right now?"

Ying Ying took Pei-hua's words as referring to her physical health.

"No I didn't mean that. I am all right. I just feel lonely sometimes. Life seems so vacuous."

"I understand, Pei-hua." Sympathetically Ying Ying tried to find words to console her friend. "I am sorry that Kang Wei has occupied some of my time that used to belong to us. But Pei-hua, he has not taken me from you, not in the least."

"I know, I know. Don't be silly. You are married. You should spend time with him and allow him to occupy your mind and heart. Don't apologize to me. We are good friends. But you and Kang Wei are husband and wife, and lovers."

Kang Wei had been a good friend to Pei-hua and Li Yong. Whenever Li Yong came to Boston the four of them would get together in their home in Cambridge. Kang Wei would prepare a good dinner. He was a better cook than Ying Ying. They always had such wonderful conversations over tea. Sometimes they drank a little wine. Ying Ying, however, couldn't join them because wine did not agree with her palate"

"Pei-hua, when will you and Li Yong be married?" Ying Yiing had brooded over this question for some time. It hit the sore spot in Pei-hua.

"How do I know? Ask Li Yong." She said ruefully.

"I meant to bring it up to him. If you allow, I will when he comes up here the next time."

Pei-hua made no comment.

A week later Pei-hua and Li-Yong were in Ying-Ying-and-Kang-Wei's home. Ying Ying put out a plate of hors d'oeuvres, a bowl of cut fruits, and a bottle of wine. Kang Wei poured it in three glasses and in the fourth glass he filled it with Seven Up and handed it to Ying Ying.

"Pretend this is wine," Kang Wei winked at Ying Ying.

"I don't need to pretend. Tea tastes so much better."

"Ying Ying doesn't care if it's socially fashionable to have a glass of wine in hand at parties and functions. She is always herself," Li Yong commented.

"Yes, she is always her lovely and admirable self. She doesn't follow the crowd." Kan Wei could never refrain himself from lauding his wife every chance he got.

"Everyone admires Ying Ying," Pei-hua acclaimed with sincerity.

"All right. That's enough. For all these sweet talks I'll have to treat you with my favorite dish, the one I can cook well," Ying Ying conceded with a smile.

"Thank you. Great fortune will descend on our taste buds," Li Yong said cheerfully.

"*hui-guo-rou* (Return-to-the-Pot Pork) ? Mmmm, that's my favorite" Pei-hua exclaimed.

"Wait till you see what Kang Wei is going to cook," Ying Ying offered.

"We can't wait. Which of your specialties are you going to cook for us," Pei-hua asked.

"As a starter, Hot and Sour Soup with tiny tofu dices, finely sliced pork, parched tiger lily petals, tree ears, parched mushrooms, and minced scallion.

Then diced chicken breasts with pine nuts and shredded red pepper and scallion. The others I will keep as a surprise."

"My mouth is watering. Kang Wei, when is you restaurant open to the public," Pei-hua jokingly exclaimed. "Ying Ying you are so lucky to have such a good chef cooking for you everyday."

"But I have to curb my appetite and watch my weight. That's not so easy." Ying Ying was half serious.

Kang Wei excused himself and retreated to the kitchen. Pei-hua suggested that they all go to the kitchen to help him.

"It's not fair to let him do all the work by himself. We should at least give him a hand on small things, like handing him a bowl or something."

"Yea, good idea. He can cook and talk with us at the same time," Ying Ying said. So they all got up and moved to the kitchen with their wine and hors d'oeuvres.

Kang Wei had already prepared all his ingredients and was ready to cook. Yng Ying took out a big slab of pork with skin and fat for making "Return to the Pot Pork." She put it in a pot of water to boil while getting the other ingredients ready. The pork was boiled till just done. She cut it into thin slices and proceeded to the steps in cooking that dish.

"It's a complicated process. Must you sauté each ingredient separately? Can you cook them altogether at once?" While watching Ying Ying Li Yong noticed the tedious process. "My style is called 'All in One Pot.' Everything is dumped in a pot at the same time and I let it boil," he laughed.

"That can't be called a style. That is survival food," Kang Wei smirked. "I am the cook in this household. Ying Ying would fire me if I served her survival food."

"I can't believe it. Ying Ying is spoiled rotten by you. All-in-One-Pot was what she used to do," Pei-hua protested.

"Look who's talking? At least my meals did not consist of Kentucky Fried Chicken, McDonald hamburgers and Taco Bell Sandwiches like somebody I know," Ying Ying retorted.

As they were bantering Kang Wei already made the Hot and Sour Soup, salted the flounder, sliced stalks of scallion and pieces of ginger, minced sections of garlic and covered them on the fish. Then he was ready to prepare and cook his other dishes of meat, poultry and shrimp. Li Yong admiringly remarked:

"Ying Ying you are so fortunate to have such a husband. You didn't wait in vain."

Kang Wei smiled and said: "I am the fortunate one. I have waited so long to show her my cooking prowess. Fate did not disappoint me." He reached out his arm to encircle Ying Ying's waist and give it a squeeze. The bowl of liquid spice-mixture Ying Ying was going to hand to Kang Wei almost spilled at his jerky motion.

"Watch it," she alerted.

"Sorry," Kang Wei apologized. He turned to Pei-hua and asked: "Pei-hua, when will you make Li Yong a fortunate man like Ying Ying has made me?"

"Yea, when will you two let us drink your wine-of-happiness," Ying Ying asked.

Li Yong was caught off guard. Pei-hua evaded the issue. Silence befell among the three for a second. Not allowing the atmosphere to freeze Ying Ying jumped back to salvage the situation.

"Anyway, we want to have our gatherings at your house."

"I ... I am afraid..." Li Yong stuttered: "We won't be ... " As all three were disappointed and stunned by his abrupt answer, he continued: "living in Boston or its suburbs."

A silent sigh of relief was let out by the three. Ying Ying broke the ice by casually remarking:

"Well, that doesn't matter. We will chase you wherever you are. New York?"

"This is a hard issue. And it's why I have not brought it up to Pei-hua. Boston is not conducive to my career as an actor. But Boston is where Pei-hua's career is based."

"For you New York is best. Pei-hua doesn't have to be rooted in Boston either." Kang Wei sensed the time was ripe for him to push. "I relocated because of Ying Ying and at that time I wasn't even sure whether she would have me."

"It only takes a bar examination for Pei-hua to get a license. That will be easy for her. And New York is not that far. We can still get together as much as we want." Ying Ying gave it another push.

"Pei-hua, would you consider it?" Li Yong turned to face Pei-hua.

"Hey, that sounds like a proposal. Do it right. Drop on your knees," Kang Wei jested. Pei-hua smiled with a blush.

"Would you prefer to do it in private or do you mind having your best friends witness this memorable moment," Ying Ying demanded.

Without responding to Kang Wei and Ying Ying, Li Yong dropped his right knee in front of Pei-hua and held her hand:

"Pei-hua, would you marry me?"

Pei-hua was not expecting it to happen so suddenly. She glanced at Ying Ying and Kang Wei and turned her eyes on Li Yong:

"I ..." She paused.

"Say yes, Pei-hua, say yes," Ying Ying and Kang Wei both urged.

"I didn't prepare a ring tonight. Please say yes and we will go get a ring together tomorrow," Li Yong pleaded.

"Yes," Pei-hua said in a whisper. The most major event in a person's life as the Chinese labeled it, was settled right there witnessed by her best friends. It was meant to be. And it was what she wanted for a long time. She was exhilarated, feeling blessed and looking forward to a life-long of happiness. Li Yong rose to his feet and pulled Pei-hua from her seat. He kissed her. This kind of behavior, kissing in front of people, was rare among the Chinese. Pei-hua blushed and drew away from his embrace. But everyone knew how much she enjoyed that kiss.

Pei-hua was not an ostentatious woman who relished showing her things with flourish. But the wedding was such an important event in her life. She must mark it in grand style short of breaking her and Li Yong's financial limits. She picked out a two-carat solitaire as her engagement ring and an eight-diamond channel set wedding band. Li Yong's wedding ring echoed hers. Her custom-designed and tailored gown had a thirty-feet-long train. As the figure ten signifies completeness, she was to have ten bride's maids including Ying Ying as her maid of honor. Kang Wei was to be the best man plus nine groom's men.

Their parents came and stayed at the Ritz. Pei-hua's mother brought five designer-dresses for her to change into during the banquet. In order to get the visa Li Yong's parents had to show the U.S. consulate their son's wedding invitation and a letter from their daughter-in-law-to-be, Pei-hua, written on her law firm's stationary, inviting them to attend the wedding. They wouldn't have asked Pei-hua for the letter had she not been an attorney of a reputable law firm in Boston. They thought the letter would carry much weight. It had indeed. Their interviewer at the U.S. consulate in Shanghai, even made a friendly remark about it:

"So you will have an American lawyer as a daughter-in-law!!" The tension at the interview was thus eased. The interviewer followed with a routine question.

"You don't intend to stay in the United States. for long, I mean you have no intention of immigrating to America, do you?"

They swore that they did not.

The wedding ceremony was held at Trinity Church in Boston. Although both Pei-hua and Li Yong were not Christians yet they like the solemn atmosphere of the church.

The wedding banquet was held at the Ritz. Imperial China Restaurant in Chinatown catered the food. The restaurant's owner and chef recommended a fifteen-course menu. A new dish called "Lung Feng Pei" (Dragon Weds Phoenix) was created. In Chinese tradition Dragon was a symbol of the emperor and Phoenix the empress. The commoners were not permitted to use these symbols except at a wedding. Dragon and phoenix were also borrowed to symbolize the groom and the bride. A bride could wear a headdress adorned with a filigreed phoenix.

They invited all their friends, acquaintances, and Pei-hua's college alumni to the wedding. Denis had kept in close touch and friendship with Ying Ying, Pei-hua and some others although he was back to school and not working at China Society. He would not miss Pei-hua's wedding for the world. And his well wishing couched in most sincere words and expressed in his eyes touched Pei-hua's heart.

Pei-hua dazzled her guests each time she changed into a Chinese dress her mother brought from Taiwan. It was customary for brides to do this quasi "fashion show" at her wedding banquet in Taiwan. Pei-hua's five dresses were specially designed for her fashioned after different styles of ladies' robes of different periods--Manchu royal robes of the 18th and late 19th century complete with the court lady's headdress and elevated flower-pot-soled shoes; a dress of Han woman during the Manchu dynasty; a hundred-pleat-skirt and bell-shaped-sleeves of the early 20th century; and a beaded and limestone-studded red silk long dress of mid-20th century.

For their honeymoon they went to Europe for a week. Pei-hua would have preferred a longer one but Li Yong was doing a show on Broadway and one week of leave was all he could get. The parents were sent on a European cruise for two weeks. Kang Wei booked the cruise and made all the necessary arrangements long before they came to the wedding.

*   *   *   *

Through the years Ying Ying had published several scholarly monographs on Chinese vernacular architecture, Ming dynasty gardens, and the influence of Chinese art on European decorative art, and numerous other articles. Her reputation as a recognized scholar brought her many speaking engagements in New England and elsewhere. As Herald Schmidt was retiring from the Board he nominated Ying Ying to succeed him as International Foundation's president. At the same time several other arts establishments and museums invited her to join their boards or committees. The city asked her to chair the Public Arts committee, and join other special project committees. She was indeed a prominent leader in Boston's arts and cultural communities, and accordingly was awarded medals and citations for her contributions.

She initiated a number of new programs for the Foundation. A monthly jazz concert series, a contemporary music series, an international folk music series, and a modern dance series strengthened the Foundation's music and dance offerings. The Boston Jazz Orchestra was formed to give monthly concerts. It consisted of twenty high-caliber musicians. The contemporary music series was curate by a committee of five members. In addition, she also opened the Foundation's facilities to other jazz and folk musicians to apply for their use.

The media quickly noticed Ying Ying's patronage of jazz music. Articles in the papers elaborated on the jazz series and favorably reviewed the concerts. More than once was Ying Ying thrust into the center of attention. One newspaper printed:

> Due to the International Foundation's sponsorship jazz is once again thriving in Boston's cultural landscape. What's amazing is that this long overdue revival has been brought about by a Chinese woman.

But why was it unusual for a Chinese to sponsor American jazz music? Asian impresarios sponsored western classical music all the time and it did not raise any eyebrow.

Among the thick pile of daily mail on her desk Ying Ying notice one from the Ministry of Culture of the People's Republic of China. She opened it with curiosity. It was a letter from the Minister inviting her to attend the biannual arts symposium in Beijing and to give a series of lectures. She wondered how the Ministry of Culture knew of her.

The following day she received a call.

"Hello Dr. Fang, How are you? I am Chen Lo, Cultural Attaché at the office of Chinese Consulate General in New York," the gentleman introduced himself.

"Hello. How are you," Ying Ying returned the greeting. *Oh, that must be it. They recommended me to Beijing.*

"I am well, thank you. Have you received a letter of invitation from the Ministry of Culture?"

"Yes, I received it yesterday. I was wondering how they knew about me. It must have been a recommendation from someone in the Consulate General's office. It was you, wasn't it," Ying Ying said in a pleasant voice and smiled.

"No, no, no. You don't need our recommendation. You are a famous scholar and a leader in the arts in Massachusetts. People knew you from newspaper reports and TV interviews. Your accomplishments and your position in the mainstream society have brought pride to us Chinese people." Chen Lo spoke in the usual government bureaucrat's rhetoric.

"No, you overstate it. I don't deserve it," Ying Ying replied with humility.

"You are too modest, Dr. Fang. That is because you have all the virtues of a highly educated Chinese. Our government pays close attention to every one of those distinguished overseas Chinese. They know a lot about you," Chen Lo said.

Wow, great intelligence work. I am being watched, Ying Ying thought. Chen Lo continued:

"The Ministry of Culture has informed us to assist you in anyway we can to make your travel to China as convenient and pleasant as possible. I am glad that I have the honor to assist you before you go. Your lectures will be presented in September. After you purchase your plane ticket please send me your passport and I will see to it that the visa will be issued immediately. In the mean time please don't hesitate to call me if I can be of any help at all."

Ying Ying was impressed with Chen Lo's polite language. She often heard people commenting on how the Chinese officials were lacking in courtesy even to the point of being blunt.

"Thank you Mr. Chen. I am sure I will need your help."

She replied to the Ministry of Culture, accepting the invitation with gratitude. The Ministry wrote another politely versed letter to let her know that her hotel room would be reserved in the five-star Great Wall Hotel. Her traveling expenses would be reimbursed. She would be accompanied by the hosts to visit many scenic and historical sites.

The trip was three months away. September was a busy month. She had to make plans and arrangements thoroughly so that smooth operation of the Foundation and its programming would not be affected by her absence.

Chapter 8

With Ying Ying being appointed to succeed Harold Schmidt's position as International Foundation's President, her post at China Society was vacant. The Board had not found a suitable candidate to fill it. As such Ying Ying was asked by the Board to temporarily assume the role of Acting President and Trustee until the search for her successor succeeded. She had offices at both China Society and International Foundation. The Chinese community still regarded her the head of China Society and people from China continued to go to her for advice and help.

There were some writers including poets who were labeled as dissidents by the Chinese government and fled to the States. They lived a meager bohemian life, often got together in an artist's cluttered studio to drink, smoke and discuss politics, and vent their dissatisfaction and pent up feelings. They had no regular income except for small pay from odd jobs here and there. Civil-minded attorneys donated services to help a couple of them get political asylum and permanent U.S. residency. It was quite unexpected to most people because of the stigma lawyers sustained of gauging clients rather than helping them on a voluntary basis.

Ying Ying read some of those writers' works. She was fetched by the work of one poet, Liang Hai, with his seemingly austere, unpolished diction and transcendent oracular implications. She nominated him for writer-in-resident to China Society's Board. The Board voted unanimously to grand him the position, a stipend, and a room as his study. It provided him with a simple but stable life and an obligation to write. He came to his study everyday like a staff only to sit in the room with pens and paper. He refused to use a computer saying that a computer would deprive posterity of the writer's manuscripts and thinking process that was revealed in his corrections and changes made on the manuscript.

"A whole branch of research would deem extinct in human civilization," he said. He also refused to learn how to drive a car. "I prefer a more *primitive* way of life." Ying Ying had no comment on this. But when Liang Hai refused to learn English Ying Ying thought it was too extreme.

"What's wrong with learning English? You are living in an English-speaking world. How could you isolate yourself from the society at large?" she questioned.

"I don't want it to interfere with my Chinese language. I am afraid to lose the purity of my native language with which I write poetry." He made his point.

"But it will not. Many writers write in different languages. I move between English and Chinese languages easily, for example. I feel no impediment from one to the other," Ying Ying argued. Liang Hai just smiled, without a reply. Since then, however, Ying Ying noticed an English-Chinese dictionary on his desk. And he would come to Ying Ying's office sometimes to ask about the meaning or spelling of a word. Ying Ying did not make a comment but was happy that he had agreed with her.

Zhou Ping was a self-claimed journalist and publisher. He proposed that China Society form a new publishing department. He also recommended himself as director of this new department. He showed Ying Ying his many citations and photographs of him taken with important Chinese political leaders. Ying Ying was not the least impressed, contrary to what he had expected. She had a particular distaste for such inane show-offs. She knew the kind who pushed their way into having a picture taken with the illustrious, to steal a little glory from those famous people. *Rubbing shoulders with important people won't get you too far, at least not here.*

"Although I am the Acting President, I cannot dictate our programs and activities. The Board must vote on it. I am afraid we have no plan to start a publishing department." Ying Ying declined Zhou Ping's proposal.

How much did he really know about publishing? He wishes to head the department. But he does not even speak English. However, she allowed him to use a desk and telephone everyday as if he were a volunteer.

"Thank you." Zhou Ping said, disregarding Ying Ying's assertion of not being the sole decision maker. In his mind, Ying Ying had the power. "It's all right that you don't pay me now. I will work on the idea. One day soon you will see my result and gladly offer me the job."

A few weeks later he spoke with Ying Ying again persuading her to invite a Tibetan priest who was also a respected herbal medicine expert, as he claimed, to come and give lectures and lead workshops.

"I knew this priest very well. I can ask him to come. There will be no expense on your part. It's an exchange of favors. You give him a way to come and see America, he gives you his service in return."

After some consideration Ying Ying recommended the idea to the Board. "I guess we can present the lectures. But we must make sure that he will not overstay his visa," one Trustee said. Ying Ying said she would convey this point to Zhou Ping.

She said to Zhou Ping: "He has to go back to China after the event. You must guarantee that. We wouldn't want to infract the immigration law." Zhou Ping gave her his staunch promise.

Some time passed, Zhou Ping told Ying Ying that he had found a job in a restaurant. He left that day. Ying Ying never saw or heard from him again. As for the Tibetan priest, he never showed up. It was a mystery whether he had come or not.

Liang Hai was prolific in the peaceful and quiet environment, free of all worries and responsibilities. His new works and some selected older pieces were compiled for publication. An American friend of his translated some of them for a poetry periodical. This friend was also a writer.

One day after an art opening, Liang Hai showed Ying Ying a sleeve of slides. and said: "This artist is an old acquaintance of mine. I first met him in Yunnan. We have kept in contact. What do you think of his work?"

Ying Ying lifted the plastic sleeve up against the light for a quick glance and said, "I will tell you after I look at them on the light table."

She strode to the slide-viewing-light-table and turned it on. Then she laid the slides on it and carefully reviewed them. The paintings were sweeping gestures of broad ink brushes on paper. In each vaporous piece was a tenuous form emerging from the amorphous, atmospheric, hazy surface. There was also tension and strength emitting from the pieces. Ying Ying liked the work.

"Where is he?" Ying Ying read the label on a slide. "Fang Kuei, that's his name? What does he want to do?" Ying Ying sensed that Liang Hai was trying to get a show for his friend.

"He is in Italy. Yes, Fang Kuei." Liang Hai grinned: "Uh, he and you have the same ancestor five hundred years ago. He sent me these slides, sort of like 'throwing a stone to feel the road.'"

A very good analogy, Ying Ying thought. In the darkness of night when nothing ahead was certain, you had to throw a stone to find out if there was a creek, a ditch awaiting for you to fall into, or a rock, or a large tree blocking the way. The Chinese had a saying for every occasion and situation. By extension, in this case it was Fang Kuei testing if his work would interest some galleries in Boston.

"Do you think he is good enough to deserve a show at your gallery?" Liang Hai finally asked.

"Yes, he is quite good," Ying Ying replied. "I'll see if there is a slot I can give him."

She and Fang Kuei had several telephone conversations. He sent her his dossier and additional slides. She decided to offer him an artist-in-residence for three months beside an exhibition. The residency would start in January of the following year, six months from the time they talked. During the interim she planned a series of activities for him. He was to create a body of new works at a studio provided to him; head a panel discussion with four Boston artists with audience from China Society's membership; give three workshops for students participating in China Society's Education Outreach program; and he would be visiting the museums and galleries or attending opening receptions in and around Boston.

The pieces to be shown were selected from his slides. Announcements were sent out a month before the show opened. Press interviews and TV appearances were arranged. Two weeks before the show opened, a very tall and dark Chinese man stood in front of Ying Ying's office when she arrived shortly after 9am.

"Hi." Ying Ying nodded at the man as she opened her door.

"Hi, Fang Ying Ying. I am Fang Kuei.," the man said as he followed her into her office.

Rarely did people address Ying Ying by her full name. They either called her Ying Ying or Dr. Fang. Did the artist add the last name just to show that he had the same? It did cross Ying Ying's mind.

"Yes. When did you arrive? Did you see Liang Hai yet?" Of course he must have seen Liang Hai. Why ask? But it seemed the natural thing to say.

"Yes, I was in his studio talking earlier. I came here yesterday. I am staying with Liang Hai."

"That's good." Ying Ying hung up her coat; took a couple of folders from her briefcase to put on her desk. She often brought work home. She took her seat behind the large desk. "Did Liang Hai show you your studio?"

"Yes, it is very nice. Big." Fang Kuei pulled a chair close to Ying Ying's desk and sat down. "What should I do now?"

"Officially art exhibits are our Curator's territory. Although your show was arranged by me, I still should introduce you to Dr. Joseph Lee, the Curator. But first, you can start bringing your paintings to the frame workshop, and painting materials to your studio. I assume your paintings need to be stretched or framed or prepared in some way before they can be hung. Those should be done in the workshop." Fang Kuei's paintings included oil on canvas, and ink-and-color on paper, all unframed.

"I need to stretch the canvases because I have taken them down from the stretchers before the trip. The works-on-paper are mostly mounted on scrolls. There are some smaller pieces that have to be framed."

Three different formats!! Ying Ying immediately put her mind on how to set the show up so that the formats would not clash.

"Okay. We have work to do. I suppose you can stretch the canvases yourself. Can you frame the small pieces? If you can we have all the tools and unassembled frames of various sizes in the workshop."

"I always stretch my own canvases. As for framing I don't see why I cannot do it. Artists should be doing these things themselves. It would be cheaper, for one."

"We will need at least two days to hang the show. You have to get ready."

"No problem. I can also help with the hanging. It may not take two days." Fang Kuei sounded very confident and experienced.

"All right. Get on it then. Do you need a car to bring your things in?" Although she asked the question she did not have a way to provide him with a car unless he or Denis used her car. But Denis was busy on another project, and Fang Kuei must not have had a Massachusetts driver's license.

"I will call a taxi." A good answer!

Fang Kuei worked diligently, following Ying Ying's instruction. He found the hardware store nearby to get what he needed for stretching and framing his pieces. He spent all his time in the framing workshop. Occasionally he went to talk with Liang Hai in his study. Ying Ying did not see him much.

The two days intended for hanging the show was more than sufficient with

Fang Kuei's assistance. Ying Ying and Fang Kuei worked together laying out the show with three formats separated, moving the pieces around until the show looked pleasing and coherent in the gallery.

Over a hundred people attended the reception. Many were the gallery's regular attendants. Ying Ying was surprised when Dong Fei-yan walked up to her.

"Fei-yan, glad to see you. Where have you been all this time?" Ying Ying smiled and asked.

"Everywhere. I have come back a while ago though. Just didn't have time to drop by. I got your announcement and thought I'd come to check it out." Dong Fei-yan smirked. "The artist is so handsome." She whispered with a naughty titter. She did not make any comment on the art. Fang Kuei's six feet two inch height and hundred eighty pound frame, a full head of wavy dark hair and bushy eye brows, angular feature, firm jaw and piercing eyes arrested Dong Fei-yan on the first sight.

"Oh? I paid no attention to any of the artists' looks." Ying Ying said plainly. She remembered how excited Fei-yan was when she saw Meng Song in her office that time.

"You are not a woman then." Dong Fei-yan cast another glance at the artist standing a few feet away with a glass of wine in hand talking with his audience.

"Oh, I see. I didn't know that constantly falling head over heels for men is a criterion of being a woman." Ying Ying's annoyance over Dong Fei-yan's laxity was obvious.

"Ai, don't be so serious all the time. But it's natural for a woman to desire men," Dong Fei-yan spoke self-righteously. "I am going to speak to him." Before Ying Ying could utter another word Dong Fei-yan had already scooted toward Fang Kuei. She did not speak with Ying Ying the rest of the evening. The next day Dong Fei-yan came to fetch Fang Kuei. She was to take the latter to the Museum of Fine Arts, after that, to elsewhere sightseeing.

"Shall we let Fang Ying Ying know? I am supposed to be working on my new work," Fang Kuei asked.

"No need. She is not your boss. What could she do to you? Let's just go," Dong Fei-yan urged.

"I still think we should let her know. In case she wants to speak to me about something."

"All right, if you insist." Fei-yan was a little impatient.

They went to Ying Ying's office. She was on the phone. Dong Fei-yan interrupted her and interjected:

"Ying Ying, I am taking Fang Kuei to the MFA, okay? See you later, may be,"

Ying Ying did not hear what she had said. She only saw Dong Fei-yan tugging on Fang Kuei's sleeve and pulling him away while his head was still facing Ying Ying intending to speak to her.

After Ying Ying finished her phone conversation she could not find the two. She went to ask Liang Hai.

220

"Where did Fang Kuei go? Did Dong Fei-yan take him somewhere? I didn't hear what she said because I was on the phone when they came to my office."

"Dong Fei-yan is taking him sightseeing, and going to the Museum as well, I think." Liang Hai replied innocently.

"Did he know that he was supposed to be working on his new paintings?" Ying Ying was vexed. But she should not have spoken to Liang Hai; she should speak to Fang Kuei directly.

Fang Kuei did not come back that whole day, or the next day. Ying Ying was acerbated. *Does this man have any sense?* She called Liang Hai to her office.

"Is Fang Kuei staying with you? Why does he not come to do his work? The panel discussion is coming up. Is he going to be present? Does he know that he has certain responsibilities to fulfill? Our organization did not sponsor him to come here so that he could have fun."

"He did not come to my place after the opening. I did not hear a word from him. I thought he must have gotten your permission to take time off," Liang Hai conceded. "I will give Dong Fei-yan a call. She must know where he is."

"It is preposterous that she knows where he is and we don't. Who is his sponsor?" Ying Ying said irefully.

Fei-yan had not been so excited for quite a long time. Deep down in her heart she thought she had captured a prey.   She pulled in the driveway of her house in Topsfield. Fang Kuei had never seen a colonial-style house before. He walked around to see the snow-covered backyard before following Fei-yan into the house. Fei-yan gave him a pair of slippers. He declined.

"I'll just take my shoes off. No slippers. Socks are comfortable." He looked around as he followed her to the kitchen.

"Your husband is not home?" The total silence spoke of an empty house.

"No, he is at work. He still has one class in the afternoon." Dong Fei-yan pointed to the sofa: "Have a seat and feel at home. Would you like some tea?" She put the teakettle on the burner; put tealeaves in a small teapot and began to take things from the refrigerator.

"I will make a salad and fried noodles for lunch. How's that?" she asked while pouring the boiling water into the teapot.

"Let me help you." Fang Kuei strode over to carry the teapot and cups to the table and filled the cups with tea. "Come here and have tea with me. I will cook the lunch for you." It was a command. Yet those words sounded awfully intimate to Dong Fei-yan's ears. Her senses were soothed, a tingling feeling aroused. After all, she was the kind of a woman most sensitive to masculine attractiveness.

Radiance beamed on her face; sweetness surged in her heart. She moved to sit close to him on the sofa.

A kiss? An embrace? Perhaps more? Dong Fei-yan expected it. But Fan Kuei made no such move. *Not on the first date*, if this could be called a date. A man of ample experiences with women, he knew better. That would be too hasty, too easy. *This woman obviously had a crush on me. Why not let her itch and be inflamed?*

A day later Liang Hai put a call to Dong Fei-yan, but to no avail. He tried several times. Finally Brandon answered the phone. He told Liang Hai that Fei-yan had just taken Fang Kuei to New York to see exhibits at the Met, the Guggenheim, Whitney and some other art galleries. She was also taking him to visit tourist attractions.

"I don't know when they will be back. She didn't tell me," Brandon added dispassionately. Liang Hai had to convey this information to Ying Ying. She was not surprised but one thought hit her: *Letting the two go out of town together? Brandon, you are inviting trouble.* She did not reveal that thought to Liang Hai. She only said:

"It doesn't sound like he will be back for the panel discussion next Tuesday. What do I tell the other panelists and the audience?" She was not asking Liang Hai for suggestions but to vent her indignation.

"I think you may have to prepare for the worst." Liang Hai offered a suggestion anyway, warily. "Maybe you'd better get one or two other Chinese artists to take his place in case he goofs off."

"That is the only option now. I will ask two artists to prepare for the discussion and cancel the translator." Ying Ying was speaking to herself. "I am going to cancel his other engagements and withdraw our sponsorship. He is on his own from now on."

Ying Ying picked up the phone and called two other artists to replace Fang Kuei. The panel discussion was on the following Tuesday, only four days away. Yet the two artists happily accepted the assignment.

On Tuesday morning Fang Kuei came to Ying Ying's office in an insouciant manner.

"Hey, how are you? Is the panel discussion still on?" He asked.

Ying Ying lifted her eyes from the document she was reviewing. She was irate. *Still on? Do you think a scheduled event is a child's game? It can be scratched because you irresponsibly walked away?*

"Is the panel discussion still on? Of course it is still on? Why wouldn't it be?" Ying Ying replied to his question with a question in a cold tone and indifferent manner. "But you are not. I have asked two other artists to take your place."

"Oh." Fang Kuei was obviously stupefied. Had he talked with Liang Hai first he would not have been. But he came in late already and did not have a chance to stop by Liang's study.

"I don't know about China or Italy. But here in our organization everyone must be responsible and self-reliant. There are rules and regulations to abide to. China Society did not invite you here to tour the scenic sites. You can do that after you have fulfilled the requirements of an artist-in-residence. You have broken our rules, taken our sponsorship lightly. We can't but withdraw our sponsorship. I am also going to cancel all the workshops and museum visits for you. I suppose you don't care about them anyway."

Fang Kuei did not expect the situation to deteriorate so. As if his tongue

222

was tied. He could not utter a word.

Ying Ying rose to her feet, picked up her bag and strode to the coat hanger. "Sorry, I have to attend a meeting. You can talk to Bruce and Liang Hai about what to do." Ying Ying left her office leaving Fang Kuei gaping in bewilderment. He could not communicate with Bruce, the visual arts coordinator, nor did he have the interest to speak with him. He went to Liang Hai.

"Fang Ying Ying has a hot temper, hasn't she? How does she treat you?"

"No, she does not have a hot temper. In fact she is even tempered and she treats people very well. But she does not tolerate irresponsible and unreliable people," Liang Hai stated candidly. "She made all those arrangements for you. And you left without a word. Now at the last minute, she has to call some artists to replace you."

"Those activities are not important to me. It's not what I want. I only want to have the show," Fang Kuei said apathetically.

"But the artist-in-residence program is not just to mount a show. There is an agreement between you and China Society. She meant to make your visit more fulfilling and meaningful. You should not have treated it so lightly."

"What now?" Fang Kuei asked

"She said she would withdraw her sponsorship. You have no more association with China Society. I suppose you should move your things out of the art studio."

"Just as well. It will be difficult for me to come anyway. Dong Fei-yan asked me to stay in her house. I have no transportation to get here." He seemed relieved.

"What is going on between you and Dong Fei-yan? Remember she is married. Don't get yourself in a big mess." Liang Hai gave him a friendly advice.

"Nothing," Fang Kuei lied. "What can go on between she and I? There is nothing about her that attracts me. But it's good to have someone so eager to please me. She takes so much pleasure in catering to my needs. Without her how would I get to go to New York, Washington and other places? Who would take me? Certainly not Fang Ying Ying."

"How could you even mention Dr. Fang in this context?" Liang Hai was irritated by Fang Kuei's flippancy. He demanded poignantly.

"I know, I know. Fang Ying Ying is the president, a big shot. Of course she wouldn't take me sightseeing," Fang Kuei mocked sarcastically.

"Don't even think of comparing her to those women you can exploit, okay?" Liang Hai was annoyed. "But let's not argue. Just be grateful that she gave you the opportunity to come here and have a show. Do you know how many artists send in applications regularly?" Liang Hai exclaimed.

Fang Kuei ignored Liang's remark and said: "Let me call Dong Fei-yan to pick up my things." He used Liang Hai's phone to make the call. Before the morning drew to an end Dong Fei-yan had already put Fang Kuei and all his painting materials in her car and sped away.

"What is it with Fang Ying Ying?" Dong Fei-yan turned to give him a leer and asked.

"Who knows? She had a fit and fired me," Fang Kuei jeered scornfully.

"She can't fire you. You are not her staff. You are an artist-in-residence. She should treat you with respect and politeness." Such a remark definitely kindled Fang Kuei's resentment.

"Never mind her. She can't do anything to you. Don't ever see her again," Fei-yan further provoked.

Fei-yan took Fang Kuei to the Museum of Fine Arts, the Gardner Museum, the Peabody Museum in Salem, and galleries on Newberry Street. She also took him to see a ballet at the Wang Center, and *Sheer Madness* at the Charles Play House. She had to scratch her plans for plays at the Huntington Theatre and American Repertory Theatre because Fang Kuei did not know English; even *Sheer Madness* made no sense to him. All this time Brandon treated him like a member of the family, never questioned Dong Fei-yan how long was this guest going to be in their house.

After three weeks Fang Kuei felt sated. He also felt like a pet on a leash. He called Liang Hai.

"What? Tired of the lady's boudoir?" Liang Hai jeered pointedly, mercilessly penetrating into Fang Kuei's heart.

"You rascal. Don't make fun of me," Fang Kuei replied in his usual carefree manner. "Let's go to some bar tonight. I am tired of those museums, ballet, and opera stuff. Who can take that much culture anyway?"

"Ha ha," Liang Hai laughed. "You are all cultured out, eh? It's a stigma of ours. We are supposed to be immersed in culture day and night." Liang Hai was speaking his mind. He liked to frequent the bars and strip joints from time to time and had to hide the fact from Ying Ying. A poet was supposed to be beyond such vulgarity.

Fang Kuei told Fei-yan that he wanted to move back to Boston.

"Why? You don't like it here with me?" She was very disappointed. "I just told Brandon that you would stay put with us. He had no objection."

"That's just it," Fang Kuei commented impatiently. *Stay put with you? Have you consulted with me first? Do you own me?* "He is such a good man and so nice to me. I should not take advantage of him like this, living in his house, taking his wife, making him a cuckold. That's not the way I operate. Beside, I don't like to sneak around. If I want a woman, I will have the woman, not steal her from another man." Fang Kuei said irefully: "Please take me to the subway station. You don't have to drive me all the way into Boston."

Fang Kuei's stern words and bone-chilling tone stabbed Dong Fei-yan's heart like knives. *How despiteful a man can be!! Only a few hours ago he was lying in my bosom and now he speak in such sub-zero frigidity. What should I do? Well, I will not be a weakling; I will not beg him; I will not let him feel superior to me.*

"All right, suit yourself," Dong Fei-yan said impassively. She had guts. She would love without reservation when she felt the love, and turn love into hatred without hesitation. At the moment her heart was as cold and hard as a block of ice.

"Pick up your stuff. I will take you to the subway right now." She stunned Fang Kuei no less than Ying Ying did when the latter rescinded her sponsorship on him.

"What has America done to these women?!!" After describing what had happened, Fang Kuei further commented to Liang Hai that he had not met a Chinese woman with such bull-headed obstinacy: it must have been America that had changed these women, he thought.

"It's not that America has altered the characters of these women. These women were born with strong characters even though their individual personality may be entirely different." Liang Hai made a sensible assessment.

*   *   *   *

After being liberated from Dong Fei-yan's smothering passion Fang Kuei was refreshed by the feeling of freedom. The desire for doing something wild permeated his senses. He persuaded Liang Hai to take him to a topless bar on Washington Street a few short blocks from the Boston Common.

Liang Hai was a longhaired, fair-featured gentle soul. He appeared to be shy and quiet. But in the topless bar he was a different person. After a few drinks he began to flirt with a waitress, touching her hair and bare skin. The waitress brushed his hand off. He ignored that, and put his hand right back on her again while mumbling something indistinguishable. The waitress batted his hand away. He lurched forward, his body bumped into hers. The waitress became livid. She clenched her teeth and let out a repressed yell:

"Please, don't touch me."

At this moment two big security guards, one white and one black, about six-feet three or four-inches tall and weighed around 250 pounds, shaped like refrigerators, rushed over and grabbed Liang Hai by the arms and lifted him up, his feet kicking in the air as he struggle to free himself. The two big guys wouldn't let go of him. They scooted him out of the bar. Fang Kuei jumped over quickly and overtook the two big men outside the bar. He jerked his index finger first at Liang Hai and swiftly thrust toward the ground and shouted in Chinese:

"*Fang ta xia lai*!" (Put him down.)

The two guys could not understand what he said and did not care. At their toss, Liang Hai fell on the ground. Fang Kuei rapidly threw a fist on the white guy's face and flew a foot on the black guy's chest. Like two large pieces of timber the guys lurched and fell. It happened so quickly and off-guardedly that the two men didn't know what had happened. They scrambled to get up only to be kicked and knocked down again by Fang Kuei.

"*ta ma de, xiao zi, ni gan qifu zhongguo ren*?" (You goddamn son of a bitch, you dare mess with the Chinese?)

The two huge guys crawled several feet away before they scrambled to their feet and ran into the bar. There were some by-standers, some whistled, some clapped, all amazed at the martial prowess of this tall Chinese guy.

"All right!!! Martial art stunt."

The next day Fang Kuei and Liang Hai were strolling on Shawmut Street after having supper in a restaurant when suddenly a ruffian grabbed Liang Hai's bag and ran. Fang Kuei told Liang Hai to wait there, and he ran after the guy. He passed by a building under renovation with some construction debris in front of it. He picked up two broken pieces of cement block and continued running after the guy. The guy made a turn at a corner into a narrow side street. Fang Kuei followed him and saw three other guys, one with a knife in his hand the other two each had a piece of three-feet-long 2" x 4"s. He quickly slung one piece of his broken cement block and hit the guy with the knife on the chest. The guy stumbled and tried to run away. Fang Kuei slung the other piece of cement block at another guy and hit him on his neck. The guy dropped his lumber and fell on the ground. Fang Kuei jumped ahead and grabbed the two wounded men by their hair and knocked the two heads against each other several times. He yelled at the two running for their lives:

"*zhan zhu*!!" meaning "freeze." Of course the two did not understand and kept running. Two policemen ran into the fleeing rascals and grabbed them. Liang Hai was behind the cops.

The police asked Fang Kuei what had happened. Liang Hai translated the questions and answers with his limited English. The police got the gist and said to Liang Hai:

"Your friend has a lot of nerve chasing those gangsters. It's very dangerous, you know? They may have guns. Tell your friend not to be so foolish again."

Fang Kuei asked Liang Hai in Chinese "Did you call the police? Why?"

Liang Hai replied: "I was afraid you might kill the guys."

Fang Kuei also liked to roam the combat zone at night and watch the prostitutes accosting customers, and watch the flimsily garbed young women go in and out of nightclubs in the theatre district. Sometime he and Liang Hai were mistaken as a gay couple. He was so irritated that he wanted to beat up people again. Liang Hai stopped him.

"If you keep it up like that you will be in big trouble, I am telling you."

Dong Fei-yan's amorous snare never did catch Fang Kuei, not even for a moment. He had seen too much, experienced too much to fall into such a trap. He wasted no time to captivate several women. Magnetism was his innate attribute. Women easily fell spellbound by him.

He had only a few weeks left before his visa expired. He needed to legalize his stay after that.

Asking Ying Ying to extend his artist-residency was out of the question. He was fully aware that his offensive behavior had negated all chances for such a favor. The last resort would be picking a U.S. citizen to marry. Kathy Harris, the art consultant, or Marian McArthur, the manager of Hamel Art Gallery, would marry him at the drop of a hat if he would ask. He met them at the opening of his show. They asked him for dates lately and threw themselves at him with no effort on his part.

Kathy already sold a few pieces of his work to her clients. Marian told him

226

that the gallery would consider representing him. Both women were useful. Marrying either would not be a bad idea. Beside, it would only be a temporary arrangement, a marriage of convenience. That could end any time after it served his purpose. No need to be too concerned.

Kathy was a better choice, with her sensuous figure, seductive voice and sultry movement that fetched him. But he wanted the woman to propose to him rather than the other way around.

He called her: "Kathy, Fang Kuei. Tonight. See me?" With only very limited vocabularies he was able to communicate with his women. Kathy understood him and was joyful. She picked him up from Liang Hai's apartment. After having dinner in a restaurant they went to Kathy's condo.

"I go Italy. No visa stay here." He kissed and caressed Kathy's nudity in her bed and she said, "don't go. I don't want you to go," Kathy muttered in her dreamy voice, resting her head on his chest, her right arm around his waist.

"No visa. I back Italy." Fang Kuei kissed her more. His right arm circled her shoulder; his left fingers tracing the curve of her back and hip.

"I know you cannot stay without a visa. But if you marry me you can." She made it very simple and straightforward so that Fang Kuei would understand her.

"Marry?" Fang Kuei knew that was a proposal, just as he had expected.

"Yes, marry me. Then you can stay. I love you. I don't want you to go." She did love this man. This was a God-given opportunity for her to get him.

He agreed to marry her.

After the wedding he hired an attorney to handle his application for permanent residency. The immigration officer routinely investigated the legitimacy of their marriage. They passed. His application was accepted. But he had to wait for a year or two to get the green card.

Promoting and selling Fang Kuei's work undoubtedly preoccupied Kathy's full attention, not only because she loved and admired this artist, but also because their interests were intimately intertwined now. She extended her tentacles to all nicks and crannies in the collecting community; took Fang Kuei's work to public and private collectors, art galleries near and far, local and national art fairs; and entered his work for various competitions. Fang Kuei was against competitions. The idea of subjecting himself to being judged did not sit well with him. If he lost it would compromise his confidence and pride.

Fang Kuei was a versatile painter. Abstract art in various media was what he preferred to be recognized for. But he was equally at home with impressionistic depiction of landscape and realistic representation of portrait. It surprised him greatly when he received the highest award in a portrait competition. Instead of being pleased he complained to Kathy:

"I say no competition. No portrait."

But it was too late. His reputation as one of the top portrait painters in the nation stuck with him. Commissions poured in against his will. He refused them. Kathy had to deal with the clients; lied to them saying that there would be several years of waiting because of the large number of commissions on the artist's hand.   But there was one particular commission that Kathy could not but beg Fang Kuei to accept.

"Kuei honey, this one is very special. It's from Dr. Morrison's wife. Dr. Morrison is a wealthy and powerful man. His wife Ching Ju is a Chinese, a highly admired, fashionable lady in Boston's rich circle. We are lucky to have them as a patron. They will be most useful in advancing your career. Please just paint a portrait for her."

Fang Kuei did not understand all that she had said. But he gathered that the man was rich and the woman was a Chinese. *Another Chinese woman married to a white American. I wonder what she is like.* After groaning a bit he agreed to do it.

Ching Ju, was the young Chinese dancer from Japan accompanied by her wealthy American husband Dr. Jack Morrison to China Society to audition for a spot in the Chinese New Year program in 1989. Jack Morrison's company, JM Bio Tech, had grown steadily through the years. Beside biological and pharmaceutical research, products and supplies, the company expanded to include medical equipment and supplies. Ching Ju's charm and style coupled with her husband's wealth and social status made her a glistening stud of Boston's opulent society.

Kathy made an appointment for Fang Kuei to meet Mrs. Morrison in her twenty-million-dollar estate in Westin. The estate, sitting on twelve acres of well-landscaped ground, consisted of a magnificent mansion, several secondary buildings, and horse stalls, nothing in common with Dong Fei-yan's house, of course. It was the kind of edifice Fang Kuei had only seen in movies about the ultra-rich Americans.

A bearded man in formal wear greeted them and led them to a large sitting room with a marble fireplace, heavy drapery, and silk upholstered sofa and chairs.

A woman in a black uniform, with white apron and a little white fan-shaped crown perched on her hair, brought in tea and scones on a silver platter. Even as she was politely uttering: "Please have some tea. Mrs. Morrison will be with you momentarily," Ching Ju entered the room wearing a bright smile on her face. Pleasant as well as pleasing, her lilting voice uplifted the spirit of those who heard her.

"Kathy, Mr. Fang, welcome to my house." She extended her right hand to shake Fang Kuei's. Then she quickly turned around to catch Kathy's hand with both of her hands. Kathy quickly greeted Mrs. Morrison.

"How are you Mrs. Morrison?"

"Sit down, sit down. Excuse me for not meeting you at the front door." In fact she never greeted her guests at the front door.

"Jack wants to have a life-size portrait of me in this room," she laughed. "He has been looking for a good portraitist but hasn't found one that meets his standards."

"Mr. Morrison has exceptional taste." Kathy carefully chose her words. "We are honored that you have picked Fang Kuei. He is certainly the best."

228

"Oh, yes. And we are honored that Mr. Fang has agreed to do it for me." Then she spoke directly to Fang Kuei in Chinese: "We heard that you had turned down every commission." She laughed again. Fang Kuei replied in Chinese.

"I am sort of busy."

"Thank you so much for being willing to take the time to do mine." As a seasoned socialite, she was very sensitive about leaving Kathy in the dark while she and Fang Kuei conversed in Chinese.

"Kathy, excuse us. Mr. Fang seems to prefer his native language."

"Oh, Mrs. Morrison, don't worry a bit about me. It's my fault for not being able to speak that beautiful language. Please continue your conversation in Chinese." Kathy conceded apologetically.

After several minutes of social talk the conversation eased in on the portrait.

"It is quite usual nowadays that the artist paint from a photograph he takes of his subject because the subject has no time to sit. Well, not only one photograph, but several. The artist studies the subject from a series of photographs. But it can never be as good as when the subject sits for the artist. Better yet, if the artist has the opportunity to observe the subject on various occasions, he would understand the subject's mood, emotions, feelings, then the portrait would come alive, would have much more depth." Fang Kuei expatiated his point.

Ching Ju was elated. "I will sit for you. And I will let you get to know me before we start. It is important that the portrait truly represents me."

The remuneration for the portrait was many times more than what an established artist would charge. Kathy envisioned the large portrait hanging in that grandiose room and the awe-stricken guests at Morrison's who would fight for Fang Kuei's work. Fang Kuei's career would take off to a new plane. Deep down in her heart, a seed of worry was planted. Would she be able to hold on to Fang Kuei?

Ching Ju and Fang Kuei agreed that they needed to spend some time together to get acquainted with each other, a couple of months, perhaps. During this period Ching Ju would take Fang Kuei to many of her parties, functions, and events, and include him in all the parties she and George were to throw. Whether Ching Ju realized, or admitted it or not, she would definitely not be embarrassed by having Fang Kuei by her side. In fact, she would feel proud to show him off, just like showing off her magnificent diamond.

Fang Kuei did not have the proper getups for many of those occasions. But it did not matter to him. Ching Ju, on the other hand, insisted that she must furnish his wardrobe; it's all part of the job. Fang Kuei resigned without arguing.

He attracted much attention from the ladies at the first large event he attended with the Morrisons. Ching Ju introduced him as "my portrait painter." The ladies were curious and asked about the portrait.

"It has not been started yet. Kuei needs to know every aspect of me in order to put the whole real me on his canvas." Ching Ju gave her famous laugh and put her left hand in the crook of Fang Kuei's arm and rested her right hand on top of her left hand. She raised her head to look at the grinning Fang Kuei proudly.

"Woo, you must throw a large party to reveal the portrait once it's finished," one lady said.

"Of course, darling. You will be the first to be invited."

"And I hope I will have the fortune to ask Mr. Fang to paint my portrait too," The lady said.

"If he is not completely occupied," Ching Ju said with a dazzling smile. She glanced at Fang Kuei and returned her eyes to the lady and whispered: "I will put in some good words for you."

Jack Morrison happened to be striding by and heard his wife.

"Darling, showing off your artist? Careful. You are making all the ladies jealous." He winked at Fang Kuei and put his arm around his wife's shoulders.

These social circles were totally unfamiliar to Fang Kuei. He enjoyed his new experiences immensely, even if most of the time he had to rely on Ching Ju filling him in about what people were saying.

"That lady wishes to have a portrait by you. I am sure before the evening is over there will be more commissions than you care to have. I hope you will not decline them. These are people in high positions. Having your work in their houses is the best publicity, to say the least."

Fang Kuei did not abruptly object as he did with Kathy. He was no fool. Although he knew nothing about America, he knew more than enough about money and power. He had learned much in China where power was everything. He could see that Kathy was only a poor gofer whereas Ching Ju could wave her magic wand and make his dream come true. He wanted to see his work permanently in all major museums.

Although portrait painting did not interest him it would open the doors to bring his abstract work to the fore. In the meantime he must work hard to please Ching Ju and her rich lady friends.

For two months he was constantly with Ching Ju whether there was any party, or function, or event, or nothing at all. Every morning a limousine would come to pick him up to have breakfast with Ching Ju. Sometimes her eight-year-old son Chris and five-year-old daughter Annie would be there with them. Only occasionally would Jack Morrison be present. He was busy with his company and had no worries whatsoever about leaving his lovely wife with this hunk of an artist.

On the rare occasions when there were no social activities, Fang Kuei would accompany Ching Ju to shop in boutique stores; saunter in the garden; sit in the solarium sipping tea and chat; or listen to music or watch a little TV in the entertainment room. Little Annie came to like her uncle Fang Kuei a lot. She insisted on teaching him how to speak English. He actually picked up some words from her.

After a couple of month when Fang Kuei felt that he knew Ching Ju quite well he was ready to start the portrait. Ching Ju asked for Jack's opinion on what dress to wear, and discussed with Fang Kuei about what pose to choose.

She sat one or two hours for him each day. After he quickly sketched in her pose she could talk and laugh and was relaxed instead of being stiff and motionless. He also took many pictures of her as reference when he needed to work more in her absence. When George was home during the painting session he would strode into the studio and watch the artist at work for a while, making a few favorable remarks.

The work took him one month to finish. Ching Ju asked Fang Kuei to paint each of her children too. The kids were excited. Fang Kuei only asked them to sit for thirty minutes or so each time. He also used the pictures he took for help. Their innocent expression and playful manners were deep in his mind. The portraits captured the essence of their spirit and their adorable likeness.

About a hundred guests were invited to the party revealing the three portraits. When Ying Ying got the invitation addressed to her and Kang Wei, she hesitated for a long time. She had no time to attend those "fun" parties, a pastime of the rich and leisurely. She usually just sent regrets in RSVPs. However she could not decline this invitation, as much as she was uninterested, because that might cause Fang Kuei to think she was holding a grudge, and Ching Ju to think… something, she was not sure, but it might be something entirely untrue. She had to accept this invitation. She and Kang Wei went. Ching Ju welcomed them with such warmth as if they were her closest friends.

"Oh, Ying Ying, my dear." She hugged and air kissed Ying Ying. "And Kang Wei, I am so glad that you are able to come." She shook Kang Wei's hand.

Jack Morrison saw his wife chatting with those two special guests. He strode over to greet them. They pleasantly alluded to the time when Ching Ju first went to audition for China Society's dance presentation. He thanked Ying Ying for her friendliness.

"We know what great work you have been doing through the years. Very admirable," Jack added.

"We really should have kept closer i n touch, my dear. It's our fault. We are always involved in a lot of frivolous social events," Ching Ju conceded to Ying Ying. Of course, it was only polite talk.

"No, Ching Ju, you are popular and being admired in the affluent circles. And you are a philanthropist. That in itself is highly respectable," Ying Ying reciprocated Ching Ju's polite talk.

Ying Ying and Ching Ju were both active and respected in Boston but in different circles. Even when their paths crossed, for example, at the MFA, Ying Yng was respected as a scholar and curator, Ching Ju as a philanthropist and patron. When they occasionally appeared at the same events, they did no more than exchange a few words of greetings. Then they would be off to talk with other people.

"We will be honored if you would come to more of our parties. We really should keep in closer touch. I promise that if you let me know your events, we will definitely attend," Ching Ju said with sincerity.

Fang Kuei talked with Ying Ying as if they had just met, with proper politeness and distance. Ying Ying couldn't but laugh inside. *Fang Kuei, who are you fooling? You think pretending you had never met me before would negate your infamous history? You may be a good artist, or I would not have sponsored you to come here, but you are also an unabashed user. You use people as steppingstones to cross turbulent waters. You are a ruthless opportunist. No matter how successful you become as an artist, you will never be successful as a good human being.*

The party was an opulent black tie event, needless to say. The gents were in tuxedoes and the ladies in gorgeous evening gowns. The chef prepared a sumptuous banquet preceded by a champagne reception. Waiters in red jackets, white ruffled shirt, black trousers and bow ties; waitresses in white uniforms weaving among the guests serving exquisite hors d'oeuvres and champagne. Praise poured like wine. The ladies waited so long for Fang Kuei to paint for them, they asked when they might invite the artist to their homes:

"Ching sweetie, when can Kuei paint my portrait? I have waited for so long. You promised," one lady asked.

"Mine too. You said last time that you would put in some good words to the artist for me.," another lady chimed in.

"Darling, I am sorry but you have to be a little more patient. Kuei has to do Jack's portrait before he can do yours," Ching Ju said to both ladies.

"Do I get a portrait too, darling?" Jack Morrison turned his head away from his friends to ask Ching Ju.

"Yes darling. Your conference room needs to have a portrait of you. It will make the room look good." No one could argue about that.

Fang Kuei appropriately portrayed Jack as a president, official, formal and dignified, like the portraits of university or bank presidents. Yet Jack's magnanimous personality, humor and intelligence shone through. When the portrait was hung in the conference room of JM Bio Tech's building, all the staff, colleagues, associates, and visitors incessantly lauded it. Ching Ju was happy and proud. *Why not put more of Kuei's paintings on the wall?* She made a suggestion to Jack:

"Darling, do you think it would be a good idea to replace some of the paintings in the building with Kuei's works? I think Kuei's paintings are far better than those."

"The art consultants selected those for the building. I didn't pay much attention to those things. If it makes you happy by all means tell Kuei to look around the building and decide what he could do," Jack said. He would not mind spending the money. After all money was no object to him.

Ching Ju was happy to convey the message to Fang Kuei. The two of them toured the building. Fang Kuei tactfully kept many of the paintings by different artists that were on the wall and only replaced a few at the most noticeable and spacious spots. So he was only one of the artists represented in that building. The contrast between his large and eye-catching work and the other artists' pieces was glaring. Ching Ju threw a reception and invited many guests, among who were art critics and collectors.

A few days later several reviews came out, nothing but favorable comments. And they called Fang Kuei "emerging artist deserves watching" or simply "an artist to watch." These foretold Fang Kuei's future. He was very pleased that his "real" work was finally being put in the public's eye and getting attention. Ching Ju told Jack that she would like to get the NewArt Museum in Cambridge to mount a show for Fang Kuei. She needed Jack's help. The artist's work certainly could speak for itself. But without the Morrisons' influence, he would easily have to wait years before a slot would be given to him. Morrison was a major benefactor of NewArt Museum. With his request plus good critical reviews of Fang Kuei's work, the museum promised to show him in the following year.

As a repayment to Ching Ju's generosity, kindness, and patronage, Fang Kuei willingly accepted commissions from the ladies in her social circle. Each one took him several weeks to do   As usual, every one of those ladies threw a large party to reveal her portrait. The lady invariably was gratified by admiring and envious eyes and warm encomia. More commissions were offered to Fang Kuei. But he declined them all. To everyone's regret, he announced that portrait was only one branch of his oeuvre and one that he did not intend to do anymore. He suggested people to view his work at JM Bio Tech building and attend the opening of his solo show at NewArt Museum the following year.

He had several months to prepare for his solo show. He was to create a corpus of new work specifically designed to suit the exhibition space assigned to him at the museum. He needed a large studio suffused with natural light. Kathy's condo certainly would not cut it. The proceeds from his many commissions would easily enable him to buy a studio space. But no studio can compare with the one at the Morrison's estate. Using that studio was a matter of course since the Morrisons were doubtlessly his patron. Ching Ju also suggested that if he preferred not to commute back and forth everyday he could stay at their guesthouse, a beautifully appointed, separate edifice from the main house. Fang Kuei accepted the offer without a question.

Kathy had, for a long time, sensed that she was of no use to Fang Kuei anymore and she could no longer hold onto him. She did not exist in Fang Kuei's life. She was never asked to attend any of those parties and functions. She doubted any of the ladies knew Fang Kuei was married. And apparently his being married mattered nothing to Ching Ju.

Kathy regretted that she had brought Fang Kuei to meet Ching Ju. Yet she had to admit that an artist, a man, like Fang Kuei would meet Ching Ju sooner or later without her bridging. She suspected that Ching Ju had kept Fang Kuei as her lover. She was fully aware that she could not compete with Ching Ju. But she was legally Fang Kuei's wife. And Ching Ju was the wife of a powerhouse of Boston's society. Why would Jack allow his wife to have a lover? She wondered what gossip was circling around the affluent world. Did Jack Morrison know about it?

"Kuei, do you want a divorce? You don't need me anymore." Kathy was in tears. She loved this man. There was so much that she wanted to say. But the communication impossibility always stood between them like a stumbling block. She could only say the most simple and direct words.

Divorce? She wants a divorce. Without thinking, Fang Kuei just assumed perfunctorily that she was not happy and wanted to divorce him.

"Okay. Divorce." He continued to pack his things. The limousine was waiting downstairs. He did not want the chauffeur to wait for too long.

Kathy's heart sank. She regretted to have brought up the divorce. It was the last thing she wanted. But it was too late. She burst out crying and began to stammer things not caring if he understood it or not. She needed to vent her emotional maelstrom.

"Kuei, it's … it's … so unfair. You … are treating … me so…badly. How … how could you be so … heartless? Are you … are you … in love … with Mrs. Morrison? But she is … is married. And … and … you are … married. Does our marriage … mean … anything to … to … you? I love … you so … so … much. And I … I … I thought you … loved me too. But you … want … to … to divorce me, …just like that. You have not … gotten your … your … green card … card yet. And you … you… cannot even wait … till you get it." She knew she did not make much sense and Fang Kuei did not understand her. But she didn't care

"Green card. No want." He thought Kathy was using the green card as a weapon to detain him. A green card was not a concern to him anymore. He was about to be rich and famous. Rich and famous people had no need to worry about such a thing. "Money can buy ghosts to push the grinding stone," as the Chinese saying went. Beside, Ching Ju would pay their lawyer to handle it for him if he mentioned it to her.

Ching Ju helped him settle his painting materials in the studio. The guesthouse was already well appointed. Ching Ju could only add some small personal items there for him. He had never felt so comfortable before. The Morrisons treated him as a member of the family. The children were immensely happy. They would drop by from time to time to play with him. Ching Ju had to constantly remind them not to disturb their uncle when he was working. Because of the intensity in which he worked and the tightness of his schedule, he asked Ching Ju to excuse him from some of the events and functions. He was a bit rushed even, as the opening date rolled near.

Ching Ju hired an art moving company to move Fang Kuei's paintings, except the large triptych, to the museum. The museum staff hung the show according to Fang Kuei's layout leaving one wall empty, reserved for the large triptych he was still working on. It was delivered to the museum two days later. The show looked smashing.

At the opening, newspaper reporters interviewed him through Ching Ju's translation. Art critics, because of professional integrity, avoided speaking to him about his art.

The show was on view for three months. All the reviews were favorable. Newspapers gave significant space for his news and pictures. The attendance was better than usual.

The museum's policy was not to sell the works in the shows. But that did not deter collectors from getting Fang Kuei's contact information and dealt with him directly after the show closed. Fang Kuei made a great kill. He donated the proceeds from one large piece to the museum. The museum graciously accepted it and made him an honorary lifetime member.

Gallery owners, curators, collectors from New York, San Francisco and other cities called on him. Show upon show opened in those cities. He, sometime Ching Ju too, attended the openings of those shows at which he met more important people in the art circle. Galleries asked to represent him. But he only agreed to send works to some of them without giving any one exclusive right. He would not be bound by contracts. He must have total freedom to show and sell his work as he pleased. No gallery ought to have the honor to be his sole agent, or any right to claim a share of his proceeds.

His name spread quickly to Europe and Asia. His work was collected by internationally renowned museums in three continents. Some of his works were sold at auction houses in New York and Hong Kong at prices several times higher than those private collectors had paid him for. That served as an indicator of where he stood in the art market.

He began to enjoy these. They were in fact exactly what he had hoped for—money and fame. Now that he had achieved them, what else did he want? Should he be content?

No, he needed more. Money and fame were the basic stuff a person of his ambition must acquire. They were transient, however. Time would extirpate them without mercy. He was a person of vision, a vision for greatness. He needed to occupy a significant position in history.

He contemplated this issue constantly: *What would it be? one major piece of work or a corpus of work to be shown together? I must create something that is so powerful as to exert a mighty impact on the art world and leave an indelible mark in history.*

He set his mind on this goal, constantly thinking about the shapes and forms and the scope of this work. *It's best to be in the form of a complete exhibition, not a single piece. It must be large. Large in terms of the richness of content, in terms or dimension of the pieces, in terms of exhibition space required, in terms of the impact felt by the audience and critics.*

He decided to name this group of work Humanity And History. It would consist of various forms of art—two-D and three-D objects and installations to delineate his reflections, ideas, opinions and commentaries on man and his world past and present.

He worked diligently without disruption for two years in his own studio. He had told Ching Ju that he needed to have a huge space and a peace and quiet environment. Ching Ju understood how important it was for him to create this upcoming monument. She had no objection but to help him realize his idea of buying a section in a closed-down factory and rebuild the interior into a studio space. This huge space has a tw-story ceiling and ample natural light. She occasionally visited him while he was working. But she never asked him to attend any of her parties or functions so as not to waste his time.

As China continued to develop and prosper more and more Chinese in Boston, including those artists and musicians who came in the 1980s, anxiously rushed back there to find their opportunities like the Forty-Niners in America in the nineteenth century during the gold rush.

What happened to their ventures? Did this "gold rush" award them richly? Was China now a land of dreams? We knew at least the stories of those associated with China Society.

Tan Jin, the stage designer for *The Wild Land*, could not get a job in Hollywood for quite some time until he finally joined the set designers union. Then he was hired by Walt Disney Company's Animation division. His forte was translating a design on paper to large-scale finished sets. Scene construction, scene painting, property design/building, lighting design and installation were also his expertise. These skills were better suited for the Company's Theme Park department. He was transferred to that department and often sent to other countries to supervise the installation of the scenery created by his group.

His work was satisfying and well paid. But the enticement of China was too powerful to resist. There was a cluster of aspiring Chinese, some schoolmates of his, some burgeoning businessmen, and one government official whose name was concealed, that came up with the idea of emulating the Disney theme parks. They proposed to partner with him in the project. He would contribute his design ideas and technical know-how, the others would take on the full responsibility of finance. He was offered a 30% partnership. As projected, the theme park would be a huge moneymaker.

He took a leave of absence from Disney and went to Shanghai. His name, resume, and design, coupled with the influence of that government-official-partner, was able to obtain a large sum of money from the city of Shanghai. The project was promising and all set to go. Yet the project leader told Tan Jin that they lacked sufficient funds and must try to raise more; in the meantime Tian Jin should go back to Los Angeles and wait for further news. They would select contracting companies for the various components of the theme park before Tian Jin returned to Shanghai.

Tan Jin needed to make arrangements with Disney. He must keep his job and a good rapport with the company even if he was anticipating wealth from his new venture in Shanghai. The company's international reputation would enhance his credentials and demand more respect from his compatriots.

In China at this time, there was a special label reserved for those educated abroad and went back to work in their native country. It was called *hai gui-pai* 'The School of The Returned-from-Abroad.' Held as experts, these returnees were awarded exceptional respect. But once settled in China permanently the luminosity dimmed. Therefore, it would be important to keep a job abroad, and return to China only occasionally.

Years later when more and more individuals, without any special talent or ability to speak of, took advantage of the opportunities and had nothing to show, China was disillusioned by their mediocrity. Eventually The School of The Returned-from-Abroad was tauntingly and seamlessly changed to The School of the Sea Turtle. It was a play of Chinese homonyms,

Tan Jin negotiated with Disney Company, asking for a two-year leave and a guaranteed a job for him when returned. The company's condition was that he must first finish the undergoing project he was involved in. It meant a few months of time. That was reasonable and doable.

As he was winding up his project and ready to go he heard from Shanghai that they had to cancel the project due to lack of additional funding. He asked about the money they got from the government before. The answer was that it was expended. A report was already submitted to the city of Shanghai. As Tan Jin knew, the sum allocated to the theme park project was sizable. *How could they have expended it before the construction had begun*? He thought. His travel and hotel didn't cost much. He should have been compensated for the two months of service. But they said there was no money to pay him. He lost his two-month salary from Disney during the leave of absence. A moneymaking idea turned out to be a pipe dream. He was a victim of exploitation.

Lu Wen, one of the artists who had painted the costumes for *The Intrigues in the Manchu Imperial Court*, had developed a successful career as a portrait painter in the West coast. He was well connected in China that enabled him to get jobs designing hotels and public buildings while he had no experience in such work before.

"As long as they pay me well and I do a good job for them, that's all it matters," Lu Wen said. Traveling between China and Boston was a regular occurrence for him. He also proposed to build an enclave in the outskirts for Beijing, a cultural establishment including a modern art museum, several art galleries, upscale shops, restaurants of international cuisines, and a five-star hotel. Objects to be shown in the museum would be borrowed or rented from museums around the world. The idea was very good, as Chinese museums did not have collections of art from other countries, past or present. The public and art students were impoverished due to this lacuna. Enormous revenue was projected from admission proceeds alone since China had over a billion people, if one percent would frequent the museum once in their lifetime.

His proposal was seriously considered by the city and some wealthy individuals. Yet due to insufficient funds, as the core people claimed, the project was abandoned.

Chong Teng, The carpenter who built the sets for China Society's theatre production, was a graduate of Shanghai Conservatory of Music and Boston Conservatory. He turned to carpentry because his mediocre skill in music could not make him a living. Beside carpentry he was also hired by a licensed home remodeler to paint houses and do a little plumbing and electrical work. He could make a lot more money if he had plumbing and electrical licenses. But he said it was too hard for him to pass the tests. His work was keeping him very busy. As he accumulated enough experience he became a home remodeler himself, albeit unlicensed. A nicely designed business card and a good-sounding company name led people to believe that he had a big construction company. He did most of the work himself with only some help from a hired hand. When he had to do plumbing or electrical work he would pay a licensed workman to sign the required documents as if the latter had done the job. It worked well.

He was no less drawn by the golden opportunities in China than the others. He went to Shanghai where he was revered to be a successful owner of an American construction company. With the help of his old schoolmates that had become government officials holding rubber stamps, he entered the interior-construction industry effortlessly. Interior finishing work was a big business because new houses and condos, commercial and government buildings in China were sold to consumers with only the shell, leaving the interior an undefined, blank space. The eye-catching name of Boston Interior Construction soon became well known. His powerful rubber-stamping friends steered the biggest and best projects to him. He knew how to reward them with kickbacks. The operation was beautifully smooth.

Some major projects came to him through his pivotal government friends. It was restoration of some historically important architecture. The budget for the work was enormous; the profit was sizable. However, the scope of the work was far beyond Chong Teng's capability. He was reluctant to take it.

"Old Chong, why are you hesitating? This is your big chance. Make it or break it. It's your call. Hey, let's not toss it away without trying, ok, brother? Why not look forward to a comfortable and affluent second half of our lives?" A communist cadre, his old friend, urged him.

Chong Teng was still very cautious. He thought about it for some time. *I should ask Ying Ying to connect me with the right architectural firm then I may be able to take this on.*

He went back to Boston to see Ying Ying. He described the nature of the project and the importance it would bear on his business growth.

"I think you must have connections with many large architectural firms. I hope you will introduce me to the appropriate ones that can do the job." Sitting across the desk from Ying Ying in her office Chong Teng plainly made his request.

"Yes, I do know many architects in large companies. I can think of a few right now that can do the project easily. Their specialty is restoring historical buildings and architectural details," Ying Ying said. "But according to your description, the project in Shanghai is very large. Will the authorities not have a competition to choose the best-qualified company? Will architectural firms in different countries not know about this project?"

"You don't know China," Chong Teng smiled. "Everything depends on having connections. I happen to have this golden connection. My closest friend since college, sort of a blood brother, is in charge of this. Who would he give it to but me? Oh, yes, they may hold a competition, but it will only be a surface pretense, a false front. We will take their ideas and synthesize them for our own benefit. The firms that lose the competition cannot complain because everything we will do is legal."

238

"That is so unfair, coaxing people to send in their proposals and steal their ideas!!!" Ying Ying protested.

"Well, we don't look at it that way," Chong Teng said complacently.

"I just remembered something. Mr. Qian De of Qian/Wilson Architects told me about a major project in China. He entered a competition by invitation. There were eight entries from renowned architects of Europe and the U.S.. They were invited to a conference in Beijing where they presented their designs. In the end, none of the entries was selected. Instead, China took something from each of the proposals and used their local architects to build the building."

"Oh, that is a common practice in China. It's not illegal. Borrowing some ideas is different from stealing a complete design." Chong Teng snickered at Ying Ying's excessive uprightness.

"If I recommend some architects to you I hope you will not exploit them that way," Ying warned half jokingly.

"No, I won't," Chong Teng grinned, "because of you."

"How are you going to work with them?" Ying demanded.

"My company will sign the contract with the authorities and handle all logistics and legal procedures. The American company is not going to contact the Chinese authorities directly. They will sign a contract with me. They will take orders from me and do what I ask them to do."

"They will be a subcontractor?" Ying Ying asked.

"In a way, yes. But the Chinese authorities must not know that. They should think that the American architects are my employees."

"I see, because you poise yourself as a big company with many American architects? Right? Now I understand." Ying Yling chuckled. She wondered how Chong Teng was going to manipulate the American company and hide the truth from the Chinese authorities.

Ying called three architects; gave them a briefing and asked them to contact Chong Teng if they were interested. Then she put it behind her.

Han Tu broke his contract with the San Francisco Opera house to open a vocal music training school in Beijing hoping to make big bucks because education had become a flourishing business in China. There were too many young aspiring students being barred outside of college doors due to a disproportionate ratio of high school grads to colleges admissions. Slipshod schools and training programs of all sorts mushroomed in this fertile ground like "bamboo shots after the rain in the spring," as the Chinese saying described it. They all promised to prepare the kids for passing college entrance exams. These schools and programs were always crowded with students, thus money kept rolling in.

During one of his frequent visits Meng Song was persuaded by his friends and relatives to establish an all-encompassing art complex on Nanking Road in Shanghai. To be more specific, the complex would include a large, first-rate gallery, a design company to offer 2D and 3D works; interior design as well as architectural designs; a bookstore of arts and humanities subjects in different languages published in the United States, the United Kingdom, Sweden, France, Germany and Italy and of course in China; a store for selective craft items from around the world; a classical music café; and a few artists studios. The idea was very appealing to Meng Song as he had an earnest penchant for books, classical music and all realms of the arts.

Despite the intense demands on him by the galleries of his new works, he chose to take on the challenge and opportunity to pursue the art complex project. He did have to create many pieces of paintings to satisfy the galleries' needs. But moving back to Shanghai would not affect that in any way. He just had to travel between China and America frequently.

His parents certainly were happy to have him around. They would put up a good amount of money to help him get the business off the ground. A number of friends asked to invest in it. Capital was not an issue. Soon they secured the location, and renovation of the buildings began. He oversaw the process himself making sure that every detail adhered to his specifications. The workmen moaned and groaned under his criticism and pressure.

At the opening of the complex VIPs from the government, art circle, major businesses, and reporters from news media filled the reception room. Art works exhibited in the gallery, crafts items displayed in the shop, the décor of the café and bookstore were all exceptionally tasteful. Soon the Meng Art Complex, as it was called, caught the eyes of tourists and local wealthy. Business could not be better. It was ironical that the one artist who was always aloof to wealth and fame, and not only was disinterested in but slighted all commercial activities, would become a successful businessman.

Like Han Tu, Li Yong went back to Shanghai to open a school too. His was an acting school. With his fame as a Broadway star success was guaranteed. He hired the teachers from Shanghai Drama Institute to teach part-time. Students waited in long lines to enroll. Soon a second school was opened in Beijing. At the same time film contracts came his way one after another. Only rarely did he return to the U.S.. He and Pei-hua lived apart most of the time. Understanding the nature of his career as an actor Pei-hua had always been accommodating to his absence from home. But spending ninety-nine percent of the time in China plus having a flourishing new career there was hard for Pei-hua to deal with.

"To keep our marriage intact, I think we should move back to China," Li Yong said during his one-week stay in New York.

Move back to China? China was not where I came from. It would not be "going back" for me. Beside, my career is here. My friends are here. However, Pei-hua did not voice these thoughts to Li Yong.

"Li Yong, It's a hard decision. But I am afraid that I can't make that move." She made a curt and determined statement.

"But I must be in China. As you know, my career is there. In New York, I have achieved what an Asian actor could hope for. But how many lead roles are there for an Asian actor? The TV offers are only small parts. You know that. And Hollywood is worse. In China, I have offers more than I can take. And the acting school is doing so well. You will have a very comfortable life there. No need to work any more." What Li Yong said was true. But Pei-hua felt belittled. *Is that all I am worth? I work only because I need to make a living? When you make plenty of money I will be a useless idler?*

"I didn't go to school to end up a rich man's wife. I have a thriving career and I want to keep it." Her voice was many degrees below the usual warmth.

"You can practice law in China. I am sure you will have a great career there." Li Yong tried to mend the damage he had made.

"But Li Yong, I am afraid I can't."

Why was Pei-hua so obstinate? Has her love for me waned because of frequent separation? He knew argument would not get him anywhere. He must use other tactics.

"Pei-hua, sweetheart, please, for the sake of our love, would you please try it? Just go and live there, with me, for a while. Mmm? Okay? You know how much I miss you." He reached a finger under Pei-hua's chin and lifted her face to his. His gentle voice, tender gaze and loving kiss softened her. She was silent. Li Yong knew that he had won her over.

"That's my girl. I will call the travel agency to get your ticket. Can you be ready for the trip in a week?" He had to secure the opportunity before Pei-hua changed her mind.

"That's too soon. I have to ask the firm for a leave of absence. I have to give them at least a month." Pei-hua gave in.

"All right, I will reserve the ticket for a month from now. I will change my ticket and tell the producer to extend my leave. I hope it will not create too much of a problem for them. You know how tightly they keep the production schedule." That was true, each day of delay was a big loss of money. Li Yong begged for the producer's understanding and help to find a better apartment for Pei-hua and him. He wanted Pei-hua to be as comfortable as could be. The producer, Mr. Lin, understood that perfectly.

Li Yong told her that Meilan, like himself, had established her business in both Beijing and Shanghai. Currently she was in Shanghai.

When they arrived at the international airport, a file of people from the TV production was there to welcome Pei-hua. They sent the couple to their luxury apartment on Huai-Hai Road West in a chauffeur-driven Audi. The next day Meilan invited Pei-hua and Li Yong to her apartment on Heng-Shan Road in Jing-an district. Meilan, that fascinating person who never failed to light up a room with her presence and colorful stories, was now interested in only one subject -- her success and big business. The big advantage of returning to China before others did and having the best contacts among the Chinese leaders had given her a sharp edge in achieving all she ventured to do. After her third tour she formed Meilan Development Incorporated, with money from two investors she met in Hong Kong. One was a Japanese businessman and the other was a Hollywood filmmaker. She unfailingly used her magic power to sway the gentlemen into forming a partnership with her. Under her management and resources the company grew quickly. Knowing her own ability, the partners became useless profit sharers to her. She resorted to buying them out.

Her company was a conglomerate with a TV production company, a dance troupe, a recording company, a fashion manufactory, a chain of fashion boutiques, and a school for the arts. She also imported high-tech equipment to China, and help foreign investors by identifying appropriate opportunities for them. Many foreign companies crossed the immeasurable gulf lying between China and them through Meilan's bridge.

"My business and expansion came effortlessly like wind sweeping fallen autumn leaves. There is no stopping. Everything I touch succeeds and money follows." Meilan said, not bragging, but reporting the facts.

"Meilan, where does Mr. Hemmingway fit into this grand picture? Is he still waiting to marry you?" Pei-hua inquired?

"I told him that I could not give up my career to marry him. Since he could not give up his and move to China we just have to forgo our promises."

"Oh, Mr. Hemmingway was so much in love with you. This must have broken his heart." Pei-hua was saddened by how easily money and ambition could break a loving relationship.

"George is a good men. Yes, he really loves me. But there is no other way. Even if I had married him and allowed him to live in Boston, he would not want to have a wife thousands of miles away. No American man would accept that kind of a life. He wanted me to go back to Boston and treat my business as a pastime. How could I? I am not content to just be a rich man's wife."

Her situation struck a cord in Pei-hua. She would not be content with being a rich man's wife either.

"How did he take it? Did you talk to him face to face or just through a phone?" Pei-hua asked.

"Oh, I couldn't just give him that news by a phone call. I broke the news to him gently when he was visiting me. It was not without regret on my part. I was caught between love and ambition. And the timing is really lousy. I said we would remain good friends if he wanted. He was very saddened. And he insisted on giving me a designer million-dollar diamond necklace as a token of friendship. I accepted."

"Do you still keep in touch?"

"Yes. He calls me and sends me cards and small gifts from time to time." Meilan appeared wistful.

"I understand. Li Yong and I are in a similar situation. He has his career here and I have mine in America. Neither of us is willing to compromise. So, you can see where we are going." For the first time Pei-hua and Meilan were talking heart to heart.

"Oh, Pei-hua." Meilan patted Pei-hua on her hand. "I thought you were moving to Shanghai for good. You will easily develop an enviable career here. China needs good lawyers. I need a good lawyer." She smiled.

"I don't feel this is where I belong. I am accustomed to the American society and way of life. Beside, I studied American law, not Chinese law."

"I see what you mean. When I first came back here, I was not used to it even though this was where I grew up."

"What is your big project now?" Pei-hua changed the subject.

"Right now?" Meilan replied in high spirit: "I am helping put together a large deal between China and the U.S.. It's a two billion dollar project. My commission will be the usual rate of two percent. Imagine that. But I have competitors too. There are companies in France and Germany fighting for the project."

Two percent of two billion!! That was forty million dollars. Pei-hua was overwhelmed by it.

"Pei-hua, think it over. Shanghai is not a bad place to be. It will take you a little getting use to. But if you come here we will work together. Ying Ying should come too. How nice it would be!! If the three of us are to work together. Li Yong will join hand with me in operating the arts school. He has a theatre arts training school in Shanghai and Beijing. But they are not in the scale of my school. He does not have the energy to run them alone. If we join forces our school will be on a par with Shanghai Drama Institute. What would you like to do? Pick any one. Import/export? Fashion? Dance Company? Film and TV Production? Join Li Yong and I in our school project? Or if you have any good idea, let's do it" Meilan enticed Pei-hua.

"Meilan, I admire your success. But I'd better stick to my own field. What background and qualifications do I have for those works?"

"Ai. Who has any background? Do I have it? Learn it while doing. That's it. If you don't like those things how about just be my legal counsel?" She paused for a second and asked: "Do you think Ying Ying would come and join me?"

"She is very busy. You know that. I seriously doubt that she would leave her work and Kang Wei to come here," Pei-hua replied.

"Of course Kang Wei must come too. He definitely can get a job here."

"People make moves for specific reasons. Kang Wei is on the faculty of bio-medical science at MIT. He is bright and has published many papers. Clearly his interest and future is in the academia. Even if he can make much more money in Shanghai, he is not going to leave MIT."

"There are famous universities in Shanghai and Beijing. Why can't he teach in one of them?"

"I can't speak for him. And MIT is MIT."

"You are right. I guess I am being selfish. I would like to have you and Ying Ying be here with me. You are my best friends." Meilan was wistful. "Ying Ying and Kang Wei are a happy couple. I know."

"Yes. You know, he was in love with Ying Ying since college. They are very happy together."

"They are lucky. Now I am single, without a man who cares for me. Sometimes I feel lonely."

"You? Lonely? You still live under the limelight. Your suitors and business are more than occupying all your time. When do you have a chance to feel lonely?

"Those are nothing. At the end of the day, when I am at home by myself, I feel lonely and empty. Without someone to share your success and failure, you feel meaningless."

"Contradictions, contradictions."

"Yes. I chose my career, to fulfill my ambition over marriage. And now I feel empty."

"If you marry someone local the problem would be resolved. Why don't you? There must be a some suitable men around you."

"No, it's not easy. The more successful I am the less likely a man would want to marry me. They are overwhelmed and threatened by my fame and success. Frankly, I would not marry a man who is incomparable to me in every aspect either. There have been a few suitors, overseas Chinese in foreign countries where I performed. The sparks were not strong enough to ignite my feelings." Meilan brooded for a moment and sighed: "I do want to rebuild a home."

"Life is fickle. We can never predict what will happen. I used to have such romantic notion about the much eulogized eternal love, 'until ocean dries, rock rots.'" Pei-hua was thinking about Li Yong and herself. Once Li Yong was her love and life. He occupied every minute of her thoughts. Now she was contemplating divorce.

"An innocent young girl's dream. We all had it." Meilan spoke for both of them.

*   *   *   *

In the following weeks Li Yong was busy filming in the studio. Pei-hua went with him a few times to see him at work. Oddly, she distinctly felt that the people in the studio treated her with excessive politeness as if she were a foreign dignitary while they acted like sworn brothers with Li Yong. It made her feel uneasy. She tried but could not fit in. Li Yong had to look after her wellbeing all the time. She felt that she was in their way, costing too much of their time and effort. It would be best if she were not there. So she chose to occupy her time by sightseeing and shopping.

This Shanghai was a far cry from the one she and Ying Ying had seen years before. Numerous magnificent high-rise buildings, large shopping malls with famous brand merchandise, luxury hotels, restaurants, bright lights at night, it was a cosmopolitan city of the first rate. She called a taxi. When she entered it the driver used his forced and broken English to ask:

"Where go?"

Pei-hua was puzzled. *Why did he speak English to me?*

"I would like to go to a mall. Please just take me to one," she replied in Chinese.

The taxi driver turned his head to face Pei-hua, smiled and spoke Chinese to her: "You can speak our language?! And you speak it very well. Where did you learn it?"

"Why? It's my native language." Pei-hua was confused and amused.

"But you are not a Chinese, are you?" The taxi driver took a hard look at her and questioned.

"Why not?" Pei-hua chuckled.

"You don't look like a person from our country," he said. Pei-hua could not figure out why she gave the taxi driver such an impression.

"I am a pure, one-hundred-percent Han Chinese," she said with a grin.

"Not even a mixed-blood?" He seemed disappointed and disbelieving.

"No." She confirmed her claim. "But I am not originally from here." She paused and continued: "I am from Taiwan."

"Oh, Taipei?" He asked

"Yes."

"Which area? What street?"

"Why do you ask? Do you know Taipei?" She was curious why he asked so many questions. What difference would one street from the other make?

"I was in Taipei several times. I know the city."

"Oh? Really? Why were you there?" Pei-hua was interestedly surprised.

"My mother lives there."

"Really??" Pei-hua was more surprised because Taiwan did not allow the Mainlanders to travel there.

"Really."

"Why is she there and you are here?" It was a logical question.

"Both my father and my mother were soldiers of the Eighth Route Army. The Party denounced them as anti-revolutionists. My father was put to death. My mother fled to the countryside and hid for months. Then she sneaked out of the country with the help of someone. I am not sure whom. She went to Taiwan where her brother, my uncle, was. He had gone there with the Nationalist government in 1949. My mother could not take me along, understandably. In recent years she's contacted me, and I pleaded with the Overseas Chinese Affairs Authority to allow me to visit her."

"Wow, that was awesome. Why didn't you stay in Taiwan with your mother?"

"I have my own family, I mean my wife and a kid, here. It would not be feasible to immigrate there. It was not allowed either."

Pei-hua was moved by his story. All similar bittersweet stories flashed through her mind--families reunited temporarily after being separated by the Taiwan Strait for decades. When Taiwan and the mainland opened a slit between their doors many mainlanders took the opportunity to visit their family in Taiwan. She only read about those in the newspapers but had not witnessed one with her own eyes. After a minute of silence Pei-hua asked the driver:

"Where are you taking me? Where is a nice mall I asked you to take me to?"

"I don't know. I will just drive you around." He said in a humorous tone. Pei-hua was not sure whether he was serious or being funny. She had heard much about taxi drivers deliberately driving the customers in circles to boost the fare. She did not like to be taken yet she was too embarrassed to say anything.

"I was only kidding." The driver turned his head around and smiled brightly. He must have guessed what was in Pei-hua's mind. Pei-hua noticed that he was a good-looking man. He stopped at a large new mall and said:

"This is a good one. It has all luxury stuff. You can afford to buy. I cannot," he grinned. "Maybe I will have other chances to drive for you again."

"Yes, I hope so. Thank you very much." Pei-hua paid her fare and got off. The driver waved to her and she waved back. She felt a little lost as if saying goodbye to a friend whom she would not see again.

The mall looked similar to the malls in American cities. Famous name-brand merchandise was displayed nicely in different sections. She ambled around, browsing from store to store. The prices were generally higher than those in American malls. She wondered how the average Chinese consumers could afford them. She was checking out some casual wear. when a salesgirl strode over to help her. Interestingly she also spoke English to her.

"Miss, good shirt. Want buy?" Pei-hua was not perplexed anymore. She only hesitated for a moment about whether she should speak Chinese to disappoint her. No. She decided to play along:

"Yea, but let me look around a bit. Thank you." She left the store after a minute. She had no interest in buying things that she could buy in Boston. Chinese quilted jacket, cloth shoes, authentic crafts items made by ethnic minorities, hand-made custom jewelry with Chinese flavor and such. Those were what she liked to buy as presents for her friends in Boston. But none of those could be found in the mall.

She was taken as a mixed-blood or some foreigner by clerks in the food market, fruit-stand owners, street-corner knickknack peddlers too. By then she was used to it already though still mystified by it.

When she asked Li Yong and his friends about it, some said it was probably because of the way she dressed. Yet she did not dress differently from the local girls. Some said it was her mannerism, the way she walked and moved that separated her from the local females. Some said it was because of her fair complexion, and her facial features--wide eyes glittering with black pupils and hooded by thick lashes, a turn-up nose with a bridge more prominent than those of many Asians, and her multi-shaded, streaked hair colors. Her cousin in California joked with her more than once calling her a ghost because her skin was so light. In the subway in New York people sometimes spoke Spanish to her only to be surprised when learning she was not a Spaniard. It must have been a combination of all those reasons that misled the locals into taking her as a foreigner.

She visited the "water villages" and other small villages near Shanghai. The natural beauty of the landscape and the originally built Chinese-style houses unspoiled by tourist commercialism were enthralling. She was glad to have seen them before the tourist industry eagerly wiped them out.

Dinner engagements occupied her evenings. They were invitations from

246

the production company's personnel, and Li Yong's old schoolmates and friends. Once in a few days she and Meilan would meet or talk on the phone. There were some old schoolmates of hers from Taiwan University living in Shanghai. But she had not kept in touch with them or had their addresses, or phone numbers. She mentioned it to Meilan.

"Oh, yes, there are so many Taiwanese settled here. They don't mingle with us much. They have their own community and schools. Their children learn traditional Chinese script instead of our simplified one. The Taiwanese has a superiority complex. They still think we are poor and backward, far below them." Meilan snorted.

"How could they think that? Haven't they seen China with their own eyes?" Pei-hua questioned. But she was not surprised by the superiority complex of those people. For so many years a spiteful attitude had been firmly planted in the minds of people in Taiwan.

"How can I find my school-mates here?" Pei-hua asked.

"The telephone directory would be a start," Meilan replied with a straight answer. She brought out a phonebook for Pei-hua. Pei-hua flipped the pages and said:

"I suppose if I find one of them I will find them all." In a few moments she exclaimed: "Here she is, Chen Bi-wei. She was my classmate. Let me write down her number.... Let me see. Who else I should look up," She jotted down Chen Bi-wei's number and turned the pages. "Oh, Zhang Guo-qiang. He is from the Business School. I knew him well. Okay. That's enough. They will let the others know that I am here."

She called both Chen and Zhang to no avail. She left messages on their machines. In the evening they called back. Two days later twenty some old schoolmates invited Pei-hua to a banquet at Jing-jiang Restaurant. Some of them came from the U.S. in recent years to seek business opportunities. Others moved there from Taiwan. Several of them settled there by chance. They were enticed by the low real estate prices while a tourist in Shanghai so bought houses there.

"It is difficult to do business here. Even the big foreign companies after many years of operation still have not broken even. Only the local Chinese have made money. They can go every which way and open every door. We cannot. All roads lead to dead ends and all doors are sealed to us. They make things especially difficult for us and take full advantage of us. They call us "Taiwanese target" to be screwed. On the surface they treat us nicely. We have already sunk too much money here. If we back out we lose everything. There is no alternative but to hold on."

Pei-hua was astonished to see such fissure between the Mainland- and Taiwanese Chinese. She did not feel it with Li Yong's colleagues. They all seemed to welcome her with extra warmth. Of course it's mostly because she was Li Yong's wife; she was a guest here; and she was an American lawyer. They hardly thought of her as a Taiwanese or a competitor in any sense.

                    *   *   *   *

Some people who were friends of Li Yong's friends asked to invite Pei-hua to lunch. Li Yong blocked many of them. He knew what those people wanted. He also knew that those would be bothersome to Pei-hua. Some asked Pei-hua directly during the dinner parties they hosted. In such cases Li Yong could not decline on Pei-hua's behalf.

"They are going to ask you for help or a favor. I am not sure what. I hate to see you being bothered and be put on the spot. So I have blocked many such requests already. Just beware not to be snared by them. Don't hesitate to tell them no," Li Yong warned Pei-hua.

"Don't worry. I am not a fool. Remember, I am an attorney." Pei-hua smiled and felt the warmth when Li Yong worried about her wellbeing like a big brother.

"Attorney Liu, I am truly grateful for having the honor to lunch with you. I know that your evenings are filled and I will not have the chance to invite you and Mr. Li to dinner," Zhen sycophantically stated. Then he presented Pei-hua with a small gift box. "This is a humble gift I respectfully beg for your kind acceptance."

Pei-hua felt a pressure from this man. He must have something major to ask of her or he would not have given her a present. Whatever was in the box it must be more than a mere gesture. Should she open it right there and then or not? According to American custom that she was used to, a present should be opened in front of the giver so as to allow him to see the joy and gratefulness on the recipient's face. The Chinese tradition, on the other hand, is not to show the eagerness on the receiver's part; a gift should not be seen as important in the scheme of things. So, she put the box aside and not open it in front of him.

"You are too thoughtful. You shouldn't have given me any gift." Pei-hua said casually.

"It's insignificant, not worth mentioning."

The so-called lunch, in fact, was no different from a dinner. The setting was a luxury restaurant. The dishes were many and exquisite. The waiter filled their cups with wine. Pei-hua did not drink wine so he brought a glass of fruit juice for her.

"Attorney Liu, I have this plan, a project, I hope to bring to you for collaboration." After a few exchanges of casual remarks Zhen came to the point. "There is a keen need of our youth to be better prepared for college in America."

"Undergraduate or graduate school?" Pei-hua asked absently.

"Undergraduate," Zhen replied. "The graduates from top colleges have their way to go abroad. There are many high school graduates whose parents are loaded with money and wish to send them to America for college. They don't know how to do it. And the students need preparation before attending an American college even if they find the way to go."

"I don't think it's easy to get visas."

248

"For sure," Zhen grinned. "That's why many people have the idea and no one can do it. If you will partner with me, we will be successful. You are an attorney in America. Who else but you can get the students to go there?"

"I am not an immigration lawyer." Pei-hua said.

"But I am sure you can get them to go there." Zhen did not give up. "There is a lot of money to be made because the need is big and the competition is zero. Ours will be the first company to assist youngsters to attend a pre-college-preparatory-camp, for a few weeks in the summer, and apply for college entrance and get visas for them."

"How much money is *a lot of money*? How many can you send? What are you going to charge them?" Pei-hua had no interest in collaborating with him. But she was interested in finding out what he had in mind.

"We can easily make $30,000 to $40,000 from each head. As for how many we can send depends on how many you think we can send without alerting the U.S. consulate's suspicion. Of course the more we send the more we can make."

"You can make that much from a kid? Expenses in Boston are high--room and board, transportation, fees for teachers and materials and so forth. I am surprised that Chinese kids can afford to attend the program, much less paying $30,000 or $40,000 above and beyond those expenses," Pei-hua stated.

"Oh, that's what you don't know about China. The poor people are still poor. But there are many, many rich people and super rich people. Their children are at the age of graduating from high school. Those kids are the only children in their families due to the One-Child Policy."

"I see."

"The parents can't do enough for these kids. They are more than willing to lavish over them with money."

"So people come up with ways to gouge the parents," Pei-hua taunted.

"We are providing them with services that will make them feel good," Zhen countered with humor. Then he turned serious. "Attorney Liu. It is my great fortune to know you. The good old heaven is kind to me because I am a good person. He sends you here to help me. With your help my plan will be realized. It will be our joint business. We will succeed together."

He asked to incorporate a company with Pei-hua and let Pei-hua be the president. He would be vice-president. Pei-hua's responsibilities would be setting up the short-term study camp, hiring teachers and staff members, arranging hotels or dormitories for the students, drawing up a curriculum and activity schedule, and handling all legal issues. Zhen would be responsible for selecting students from a large number of registrants he anticipated, collect their money and get them ready to go.

"I trust that once announced, many parents will register their kids. We will let them know that we have a stringent screening process. Only 30 or so students will be send off, that's if you think 30 is a good number, if you think we should have more or less, we will do as you say. We will set a fee schedule for the participating students. The registration fee alone will be substantial, as I have estimated. I will keep the registration slip, of course, so that you will know exactly how many there are."

Pei-hua did not accept or reject his proposal. "I will think it over and let you know."

"Of course. You need time to think. But as you can see, there is nothing negative about this project. I hope you will make a decision soon. We have a lot of work ahead of us."

Pei-hua opened the gift box when she got home. It was a pair of jade bracelets. From the purity of its color and its translucency, the jade was of top quality.

Another proposal was from a team of woman: "Attorney Liu, we are planning to hold a nation-wide arts competition to select young musicians and dancers. We expect to have tens of thousands of registrants if we tell them the winner would be sent to America for cultural exchange. The registration fees will be quite sizable even if we only charge 150 *yuan* each. We will send any number of them to America, with your help, that is. Without the American component the draw would be limited. So we need your help, your sponsorship actually. You tell us how you would like to share the profit. We will do it."

It was much like Zhen's proposal except the name was changed from college prep to cultural exchange. Those people had superb schemes to coax money out of aspiring parents.

"Arts competitions? Will it include visual arts?" Pei-hua asked.

"Huh? Visual arts? What is that?" one woman asked. It astounded Pei-hua that these women had the gall to organize national arts competitions while they did not even know what visual arts were. *Isn't it a little ridiculous?*

"Painting, sculpture, calligraphy, decorative art, graphic design, and so forth." Pei-hua replied.

"Oh, those. Can those make money? Can people make a lot of money doing those?" one woman eagerly asked. No surprise. Money was the sole driving force for every plan, every activity.

The third proposal was to take a team of young and beautiful models to America for touring fashion shows. The models would be selected through a competition, again "nationwide." The registration fees would not amount to hundreds of thousands of *yuan* because there were not tens of thousands of models to register. The bulk of the money, they anticipated, would come from corporate advertisements, endorsements, and ticket proceeds from shows in China and touring shows in America. Since the models would be winners from national competitions to tour American cities, they certainly could attract corporate money and audiences. The models would not be compensated, of course. Not only that, they were required to pay their own way to America too because this was a great, valuable and rare opportunity that would further their careers, the women said.

"In principle they should pay us for the opportunity," another woman said. Pei-hua was amazed at how these people had every trick to exploit young people. She had seen model competitions and shows on Shanghai's TV almost everyday. The girls were about six feet tall and weighed nothing. They looked like bamboo poles. Yes, they were gorgeous.

Since when have Chinese women grown that tall? And how did they learn to catwalk like that? Pei-hua wondered. Little did she know, modeling had become a big industry in China. Modeling schools and training centers had sprouted and spread to even very small towns.

*   *   *   *

Pei-hua heard a buzzword, *shi-shang* (vogue) in every context. She could accept its widespread use in clothing, shoes, handbags, hair styling, even furniture, decorative motifs, interior design, and such. But in classical music, folk dance, academic training, and food?

In Meilan and Li Yong's circles there were people even more ruthlessly aggressive and voracious than those Pei-hua had lunch with. Beside money, nothing had any value to them. Faithfulness, trustfulness, honesty, loyalty, altruism, etc, qualities that used to be held dear by the Chinese, were completely extirpated from people's mind. Beguilement, machination, and betrayal were acceptable. Broken promises, selfishness, and damaging others in order to benefit oneself were commonplace. Trustfulness was scoffed at as being stupid because no one was trustworthy. Conversations were vacuous and magniloquence-laden. What was said was not meant since honesty and sincerity were things of the past. Honesty and foolishness were synonyms. A negative adage, *ren bu zi si, tian zhu di mie* "One who is not selfish will be executed by Heaven and eradicated by Earth" or "The unselfish one will be damned by Heaven and Earth" that used to serve as a reflection of the treacherously selfish mind that regarded evil as virtue, was meant to expose and criticize such selfishness then, was hailed to be the truth now.

"They all talked about doing business in frightfully large sums of money, in the realm of hundreds of millions of U.S. dollars. It sounded inconceivable to me," Pei-hua commented over her afternoon tea in Meilan's commodious sitting room.

"Who knows which is real and which is bullshit? I believe most of them are humbugs. But there is no choice if you want to do business. If you don't talk big no one will pay any attention to you. If you make tall talks people tend to think there may be some level of truth in it. They wouldn't want to miss the boat in case you are real." Like a teacher in a classroom Meilan was giving a valuable lecture. "This is how China is doing now. You'll just have to accept it and learn to behave accordingly if you intend to exist in this society. This is your lesson one."

"Those phonies, how do they get out of the embarrassment once the truth is exposed? Who will believe them anymore?"

"No matter what, the person has his moment, right? The real experts can extricate themselves from every quandary without a sweat. They can even metamorphose and come back stronger. Ah, there is so much to learn about the society, the way people operate. It's not something I can tell you in one sitting. You have to come here to feel it, taste it, savor it." Meilan gave Pei-hua a mysterious smile and insouciantly sipped her coffee.

"What is the level of truth in your image, Meilan?" Pei-hua half jokingly pricked with a sharp needle.

"Who, me?" I don't have to put up a false image. My fame and wealth are one hundred percent real. Everyone knows it. And you should not have doubted it." Meilan was serious.

"I was only joking," Pei-hua conceded. Meilan softened and smiled.

"The two-billion-dollar deal that will bring you forty million dollars of commission. That is totally real?" Pei-hua still could not believe that one.

"The deal is real, of course. But I didn't say that I would definitely succeed in bringing it to fruition. There is a lot of hard work ahead. My advantage is that these opportunities come my way because of my name and proven ability. You don't now how many people are eagerly searching for such opportunities. But even if they get them, the chances of success is almost nonexistent," Meilan earnestly defended.

"I believe so. No one can compete with you. Would you give me a tour of your office building?"

"I will take you tomorrow," Meilan said. Then she jokingly asked: "What? You want to make sure that I have an office, don't you?" Meilan grinned.

"I know you have an office," Pei-hua chuckled. "Unlike when you were in Boston and your clients from China suddenly went there to talk business with you, remember?"

Meilan laughed convulsively. "Of course. How can I ever forget that? I had to pretend to be doing well while indigent, uncertain of anything and had to appear confident. Those were trying times for me. I told those Chinese I could help them with this and that. They thought I had a large company in Boston, not knowing that I shared an one-bedroom apartment with someone else."

"You asked Ying Ying what to do. Ying Ying offered her office to you but you said it was not plush enough. You needed a stylish grand office to impress your Chinese clients and associates," Pei-hua reminisced in humor.

"So I had to rent an office in the financial district for one day." She took over from Pei-hua, and continued: "And when they asked where was my car I pointed at a Mercedes parked on the street. I said that I did not want to move my car because a parking space was too hard to find. So I called a taxi." Pei-hua laughed to tears. Then she said: "Now you have everything. You sure are the most successful and capable woman I know."

"Yea, beside you and Ying Ying." She was happy to hear Pei-hua's praise. Her reply was a mixture of pride and humility. Yes, a tiny bit of humility in front of her old friend.

"Me? Huh, there is nothing to speak of. Ying Ying maybe." Pei-hua answered matter-of-factly.

*   *   *   *

The next day Meilan sent her chauffeur to pick up Pei-hua.

This visit opened Pei-hua's eye to a different Meilan. Her office building on Nanking Road was large and modern. Apart from offices, it housed her TV studio, recording studio, film studio, and dance studio. The boutique shops, art school, and fashion manufactory were located in other areas of the city. What surprised Pei-hua were not those grand establishments, but was the Meilan that she did not know. Unveiled to her was a dictator whose petulant temper, condescending manner, and unstinting use of truculent language on her staff, imputing all mishaps to them. Pei-hua was completely stunned.

"What a bunch of Godddamn useless and careless scum you are. Your stupidity cost me dearly. How could the budget you did for the last European trip be so far off the mark? We should have made 200,000 *yuan*. Instead, we only made 160,000 *yuan*. Who is going to make up this difference?" Meilan yelled at her tremulous assistant. She was referring to her performing group's engagement in the international arts festival in Spain.

"Where is the contract? What did the contract say? Why did we end up 40,000 *yuan* short?"

Her assistant scrambled to look for the contract. Pei-hua wondered why he did not put it in the proper file that would be easy to find. But she did not utter a word. *This poor guy would be chopped to pieces by Meilan if I mention it*, she thought.

Finally the staff found the contract. It was in the Spanish language that no one understood. But they could figure out the amount of money Meilan was to be paid. It was equivalent to 200,000 *yuan* at the time the contract was signed.

"Our RMB exchange rate dropped against the Euro, and you brought along a guest star whose compensation, traveling expenses, hotel and meals came out of our side because Spain only paid for the ten members as agreed. You also bought instruments and costumes in Spain." The staff timidly hazarded an explanation for the shortfall.

Meilan was nettled: "You are blaming it on me?" she shouted. "I was tricked into a losing deal. His mother's!!" *His mother's* was a scurrilous profanity comparable to the "f" word in the English language. Pei-hua was shocked to hear that coming from Meilan's mouth.

The staff was silent.

That afternoon, all of Meilan's staff were scrubbing floors, vacuuming the carpet, cleaning the furniture, the windows and glasses, scrubbing the toilets and wash-basins. Pei-hua was perplexed and asked:

"Don't you have custodians and maintenance people? Why are your whitecollar staff members doing cleaning people's work?"

"Lesson two. Pei-hua. Don't bring your American way to China. Instead, you must learn to be conversant with the Chinese way. I train my staff to do everything. What white collar? They are lucky to have jobs. I had to feed pigs, carry water from the well and walk miles to our compound, chop firewood, and do a lot of other chores during the Cultural Revolution. Did I complain?" Meilan said unequivocally.

"Are all companies having their staff do cleaning job?" Pei-hua was still seriously curious.

"Perhaps not, but I don't care what other people do. One time I had a staff member that complained about having to get on her injured knees to scour the floor." Meilan recounted. "I told her, 'Madam, you go home to have your servant wait on you.' And I fired her on the spot."

The staff accepted their fate resignedly.

While Pei-hua was trying to take in what she was witnessing, a knock sounded on the door. There entered another staff member holding some paperwork.

"Boss. This is a bill from the framing company for the work their men did yesterday. Would you like to take a look and see it they have done a good job and if they have finished as many as they claimed? And should I pay them today?"

Pei-hua was wondering why the staff needed to bother Meilan with such triviality. Shouldn't they know the framer's fee beforehand? As the staff, should they be responsible in overseeing the job and know how many pieces were done? Did they have a rule on when a bill should be paid?

"What? They charged for a day and half? I told them to finish the job in a day." Meilan looked at the bill and was angry.

"They were here till 7pm yesterday. They couldn't finish it. So they came back today and worked for several hours," The staff member said.

"They took time to eat lunch. I saw them. Why should I pay for that time?"

The staff timidly said: "But they worked till 7pm. and more than five hours today."

"Nonsense. They were just dragging their feet so that they could swindle money out of me. No way. You just give them one day's pay and tell them to get out. Tell them not to get on my nerves. Nothing good will come of it," Meilan yelled. She did not give her staff member the answers he needed. He was hesitant but exited without another word.

Pei-hua returned to Li Yong's apartment. A question marked in her mind: *what happened to Meilan?* The next morning as she was getting ready to venture into the city again the phone ran. It was Meilan.

"Pei-hua. I am glad to have caught you in time. I need you to help me at a business meeting. In fact I need you to help me with that large business deal. It is urgent. I will send my chauffeur to pick you up." She did not ask if Pei-hua had made other plans. It wouldn't matter. Her need was more important than Pei-hua's plan, naturally. Pei-hua wavered. Meilan spoke again.

"Hurry up. The chauffeur will be there in a few minutes." So, she had already sent her chauffeur before she called. Even as Pei-hua was calling Li Yong to let him know where she would be the chauffeur rang the bell.

As soon as Pei-hua stepped in her door Meilan hastily poured out her plan:

"Pei-hua, I am having a meeting with the Americans and Japanese this morning. There will be a few Chinese too. The meeting is at Ritz-Carlton Hotel where the Americans and Japanese are staying. This is the big two-billion-dollar project I told you about. I want you to go with me. You will be my translator."

"Is this your first meeting?" Pei-hua asked.

"No, we have met many times. It is complicated. No single meeting can resolve anything," Meilan answered as she grabbed her brief case.

"You don't have a translator?" Since she already had several meetings why did she not have a translator?

"I used several and fired them all. None of them was good enough. You will be perfect." Meilan locked the door behind them as they were leaving the apartment.

"But I won't be here for long. What do you do when I am gone?" Pei-hua asked as they stepped in the elevator.

"I will get another one. But for now I want you to do it." Meilan glanced at her watch.

Pei-hua walked into the meeting with no knowledge about the project. For a translator it would be most difficult under such circumstances. No wonder Meilan's translators could not do a good job! It was not the issue with the language but rather the content of the project itself that had perplexed the translators. Of course with Pei-hua's mental acumen, legal training, and knowledge she quickly apprehended the whole picture of the project. As such she not only translated but also expatiated in many instances. She clarified several major cruxes that were confusing to Meilan and the others.

Pei-hua was curious why the Japanese delegates were able to speak English, though with a very thick accent, while the Chinese representatives of a government unit could not at all.

Meilan was very pleased with Pei-hua's help. She asked her to take home a thick stack of documents to translate for her. Pei-hua told Meilan that she did not have a computer in Li Yong's apartment Furthermore, she was absolutely ignorant of the ping-yin system. As such it would be impossible to enter Chinese text in the computer.

"That's simple. You can stay here and use the computer. I will tell my secretary Li Ya to enter the Chinese text for you." Meilan made the arrangement complacently.

"These will take many days to do. Look how thick the pile is. Can you pick out the more important and urgently needed documents? I will do those first. If there is time I will do more," Pei-hua suggested with reason.

"I don't now which is more important. Can you read them and decide which to translate first? We have another meeting tomorrow. We need those documents." Meilan insisted on her unreasonable demand.

"Unless I read every document I can't be sure which are more important. . All right. I will try to do my best." Pei-hua gave in.

Pei-hua was used to reviewing lengthy legal documents regularly. She was a fast reader. Yet she could not go through that big pile in three hours. She picked out a dozen English documents and several Chinese ones including a detailed contract and an explanation of the projected budget. She and Li Ya each used a computer. She typed in the English translation of the Chinese documents and verbally translated the English documents for Li Ya to type into Chinese *ping-yin* in another computer.

At 6:00 pm Li Yong called and asked when she would be home. She told him that she was helping Meilan with a translation.

"Do you want me to buy some takeout for you and Meilan?" Li Yong asked.

"It's all right. I think Meilan may get something."

"Is she there with you?"

"No, she is in her office. I am in a different room with her secretary. I have a lot to do."

"May I come over? I will wait for you." Li Yong was concerned and sweet like a good husband.

"If you want. But you don't have to."

"I will come."

Li Yong came. Meilan called a restaurant to deliver dinner for four to her office. After dinner Li Yong and Meilan chatted in her office while waiting for Pei-hua to finish the translation in the other room. She and Li Ya worked till midnight.

"You must be very tired. Meilan should not have asked you to do so much work for her. You are on vacation. Why doesn't she hire translators? There is no shortage of well-experienced translators. They only cost more," Li Yong commented as they were on their way home in his car.

"I didn't expect that she would ask me to do this much. The project is large and complex. Her translators had no idea about the project and were not able to do a good job for her. I have to go to the meeting with her again tomorrow."

Pei-hua attended not two but many meetings with Meilan. She instinctively felt that the Chinese and the Japanese thought of her as a hired hand and treated her accordingly, as they usually did with their subordinates, without proper respect.

"I am amazed at how much I am not used to the way people in a work environment act here," Pei-hua spoke to Li Yong at home.

"You mean...?"

"Maybe it is the traditions and customs of the Chinese and Japanese societies, or the other Asian societies as well. There is this strong, well-defined distinction of class between the boss/superior and the hired-hand/subordinate or inferior. Caste is unbreakable. Hired hands must be submissive, servile, and enduring rudeness and harshness of their superiors."

"Something at Meilan's office prompted your comments?"

"Yea, but not only that. It is obvious. Secretaries are servants. They make tea for the boss, clean her desk, hang up her coat, not dare to exonerate themselves when being wrongfully blamed and verbally abused. I wouldn't be surprised if the boss hit the secretary."

"No, not that far," Li Yong chuckled. "I understand how you feel. The subordinates can never talk to the bosses as an equal. They are always very vigilant about what may displease the boss. The bosses treat them like slaves without concern or basic respect."

256

"Would you like to be in a subordinate position?"

Li Yong smirked and said: "No one would like to be in that position but a large number of people are. And they understand and accept that as the way it is."

"I don't."

"You don't have too. You are always respected by people as a corporate attorney in Boston. More so here."

"No, not so here. I have been treated like a hired-hand with all the consequences."

"What? I don't understand."

"I am Meilan's translator. Everyone treats me as such. I feel extremely uncomfortable in that situation."

"Really?" Li Yong was a little irked: "That is awful. You are giving her so much help and she has not properly introduced you and seen to it that people pay you proper respect and gratitude? I am going to have a talk with her."

"No, Li Yong. Don't make a federal case out of it." Pei-hua smiled, feeling good about Li Yong's concern. "I will talk to her myself."

"Of course. I know what you mean." Li Yong said understandingly.

The next day Pei-hua did talk to Meilan: "Meilan, can you let the people know that I am your friend, vacationing in Beijing and giving you help at your request? The Chinese and Japanese treat me as a hired-hand, a servant, no respect at all."

A usual response would be something like "I haven't noticed that. I am sorry. I will re-introduce you to them" was what Pei-hua expected. Yet it was not Meilan's response.

"Ai-ya, why do you care so much about that? No one is treating you as a servant." Meilan's brash reply astounded and irritated Pei-hua. The ruthless dictator had lost her temper many times at the meeting and during breaks when things did not go smoothly, when the Chinese representatives were distrait, displaying an insouciant attitude that acerbated her anger. But she had no right to unfurl her insolence on Pei-hua.

"Meilan, I do care. I am not used to your Chinese pomposity, especially when I am being taken as an inferior while spending my vacation time and effort trying to help you."

Meilan was astounded by Pei-hua's sudden show of intolerance. She stared at her for two seconds.

These government bureaucrats were not motivated to push the project through because there was no personal benefit in this government project unless Meilan tactfully bribed them. Yet there was no sign that Meilan had such a plan. The bureaucrats could not but resent Meilan for making a huge commission.

"These bastards have no intention to see the project succeed because they cannot make money from it openly. Little do they know, I will let them make a bundle. When I drop that on their laps they won't know what hit them. But now I cannot talk about it. They will be put in jail for taking bribery. I would be implicated too. There is a whole book of tact for bribery. You will never learn it. But I know the highly sensitive maneuver."

Meilan overlooked Pei-hua's confrontational remark and went on boasting about her business prowess.

"How do you do it then?" Pei-hua suppressed her vex and asked

"Well, there are many ways. I can offer several of them. I can guarantee to get their children to America for schooling, deposit money in their bank accounts abroad, buy houses for them wherever the schools are, and so forth. I will hire housekeepers, cooks, and chauffeurs to take care of their kids. Their names will not be inferred. These son-of-bitches, because I could not openly promise them these things, worry about not getting any goodies" Meilan expatiated adeptly.

"That's how those pretentious young kids flaunt and squander their unwarranted wealth." Pei-hua was talking to herself. She had seen too many youngsters going to expensive private schools in Massachusetts. They lived like royalties, in large expensive houses and served by several household staff, chauffeured around in Mercedes, Audi, and Bentley.

"Can you invite them to your apartment individually and lay it out for them?" Pei-hua questioned.

"No. It's risky that way. They would not trust me. They might think that I plot to expose them. And I would worry about them suing me for bribing government officials."

"Then there is no way out. What do you do?" Pei-hua failed to see any other options.

"I have no good plans yet. But I must come up with one." They sat in silence for a while. Then Meilan had another demand.

"Pei-hua. I need you to be my legal council. My lawyer is useless as you probably sensed. He doesn't know English either. I need you to handle the whole project for me, especially the bribery part." Meilan openly made her demand. Pei-hua was alarmed by her boldness.

"Meilan, you know I don't have much time left here. I must go back to my work in New York. I cannot do it for you. And bribery is way out of my alley."

"Hai. Don't you reject my request so off handedly. Don't you think I am exploiting you? Don't worry about a thing. I will pay you handsomely." Meilan made another surly remark. Then she tried to coax Pei-hua: "Beside, Li Yong will be happy to keep you here. Think of your marriage."

"Meilan, I don't care about pay. I am always willing to help friends. I will help you as much as I can. Friends don't help friends because of money. I am not going to charge you. Really. But I must go back to New York. I cannot change the course of my life because of your project." Pei-hua's and Ying Ying's upbringings were different from that of people in Mainland China. That was why those people could never understand the two women's sense of value.

"Don't give me that lofty talk." Taking Pei-hua by surprise, Meilan snapped, and pounded on the table: "not caring about money; not going to charge me. How can I listen to this bullshit? You set yourself up so high and haughty. You make yourself seem so pure and different from everyone. Who can believe that? Everyone wants money. Don't make me seem reek with the odor of coins." Pei-hua was so petrified that she lost her words. Melian's gruff scurrility continued to assault her ears:

"I don't believe a shit of what you are saying," she shrieked: "You are no different from those dog fuckers, jealous of me, hate to see me succeed. I was going to make you a partner and share my commission with you. But before I had a chance to tell you, you thought I was going to get a free ride from you. OK, reject me. You think I cannot find someone as capable as you?" she stomped out of the room leaving Pei-hua paralyzed in disbelieve.

What has happened to her? Has money and power poisoned her? Pei-hua was beyond feeling hurt, insulted, and abused. She was indignant and sad at the same time.

Without seeing Meilan again, she called Li Yong to pick her up.

*   *   *   *

Pei-hua found herself more and more at odds with Shanghai. She told Li Yong that she must go back to New York and reassess her values and direction before making a decision on where she would be. An ominous portent haunted him. He knew he would not be able to sway her this time.

In order to avoid speaking with Meilan, Pei-hua did not answer phone calls. She briefly described to Li Yong what had happened and asked him to tell Meilan that she had already returned to the States.

After she announced her leaving, came a slew of dinner invitations of which she only accepted a few. The night before her departure Li Yong and her had a romantic candlelight dinner at a French restaurant. Pei-hua was especially gentle and sweet the whole evening. This was a farewell to Li Yong. He knew it.

She flew to New York and returned to her apartment feeling lonelier than ever. She couldn't help but cry. She loved Li Yong. But they hardly ever had a normal married life. And now if she wanted to be with him, she had to sacrifice her career, her best friends, her sense of values, and the place she loved, to relocate to China where people's views, ideas, behaviors, and most of all, sense of value were diametrically opposed to her own. She resolved that she could not succumb to that.

A short pain is better than a long pain, she told herself. She immersed herself in work for a week before she called Ying Ying.

"Ying, I think I am going to divorce Li Yong."

"Are you in Shanghai?" Ying Ying thought Pei-hua must have had some words with Li Yong.

"No, I am back. A week ago."

"You're over the jetlag?" Ying Ying asked. After a short pause she asked again, "How was the trip? How is Li Yong? What happened?" She got to the point.

"Li Yong is fine," Pei-hua spoke, and paused, and spoke again. "But I felt distant. I wouldn't want to be in Shanghai.... There is no other option." She meant her divorce.

"That bad!!"

"You would not want to be there either. The people are opposite from us. The society, beautiful on the surface.... But rotten to the core." She also told Ying Ying about Meilan, her presumptuous behavior, her truculent treatment of her staff, and her collaboration with Li Yong.

Ying Ying empathized with Pei-hua. Yet it hurt her to foresee her best friend suffering from a divorce. She could feel for Li Yong's loss too.

"But Pei-hua, aren't you a bit precipitous? Give yourself a little more time to think through it. You and Li Yong were so much in love and have gone through a lot. I know you are distraught now. But... Just give it a little more time before you decide. Okay? I will come to see you this weekend." Ying Ying's gentle voice soothed Pei-hua somewhat.

Pei-hua's mind was made up. A weekend with Ying Ying did not change it. "Ying, a short pain is better than a long pain. You know that. My love for Li Yong and our constant separation have consumed me already. Now, I feel he and I don't belong together. Maybe the difference between them, those who grew up under the Cultural Revolution, and us are irreconcilable. It was not so blatant while they were here. Once they are back to their homeland, their true selves are nakedly exposed. "

"You mean Li Yong too?" Li Yong was a true artist, in Ying Ying's mind.

"I think he hides that side of him from me. I believe his joining Meilan is motivated only by money and power instead of any noble cause such as providing better education to aspiring young theatre enthusiasts." Pei-hua revealed her deep suspicion.

"I hope you are wrong about him." Ying Ying was still hopeful.

"You know how many people, friends of his friends, approached me, asking for collaboration in all kinds of money-making schemes?"

"You? What kind of money-making scheme could they propose to you, beside gouging the clients." Ying Ying made a cliché joke.

"Sponsoring music and dance competitions and bringing the winners to Boston for arts exchange, organizing young models to stage fashion shows here, bringing rich college-bound youngsters to Boston to join the study-abroad preparatory camp we would provide, etc, etc, etc." Pei-hua ignored Ying Ying's facetious joke and answered her question solemnly.

"These are good projects. Why do you discount them?" Ying Ying asked.

"Oh yes, the projects sound worth doing. But those people's intention is not on the projects. Those projects were carefully thought out to entice the zealous parents into spending money. Their sole purpose is to make money inequitably under false pretenses. They will gouge the selected participants by charging large registration fees. Yea, you are right, *gouge,*" Pei-hua vented.

After hearing a detailed account of those proposals, Ying Ying sighed:

"That's not right. In most instances, moneymaking is appropriate, even imperative, for example running a business, or investing in real estate and stocks. But using a public benefiting project as a pretext to unjustly gouge people is contemptible."

"What a difference, like day and night, between you and them, Ying." Pei-hua spoke her true feeling.

The morning after Ying Ying left, Pei-hua called Li Yong in Shanghai, but at no avail as expected. She left a message for him to call back. There was a certain chill in her voice that Li Yong immediately knew what Pei-hua was about to say to him. *She has made up her mind to leave me.*

He did not return the call until two days later. His excuse was that he was out of town. He knew that Pei-hua knew it was a lie. When the word "divorce" hit his eardrum through the airwave he was not surprised.

"Pei-hua, I have begged you not to leave me. Does our marriage mean anything to you? I am sorry that America is more important to you." He was unusually disimpassioned. "However, China is your country too. You should be pleased and proud to see our country stepping out of the past shadow toward a bright future. There is so much that we can do here. But you refuse to consider. You have made up your mind. I respect that."

That was it. That was it!!

Although it was her own decision she couldn't stop feeling that she had been completely drained. Frightening vacuity swelled her mind and broken heart. She collapsed on her sofa, tears streaming down her checks. She did not know whether she had fallen asleep or was lost in a deep, dark abyss of despair. When she opened her eyes it was completely dark.

She called Swanson, Williams and Murphy, her old law firm in Boston, and spoke with the main principal. He welcomed her back with both arms. In a few weeks she resigned from her job in New York and re-joined the Boston law firm. She rented in Tremont-On-The-Common again, though a different apartment. It was facing the Common, like the one before. She often invited her old friends over for a simple dinner and chat. The sadness of the divorce and the feeling of desolation were eased by having those friends around her.

The news of her divorce broke her parents' hearts. Her mother cried while asking how she was doing and offered to come and keep her company for a while. Pei-hua's parents were separated for many years because of that Peking opera singer. They did not divorce. That thread connecting them was always there. And there was the old-fashioned notion of marriage that bound the couple together. Pei-hua's father just strayed away. His wife knew he would be back. Eventually after the kids left home he came back.

"Ma, why don't you and dad just move to Boston? Dad has retired. You don't have to stay in Taipei," Pei-hua urged. It was true. What would be better than moving to where their daughter was? So a short time later they rented out their house in Taipei, moved to Boston and rented an apartment in the same building as Pei-hua's. They wanted to buy a large house in the suburbs and have Pei-hua move there with them. But Pei-hua preferred to live in the city close to her work. Eventually her parents compromised and bought two spacious luxury condos on Beacon Street near the Common. The mother said:

"This way you have your own place and only next door to Dad and me. You have to take care of us." In fact the mother wanted to take care of her girl. It was a perfect setup that pleased everyone. Pei-hua had her meals at her parents' place and spent as much time as she had with them. Ying Ying and Kang Wei also felt comfortable and at home when visiting Uncle and Auntie Liu. Even the old gang from China Society relished the warmth and comfort in the Liu household. Following the Chinese custom they also addressed the senior couple as Uncle and Auntie Liu.

*   *   *   *

Once a year, like all green-card holders, Meilan would take a trip back to the U.S. in order to keep her status valid. This year, Meilan came to Boston shortly after Pei-hua and her parents settled down in their new homes. She seemed to have forgotten her scurrilous manner toward Pei-hua in Beijing, or she pretended it never happened. She called Pei-hua and said:

"Pei-hua, you left Shanghai without letting me know. Was that what a good friend should do? I felt so sad. I thought about you every day." It was her old mellifluous lilt.

She gathered some of her old acquaintances at her hotel for tea and dim sum. She also went to Pei-hua's parents' home with other friends to make dumplings or cook a meal together. She was sweet, pleasant and full of fun, a completely different person from the one in Beijing. Her wittiness and charm quickly won Mrs. Liu's heart. Her many colorful stories amused the elderly couple who had never heard anything about life in China during the Cultural Revolution.

"She left the other Meilan in Beijing." This was Pei-hua's answer when Ying Ying asked what happened to her characterization of the new Meilan. The Meilan in Boston was as lovable as before.

One of those old acquaintances who intrigued Meilan was Susie. She was one of the dancers Meilan had led in rehearsals for China Society's dance showcase in 1989 for the celebration of Chinese New Year. Susie was not a shiny star or award winner like Ching Ju and Ailing who were featured as soloists in the event. Nor was she good looking or well trained like those mainland dancers. She played an insignificant role in that event.

For years she struggled to make a living for herself and her young son and tried to study English at the same time. The only work she could find was low paying menial jobs. Then she got a small but steady job at Boston's City Hall. Without a marketable skill, or an advanced degree, or good command of the English language, there was no prospect of a better future. However, she was content, and hoped for nothing more.

Yet Fate was kind to her. Luck came knocking on her door. One day a co-worker of hers, a Chinese woman from Singapore, asked for her help.

"Susie, I hope you can do me this favor, to pick up a couple at the Logan airport. I don't know this couple. But they are from Singapore as I am. My friend has asked me to pick them up but I am not free tomorrow. Can you do it? I am sure they will tip you," Susie's co-worker asked.

"I suppose. I got nothing to do to morrow." Susie replied.

"I have to find a hotel for them. That won't be too hard," the woman said.

"It may not be too easy either. Booking a hotel room usually needs a few days in advance," Susie commented.

"Oh, gee. Can you make a few phone calls, please?" the woman further demanded.

"What kind of a hotel? I mean what price range?"

"I don't know. I guess not the expensive ones."

Susie reserved a room in a two-star hotel in Inman Square, Cambridge The next day she went to the terminal, holding up a sign she made, with the couple's name on it. This was the only way she and the couple could identify each other. She took them to the hotel and gave them her phone number. She promised that she would help them in any way she could if they let her know. The lady, Mrs. Deng, thanked her and gave her a hundred dollars. She pushed it back to the lady and said that she was happy to help. She did not accept the tip.

The lady said that they needed to hire a guide to show them around. She asked if Susie could be their guide.

"I would love to show you around. Let me ask my boss if I can use my vacation time."

A city government's job is lightweight. No one would miss her for a few days during her absence. Her supervisor let her take her vacation. For two weeks she showed the couple around Boston, and accompanied the lady on her shopping sprees. She was in awe when the lady purchased jewelry at Tiffany for tens of thousands of dollars each. She pondered: *This couple must be very rich*. Yet they stayed in the inexpensive hotel she reserved without saying anything.

At the end of the two weeks, Mr. Deng gave Susie $5,000. Mrs. Deng gave her some nice gifts. Susie declined saying that she made $2,000 a month at work. $5,000 was way too much for two weeks. She would accept the gifts, but not the money. Mrs. Deng insisted and said they were very appreciative of her help; she had made their visit to Boston a very pleasant one; that alone was worth more than the money they offered her. She could not decline further but accepted the money and thanked them.

They exchanged addresses and phone numbers with Susie and said that if at any time she wished to visit Singapore she would be their guest. Shortly after the couple returned home Susie received two open-dated roundtrip plane tickets to Singapore. Susie was very surprised and happy. She requested another week of leave of absence from her supervisor and asked her son's school to excuse him for a week. They flew to Singapore.

They stayed at the Deng's huge mansion. They were taken in a chauffeur-driven Rolls Royce to see the city and other small islands that made up

Singapore state. Mrs. Deng told Susie that they were brought together by kismet. She and her husband were fond of Susie and believed that she was a nice woman who was also worthy of their trust.

They asked if Susie would do some work for them in Boston.

"What kind of work? I would be happy to do it for you if you think I have the ability." Susie also liked the couple. She thought they were very kind and generous. They certainly would compensate her well if she did work for them.

"Handle some business for us," Mrs. Deng said. "We may want to invest in something in Boston, but are not sure what. We will not be there. So we need to have someone whom we like and can trust. We think you are that person. My husband and I have considered a number of people. But we like to ask you to do it."

Susie was completely astounded. She had never thought about doing business because she had no money or opportunity. But she was diligent and dedicated to whatever she did. She believed that she could handle it, if she was given the responsibility.

"Thank you for your trust. I will do my best."

"That is good enough. You have lived in Boston for some years. Do you know anything about the real estate market there?" Mrs. Deng asked.

"Oh," Susie smiled: "I do know a little. I have a real estate license. But it's expired because I have not renewed it after I got a job at the City Hall."

"That is very good. It means you have knowledge in real estate. We want to invest in some properties. I would like you to help us find the good ones. This is a start. If it goes well we can do more."

"This I think I can do well." Susie said with ample confidence.

Upon her return Susie wasted no breath in searching for properties in Cambridge and Brookline. She carefully evaluated and compared many of them and recommended only four to the Dengs. Mrs. Deng told her to go ahead and purchase the four. She made her offers. All purchases were in cash. There was no waiting for mortgage approval. The transactions were fast. The sellers were pleased.

Susie asked Mrs. Deng to come for the closing when all the papers would be signed. Mrs. Deng replied:

"We want you to be our power of attorney. We will send you the paper immediately and you are authorized to handle the transactions," Mrs. Deng said.

After completing the legal process Susie called the Dengs asking about what to do next.

"Pick the best one for yourself. Rent out the rest. You manage them for us," Mr. Deng said.

"One for myself?" Susie was not sure what Mr. Deng meant. "Manage your properties?"

"Yes, One for yourself. Move in it. It's yours. Your apartment is too small and Roxbury is a bad area for your son. If you like Brookline pick the house in Brookline," Mr. Deng said unequivocally.

Susie was moved to tears. Her voice quivered:

"Mr. and Mrs. Deng, you are too generous. How can I thank you? What should I say?"

"Don't say anything. You are helping us. It's very fair," Mr. Deng said.

Susie rented out the three houses and moved into the one in Brookline. Nothing could make her happier than taking Ricky out of the rough school in Roxbury and put him into a Brookline school. She felt blessed and wanted to do more for the Dengs. During their frequent telephone conversations she asked about the Deng's investment objective. The Deng's had a network of people they trusted working in different cities in the U.S. and other countries for them. They were testing Susie at this time to find out her potential and trustworthiness. As soon as they thought Susie had the ability and dedication to do the work they entrusted her, they gave her the power and freedom to do what she saw fit.

"You study the market and decide what to buy. When you see a good opportunity, grab it. Tell us how much and we will wire the money over." Beside unwavering trust, the Deng's placed a tremendous duty on Susie. The financial resources seemed limitless. Susie was enormously grateful for their trust and willingly accepted the duty. Within a matter of over a year she purchased a five-star hotel, a two-hundred unit plush apartment building, two large office buildings in the Financial District in Downtown Boston, four storefronts on Newberry Street in Boston, and several nightclubs and restaurants near the Theatre District. These cost hundreds of millions of dollars. She had an in-house maintenance team of various workmen at her disposal at any moment, and a management team of skilled professionals. She contracted a large law firm to handle legal issues. The operation system was well laid out.

The financial gain on her part was considerable. The Deng's gave her 20% of ownership of the corporation they formed, with Susie as the president. In addition she got 2.5% to 5% of commission from every building she purchased because she acted as the buyer's agent. She also made a handsome salary.

She became a big shot in the real estate agencies because of her quick decisions, fast actions, and cash transactions. Mr. Deng did not like to borrow money for mortgages. All purchases were paid in cash. After the real estate acquisitions, she set her mine on banks and shopping malls.

Chapter 9

$\mathscr{M}$arket economy reversed the course in China. "Ample opportunities and lawlessness" was a fitting portrayal of that country. Without an effective tax law threw the doors wide open for sly individuals to abuse the opportunities at will. In that environment, some mega riches emerged. Most of these new riches desired to send their children to America. The environment fitted perfectly for those vulpine "Returned from Abroad" Chinese to cajole money from the wealthy. Promising to get the rich men's kids to America was a magic wand that worked in all instances. In exchange, the rich men must enter into a business partnership with these returning Chinese, several of whom were associated with China Society at one time or another. With money from China, these people opened restaurants, grocery stores, Asian import companies, Chinese furniture stores, and real estate agencies among others.

Woolan struck the biggest gold mine. During his visit to Beijing he discovered that one of his fellow brick-bakers named Tian Kun had become a multibillionaire. He quickly found out this rich chap's address and phone number and made a call.

"Old Tian. This is Woolan. You remember me, of course. I just came from Boston to visit some friends, including you definitely." The way he addressed the guy as old Tian and spoke in such intimate tones and words was to close the distance between them. It worked well. Tian Kun was surprised and elated. The images of twenty years before rushed vividly to the front of his eyes.

"Oh! Woolan, of course, you rascal you. You damn kid ran away from us. You know we were all sent to look for you?"

"Ha, ha, ha," Woolan gave the best answer. "How were things after I ran away? Did you stay there long?"

"What else? The same as always. You inspired me to escape that hell too." Tian Kun laughed.

"Oh, then you owe me for your financial empire. If you didn't escape you would probably still be baking bricks," Woolan joked and laughed.

"You are not kidding. There are still some stupid ones left there." Tian Kun was a clever guy back then. Woolan sensed that as soon as he met him.

Had Woolan not fled he would probably have been the first one to do so. In their miserable existence Tian Kun had thought that one day Woolan would become someone important; and he promised himself that he would achieve greatness in some way too. He looked up to Woolan for his decisiveness, courage, and success in plotting and executing the escape. He followed his inspirer's footstep soon after.

"Let's not chat through the telephone. Come to my house. We will have a good open-bosom talk. We need that. It's been twenty years," Tian Kun said in high spirit.

Woolan went to his house. A large quadrangle residence (*si-he yuan*) with three courtyards, one behind the other, and edifices surrounding each of the courtyards, that used to be the home of a Manchurian prince, completely restored to its original grandeur. It was situated near the center of Beijing and yet city noises were buffered by the high brick walls and the large first-layer courtyard. The world inside the walls and bronze double doors with animal head knockers was one of elegance and luxury. A pair of marble lions crouched on both sides of the doors. A servant dressed in Chinese man's long dress in the style of a hundred years or so ago opened the door. White undershirt's collar showing behind the man's dark blue outer dress's "mandarin collar," and the white undershirt's sleeves folded over the outer dress's sleeves. Black pants shown from the high slits on both sides of his dress. The man also wore a pair of black cloth shoes and white cotton socks. He seemed to have walked out from about year 1900.

Woolan smiled at the reverse anachronism or time-game. But he knew it had become fashionable, among the wealthy, to hold nostalgic reminiscence of the past. It was a romantic yearning reflected in TV dramas as well as some restaurant and teahouse decors.

The servant led the way to the hall of the first layer of buildings where another servant walked swiftly through the second and third courtyards and halls to announce the arrival of the master's guest. Woolan walked slowly stopping to admire the antique artwork displayed in cases and shelves and paintings and calligraphy pieces hanging on the wall. He was giving time for Tian Kun to come and meet him half way. As he entered the second hall Tian Kun was striding quickly toward him in broad smile.

"Ha, brother Woolan, finally we meet again." Tian Kun warmly grabbed both of Woolan's hands, holding them together and tightly, and shook them: "Welcome, welcome."

"Brother Tian. Prosperity agrees well with you. You look wonderful, almost young as you were twenty years ago."

"Foreign water agrees with you too. I am sure you are just as prosperous in America."

"Ha, ha, ha," Woolan laughed. He did not want to appear awestruck by Tian Kun's enormous wealth. He needed to have Tian believe that he was also rich and successful. He gave a benign answer: "I Cannot compare with you. None can compare with you."

In their conversation Tian Kun told Woolan that he had a sixteen-year-old son whom he would like to send either to Europe or America for schooling. It was Woolan's chance to offer help.

"If you are serious about sending him to America, Boston would be the place," Woolan suggested in a seemingly casual tone.

"Yes, I heard that Boston has the best schools. And more than anywhere else."

"That's true. But some schools are better than others. Han-han is in senior high, isn't he?"

"Yes, the first year of senior high. He has two more years before college. I hope he can enter Harvard or MIT."

Woolan had heard people talking about how demanding Harvard or MIT were. But he was not about to discourage Tian Kun with that information.

"Of course. Those are the best universities in the world. I am sure Han-han is a good student and can get in."

"Can he go to Boston now?" Tian Kun had no clue how to send the boy abroad. Woolan had heard about investment immigration. He offered his opinion:

"The best and surest way is that you invest in some business in America. Then you and your family will be eligible for immigration. Of course you will not be interested in that but Han-han can have a green card and study there. And it will be very convenient for you too. You and your wife can vacation in America any time you want."

The idea sounded attractive. "How much should I invest and in what business?" Tian Kun asked.

"One million. The business must create ten job opportunities to Americans. This is called Investment Immigration," Woolan explained.

"One million. That's nothing. Easily done. Specifically what business do you think we can do with this one million?" Tian Kun's interest was heightened.

"I think the easiest would be a mid-size restaurant. Chefs, waiters, cashier, factotum, there will be more than ten jobs created." Restaurant business was familiar to Woolan.

"Would you, brother Woolan, see to it that this is done? Would you be willing to partner with me in this venture? I will lay out the million. I know it's too small for you. But it wouldn't hurt to add this to your other businesses. When this is successful we can collaborate on many other ventures. That is if you don't mind working with me." Tian Kun coached his request in mellifluous terms.

Woolan accepted this suggestion placidly so as not to show his zeal. He achieved his scheme with more ease than he had hoped. Tian Kun found a way to send his boy to America unexpectedly. He was elated. One million U.S. was such an insignificant figure to him. Any profit from the restaurant would be an extra bonus.

A sumptuous dinner in an expensive restaurant was what Woolan was expecting from Tian Kun. But Tian Kun ordered his kitchen to prepare the dinner instead.

"It is a humble home-made supper. Very disrespectful," Tian Kun said as he showed Woolan to a seat at the dinner table. There were only the two of them as his wife had gone to Hong Kong shopping and his son was out with friends.

The dining room was large and richly appointed with antique furniture. The sumptuous and exquisite food paled even the best restaurants banquets. Tian Kun had under his full-time employment the best chefs in Shanghai and Beijing. They claimed to have apprenticed with the old master chefs of the Forbidden City.

With the million dollars Woolan opened a nice restaurant in Cambridge. As promised, he helped Tian Kun's son to come and enroll in a private school in Newton. He was going to find a host family for the boy but Tian Kun wanted to buy a house near the school, hire a housekeeper, a cook and a chauffeur for his son.

"We have suffered so much in our youth. Why let the kids go through any hardship and inconvenience? What is money for?"

Spending money was not a bit difficult. Woolan found a new fifteen-room house on the carriage lane of Commonwealth Avenue in Newton, bought a Mercedes, and hired two household staff before the boy and his mother came. He only bought a few pieces of furniture and left the furnishing to Mrs. Tian.

"I heard that there are interior designers who have good ideas about decorating the rooms. Why don't we let them do it? I don't have the time to shop for all the things. And to tell you the truth, I don't know what is fashionable in Boston," Mrs. Tian conceded. So they hired an interior designer.

The restaurant's business was good. Before long a second one was opened in Boston. Tian Kun would entertain other joint ventures with Woolan as he had indicated. Real estate investment caught Woolan's fancy. He suggested it to Tian Kun who accepted it with a request to form a legal partnership. As equal partners Woolan's investment would be his effort in finding appropriate buildings, and management of the businesses, not cash. Tian Kun was more than generous. Yet he regarded it as being fair and just.

Modeled after Susie, Woolan started with buying multi-family dwellings and rented them out. Next he acquired apartment buildings, then office buildings, commercial buildings in shopping malls, hotels, and finally he bought a bank. Like Susie's backer Mr. Deng, Tian Kun also had unbounded capital at his disposal. Woolan did not fail him. The real estate appreciated, rental income was substantial, and the bank was profitable. Woolan was now a rich man himself and a big shot. The real estate brokers in Boston, Cambridge, Brookline and Newton were in awe with the two powerhouses, Susie and Woolan. They respected these two Chinese as astute and decisive investors with unlimited resources. They tried to ingratiate themselves with the two to ensure a share of their patronage.

*　　*　　*　　*

Sun Sang also became a financial success. With only an elementary school education in China and knowing no English, his chances of making it in America were slim. He did not take the usual beaten path of finding a wealthy investor in China. He tried importing Chinese goods without success before settling on restaurant work. Many Chinese restaurant workers often gambled at Fox Wood Resort Casino and Mohegan Sun Casino in Massachusetts and Connecticut respectively. Since they usually lost money they facetiously referred their gambling lost as "depositing money."

Sun Sang resisted the temptation. "Why throw hard-earned money away? I would rather do something useful in my spare time," he declared. His second cousin was a computer technician who traded stocks online after work. He had made some easy money. Sun Sang asked this cousin to show him how to do it. Then he bought a computer and began trading. At the same time he tried to learn English in order to read and listen to reports on TV about stock market movements and the economy in general. He was thrilled when he made a hundred dollars one day.

"I will make one hundred each day. Three thousand a month!!! That's equivalent to waiting on tables," he told friends with joy and confidence. He continued to hone his trading skills and tried to read news about stocks. He was able to make out the content of the news articles from the little bits and pieces he did understand. He also had a clear insight of world economy and international affairs that helped him in making astute decisions in regard to trading. One time he told Ying Ying that he was thinking of buying a house in Newton for $600,000. He had to sell his stocks for that. Ying Ying encouraged him:

"Yes, Sun Sang, buying a house is a good move. The house will always be yours. And it will increase in value. Stocks go up and down. You will never be sure whether the money is yours until you cash in. My father warned me not to play with stocks or do anything in the nature of gambling."

"Yes, you are right. I will take money out and buy this house."

A few weeks later when Ying Ying saw him again and asked about the house, he smiled shyly.

"I, I did not buy it. I was reluctant about depleting my stocks for the house. Then I would have had to start without capital again, and lose the chance of making more in the mean time."

"Oh." Ying Ying was disappointed. "Did you make more during these weeks?"

"No, on the contrary. I lost $550,000." Sun sang seemed embarrassed. But he was not discouraged. "I will make it back. I have learned a lot from this loss."
He was a very intelligent man who learned from his mistakes. In no time he made back all the money he had lost. As he continued to trade, he won sometimes, lost sometimes. But always he learned a great deal from losing and became a highly perspicacious trader. Other people followed suit but lost all their savings. Since he became so successful he accumulated a sizable sum. He bought a house for two million dollars. In a few years he became a private hutch fund manager.

*   *   *   *

Another one of those very rich Chinese who invested money in Boston was Dai Tong. Dai Tong was a bare-foot peasant in the mid-1980s. In a matter of only ten years he amassed an incredible amount of wealth. He started as a small peddler of various goods he bought from one town and sold at another for a small profit. He was endowed with keen eyes and an astute mind albeit without an education. No opportunity eluded him. The one venture that turned his fortune was building apartment complexes with little capital. He started selling the units as soon as the architectural drawings and blueprints were ready. Before construction even began he had already sold all the units. He stayed in the real estate development business for a number of years and moved on to other even more profitable ventures such as coal mining and oil extraction in Manchuria. Like Tian Kun, with the help of a Chinese in Boston he got his son to enroll in a college there. He bought multi-million-dollar homes in Weston, Martha's Vineyard, and Cape Cod, furnished the garages with a Bentley, a Bugatti Veyron and a Ferrari.

Because Dai Tong and his wife only spent two or three weeks a year in the States, he entrusted An Kai, the man instrumental in getting his son to Boston, to manage his properties. An Kai's duty was managing the household staff at each of the three locations. Of course he was amply compensated.

For years An Kai's income reported to the IRS was below poverty line. Ever since his wife Hu Ning had a baby they qualified for government-subsidized housing, free health care and other benefits. Hu Ning's mother was brought from China to watch their granddaughter so that Hu Ning could work under the table without reporting her income. They lived a pretty comfortable life with all possible benefits from the government. As Hu Ning said, there were so many people doing exactly what they did. Only fools did not take full advantage of the system, a very familiar saying among those welfare recipients.

Hu Ning was the actress playing the role of Empress in *Intrigues in the Manchu Imperial Court* and fell in love with Meng Song afterwards. The biggest joy of hers as a result of her husband managing Dai Tong's houses was that she got to drive those luxury cars, entertain her friends in the magnificent mansion in Weston, and take vacations in the gorgeous houses on Cape Cod and Martha's Vineyard. She did her best researching for the most luxurious cruises, hotels, restaurants and fun vacation places throughout the country so that when the Dais came each year she could recommend those to them. The Dais always took Hu Ning, An Kai and their daughter along as companions on their vacation trips. After each vacation the Dais would give Hu Ning expensive gifts such as LCD HD TV, jewelry, designer clothing, a sound system, and various other electronic gadgets as gratuities in disguise.

In Las Vegas the Dais threw away half a million dollars in the casinos without frowning. An Kai's and Hu Ning's losses were on the Dais's tab, without a question. Hu Ning became used to seeing the Dais squandering large amounts of money. She felt like a rich lady herself and sneered at people for being frugal.

Dai Tong's son liked the nightlife of the city. He lived in a two million dollar luxury condo on Marlborough Street in Boston, drove a Porsche Carrera, and frequented fancy nightclubs and restaurants, with a different blond on his arm each time. When his father admonished him to pay more attention to school he said:

"Why? You didn't go to school. And you are not doing too shabbily." He winked and grinned: "Beside, am I inheriting all your wealth?"

*   *   *   *

Hu Ning hosted parties and gatherings in Dai Tong's houses. She had a big circle of a widely diverse assortment of people. She often invited Ying Ying and Pei-Hua. But the latter rarely went. In one party Ying Ying and Pei-Hua attended, they saw and heard about things that they would not have imagined. Some women were made up like models and dressed in cocktail dresses, evening gowns or Chinese long dresses. Others were sloppily garbed. Hu Ning wore a tight fitting evening gown with a high slit on one side, and glittered with limestone jewelry. Her hair was adorned with silk flowers and dripping strings of beads. Ying Ying and Pei-hua were casually and respectably dressed. They did not know what the occasion was.

Most of the people were strangers to Pei-hua and Ying Ying. They were introduced and mingled with them a little bit. When Hu Ning came over with a plate of hors d'oeuvres, Pei-hua asked:

"Why are you and some of your guests so dressed up? What kind of a special occasion is it?"

"No special occasion. We always do this. I have not told you. But those ladies and I are a team of models and entertainers. We do fashion shows and perform Latin dances on hire." Hu Ning put the plate on a table; flung her hair to the back with a hand.

"Oh? Why didn't you tell us? That's interesting," Ying Ying commented, taking a piece of shrimp dumpling and a glass of soft drink from the table.

"You won't be interested in these things. But we have done it for over a year. This guy came up with this idea. He met these women at functions and parties. Because we are all tall and shapely he said we should be models...." Before she finished talking someone in the dining room called her away.

The dinner was catered by a Chinese restaurant. Because there were too many people for a sit-down-dinner they had a buffet. People sat in small groups in the dining room, TV room, kitchen and living room. Each group was avidly chatting.

Pei-hua glanced at those women. Yes they were tall but hardly shapely or qualified to be models. *Ailing is much more beautiful than these woman.* She wondered why Ailing was not among them.

"Where do you do fashion shows?" Pei-hua asked Hu Ning who was sitting close by at dinner.

"That guy featured us in a few shows in rented spaces," Hu Ning replied.

"Which designer's collection did you show?" Pei-hua asked further.

"Many different ones. Some are not by designers."

"What do you mean?"

"We wore our own dresses. We picked whatever we liked to wear. Some are designer dresses, many are not."

"I see." Pei-hua scoffed. *That is fashion show?*

There was a ring at the door. Hu Ning went to open it. Her guest stepped in. Hu Ning exclaimed, in not very friendly tone:

"Ah, you came!?"

"I know. I am not invited. But I thought you wouldn't mind me coming," the young, tall, slim and pretty woman said.

"Xi Feng is here. She will not be very happy to see you," Hu Ning stated. The woman did not pay attention and strode toward the function room.

"Mei Shan. I warn you. Xi Feng is not going to forget what you did. Why did you have to come?" Hu Ning followed her and said.

"Hu Ning. I think Xi Feng will not be so narrow-minded. We are friends," Mei Shan maintained while popping her head in the function room door.

'Yes, you were friends," Hu Ning muttered.

As Mei Shan entered the room she noticed many pairs of eyes glaring at her then turned away. It was apparent to her that people had begun to talk about her. At the same time an angry voice and gruff words were spurted out from a woman in a long evening gown. It was Xi Feng. She had her back toward Mei Shan at first but now turned around to face her.

"How dare you come here? Are you going to sneak into the bedroom to take pictures of Hu Ning's jewelry and wardrobe too? You goddamn cheap thief and duper! If you don't leave immediately I am going to make you."

"Don't worry. My jewelry and wardrobe are locked up in my storage. They are not here." Hu Ning just returned to the function room. She tactfully avoided pointing out that the house did not belong to her although some people vaguely knew it.

"Xi Feng. Don't hold grudge forever. It was a joke. It's over. Can't you put it behind you?" Mei Shan forced a titter and insouciantly crossed to the serving table and poured herself a glass of wine. Behind the put-on front was a distressed thief caught by the victim. She saw only enemies, no friends in this room.

"Joke?" Xi Feng screamed. She turned her eyes from Mei Shan to sweep through the room, and yelled to all:

"Listen to her. She calls her stealing, robbing, cheating and lying jokes." Rage swept through her   She roared at Hu Ning:

"Hu Ning, why did you ask her to come?"

"I didn't. And I couldn't stop her at the door," Hu Ning explained.

"Good. Then she is not your guest. She is here to disturb us. I want her to get her butt out of here." Xi Feng scooted toward Mai Shan, ready to give her a push.

"You have no right to give orders here." Mai Shan pushed Xi Feng who lurched backward, then steadied herself. Anger tore through her. She charged forward. A crisp clapping sound cracked as Xi Feng's right hand slapped Mei Shan on her left cheek. Stunned, in a fury Mei Shan lunged at Xi Feng, grabbing and pulling her hair, hitting and spitting at her at the same time. Xi Feng fought back. And they both used vulgar profanity on each other.

Pei-hua and Ying Ying gaped at the display of scurrility. Hu Ning shouted:

"Hey, you two. Stop it. If you don't I am going to call the police." It was a threat. She tried to pull the two apart. A few others also went over to grab on the arms of the two women and pulled them apart. One woman said:

"Hu Ning, just tell Mei Shan to get out. No one wants to see her anyway."

Hu Ning complied and said to Mei Shan:

"Will you just leave? Look what you have done to my party. You are not invited. Why don't you just go?"

Mei Shan straightened and sneered:

"Ok, I will go. Who cares about your party? I was doing you a favor by showing up. I did not expect to meet such a bunch of animals." She made her way toward the door, turned around and threatened:

"You all just wait and see."

Mei Shan was something like a purchased bride, although that was not a common underground business practice in China. She was a clerk in a five-star hotel in Shanghai who availed herself as a call girl at night to the hotel's clientele. Her secret activities were not discovered by the management, because she employed an agent to act as salesman and manager of her business, and she paid him well enough to seal his mouth about her. She was the boss, controlled by no one.

Mei Shan was well known and was well sought after. One customer of hers, Brad Wheeler, was an American businessman. After selling her flesh to him now and then for a few months, the man offered to make a final purchase and bring her back to the States. In Boston few knew her hooker background. She told people that she was Brad's secretary in China.

"Without my help his business would not get anywhere," she bragged. Brad was in the electronics business. He made good money, but nowhere near the wealth of Ching Ju's husband Jack Morrison. Mei Shan knew of Ching Ju but the two had never met. Brad Wheeler was not in the social league of the ultra rich and powerful that Jack Morrison belonged. He had no way to enter that circle. Deep down in Mei Shan's heart, a fire of jealousy burnt fiercely. She strained to climb the social ladder by buying an expensive house in Weston and two expensive cars. She also threw large parties and tried to invite high-class guests. But no matter what she did it was like a plastic imitation of a Waterford crystal. Although she was beautiful, she had no class. Her lecherous behaviors, an extension from her prostitute career, invited scorn. She fantasized about wife swapping, multi-partner sex camps, and open marriage that she had heard about in Shanghai as a normal lifestyle of Americans. She asked Brad why they did not do those things or go to those places. Brad was not upset at her

274

dissolute interest left from her call-girl days. He only told her that it was not what regular people did. Disappointed, she took all the liberty to explore what was out there. Gas station attendants were her ready prey. Her gardener, maintenance men hardly slipped though her fingers.

Although the indulgence satisfied her carnal desire, she was soon tired of freely giving herself away to those unworthy working-class guys. She could very well throw one stone at two birds: to amuse herself pleasurably, and to be rewarded by the men who derived pleasure from being intimate with her. She proceeded to seek men she met at parties, restaurants, shopping places, even among her husband's customers. She had such discerning eyes to know who would lavish on her for her body. And she had such tact that she never failed in her quest to lure men.

Her other trait that turned her female friends off was putting them on the spot to pay for her meals, parking, tickets to theatres, and other events. She acted like a rich lady to whom money was no object. She always drove through the garage attendant's booth and told the attendant that her friend in the car behind her would pay for both, when there was a friend behind her. If not, she would just speed away. When eating in a restaurant she would avoid paying by going to the lady's room when the waiter brought the check to the table, or tell her friend that her money and credit cards were left in another purse.

"Foot the bill for me. I will pay you back." But she never did.

Those small humbugs alienated the people she socialized. They talked about her debased behavior. But those things were minuscule in comparison to other two insidious schemes she pulled. One was what enraged Xi Feng. The two women and their husbands were close friends. Mei Shan noticed Xi Feng's expensive diamonds, watches and other jewelry, minks, designer outfits, and evening gowns. She was envious and thought if she just stole a few probably no one would find out even if Xi Feng reported it to the police. Then she drummed up an innovative idea. She snuck in Xi Feng's room on several occasions and took pictures of her- and her husband's valuables and put a small and inconspicuous mark, MS, or BW, on the back of the labels of each piece of clothing, and lightly etched an M or a B with a stylus on the back of a watch, a brooch or the inside of a ring, or the clasp of a necklace. Then she made up a long pictorial inventory of her possessions. Xi Feng' and Jing Sheng's things were on that list and marked as missing.

She took the list to the police and claimed that those items were stolen. She said that she had seen some of Xi Feng's things looked like those she had lost.

"All our belongings were marked with our initials and I have a detailed inventory. You should take this list to that house and find out whether they have these things." Mei Shan adamantly demanded. Consequently the police got a warrant to question Xi Feng and her husband and search their house. The couple felt as if being hit by a thunderbolt. And they were dumfounded when looking at the pictures on the loss item list. The police said:

"We have the warrant to search your house for these things."

"You don't have to search. They are in our closets and drawers because they are our belongings. What the hell is going on? Who is playing this dirty trick?" Jing Sheng fumed.

"Sorry but the lady had this detailed inventory and pictures. She said all the items were marked. She claims that these are stolen. We have to check and see if your items have any marking or not," the cop said.

Xi Feng was panic-stricken. Some intruder must have entered their house and did that frightful thing to them. They could not refuse the police because of the warrant. But if the police were in they might find the incriminating evidence if there were in fact markings on the items. The situation was like a double-edged sword. She looked at her husband. He looked vacuous.

"We have to take a look.," the cop said.

"If there are markings I don't know who put them there. Must be whoever is playing this cruel joke. Can you tell us who reported the theft?" Xi Feng's husband asked.

"We cannot divulge that information."

The police opened the closets and drawers, identified the "stolen items," verified the markings. Everything confirmed Mai Shan's report.

"We have to take these things to the station. And you need to get a lawyer," the cop said dryly.

It took a lawyer to find out from the police headquarters about who reported the theft that incriminated Xi Feng and Jing Sheng. The Jings were furious when they found out it was Mei Shan who pulled this horrendously diabolical scheme on them. They vowed to retaliate. But first they must exonerate themselves. Their lawyer asked if they had kept some receipts of the items in question. Xi Feng knew she still had receipts of her jewelry and watches. Some other receipts might still be somewhere. But it would take some effort to recover them. She looked everywhere, desk drawers, purses, bureau, dresser, and chest. She did find some. Those were enough to prove ownership of many of the items and evidence of Mei Shan's criminal act.

Xi Feng and Jing Sheng sued Mei Shan for her insidious machination that incriminated them and destroyed their reputation. Their lawyer suggested suing Mei Shan in the criminal court for breaking in the house when they were not home to take those pictures. Mei Shan did not foresee such a development. She was alarmed. She told her lawyer to negotiate with Xi Feng's lawyer to settle the case outside of court. But this was not only a civil case. Breaking and entering a house to plot a fraud was a criminal case. Whether or not she would be put behind bar was to be seen. The story was unfolding.

The other major opprobrious stunt of hers was financial fraud. She must have been born with a devious mind. And she was quick in learning about how to use loopholes in the system for her benefit. Bankruptcy and mortgage default as ways to steal money were two tools unknown in Shanghai but readily available in America. She wondered why everyone was not taking advantage of those.

Through those machinations she insidiously agglomerated tens of millions.

Along the way she hurt many of her acquaintances who fell into her beguiling scheme. She designed an elaborate plan to take money from people. It started with incorporating two companies, one in Boston under her own name another in China under her brother's name. Then she alleged many joint ventures between the two companies. Of course no one knew that the Chinese company was hers. She had many beautifully printed brochures in English and Chinese showing the grand scale of the ventures. Then she chose, among her acquaintances, people with money and offered them opportunities to invest in these ventures.

She was smart enough to not involve her husband's business. Her personal assets were separated from her "business" and protected. From her house and cars to her clothing and jewelry people were convinced that she was a wealthy lady. The way she talked and acted with utmost confidence made people believe that she was also a capable and well-established businesswoman. After enough money was pulled in and the investors were asking about profits, she hit them with the bad news and declared bankruptcy. The money was already well hidden. The investors lost every penny. She did the same with real estate investments. She bought building after building within a short period of time with little down payments. Shortly afterwards she defaulted on mortgage payments and declared bankruptcy.

The banks foreclosed the properties and lost money leaving her with sizable gains. Those who were aware of what she had done called her the worst virulence existing on the planet.

*   *   *   *

The group of women at Hu Ning's party was certainly not professional models. Modeling is something to fulfill a vanity dream, giving them an opportunity to fantasize being glamorous entertainers on stage. The women felt beautiful and special although they were not. The Chinese social circle mimicked the society at large in its various activities. the most popular being ballroom dancing, occasional stage shows and Karaoke singing. Cultural events or life entertainments outside of their circle did not appeal to them.

Hu Ning took ballroom dancing for years and became good at it. She was active in the Chinese social circle that daubed her the title of "Queen of the Ballroom." After dinner, Hu Ning announced that the evening would include a fashion show and Karaoke singing.

Pei-hua and Ying Ying had not attended Chinese social gatherings of this kind before. They were mystified by the two distinctly different groups of guests at this party. Beside the fashionably dressed aspiring models, there were some sloppily garbed women that Ying Ying and Pei-hua noticed as they first entered the house. Those women apparently had no interest in the vanity-fair. They separated themselves from the others by staying in the TV room on the second floor. Out of curiosity Ying Ying and Pei-hua strode to that room to see what they were doing. The women paid no attention to them and continued talking.

"I hate America. I hate it, hate it!!!" Woman A with short haired and glasses said emphatically.

"I hate it too. But we all came here. All Chinese want to come here. We study English, go to school here. Why? Why don't Americans study Chinese and go to our schools in China?" woman B added in a huff.

Pei-hua was about to make a comment when Ying Ying tugged on her sleeve to stop her.

"Not only us, everyone in the world hates America because it is an evil country. It is aggressive and has the wild ambition to conquer the world," woman C drummed in.

"Yes, it is trying to destroy our country." Woman A made a forceful statement.

Both Pei-hua and Ying Ying were astonished by those strong emotions. They had never heard of such attacks on this country by their other Chinese acquaintances.

"America is not like what you described. It does not attempt to conquer the world. The people are peace loving and fair. Let me ask you. If you hate America so much why do you come here?" woman D sitting in a corner put in her question and comment. Her words immediately antagonized the other three women. They turned on her like a chorus.

"We came here to destroy this country. It does not deserve to exist." Woman A was infuriated by woman D.

"Who are you to question us? Are you a Chinese?" woman B fiercely demanded in anger.

"She is a traitor," woman C stood up, pointing a finger at woman D and shouted in fury.

"We cannot allow a traitor in our midst," woman B pounded on the table and yelled. The three dashed toward woman D who was apparently frightened.

"What do you want? Can I not voice my opinion?" woman D ask timidly.

"We want you to get out." Woman A lunged toward woman D, speaking in a threatening voice and thrusting an arm and pointing finger toward the door.

"You have no right to order me out. I am Hu Ning's guest," woman D defied.

Ying Ying pulled on Pei-hua's skirt and signaled her to leave the room. They went downstairs to find Hu Ning.

"You'd better go upstairs to appease a few of your guests. They are about to hit a woman," Pei-hua said. The "hit" bit was exaggerated.

"What happened?" Hu Ning hastily left the function room to scoot upstairs. Pei-hua and Ying Ying trailed behind.

The scene in the room was uglier than Ying Ying and Pei-hua had seen a moment before. The three women were actually hitting their enemy. Other women were trying to pull them away but instead were pushed by the three women.

"Hey, what's going on? Stop it. This is a party. Why are you fighting?" Hu Ning raised her voice and demanded.

"This goddamn traitor is selling us out," woman A cried.

"All right, all right, let's stop the fight for Hu Ning's sake, okay?" said woman E, one of the others trying to stop the fight.

"If you want to fight, go somewhere else. Don't do it at my party." Hu Ning showed her vexation.

The timid woman D combed her hair with her fingers and smoothed her shirt and snuck away. The other three were still fuming.

Hu Ning tried to mollify the roughened atmosphere in the room. She tilted her head slightly, winked one eye and said: "Everyone having a good time? Why don't you go downstairs to join the others and sing some songs? Why talk about those sensitive and boring topics? Come on. There is more food in the function room. Let's go." She left the room not caring if any of the people were following her or not.

Ying Ying and Pei-hua stayed in the room absently listening to the conversations. One utterance grabbed their attention.

"It is true. The girl was ill for years and never recovered," a woman named Kaka said.

"What happened?" Pei-hua asked. "Sorry I was not paying attention."

"It's all right. I was telling them about a college classmate of mine at Tsing-hua University ten years ago. She was very pretty and intelligent, and an award-winning swimmer as well as a pianist. She had a devoted boy-friend and many admirers. A lot of girls were envious of her. That was fine. But one girl, a close friend of hers, was insanely jealous of her and set out to snatch her boy-friend. That girl put poison in her water. It was a kind of heavy metal. It caused the victim to lose her brain. She nearly became a vegetable and was bed-ridden for years. Her parents had to massage her, and put her on an exercise machine in order to keep her muscle from deteriorating." Kaka repeated the story.

"How horrible." Ying Ying was aghast at the story.

"Was the evil girl's baleful deed exposed? Did she get the boy?" Pei-hua asked.

"Exposed? Not really. People knew it was her, but no investigation was ever conducted to nail her. You know how it is in China. Many things fall between cracks. It was worse ten years ago. As for the evil girl, she did not get the guy. He had no interest in her."

"Destroying someone else yet gaining nothing for herself!" one woman exclaimed.

"A friend of mine, a so-called friend, did a similar thing to me, although she did not poison me by putting pernicious foreign matters in my food or water. She used her mouth and tongue to destroy me in front of my boy friend, plotting to take him away from me," Kaka added.

"What happened? Did she succeed?" one woman asked.

"No, my boy-friend was not a fool. That's why he is my husband now." Kaka smiled radiantly.

"This kind of story is common. I have heard too many," another woman said.

Ying Ying glanced at Pei-hua and slightly shook her head. Pei-hua shared her feeling. *What is wrong with humanity?!*

Later Ying Ying and Pei-hua learned much more about this omnifarious assortment of people befriended by Hu Ning. Many of them were parasites of the welfare system. They lived in nice government housing. The heating and cooling system were regularly checked, repaired or replaced.. The rooms were repainted, carpets cleaned, windows and doors well maintained or replaced, bathrooms and kitchen appliances updated whenever necessary. The ground was neatly and regularly landscaped in the warm seasons; snow removed in the winter. The older people even had government-paid house cleaners and caretakers. Because the welfare recipients worked under the table and hid their earnings and savings, they were eligible for a monthly stipend called SSI. Beside enjoying all those benefits, they abused the health care system by using it unnecessarily for example going to the emergency room with absolutely no need just because "It was free. If I don't use it I would be wasting my right," as they said.

They overstocked free milk, baby food, and baby juices. Every month they threw away a lot of excess they couldn't use. They were proud of what they did. "America has too much money. We are helping them to get ride of some." There was one guy who borrowed $100,000 from credit cards and left the country. Many of those in Hu Ning's circle talked about it in admiration and tried to emulate him. "But he has to hide outside the country for many years before he can come back." That was the only drawback to them.

Those must be scum of the earth. Both Ying Ying and Pei-hua, were not aware of their existence before.

*   *   *   *

Manna and Hu Ning were very close one time. But for several years Hu Ning severed all connections with Manna because the latter brought nothing but trouble. She and her husband Roger had divorced because she cheated on him too often. Her two sons, given to her by the judge at first, were taken from her and given to Roger because Roger proved she was an unfit mother. One time Roger went to pick up the boys on his visitation day and found them home alone. The older boy told the father that their mother often left them home without a babysitter. This was a reason enough for Roger to bring the custody issue back to the court for re-examination. He wanted to be sure that the boys did not overstate the fact. So he hired a private investigator to follow Manna. He found that Manna often left the kids home by themselves when she went out to drink in the bar, dance in the nightclubs, and pick up men randomly. She was sexually involved with several men. One of them was a drug dealer and got Manna addicted. With such evidence Roger pleaded to the judge to re-open the case.

It did not take the judge much time to announce his verdict. Manna lost. Her old acquaintances ceased contact with her. No one seemed to remember her anymore.

Suddenly one day she called Hu Ning.

"Hi, Hu Ning, long time no see," Manna opened with a familiar greeting. Hu Ning's mind went blank. She could not think who was on the other end of the line. She was trying to place that voice.

"Ah, yea,..." she was still searching her brain.

"This is Manna. You have forgotten me?" The voice was insinuating and saccharine.

"Oh, Manna. I did not forget you. But I did not expect a call from you either." Hu Ning's voice and tone were tepid. But Manna did not cringe.

"I heard that you have three mansions and expensive cars. That is so enviable."

"Yes, but they are not mine." Hu Ning was suspicious of Manna's motives.

"You know, I am not doing so well." Manna plunged right in. "You know, I lost my apartment. The welfare department found out that Roger was paying me alimony."

Not doing so well!! That was no one's fault. She must have brought it on herself. Hu Ning knew it only too well.

"That's too bad. But you already enjoyed the benefit for years when you really shouldn't have. You saved a lot of money already." Hu Ning showed no sympathy and her voice became colder.

"Well, you have so much money and yet you still have your town house from the government. And you got government's senior housing for your mother too. You made out much better." Manna forgot her reason for calling Hu Ning. Her acrid tone exposed her jealousy uncontrollably

"What do you want, Manna?" Hu Ning would not put up with this pettiness from someone of no use to her. As such she needed not to hide her annoyance.

"Oh," Manna quickly came to her senses and changed to a tone full of succulence. She needed Hu Ning. How could she say anything offensive?

"We lost touch for many years and I often think about you. You are my best friend."

"What do you want?" Hu Ning did not fall into Manna's snare.

"I am wondering ..." Manna was left without choice but to plung right into the crux. "... if you can let me stay with you for a while since you have so many big houses."

"Manna. Don't even think of it. I already told you the houses are not mine. I still live in my two-bedroom apartment in a government housing project." Hu Ning's voice was glacial now. "If you need help why don't you call Ying Ying. She will help you. She will help anyone."

" But Hu Ning, we are good friends. That's why I called you. I never wanted to have anything to do with Fang Ying Ying. In fact I hate her. I have hated her ever since that year when she sponsored Chinese New Year events. You knew that."

"I never understood why you hated her. She is nice to everyone. What has she done to you?" Hu Ning demanded.

"She was not nice like you think. She thinks she is better than us, above us all because of her family and school. Now, she is the president of International Foundation, and has a good husband. She acts even more haughtily, as if she is superior to everyone. I can't stand her." Manna clenched her teeth. Hatred spiraled through her and reached Hu Ning who trembled at Manna's force.

"You are just jealous of her. I have not heard anyone say such things about Ying Ying. I don't believe anyone would agree with you." A strong feeling of detestation rose in Hu Ning. She had to speak her mind.

Manna snapped at Hu Ning's words. "You are like the others, under the spell of that rotten bitch," she shrieked: "You people don't know the real person in her. She and I are both from Taiwan. I know her better than you do. She is a spoiled brat being from a family of money and high position. Do you know that she had a maid cleaning her dorm room and a chauffeur driving her to places while in college? In high school while other kids rode public buses, she was driven to school in a limousine. How could she not think of herself as being superior? Oh, I hate those people from privileged class."

"How did you know all that? Having money is not a crime. Can she help if if her parents have money? Don't you wish you came from a rich family? I do. You just let your wicked jealousy overcome you." Hu Ning's ire escalated. She did not like to hear anymore from Manna. So she shot out her scathing remark without reservation.

"She is so uppity. That's what I cannot stand. In her school no boy could ever ask her out," Manna said.

"I don't care what she was like. Don't tell me any more." Hu Ning hung up.

All hope was snuffed out, Manna had no other choice but resort to asking Ying Ying. She was indeed glad that Hu Ning had brought Ying Ying up. It refreshed the deep rancor in her and rekindled her desire to get even. *Ying Ying, you had better let me move in with you if you know what's good for you. You are easy to manipulate any way, you stupid. A good concocted story should fool you into letting me move into you house.*

Ying Ying was surprised to hear from Manna. After a brief initial greeting Manna dived right into her plight.

"You have no idea what kind of a vicious and ruthless man Roger is. He used his money and influence to seize the boys from me, took all the money from our bank account. A lot of that money was mine, from my mother and sisters. They asked me to invest for them. And Roger took all that money and cut off my financial resources, leaving me in poverty. He got a restraining order from the judge against me. He even got me arrested. I spent many days in the women's jail in Framingham. You know why? Because I am a Chinese woman, and he is a white American man. Of course the judge sided with him."

Ying Ying did not believe that the judge would take sides in a court case. As for Roger, his amiable manners and Manna's tireless praises before impressed Ying Ying of a kind-hearted, polite gentleman. Now he was being portrayed as a vicious and ferocious man. What a polarity! How baffling!

"Manna, I think because you are so angry that you look at the case with a distorted view. It's hard to believe that a judge would be so discriminatory and so partial because of your races. And Roger, he changed from a nice kind man to a monster?" She was curious about Manna's imprisonment." What caused you to be incarcerated for days?"

"Ai, you only saw the surface of him. He was always nasty and mean. He said I abused our sons and threatened to kill them. He went to the judge and got restraining orders against me. When I went to get the boys he called the police and sued me for breaking into his house. He got me arrested and thrown in jail."

"That was preposterous. You have visitation right."

"Yes, but one time I went to see the kids on a different date. Roger was not home. When he returned and the nanny said I had taken the boys he went berserk. Ying Ying, you don't know those things. It's very dark, very unjust. Those women in the prison were all very pitiable. They were abused by their husbands; left without recourse, and then they were punished by law. Ying Ying, you are always in the polite higher society, and protected privileged environment. You have no idea what the real world is like. It's very ugly," she sobbed.

"I think there was more to those women's stories. Judges cannot put a person in jail without reason. They must have broken the law."

"The law is not just! It is interpreted by lawyers and judges. It can be very biased." After this remark Manna quickly and conveniently turned the subject to her need.

"Ying Ying, you are such a good person, always helping people. So many of the mainlanders are beholden to you. I think you must be willing to help those from Taiwan too."

"I do my best to help people. It doesn't matter where they are from," Ying Ying said honestly.

"I am glad to hear that. I am in a dire situation. Only you will be kind enough to help me. I am sure," Manna wheedled.

"What dire situation are you in? I will see if there is anything I can do." Ying Ying sincerely meant what she said.

"The Welfare Department found out that my sons were not living with me and Roger is paying me alimony. So I cannot keep the subsidized apartment anymore. I must move out immediately. You know that I can't afford a reasonably decent place. What can I do? Where can I go?"

"What do you want me to do? I don't think I can help you get affordable housing since you don't qualify for one." Ying Ying failed to see what was in Manna's mind.

"I am thinking of moving in with you."

Ying Ying was not prepared to be hit with such a demand. And it was hard for her to deny people's requests. She was speechless for a second.

"Manna. I don't have a big place, only a two-bedroom apartment. One room is a study Kang Wei and I share. It is also used as a guest room for our out of town friends when they visit. I am sorry but I cannot put you up. Please understand."

"Ying Ying, come on. You don't want to see me sleeping on the street. Give your poor old friend a little help. I won't forget your benefaction."

"It's not that I don't want to help you, Manna, but I already told you how impossible it is to put you up."

Manna persisted. Ying Ying's soft heart and magnanimity got the better of her. She conceded. Reluctantly she asked:

"How long do you need to stay in my place?"

"It won't be long. I will try to get on my feet as soon as I can." Manna threw out a vague answer.

Ying Ying instinctively knew it would not be a good idea to let Manna move in. "I can only put you up temporarily, for a very short time. Manna, please understand. If I had a larger place I wouldn't mind. But my place is very tight."

"I know, I know. Thank you, Ying Ying." Manna seemed pleased. That evening Ying Ying and Kang Wei moved their desks, chairs, bookshelves, file cabinets and other stuff from the study to cram into their bedroom. Ying Ying looked at Kang Wei with wordless apology. Kang Wei, not only had no complaint but also tried to put Ying Ying at ease:

"Sorry, Ying. Maybe we should buy a house in the suburb."

"Don't be silly. We like living in the city. It's my fault to let Manna manipulate me."

"No, don't say that, Ying. You are generous and kind. I love you for that. A little crammed doesn't bother me as long as you don't mind it." Kang Wei was sympathetic and understanding as always.

Manna moved in that evening. She could only bring the most essential things as there was no space for her belongings. She brought two suitcases and a couple of cardboard boxes with her. She begged another person to put her other stuff in his basement temporarily. Instantly the simply and tastefully furnished apartment was strewn with two empty suitcases and boxes. Ying Ying could not empty the closet in the study because there was no more room in her other closets. Manna had to squeeze Ying Ying's clothing tightly to one side to make room for her own. She cluttered the guest bathroom with makeup cases, bottles, and tubes. Ying Ying always liked her environment very neat and clean. *How long is this going to be?*

*   *   *   *

The next day, when Kang Wei was cooking Manna barged into the kitchen trying to wrangle the cutting knife from Kang Wei's hand.

"Ai-ya, why are you doing the cooking? Ying Ying doesn't do it? Let me do it," she said.

"I enjoy cooking. It's a hobby of mine. Beside, Ying Ying's work is more demanding than mine. I should take care of our household chores."

"Don't even think about cooking while I am here. It's my job. It's the least I can do to repay Ying Ying's graciousness."

284

"No, it's okay. You are a guest here." Kang Wei held onto the knife. But Manna grabbed the knife from him and pushed him out of the kitchen.

"I will do the cooking. I am a vegetarian. I can't eat what you cook."

That was a surprise to Kang Wei. Manna searched the refrigerator and freezer, took out the items she could use and made a few vegetable dishes. On the dinner table Ying Ying asked:

"Since when did you become a vegetarian?" Ying Ying knew of Manna's hedonistic lifestyle as well as her culinary skill and fondness of ambrosia.

"Two years ago after I was accepted to the temple of Devine Master Of The Universe. You see, I lost my boys to Roger. I almost committed suicide. It was Divine Master Of The Universe who saved me."

It was understandable. Losing the boys must have been an unbearable blow to Manna. Religion would bring solace to a person in despair. But what religion was Divine Master Of The Universe? Ying Ying and Kang Wei wondered. When they raised the question Manna was enthused in giving an introduction:

"Divine Master Of The Universe! Just that. She is the Divine Master of the universe. She is above Buddha, Jesus, Mohammad, and all other religious originators. She is a beautiful female form, more beautiful than Bodhisattva Kuan-yin, or Avalokitesvara as known to the Western world. She descended from above to earth to save all human beings. She first landed on the Everest of Himalayas and traveled between Tibet and Nepal, bringing her good tidings and saved multitudes of people. Then she traveled throughout Asia. Now her disciples are all over the world. She tells us disciples that eating animal meat is sinful, because killing is sinful. She is with all of us disciples every minute to watch if we live by her laws. We must be careful not to do anything wrong because she knows and she will punish anyone who does not behave according to her teaching."

"Have you ever been punished?" Kang Wei mocked slightly.

"Oh yes. In the beginning I thought it would not be possible for Divine Master to watch everyone. After all she has too many disciples. She probably wouldn't know if I ate some meat. Gosh, was I wrong. Divine Master was angry. She slugged me on the head. I almost fell on the floor. And then she pounded on the table very loudly. The floor shook. I was so scared. I knelt down and begged for her mercy. Then the floor stopped shaking. I heard loud footsteps of the Divine Master leaving my kitchen."

"She was in your kitchen? You saw her?" Ying Ying jeered.

"Yes. She was in my kitchen. But I could not see her," Manna replied.

"Of all her disciples you were the only one who made a mistake and was punished by her that day?" Kang Wei taunted.

"I don't know about that. I suppose there must be others who made different mistakes too."

"Then how did your master get to them since she was in your kitchen?" Kang Wei chaffed again.

"Oh, that's what you don't understand. Don't think of Divine Master in human terms. She is not confined by time and space. She is ubiquitous."

"I see." Kang Wei intended the topic to end here.

"Ying Ying, would you please get more vegetable tomorrow? You are low on it," Manna demanded.

"Manna, you mean we have to keep a vegetarian diet while you are here? We need to have meat, for protein." Ying Ying said.

"Beans and tofu will provide protein. Much better. Remember, killing is sinful. Meat eating is sinful," Manna professed. Ying Ying felt a little uneasy and asked:

"What will these sin do to us?"

"Condemned to the 18th level of hell, of course. And there is no chance for reincarnation," Manna sternly exerted: "The thing to do is to kneel to Divine Master Of The Universe and beg for salvation."

"So, beside your master's followers, the whole population of the world will be condemned to the 18th level of hell." Kang Wei's sarcasm was indiscernible to Manna.

"Yes," Manna exerted emphatically. "If they, and you, kneel to worship Divine Master, the almighty Divine Master will be compassionate. She will give you eternal life. She is here to save all beings. So, it's not too late for you. Ying Ying, Kang Wei, on behalf of Divine Master, I offer you the Road to Future Life. I will take you to our temple and Divine Master will bless your heart and take you in as her disciples. You see. I have been sent by Master to your home because she wants to save you."

Ying Ying could hear no more of that. She said: "Tell your master, no, thanks."

Manna's expression turned grim; her hands fidgety, twisting the paper napkin.

"Ying Ying, how could you desecrate Divine Master like that? You are not afraid of punishment? You will be condemned to the 18th level of hell below forever."

"I am not her disciple. How can she punish me?" Ying Ying lost her humor.

"You are not a disciple yet. But sooner or later, everyone will be her disciple less they be condemned forever." A demonic beam shot from Manna's eyes to fix on Ying Ying's face. Chill coursed through Ying Ying from head to toe. She remained calm and said gently:

"Manna, let's not discuss this now, okay? Religion is a personal choice. I don't like to be proselytized."

"Divine Master is not a religion," Manna snapped. "She is the True Savior Of The Universe. Why don't you accept that?" As if possessed, she screamed, rose from her seat and pounded on the table.

Ying Ying and Kang Wei gasped in fright. They were also worried. Manna threw the napkin on the table and stalked to her room, spitting curse words along the way.

Ying Ying and Kang Wei gasped in fright. They were also worried. Manna threw the napkin on the table and stalked to her room, spitting curse words along the way.

Ying Ying had cultivated a degree of sufferance that enabled her to cease the confrontation and try appeasing Manna. She knocked on Manna's door. Manna, still in wrath, opened the door to let her in.

Ying Ying was taken aback at the sight of the room. The walls were covered with many pictures of a young woman dressed in various strange costumes, some were seductively revealing, some in gauzy drapery like those seen on ancient Indian sculpture, some in Buddhist' monk's robe, some looked like ballroom gowns. Beside these pictures were painted periapts pined on the remaining spaces of the wall. An incense burner let out wisps of thin smoke; small sticks of candles were here and there.

Ying Ying, who came to placate Manna of her tantrum, became upset herself: "Manna, what have you done to the room! You should not have put nails in the wall."

"I cannot stay in a room without Divine Master's pictures and the Talisman of Salvation," she exclaimed self-righteously.

"But this is not your home. You are a guest staying here only temporarily. How could you change the room and damage the walls?" Ying Ying demanded in anger.

"Fang Ying Ying, you shut your mouth. You are an unreasonable bitch." As if being possessed, Manna's mouth twisted, eyes suffused with demonic dark flame. "Not allowing me to have Divine Master's pictures and Symbols of Salvation is worse than asking me to strip naked. How dare you?"

"You never let me know that you belong to some strange religion and would do this to my room." Ying Ying was riled by Manna's foul language. Yet she still tried to stay unperturbed.

"What? Strange religion? Shut your damn mouth." The last drop of control was drained from Manna. Consumed by rage she shrieked. "I told you Divine Master is not a religion. She is above religion. She is The True Savior Of The Universe. She sent me to your home to save you. Don't you know that? What ungrateful beast you are." Ying Ying turned blanched at Manna's scurrility. There was no hope to reason with her. Ying Ying turned and strode out of the room.

That night Ying Ying could not fall asleep. She was disturbed by Manna's strange behavior and by a rhythmic noise coming from Manna's room. It was the sound of a wooden stick tapping on a hollow piece of wood called wooden-fish, a paraphernalia of Buddhist temples. 'Divine Master Of The Universe' borrowed it from Buddhism?

The next day, Ying Ying had lunch with Pei-hua at a small Thai restaurant on Kneeland Street. After hearing about Manna's quirky behavior, Pei-hua warned Ying Ying to give heed to signs of danger.

"Ying, you haven't heard of the so called *divine master of the universe*? She is a cult leader and a master of black magic. She does have the inexplicable power to control her followers' minds. I had a client whose wife was a follower of that cult. He was scared by his wife's insistence to drag him in. He couldn't stand living with her and sued her for divorce."

"He could not resist the wife's power?"

"The wife did not have the power like her master. If he were weak and had followed her to the temple, and got the master's 'Blessing Of The Heart,' he would have been doomed and unable to extract himself. Now he watches his wife mired deeper each day into the abyss of uncanniness. She meditates day and night at the temple, not coming home for weeks at a time. When she does come home she tells him strange and frightening stories."

"Did he tell you any of the stories?" Ying Ying inquired.

"The cult members believed there was no demarcation between the living and the dead. There were ghosts amongst them. The living and the dead mingle and communicate easily with one another. They believe that they can travel in time, go back thousands of years to be with their dead ancestors. They said that they could see themselves from many incarnations ago. Their stories are all within those cryptic realms."

"What do you think Manna would do?" Ying Ying's mind was focused on her current plight.

"I don't doubt that she would do what she has said, to take you to 'Road to Future Life,' to have the master bless your heart and save your souls," Pei-hua laughed sportively.

"Don't make fun of it. It's not funny," Ying Ying scolded.

"I hope it won't happen. But you need to remind her again that her stay is temporary."

*   *   *   *

Ying Ying and Kang Wei went to the Chinese market to get tofu and vegetable as Manna had asked. When they went home they saw a large mystic talisman posted on the front door. Ying Ying felt apprehensive immediately. As they entered, they saw more talismans and the cult leader's pictures all over the living room walls. Candles were everywhere. Terror and anger tore through Ying Ying. Kang Wei was aghast. He called out:

"Manna!"

Manna emerged from her room Her eyes glinted with an evil glow. Her cheeks flushed. Her long hair spread over her shoulders. She glared at Ying Ying in silence. Ying Ying said in a sharp voice.

"What are you doing? Why did you put these things all over our apartment?" she declared. "You better take them down before I throw them out."

"Fang Ying Ying. Not that again. You are really getting on my nerve. You know I must do this. This is for our protection." Manna clenched her teeth and tightened her fist. She leveled a deadly glare at Ying Ying "Your apartment is filled with sin."

"What?" Grim rage and fear rushed through Ying Ying.

"Yes. Sin. Because you encourage killing," Manna confirmed. With a strained voice she questioned: "The vibration is very bad. Did you hear the

288

Beings last night?"

"What beings?" Kan Wei was angry and lost at the same time.

"Beings!!! Counterparts of human beings in the universe. They are here and everywhere else. They co-exist with us peacefully if we do not offend them. If we do, they will not let us off. Last night while I was meditating they stomped in and out of the apartment in anger." Manna ignored Ying Ying's reaction and continued: "They were going to cut off my feet. One was pulling on my feet and the other brandished a cleaver at me. I begged them for my feet. I tried to pull them back. It was like a tug of war."

"Nonsense. Manna, you have lost your mind," Ying Ying yelled.

"You listen to me. They were angry because I was in a place where lives were taken by slaughterers. They are Beings of pigs, cows, chickens, fish, shrimps and others. Their carcasses were mutilated and some ended up in your freezer. The Beings came crying, complaining, begging me for help. I cannot put their pieces together. But I can cleanse your apartment of sin. They let go of my feet after I made a promise to cleanse this apartment of sin." Manna strode to the refrigerator. Opened the freezer door and proudly shouted:

"You see. It's clean now." Manna's eyes gleamed with victory. Ying Ying looked at the empty freezer. Inflamed with anger, she asked:

"What did you do with the meats?"

"I took them to the community garden and buried them."

Ying Ying turned around to find Kang Wei. He was only one step away from her. He knew that Ying Ying was shocked beyond description. He stepped up to her and put his arms around her:

"Ying Ying, calm down. We will find a solution." His gentle and resolute voice eased Ying Ying's tension.

"Manna. It's not working out, apparently," Kang Wei said sternly: "Ying Ying was generous and kind to let you move in for a while despite our tight quarters. You should not have imposed your way so forcefully on us. We have our way of life. We also cannot take your verbal abuse. You'd better move out immediately."

"What?" Manna screamed. "You want me to move out? Where do I go? Don't you have a heart?"

"What do you want us to do?" Ying Ying demanded. "You are making our lives insufferable. There is no way that we can stay under the same roof."

"You cannot throw me out." Manna screamed again. "This is my home now. Don't think you can get rid of me."

"How can you call this your home? You promised Ying Ying it's only a temporary stay. But it's not working out. You have no place to go? We will put you in a hotel," Kang Wei resolved. "I will help you pack." He began to take down the talismans.

"Don't you touch them, damn it," Manna shrilled. "I cannot move to a hotel. I have no money to pay."

"It will be All right. I will pay the hotel for you. Just give us back your home." Ying Ying futilely tried to evoke reason in a demented woman.

"I am not leaving." She stomped to her room and slammed the door shut.

Ying Ying was distraught. She looked at Kang Wei. He was also without recourse.

"Her malicious and deranged behavior is alarming. We must get her out," Ying Ying said in desperation.

"Let's get legal help," Kang Wei said. "That's the only way."

"I will ask Pei-hua to handle it." Ying Ying had a glimmer of hope. "But what do we do tomorrow? We cannot leave her alone here. God knows what she will do."

"It is a problem. One of us should stay home." Kong Wei only came up with one tenuous idea.

"That we must do. But we cannot take off from work for long. And we don't know how long before the issue will be resolved." Ying Ying was contemplating a solution. "I will talk with Pei-hua. Do you mind staying home tomorrow?"

"I will call the office tomorrow morning," Kang Wei replied. Ying Ying went to Pei-hua's office the next morning.

"Manna has refused to move out. We must resort to a legal solution. Do you think it's a simple procedure?" After filling Pei-hua in with the fiasco of the night before Ying Ying sought her advice and help.

"It should be a simple and straightforward matter. You let her stay with you temporarily. It is your hospitality. But her way of life is incompatible with yours. So you asked her to move out. In Asia, this is not even an issue. She just has to move out. No law would protect her. However, the American legal system sometimes seems not logical and reasonable in our eyes. Good people are often victimized and bad people are rewarded. As a lawyer I should not be saying this. But it is true, and I can only say this to you. People with money and properties are usually victims. For instance, in Massachusetts the law is particularly biased against landlords. A tenant can do a great deal of damage to the property, not paying rent and the landlord cannot evict him. Yes, the landlord can send the tenant an eviction note. But if the tenant refuses to move the landlord cannot do anything. Even if the judge ordered the tenant to pay the arrears, for instance, the tenant can ignore it."

"I know. The system is absurd," Ying Ying added "I heard on the radio about an old couple in Cambridge whose divorced daughter lived on the third floor of their house for a while and shared a little utility cost, $200 a month. After she moved the couple asked a rental agent to find a tenant for them. The agent suggested the monthly rent should be $900. A woman took the apartment and paid rent for two months. In the third month she refused to pay. Furthermore, she went to the court and sued the old couple for jacking up the rent from $200 to $900. The judge gave a verdict allowing the woman to live in the apartment for two years rent-free; ordered the old couple to refund the two months' rent she paid; and forbade the old couple from renting the apartment for more than $250 a month in the future. The old man had a heart attack upon reading the verdict and died." The news upset Ying Ying greatly.

She wished that she could do something to correct it. But it was a wild, impossible dream.

"Look at these pictures." Pei-hua took out a stack of pictures from her file cabinet.

"These are from a couple who asked me to sue their tenant who ruined their beautiful house like this. Unbelievable. Look, big holes in the walls." She showed each of the pictures and described what it was. "They dug a five feet hole and inserted a 3D picture of batman and his bat mobile in it; they tore down the ceiling and hung a swing from the uncovered beam. Look at this, a basket ball hoop bolted to the wall; hundreds of BB gun bullets shot into the wall because the 17-year-old boy practiced target shooting; all these broken doors and baseboards. Here, you see, big black burnt holes on the hardwood floor. Black, red and blue paint drops all over the floor, a waterbed broke and soaked through the floor down to the ceiling below. The ceiling collapsed. Kitchen appliances, bathroom basin, tub and ceramic tiles were broken. And here the tenant cut off the hose of the washer; put it in a hole they dug on the wall, and let the water run. You cannot understand why some people are so evil."

Pei-hua showed Ying Ying other pictures and said: "Look how the house looked before." She put those pictures away and sighed.

"The tenants lived there for eleven months and owed eight months of rent. The house is in Wellesley, a good town. The neighborhood is a very nice, secluded, quiet cul-de-sac. These tenants let their children run bare-footed and half naked on the street, shouting, screaming, banging on pots and pans; and let their dogs run in the neighborhood without a leash. The dogs knocked down trashcans and tore apart the garbage bags, dragging the garbage all over the street. The neighbors were appalled. They complained to the owner of the house, my client. The owner pleaded with the tenants. Of course the tenants ignored him. When they were six-month inic arrear in rent the landlord tried to ask them to move. They would not budge. My client sent them an eviction notice from the court. The tenants ignored that too. When my client appealed to the judge again the judge said 'I cannot make them move. I can only give you the right to evict them. But it's up to them to decide whether to move or not.' The tenant went and got a public defender and threatened to sue my client."

"For what?" If blew Ying Ying's mind that the tenant had reasons to sue after owing six months of rent and destroying the house.

"For charging them $1,700 a month. This house is in Wellesley, as I have mentioned. it sits on over an acre of land; over four-thousand square feet of living space, twelve rooms, four bathrooms, five bedrooms, and a three-car garage. Isn't it worth $1700 a month? The public defender said the tenant could have bought a house and paid less than that in mortgage. So he was all ready to sue my client. Those public defenders are paid by our tax money. The tenant did not have to spend on legal fees. Of course they were happy to pursue. That is another social issue you and I have a problem with.

"I cannot listen to these anymore. They are disheartening. And stupid." Ying Ying was furious. Pei-hua continued:

"After several more months those people moved out. My client sought legal justice. But no attorney would take their case and said, 'what more do you want? They already moved.' My client said, 'look what they did to the house? It needs to be gutted and totally redone. It will cost over $100,000. Aren't the tenants responsible?' One attorney said: 'as a landlord, the most you can hope for is to get your house back. You cannot hope for more than that.' My client and his wife were very distressed and said: 'it's unfair. We want some justice.' That attorney laughed at them and said: 'there is no justice in the world.' Doesn't this send chills through you?"

*   *   *   *

"Do you think the judge will do that to us? Order us to put Manna up indefinitely?" Worry weighed heavy on Ying Ying's heart.

"She is not a tenant. So it may be different. It all depends on how the judge will look at it. You need to take notes on what she does every day to substantiate your claim of incompatibility and why she is a threat to your life style." Pei-hua's advice was from a legal standpoint.

"That means this has to go on for a while." Ying Ying sounded worried and disappointed.

"I will appeal for you and see if a restraining order might be possible. If the judge thinks it's necessary and issues a restraining order, she has to move out."

At home, after Ying Ying left, Kong Wei stayed in the bedroom to do his work on the computer. He thought his presence in the house should deter Manna from taking further malicious actions.

But something worse happened.

Manna, wearing a red silk shirt with the top few buttons undone, entered his room, strode to his desk, gave him a tempting smile and put her fingers through Kang Wei's hair. Kang Wei jumped to his feet, pushed Manna's hand away and backed up two steps. Manna laughed and said:

"Kang Wei, what are you afraid of? I am so glad you are home. We will enjoy spending this time together. Ha ha, I guarantee you will be completely ... Never mind Ying Ying. She is a bossy bitch. She makes you her cook and chauffeur. She is not a woman you want."

"Manna, you are completely out of your mind. Get out of my room and leave me alone," Kang Wei yelled in rage.

"Oh, come on. Don't pretend to be unaffected. Don't you want to find out how much better I am than Ying Ying? I know you want me. Come on." She pressed herself against Kang Wei's chest, smoothed her hand over his face. Kang Wei pushed her away and commended:

"Stop that nonsense."

"Ooh, you are afraid that Ying Ying may find out. Don't be afraid, she's not coming back anytime soon." She pressed on.

292

"Manna, you are totally insane. You belong in a the mental institution. I am going to call Ying Ying and tell her to send you to the hospital." Kang Wei knew that was only a threat, an expression of his anger. They had no grounds to commit Manna to a mental hospital.

"Ha, ha, ha. What hospital? Who would believe you anyway? You are a man. You took the day off from work because I am here. You wanted to have your way with me and I resisted. How does that story sound? Huh? You want to make the call? Go ahead. Why aren't you calling?" She dared him.

"You cheap sleazy ...." Kang Wei was furious. He went to the kitchen and called Ying Ying at her office, but to no avail. He realized that she must have been meeting with Pei-hua. He left a message with her secretary to have her call home as soon as she was back. He pushed Manna away and went back to his room. He closed the door and locked it from inside. Manna laughed spitefully.

Two hours later Ying Ying called. Kang Wei picked up the phone from his room.

"Ying, you'd better come home immediately," He said. At the same time Manna also picked up the phone in her room. She laughed and said:

"Yes, Ying Ying, You'd better come home."

Ying Ying knew something must be wrong. She did not ask what it was but hurried home. She entered the apartment and met Manna head on. Before she had time to react Manna shouted:

"Fang Ying Ying, how could you leave Kang Wei home with me? He tried to rape me. You are so naïve. You think you can trust him with a woman?"

Kang Wei scooted out of the bedroom, his face blanched with anger. "Listen to her. Listen to this cheap ..." His good breeding restrained him from using profanity.

"Calm down, Kang Wei. I am sorry," Ying Ying consoled him. Then she turned around to ask Manna.

"Manna, why are you doing this to us? What have I done to you to deserve this?"

"What have you done to deserved this? You don't know? You deserve to die. You treated me like dirt that year when you produced the dance showcase. Don't you remember? You think you are superior to everybody. You think you are powerful. Don't you? You want to kick me out? Let's see who is more powerful now," Manna shrieked.

Ying Ying was aghast at Manna's harboring such virulence toward her for so many years just because she had given Meilan the responsibility to lead the rehearsals. At this moment her eyes were caught by torn pictures, papers and envelops on the floor. She rushed over to pick up the shreds and found they were wedding pictures and other pictures of Kang Wei and her. The torn papers were bank statements, reports from various financial institutions, utility and credit card bills and other mails. Manna had gone through those papers and took down the information she thought might be useful to her.

"Why?" Ying Ying let out a tormented exclamation while trembling with anguish. She picked up the pieces and brought them to her room. She remembered what Pei-hua had told her: to keep a record of what happened each day. She put the pieces in a large manila envelope and noted the date and time, and what had happened.

Kang Wei tried to ease her anger while his own wrath was worse than hell. "Ying, this is what we will do. If the law does not protect us against such wretched adversity, we move. At the same time we will continue to seek a legal solution." That sounded like one way out. Ying Ying nodded in resignation.

What had happened to Manna to make her the evil woman she was? Did her adversities -- divorce, loss of custody of her kids, and her imprisonment push her into her malignity?

In Taiwan, Manna was a bar girl who also sold her body and soul to her customers. That might have explained her debauched behavior. But it did not explain her malicious actions toward Ying Ying. Was she really a case of psychosis?

Kang Wei put a lock on their bedroom door to protect his and Ying Ying's files and other important papers from being further destroyed by Manna while they were not home. They had to go back to work. Ying Ying talked with Pei-hua again. Pei-hua did not come up with a good solution.

"The law does not protect victims. We all know that. For your safety and peace of mind the only way out, I think, is to move away. Then we will proceed through the legal process to evict her." Pei-hua suggested

"That was what Kang Wei said too," Ying Ying responded.

With no choice, Kang Wei and Ying Ying went to look for an apartment to rent. When they came home they found that Manna had broken into their room again, trashed their files, and broke Kong Wei's computer monitor. Ying Ying almost fainted.

"Call the police, Kang Wei, call the police," Ying Ying pleaded.

"Did she hurt anyone?" The police asked after hearing Kang Wei begging for help.

"No, she was the only one home. She broke into our room an destroyed some important papers," Kong Wei reported. He could not bring himself to exaggerate the situation for the purpose of getting more attention from the police.

The police regarded it as a domestic feud and did not respond. Kang Wei wanted to appeal to the court for a restraining order. But the court was closed at 4:30pm.

Ying Ying and Kang Wei hastily packed their things to move out. Ying Ying said to Manna:

"Manna, I don't understand why you are doing these things. There must be some reason. But I am not even going to try to find out. We will move out tonight."

"Don't be so sure that you can escape from me, Fang Ying Ying. I won't let you. I will destroy everything for you. I will destroy you. Don't think you are better than me. Now I am the one having power over you. You just wait and see," Manna threatened.

"Ying Ying, let's concentrate on packing. This nightmare will end right here. She is a psychopath. Let's not bother with her for one more second," Kan Wei consoled Ying Ying.

"The files, documents..." Ying Ying looked at the mess of papers strewn the around the bedroom floor and cried.

Kang Wei picked them up piece by piece and put them in several large brown paper bags. "They are all in here. Fortunately she did not tear or burn them. It will take some time. But we can put them back in order."

"I will call Pei-hua and the others to help us move the stuff so that we can just get out of here without making several trips."

Ying Ying called Pei-hua who in turn called Hu Ning, An Kai, Susie, Woolan, Denis, Missy, Tonia and other stuff members at International Foundation. She did not have time to explain to them why they must come immediately to help Ying Ying move. They remained in the dark when they came. The sight of the living room as they entered terrified them immediately.

"What happened?" Missy was the first one to voice her surprise,

Manna heard people talking and kicked her door wide open. She dashed toward Ying Ying with a knife in her hand and shrieked:

"Fang Ying Ying, don't dream that you can get away from me. The Divine Master of the Universe ordered me to kill you now because you have caused so many deaths..." Everyone in the room was horror struck. Denis instantly jumped on her and wrangled the knife out of her hand. An Kai rushed over to clamp her arms from behind.

"She is possessed," Tonia backed away and screamed.

Hu Ning strode over and gave Manna a hard slap on the face and yelled:

"Are you really mad or are you pretending?" She turned her head to the others and said: "Let's take her to the nut house."

Manna tried to free herself from Denis's and An Kai's grip. She kicked and bit them. But the two men did not let her loose.

"Hurry. Let's move the stuff." Kang Wei reminded Ying Ying. Everyone except for Hu Ning and the two men went to help Ying Ying and Kang Wei. They quickly moved the important things that Ying Ying and Kong Wei needed everyday. Ying Ying felt like being extracted from the grip of a demon. The new apartment was left a huge mess when she took her helpers to Chinatown for a late night meal. All were terrified upon hearing Ying Ying's and Kong Wei's atrocious ordeal.

The next day Pei-hua filed for a restriction order on behalf of Ying Ying and Kang Wei. She detailed the extraordinary event in her complaint and cited the witnesses from the night before. The judge granted the restriction order: Manna was not allowed to harass Ying Ying and Kang Wei at their work places or apartment. She must keep 100 feet away from her victims. Pei-hua also petitioned for an eviction order. It was an unusual case because Manna was not a tenant. Pei-hua proceeded by sending Manna an eviction notice via registered mail and demanded her to vacate the premise in fourteen days.

Manna ignored the notice. She had no intention to move. Instead she sued Ying Ying for mental torment and Kang Wei for sexual harassment. Manna knew her way around the system. She knew that on paper she was low income; as such her legal fee would be foot by taxpayers, rather than herself. Ying Ying and Kang Wei, on the other hand, had to hire a powerful and expensive defense lawyer. The cost was prohibitive when the case was dragged on. It sounded preposterous to everyone. Yet no one could say for sure if Ying Ying and Kang Wei would have an easy win on the case.

Pei-hua appealed to the court to remove Manna from the condo by force. Manna figured she had nothing to lose. The more trouble for Ying Ying meant more gain to her. She went to the court to request a jury trial. After several months, during which Manna was allowed to occupy the condo, the case was brought to the court. After two days of lawyers' deliberations the jury could not reach a unanimous verdict. Ten of them wanted to evict Manna for obvious reasons. The other two maintained that Ying Ying and Kang Wei were gainfully employed whereas Manna had no job, no income and was living in hardship. She should be allowed to continue occupying the condo. A hung jury left Ying Ying and Kang Wei hanging.

Unfair and unjust as it was, Ying Ying and Kang Wei had to accept the reality for the time being.

Hu Ning felt guilty about Ying Ying's evil fortune. Had she not pushed Manna to Ying Ying for help none of these would have happened. She knew Manna was a pestiferous slut. *Why did I do that to cause Ying Ying all this trouble?*

One morning she bought some take-out to see Ying Ying and apologized to her. Ying Ying told her not to worry. She had helped many people. Manna's behavior was just an extraordinary anomaly no one could have predicted. It was a valuable, though wretched, experience to have.

*   *   *   *

"Ying Ying, as the president of this organization, you must have been paid a very high salary." It was a question Hu Ning always wanted to ask.

"Not really. A non-profit cultural organization can't afford high salaries."

"I thought a prestigious position must have a pay that is commensurate to it."

"Not always. It depends on what kind of work you do."

"There are a few college professors and research scientists living in my neighborhood. Their houses are small, their cars old and shabby, mostly Hondas or Toyotas. They are busy with research or writing, rarely have time for fun. I don't understand it. Why go to school for so long, earning one degree after another and not making a lot of money? What for?" Hu Ning commented.

"People don't always enter a profession for the salary. To some, doing what they are interested in, what they believe in is more important. College professors are in a respected position. But they are not very well paid. If money is the main concern, they should work in commercial enterprises. Do you understand that?" Ying Ying smiled.

"I really don't understand it. I think money is all life is about. You said you don't approve of girls marrying for money. But if a girl has no money, and no good education, or skills, all she can wish for is to marry a husband with money. It is her goal. Money is the first criterion for choosing a husband. Many girls from China are in that situation. I think they are right." Hu Ning made her point. Ying Ying smiled again and said:

"I had a long list of criteria. Money did not even make the last item on the list."

"Because you have money. For someone who has never been poor, money is not that important. When we were in China we had nothing. Now when we have a chance to have money, we will do everything to get it."

'I don't blame you." Ying Ying wished to say no more. The gulf between them was too wide to cross. No use trying to bring light to a blind person. Each has his/her own goal in life. If money is the only source of happiness to them, just let it be.

People usually associate only with those having some commonalities to share, comparable in educational level, nature of work, point of views, interests and so forth. When there was nothing in common they would have nothing to talk about and would feel bored. Ying Ying, being the head of a cultural organization with broad programming had, for years, interacted with people from widely diverse backgrounds. She accepted them as they were, passed no judgment, got along well with them. Her broad-mindedness, while applauded by many, was criticized by some cynical individuals:

"Of course, in her position, like a politician, she must tolerate, even please all kinds of people. Who knows how much of it is real?"

A few months after Ying Ying and Kang Wei moved out from their home, Roger went to Ying Ying's office and asked if she had heard anything about Manna.

"I know nothing about what she is doing, only that she is still occupying my home. Didn't you know that we were forced out of our own home by her? We will appeal the case to the superior court," Ying Ying said.

"You may not have to do that. I think you can just ask the court to allow you to take your condo back. Manna has disappeared." Roger brought this surprising news to Ying Ying. But he was in anxiety. "She kidnapped my kids and went into hiding. It's been weeks. I have brought it to the court. The police are looking for her. Maybe she has moved out of state."

While feeling sorry for Roger Ying Ying was happy to know that Manna had run away. She called Pei-hua to give her the good news. Pei-hua immediately petitioned the court to reclaim Ying Ying's and Kang Wei's condo. It did not take long for the court to give a judgment. However, they could not promptly move back because the place was left a ruin by Manna. It called for a complete renovation. In the process they were taken by two separate unconscionable contractors who took their money and left the work undone. Ying Ying and

Kang Wei were too tired to chase them. They just swallowed the loss; hired a third contractor; supervised him every step of the way, and did not over-pay him or pay too fast.

It took months to complete. After they moved back they threw a small party to celebrate the ending of all their ordeals.

Chapter 10

𝒯here always seemed to be reasons that brought Dong Fei-yan to Ying Ying. Ying Ying easily forgave Fei-yan for her often inexcusable actions and behaviour. The friendship that once existed between them gradually revived. Ying Ying would respond quickly when Fei-yan asked her to help with developing a project idea or something else.

Fei-yan told Ying Ying many stories about her liaisons with different men abroad and locally through the years. That year when she went to Taiwan after she breached her contract with Boston Common Summer Arts program, she brought a violinist along. She soon was consumed by a crush over him that led to a short period of romantic liaison between them. She was always looking forward to new experiences. One day she happily broke good news to Ying Ying:

"Ying Ying, I have some wonderful news to tell you," she simpered.

"What is it? Another love story?"

"I met a Russian musician while in Germany. His name is Ivanov. He is a very talented saxophone and bassoon player. We worked together on a few occasions. After that I visited him. He graciously put me up in his house." Her voice was filled excitement. "But his wife was pretty upset by it though."

"I should think so. What wife would not be upset? or what husband wouldn't be if his wife brought home a strange man? Were you just friends or something else?"

"At first we were just friends. But I could not resist his rugged virility. So I ... I... went to bed with him," she chortled. "We are lovers." Her openness embarrassed Ying Ying.

"I am not surprised."

"I invited Ivanov to come here. I want you to arrange a concert for us." Dong Fei-yan made such a demand as a matter of course.

"I'm afraid I can't," Ying Ying replied bluntly.

"Why not?" Dong Fei-yan was surprised and perplexed. When had Ying Ying declined a request so abruptly, without thinking?

"Have you given any thought about the availability of our schedule if nothing else? You also should know that the Foundation and China Society have their own programming committees. I cannot overrun everybody to put in an event whenever I please." Ying Ying was irked. Beside, Fei-yan's often capricious ideas had cost Ying Ying many times. She would not risk another of

Fei-yan's irresponsible behavior such as walking out of the Boston Common Summer Arts Program and backing out from the concert at China Society.

"He won't be here until a couple or three months later. You have plenty of time to schedule it," Dong Fei-yan argued.

"I'll be on the level with you, Fei-yan. You have put me in the most awkward situations before. I cannot repeat the mistake and jeopardize the organization's programming and reputation again." Ying Ying stressed.

"I know, I know. But Ying Ying, come on, you have to help me this time. I already promised him." Dong Fei-yan believed she could sway Ying Ying.

Two months later Ivanov came and stayed at Fei-yan's house. Ying Ying did arrange a concert for them on a weekday evening when the auditorium was available. She made it clear that the event was not sponsored by International Foundation or China Society. Fei-yan had to pay a fee for the auditorium and publicize the event herself. If she was to be overpowered by a moment of whim and the concert was canceled again, neither of the two organizations' reputation would be hurt.

"It will be a good experience for you." Ying Ying said.

"But to pay a fee? Ying Ying, you must waive the fee. I have no money to pay."

"It's the rule, Fei-yan. I don't own the organizations."

"Bad enough that you are not sponsoring it. You can't charge me." Fei-Yan ignored Ying Ying's comment and persisted.

Ying Ying was defeated by her importunity. She sighed: "Fei-yan, you are giving me a hard time. All right, I will bring this up to the committee and ask them to waive the fee for you. But I don't guarantee that they will."

"Yes they will if you ask them." Fei-Yan was confident.

Fei-yan scrambled to notify all the people she knew and persuaded them to come. The audience was small, nevertheless. At home, she had two men between them she must maneuver. She was also busy trying to promote Ivanov, find gigs for him, made CD of his music, and so forth. But she was happy. She clung to Ivanov like mucilage.

"You used to despise people for being inseparable from their spouse. You called that 'losing one's independence and self.' You never considered that love, rather than dependence, made a man and a woman inseparable. Look at you now. You two are like each other's shadow."

Fei-yan laughed agreeably: "Exactly. We are *shadow and form, never apart*, as the Chinese saying goes. I understand it now. We are in such love. The kind of love I never knew existed before."

"Brandon, he still does not mind Ivanov living under his roof and romancing you?"

"No, he doesn't. Maybe he does. But he doesn't show it. Ivanov minds it though. He doesn't want me to go to Brandon's room. He said he can't stand the thought of me sleeping with Brandon. He wants me to only sleep with him. Ha ha ha," Fei-yan laughed.

My God, how thick is the skin on your face?! Ying Ying tacitly denounced her friend and sighed.

"Fei-yan, may I say something?" Ying Ying's tone was sincere and serious.

"Shoot."

"Brandon is exceptionally self restrained. Please be kind to him. Image yourself in his shoes. What would you do? Would you tolerate your husband bringing a woman to live in your house, making love to her openly? No one can take it. He is no different."

"You don't understand him. He really does not mind." Dong Fei-yan was nettled. "He read a lot of books on anthropology. He is intensely interested in the folk cultures, traditions and customs of different ethnic people around the world. There are tribes in some parts of the world in which a woman has several men. He accepts such practice as being normal."

"Yea, for the tribal people. But he is a man of our society and culture." Ying Ying spoke gently yet did not give up on trying to persuade Fei-yan.

"I think he minds. He just doesn't know what to do. He is too gentle. Be kind to him."

As Ying Ying became better acquainted with Brandon and Ivanov she saw the two men's personalities and attitudes as being diametrically opposed. The husband was a well-educated, urbane British gentleman who treated his woman with tenderness and care. The lover was a rogue. He was gruff and insolent, and he never hesitated to lavish harsh criticism on Fei-yan in the presence of Brandon and Ying Ying. Ying Ying felt very awkward. She often spoke to Brandon, under such circumstances, about something extraneous so as to divert his attention. *Brandon must have felt awful to see his wife being mistreated by this intruder,* Ying Ying thought.

Many times Ivanov said to Dong Fei-yan: "Stop feeding me your Chinese food. I am hungry all the time."

One time he stewed a caldron of potatoes and beef Dong Fei-yan scooped out a bow of it and put it in a small pot, added water, soy sauce and some Chinese spices in it. He was peeved by it and yelled:

"Why do you spoil my food with this junk? Can you give up your Chinese food for a day?"

To that Dong Fei-yan replied: "I just made a little for me and Ying Ying. I did not spoil you food. Most of it is in your big pot, intact."

"I don't understand why you must change it," he pressed on, while Fei-yan said not another word. Brandon quickly ate his food in silence. After that he left the table to clean the pots and pans in the sink, all the while without uttering a word.

Beside his repulsion toward Chinese food, Ivanov also did not approve of Dong Fei-yan keeping Chinese friends: He questioned: "Why do you always associate with the Chinese? You are going to live a ghetto life forever?" Ying Ying felt especially uneasy at this remark. She tried to put in a few words. Experience had proved to Ying Ying that no one could finish a sentence without being hushed by Ivanov. She was not dismayed nevertheless.

"Fei-yan is not living a ghetto life, Ivanov. Brandon is a British. Their friends and associates are mostly non-Chinese. She only has a few Chinese friends." She felt regretful to have to point this out, and especially to exonerate Fei-yan for having a few Chinese friends. Why did anyone need to make excuses for that?

"No, no, no, no, no, no, no," Ivanov objected. Sometimes he would say fifteen no's to make his point. "You don't understand. Married to an Englishman and socializing with white people does't make her less of a ghetto person." He turned to Dong Fei-yan: "Your thinking, your manners, your habits are all still Chinese. You feel better with your Chinese friends." His tone became sharper.

Brandon strode over to the table to pick up the dishes and utensils, put them in the sink, walked back to the table to wipe it clean, then back to the sink to wash the dishes. He softly muttered: "Is there anything wrong in being a Chinese?" Ivanov did not hear it. He was still harshly criticizing Dong Fei-yan. When Fei-yan left her seat to make tea Ivanov was very irate. He yelled at her:

"Don't walk away when I am talking. You know how rude that is? You know how much I hate that?" Like a skittish kitten, Fei-yan froze. Her hand suspended before the cabinet door that was left ajar, not knowing whether she should get the tea canister or not. Then she withdrew her hand, rushed right back to her seat. Ivanov gave her another fierce glower before continuing with his other remarks.

Bandon took some fruit from the refrigerator, washed it and put it on a plate. He put the plate on the table and quietly retired to his study.

Ying Ying rose to her feet ready to say good night and leave. Ivanov stopped her and said:

"Don't leave yet. Sit down."

Ying Ying was stunned by his demand. Fei-yan chuckled and whispered in Chinese: "Don't leave yet. He likes you. Of all my friends he only likes you. Usually he couldn't wait for my friends to leave." Ying Ying plumped back down in her chair resignedly.

"Don't speak Chinese in my presence. That's not polite. Doesn't Ying Ying understand English? Why do you need to speak Chinese?" brashly Ivanov demanded.

"Sorry." Dong Fei-yan meekly apologized.

Why does he like me? Ying Ying asked herself, *because I always let him dominate the whole scene? He thought I was an excellent listener? If only he knew what I thought of him! What does Fei-yan see in this guy? Petulance and impudence aside, he does not even possess a pleasing physical appearance. Brandon is tall, slim, fit and has a nice-looking face. Fei-yan once said that some people thought Brandon looked like Harrison Ford in Indiana Jones. This guy is big like a refrigerator, with a big stomach and a coarse face. What is there about him that attracts Fei-yan?*

Ivanov spieled non-stop from one subject to another. Ying Ying's mind wondered far away not hearing what he was saying until these words hit her eardrum:

"Why do you go to the museum? What is the sense of going? To pretend that you like the art hanging on the wall?" Ying Ying was astonished. *Was he speaking to me?*

"What?" She blurted.

Ivanov paid no attention to her and kept talking. Ying Ying realized that he was speaking to Fei-yan.

"What do you know about Egyptian art, or Greek and Roman art? Or Byzantine Art? Or Renaissance Art? What do you know about any art?" He twitted scathingly. Ying Ying held back her displeasure while Fei-yan replied to Ivanov's demands.

"I don't know those arts. But do you think all the people going to the museum know them?" Fei-yan timidly hazarded an argument.

"Don't argue with me. Those people are stupid phonies. They don't know anything but pretend that they do. Why cheat yourself like that? No one is going to think, 'oh, look at her, she is so smart, she has such high taste.' No one will think that," Ivanov mercilessly pushed on.

"I did not go to the museum for that purpose." Dong Fei-yan gave her meager response.

Ying Ying could not let herself listen to that verbal assault anymore. She asked to be excused and left.

It boggled her mind that a self-reliant, confident, assertive person like Dong Fei-yan would succumb to such control by a man living under her- and her husband's roof. *How could she love a man who mistreats her,* holds her in contempt?

Some time later, one day, Ying Ying heard a cheerful voice on her phone. It was Dong Fei-yan.

"Ying Ying, I have persuaded Ivanov to stay here."

"Stay here. What do you mean?" Ying Ying had not paid attention to Dong Fei-yan's words.

"I begged him to stay here permanently, to immigrate to the United States. You know, he had no plan to stay for long. He could leave me anytime he chose. But I think he is probably willing to stay now. I told him that he could go anywhere he wanted but make Boston his home." She sounded hopeful and positive.

"What about his wife and daughter?"

"What about them?" Dong Fei-yan's tone flattened.

Ying Ying knew that she had touched a nerve there. "So you want him to get a green card?"

"Yes. That's why I called you. I want you to sponsor him." Again without considering the ramifications she thought her request was a matter of course.

"How? Under what pretext?" Ying Ying was not pleased.

"China Society can sponsor a musician."

"Not a Russian musician."

"Oh---." Dong Fei-yan was irked. "You must be able to find some way."

"But I cannot think of any way. Why would a Chinese cultural institution sponsor the immigration of a Russian saxophone player?"

"International Foundation can, absolutely." Fei-yan was happy that she thought of a good alternative. She made an unshakable order. Ying Ying was fretted by it.

"Fei-yan, although I am in charge of the organization, such matters must be discussed and voted on by the Board. The Board will raise many questions. It wouldn't be easy."

"Then what do I do?" Her balloon deflated. And she was exasperated.

"Just apply as an accomplished artist. You do not need a sponsor if you can convince the immigration officer. I can write a support letter for him. That's not a problem."

"Your support letter will be very useful." Fei-yan knew from other people that Ying Ying's letters always unfailingly brought desired results. She was delighted. "Pei-hua can do this for me then. Ying Ying, will you ask Pei-hua to help?"

"You should ask her yourself. It would be more courteous coming directly from you, don't you think?" Ying Ying pointed out the obvious.

"Maybe. But I just think Pei-hua would do anything if you asked her."

"I will mention that you are going to ask her for a favor."

Pei-hua's practice did not include immigration. She recommended an immigration lawyer to Fei-yan. Fei-yan was fretted and blamed Pei-hua for not being willing to help. She complained to Ying Ying:

"Pei-hua just doesn't want to help me. She is a lawyer, how hard could it be? Why can't she do it?"

"Fei-yan, be reasonable. You are a musician. Are you able to play every instrument?" Ying Ying reasoned with her.

"You always do things outside of your expertise. And do them well too." She was right on this point.

"Don't use me as an example." Ying Ying conceded.

"Anyway, I will remember never to bother her again." Fei-yan was roiled and developed an animosity toward Pei-hua and refused to call the lawyer Pei-hua recommended. She found another lawyer. After several months and many phone calls, the lawyer told her that their application was rejected by the immigration office.

Fei-yan was beyond disappointment. She was wrathful. She went to Ying Ying and said:

"Ying Ying, the lawyer is charging me an arm and a leg and the case has failed. I think he must not have given compelling answers to the questions. He said an independent artist was in a difficult category. You see, it's obvious that he has not spent any effort on the application. He used his usual formula and it didn't work in this case. Ying Ying, you must help. Take a look at what he put in and change it. You can do a hundred times better."

"You already know what caused the denial. Then you can make changes yourself. Why must it be me? I have no time." Ying Ying tried to turn down Fei-yan's demand.

"You know that I am not good at this sort of thing. You are the best. You can do everything well. Just help me." Fei-yan used her usual importunity. Again. Ying Ying resigned to her demand and re-wrote the answers. She was amused by the information the attorney put down. They were poorly written, vacuous, even irrelevant to the questions. Beside that, the supporting materials were haphazardly stacked.

"You think an immigration lawyer should have some sense about what is important, and arrange the supporting materials in order of usefulness. The lawyer did not address the specific questions either. The answers were flaccid and impertinent. The whole package of materials failed to establish the applicant as an accomplished individual who deserved to be accepted as a U.S. permanent resident." Ying Ying said to Fei-yan then handed her the application she had redone, Ivanov's resume she rewrote, and the supporting materials she re-arranged.

"See! That's why I said only you could help us. You can find the crux in every issue. You can present the case powerfully," Fei-yan said. She handed the package to the lawyer and had him re-submit the application. This time it passed. In a few months Ivanov would get his green card.

Most of the people Dong Fei-yan was acquainted with did not approve of her lifestyle. They described it as promiscuous, keeping a husband and a lover under the same roof. Some distanced themselves from her.

"One man is not enough for her? She must have two?" one woman scornfully put it.

Ying Ying and Pei-hua, however, always defended her.

"I don't think Fei-yan is a loose woman. She is in love with Ivonov. I believe she does not keep a conjugal relation with Brandon anymore," Ying Ying said.

"Right. She just does not have the means to move out with Ivanov. Neither of them has a regular job. Their music does not earn much money for them," Pei-hua added.

"You two are naïve," a man said. Ying Ying just smiled. Pei-hua was vexed at being called naïve.

The man continued: "You may not admit it, but I think like many people do, you also consider living with two men as morally unacceptable. But you don't want to believe that your friend is immoral. So you protect her by thinking she is only physically intimate with one man. Let's face it. As recent as the early years of this century men in China were allowed to have concubines. In America, we all know that the Mormons have multiple wives. Why must you resist the idea that your friend can have two mates? Just because she is a woman? How a person chooses to live is nobody's business. What right do we have to impose our ideas on someone else?" He made perfect sense. Ying Ying and Pei-hua could not argue with him.

*   *   *   *

Ever since she fell in love with Li Yong till the time of their divorce, Pei-hua's heart and attention were completely dedicated to that man. He was more important to her than her career. She moved to New York to be with him. But he was often taken out of town by his acting engagements. His success on Broadway was a dream came true. After that his interest turned to his native country, China. And he went to Shanghai.

Pei-hua's career was disrupted by leaving Swanson, William and Murphy law firm in Boston for New York, then returning to Boston after years in New York. Divorce brought her a period of dejection. Then she was saved by her strong wellpower and Ying Ying's constant encouragement. She resolved to put her personal saga behind her. She had experienced heart aching love and a painful divorce. She resolved never to be disturbed by romance and marriage again. She was determined to focus on furthering her career.

It worked. Her performance as an attorney stood out among her colleagues. She became a highly valued asset to the firm. Eventually she was offered a partnership at Swanson, William and Murphy.

Her social circle had always been small. Beside Ying Ying, she was only loosely acquainted with some of Ying Ying's friends. She felt that she should make some changes, to broaden her circle, to bring balance into her life. She joined a choral group; went to church, attended parties and other events, socialized with her colleagues. and went dancing with friends. Her intelligence and good looks inevitably attracted suitors. Yet she avoided them. At this time in her life what she needed was platonic friendship that transcended romance. She wished to have a male friend who was compatible with her intellectually, socially and educationally; to share mutual respect, trust, care and concerns; and to engage in meaningful discussions on topics of substance rather than senseless small talk. She also needed this friend to be pleasing to the eye. In other words he had to be handsome.

"Why does she require a male friend to be handsome if romance is not in her mind?" some people criticized.

Is this a weakness? Do I need to defend this peculiar trait of mine?

Some people taunted her saying that her idea was an impossible wild dream.

It may be a luxury to have what I wish. I may never get it. But I can wish for it.

Dong Fei-yan heard about Pei-hua's situation and sneered: "No romantic relation? That's a deceptive front. Who would believe her? She just wants to appear different from other people. Let you think she is pure and spiritual. Just look at the way she dresses. Tell me she is not sexy. It's obvious to me that she uses sex appeal to tease and flirt. Then she pushes the men away just to tantalize them. What a strategy! She must have mastered Sun Tze's Art of War. Why would a friend have to be handsome if she had no sensual desires in mind?" Fei-yan's harsh criticism was a vent to relieve her grudge against Pei-hua for refusing to help her on two important occasions. One was to incorporate her non-profit organization. The other was to apply for Ivanov's green card.

Fei-yan has no right or ground to vilify Pei-hua that way, Ying Ying thought. She had to defend her good friend:

"She finds beauty pleasing. She enjoys beauty in inanimate objects as well as in human forms. I don't think it is unreasonable to have such a preference."

"Pei-hua is a rare jewel. You don't find women like her anymore. She is opposite of Fei-yan anyway," Denis commented when the subject appeared in conversations. Although he and Pei-hua had not seen each other for a long time, Pei-hua's image occupied his mind nonetheless.

He had long ended his titular marriage with that Chinese waitress when she got her green card and brought her son from China. After getting his Ph.D. he taught at Northeastern University. He had kept in touch with his old colleagues, especially Ying Ying, at China Society. On one occasion Denis and Pei-hua sat next to each other at a banquet. They chatted about their work and daily lives. Denis told her about his teaching job, and the book he just started to write. Pei-hua told him about Shanghai, Meilan and Li Yong and about her current situation.

A few days later she got a greeting card from Denis. He told her how much he enjoyed that evening. Pei-hua wrote him a note to thank him. At the end of the note, as a customary courtesy, she wrote: "We should get together again sometime." He then called Pei-hua to chat a little. This back and forth writing and calling established a close connection between them. Their friendship rapidly developed to such a state that Pei-hua felt a closeness she never had with any man except for Li Yong. She felt like confiding in him with her innermost feelings. Yet she only described her feelings in her journal:

> Loss, desperation, grieve followed the parting with Li Yong.
> Wan, vacuum was my being.
> Rusted were my emotions and feelings.
> I didn't know how to live. I had to learn how to live.
> I discovered what I needed. I need friendship,
> Friendship of a man.
> I pondered the issue of friendship.
> I wondered about my naïve quest for pure platonic friendship.
> Cross-gender friendship is such a beautiful thing.
> But it may only be a wish, a yearning, a dream.
> Could it be a naïve wish, an impossible yearning, a fool's dream?
> Am I a naïve fool?
> It may be an unreachable goal.
> Where will I find a man who shares my ideas and yearnings?
> And he must possess perfect qualities in
> Intelligence,
> Wittiness, and
> Physical beauty.
> He must also be loving and caring.
> A loving relation that transcends romance.

She hesitated and did not write these words that were in her mind: "Denis comes very close."

In her broadened social circle she met a few men who also came quite close to her vision. She corresponded with them.

Correspondence, an old-fashion way of communicating one's thoughts and ideas to the other, always attracted her. Since ancient times people had been writing letters, letters between friends, family members, lovers. They carried such romantic ideas. They were read and re-read, over and over again. They were kept in personal archives. They were of literary value if well written. If the writers were well known these letters would become research materials for posterity. Many were published. To Pei-hua, writing expressed thoughts thoroughly, and reading a letter allowed one to enter into the writers' minds more lucidly.

What differed these letters from those of decades or centuries ago was that they were electrically transmitted, thanks to modern technology. She enjoyed reading them and kept them neatly in folders.

Fang Kuei did not know Pei-hua well. He only met her a few times before. Now that Pei-hua was divorced he tried to date her whenever he was in town. Pei-hua made many excuses to avoid him. She insinuated to him that she would not be physically intimate with anyone, she only wished to have friendship with men. She knew that message would stop Fang Kuei from pursuing her. No doubt, Fang Kuei plainly commented:

"That is your wishful thinking. Without physical intimacy friendship is baseless, insubstantial and fleeting."

Pei-hua disregarded that statement. She firmly believed that physical intimacy was a sacred thing only to be had between loving married couples. She also believed that friendship between a male and a female could exist. But that believe was shattered when one friend wrote her:

> I have fallen in love with you despite my promise to keep only a platonic friendship. ... a woman I won't be able to have. ... I cannot see you anymore.

And another friend wrote:

> Being around a woman whom I am very attracted to and who is also very beautiful but I cannot be physically close to is indeed quite torturing.

If this was how they feel why would they befriend me in the first place? Didn't they understand where I was coming from? Did they think I was not serious about my thoughts expressed in words? Did they truly want to be my platonic friends but changed their minds because it was too hard for them to have unadulterated friendship with a female?

It hurt her to lose those two friends. It was a small comfort that there remained a few who kept the connection with her through correspondence. She occasionally would meet with one for dinner, a concert, or museum events. She was pleased with that friendly relationship but was not sure how long it would last.

Denis knew Pei-hua's frustration. He wrote her:

> Pei-hua, your views and ideas are pure and lofty, also romantic and idealistic. They belong to the 19th century. The kind of people you envision are hard to find now. Your innocence is what sets you apart from most people. I have secretly admired you since we first met many years ago. I hope that I can be that special friend you'd like to have.

Pei-hua felt elated. Denis met all of her criteria and he seemed to know her thoughts and feelings well. She had secretly hoped that he would be the soulmate she was searching for. Now he had come to her. Ying Ying saw this beautiful friendship grow and prosper. She secretly hoped that in time Pei-hua and Denis would step beyond platonic friendship.

*   *   *   *

The beautiful and ill-fated dancer Ailing, after her ominous marriage to Ah Tu the cook, abused by his mother and sister, rescued by Pei-hua and Ying Ying, found a job as a cleaning lady at a ballroom dance studio, became a dance instructor, and finally competed in the New England regional ballroom dancing and won the gold medal. Her dance partner and she jointly opened a studio at which she also taught Chinese folk and classic dances to children. She felt beholden to the people at China Society that supported her when she saw only darkness in her life. So she offered to teach China Society's classes there as a volunteer. But the Board insisted on paying her at her old rate.

She also felt indebted to America for giving everyone an equal opportunity and freedom to develop, grow and flourish. To repay this country, she gave free dance instructions, workshops and demonstrations at various Boston-area schools. Furthermore, she brought her Chinese folk dance students to nursing homes and hospitals to entertain the elderly and the ill, free of charge. Her life was firmly set on the right track. She was far from the newly arrived young wench from Beijing who wantonly threw herself at American men hoping to get a green card in exchange. She was also no longer the timid, helpless little woman treated like trash by her husband's mother and sister. She was now a confident, self reliant, useful member of the society who often did voluntary work for the needy.

But life still treated her without compassion. She had shouldered a large share of portentous events she did not deserve. One night driving home after spending a whole day and night caring for a sick friend, Ailing was exhausted.

She drove through route 95N from Quincy to Newton after 1:00am. It was dark, foggy and drizzling. Cars were sparse on the road. The speed limit was 55mph. She kept her speed between 45mph to 55mph to avoid being pulled over by a police. There was a discussion on instrumental trans-communication and dreams being broadcast on the radio. It was a subject that interested her. So She listened to it attentively. After passing the Dedham exit, #17, she noticed a car behind her. The car followed her for quite a distance. She began to wonder if it was a police cruiser. But she couldn't tell because it was too dark. She instinctively looked at her speedometer. The needle pointed at 45. *I am safe*, she thought, *if that is a police car he must be chasing someone else.* She continued to drive at 45 to 50 mile per hour. The car was still following her. And a blue and red light flashed along with a soft siren (not the usual loud blaring) was heard. She realized it was in fact a police cruiser and he was chasing her. At that moment she quickly assessed her situation to decide what to do.

One: *Should I stop as a motorist must do when chased by a police cruiser?*

Two: *Should I not stop immediately but drive to a well-lit location? The second choice would render me misconduct of disobeying the police officer and end up with a ticket. But I would not be risking my life or being raped in case he is a fake police.*

There had been many reports of incidents of female drivers being raped and beaten half to death by fake police late at night. There were warnings to women not to risk their safety by unwaveringly adhering to the traffic law. One warning was "not to stop until driving to a well-lit place." She was always very vigilant after watching the news on the TV, hearing it on the radio and reading it in the newspapers.

She decided to keep driving until she reached exit 21, from route 95-S to route 16 in Newton where the road was lit sufficiently by streetlights. She felt somewhat safer there. She stopped, waiting for the police to come.

As he approached her car Ailing opened the window and asked:

"Officer, did I do anything wrong? I was driving at 45 miles."

"Did you have too much to drink?" His voice was harsh.

"No. I never drink. I hate alcohol, drugs and cigarettes. They taste bad to me." She tinged her remark with a little humor, not expecting more than a mild admonition. She was fully aware that there were many drunk drivers at that hour and the cops were out to catch them. She had been stopped more than once before because the angle of her turn was too wide or she came off the ramp from the turnpike too fast or something of that nature. One time she was stopped by the police on route 135, at a small commercial section in Wellesley because she failed to stop for a pedestrian who was about to step down from the sidewalk. Each of those times, the police only pointed out her mistake and said: "Drive carefully."

"You drove badly." This police was still huffed.

"Huh?" She didn't understand what he meant.

"You drove across the white line back and forth," he said. "Where did you go?" The harsh tone startled her. She wondered why he needed to know where she had been.

"Quincy," She replied softly.

"Why did you go to Quincy?" His grim expression chilled Ailing. She further wondered why he was interested in knowing why she went any place.

"To see a friend." Intimidated by his inescapable omnipotent authority she replied softly and gently.

"Did you see the flashing light on my cruiser? Why didn't you pull over but kept on driving?" He raised his voice. His countenance was grisly. His tone was very glacial.

God, what are you going to do? She was a helpless victim in his hand!!

I was not speeding so I thought you were following someone else." Ailing did not tell him about her worry of being followed by a villain impersonating a police. She was afraid that might rile him. So she gave him a simple and truthful answer.

"You were the only one on the road. Who else would I be following?" He became more lupine. Ailing was not the only one on the road. There were other cars, very few, but not zero. However, she did not dare point that out to him.

"I am sorry. I didn't know. I was paying attention to a talk show on the radio."

"Did you watch the radio or listen to the radio? Can you use your eyes while listening to the radio?" His voice was hard and chilly. Ailing's heart sank.

"I was only paying attention to the road in front of me. Sorry. I did not notice what's behind."

"Get out of the car," he ordered. Ailing obeyed. He put out a finger in front of Ailing's nose.

"Can you see my finger?' The same harsh voice and grisly look.

"Yes," Ailing said.

He moved his finger to the left and then to the right. "Follow my finger," he ordered. Ailing obeyed.

"Walk a straight line," he ordered again. Ailing obeyed.

"Give me your driver's license," he demanded. Ailing took it out of her purse and handed it to him.

"Registration too." Another demand. Ailing gave it to him.

He walked to his cruiser. Ailing waited. After a few minutes another cruiser with flashing red and blue lights came. Then another such cruiser came.

Why so serious, three police cruisers, just because I did not drive well? What did he mean by not driving well? Ailing was befuddled.

More time went by. He came out of his car to talk with the other three policemen. Then he approached Ailing's car again. With a bone-chilling fierce look and frightening voice he declared.

"Two criminal offenses. One, your license has expired. You are driving without a license. I can put you in jail for this. Two, you did not stop when I was pursuing you at low speed. You disobeyed a police officer. Don't you know that you must stop when a police officer is pursuing you? I can arrest you and throw you in jail for this. Another offense: You drove across the lines. I will notify the Registry that you are not fit to drive."

With all the alleged crimes and faults heaped on her Ailing was seriously frightened. She also felt humiliated. She thought: *Criminal offenses? I am no criminal. Why don't you go catch the real criminals? There are too many of those harming the society and get away without punishment. And here you are bullying me, for what? You should apologize to me.* Then reality hit her: *Stop fantasizing. You are only a helpless victim at his mercy now.*

He walked away to speak with the other policemen some more. Then the other three cruisers drove away. At this time Ailing thought she should tell this police what was really on her mind when she decided not to pull over. She got out of her car and began to stride toward him.

The police pulled out a gun and pointed at her. He shouted:

"Get back to your car. Go, go, go!!!"

Ailing was terrified. She couldn't figure out why he was more ferocious than before. She quickly turned around and returned to her car. The car window was still open since she rolled it down to speak to the police earlier. The police moved to the door of her car, pointed the gun through the window at her head. He shouted:

"Don't ever step out of the car without my order."

A flash back of her former mother-in-law's abuse singed her senses. She held back her tears. Timidly she said:

"I made a mistake. Please don't shot me. I was not aware that my license was due for renewal because I did not receive a notice from the Motor Vehicle Registry. It was a careless mistake. Would you please not make it a criminal issue?" She pleaded.

"Don't try to be cute. You think I cannot shoot you? Driving without a license is a crime. Criminals should be shot. But I am not going to shoot you this time. Only your car will be towed. I may throw you in jail right now. I will notify the Registry that you don't qualify to drive. You don't know the first rules. You don't

know that you must stop when a police cruiser is chasing you. They should not have issued you a license in the first place. Now they must suspend your license for good. You are never going to drive again. You are a danger on the road." He repeated his accusations.

"Call someone to get you home," he ordered. And he called the towing company in Wellesley.

Ailing had been driving for years without getting a ticket much less ever having caused an accident. She was a step-nine driver, with a perfect driving record. Why shouldn't the Registry issue her a license? Why should they suspend her license for good? It was all a joke, a supreme example of a petty cop's abusing his power over a defenseless motorist.

Hu Ning's experiences with the police were completely different. She made serious moving violations such as running red lights, driving 60 mph at a 35mph zone time and again. All she ever got were mild verbal warnings from the police. "Just be more careful in the future. Don't let me catch you again." Her secret? "Always smile sweetly to the police and make up some convincing little stories," she said. But mostly, luck was on her side.

Ailing called Ying Ying to no avail. It was 2 o'clock in the morning. She must be in bed.

"It's very late. officer, I cannot reach my friend. Could you.... " Helplessly she tried to plead with the policeman.

"Try again." He cut her off. She tried several times in vain. She was desperate. "I cannot reach anyone. What should I do?"

"You have to keep trying. Someone will wake up. When the tow truck comes I am going to leave. I am not going to wait here." His chilling voice and lupine manner crushed Ailing.

Why are you so relentless? I am only a motorist who has made a small mistake. Why are you in such rage? Do you want to kill me? Oh my God. If he killed me there would be no witness. His crime may never be discovered. Why must you have my car towed anyway? If I can get one friend to come and pick me up, I can get two friends to come so one of them can drive my car home. I don't have to waste money on the towing service. But of course you want to heap as much disaster on me as you can. These thought ran through Ailing's head.

The tow truck came. Ailing still had not reached anyone. The police and the tow truck driver exchanged a few words. He turned to her and said.

"He will drop you at the mobile station on route 95. You keep calling your friends." He drove away. The tow truck driver drove to a Mobile station. It was closed, not a single soul in sight. The driver gave her a business card showing his address and phone number and said:

"Next week after your license is renewed come pick up your car. You must pay cash for the towing and storage." He drove away leaving Ailing stranded at a deserted gas station.

This is Friday. Next week!!! That means I would have to pay at least for three days' of storage for my car. It might be several hundred dollars. Ailing did not have much money.

She wondered why the towing company would only accept cash. *Is there any shady practice? Do they report their income accurately to the IRS? It is a well-known fact that many restaurants falsify their books, evade paying full tax, because of customers' cash payments. Was this something that a good citizen should overlook?* She further wondered if the police force and the towing services were in a racket.

Her naïve respect for and trust in the law enforcement forces had been shattered by the repeated portrayal of depraved, corrupt policemen, on television shows, engaging in criminal acts of various kinds. *I would not be surprised if some shady arrangement was in place between the police and the towing guy. What if a bad guy happens to drive by and sees me? He might do any number of horrible things to me, murdering is not beyond likelihood. There have been so many gruesome murders in the news regularly. A woman cannot do enough to protect herself from becoming a statistic. And now, because of an insignificant mistake, the police, whose livelihood is provided by people's tax money, whose duty is to protect the public, would expose a young woman to such danger. If I were to be murdered, would the media find out what has happened? Would the police be responsible for such a consequence? Would it be an unsolved case even?*

She kept calling and calling. Finally Ying Ying picked up her phone.

"Ying Ying..." Ailing muttered, tears streaming down her cheeks. "It's me, Ailing."

"Yes? What is it?" Ying Ying was only half awake. She was apparently wondering why Ailing would call at that hour.

"I need your help. I am sorry to call you so late. But I don't have anyone else to call. Can you pick me up? I can't get home." She was desperate and apologetic.

"Your car broke down?" a logical and natural assumption.

"No, I don't have my car now. Please just come to pick me up."

"Where?"

"I am in Newton, at route 16 from exit 21 of route 128 South. Do you know where it is?"

"Yes, I think I do." Ying Ying said. She quickly put on her clothes after hanging up her phone. It took her 45 minutes to get to the Mobile station. She was astonished to see a trembling and tearing Ailing.

"What happened?" Ying Ying urgently asked. Ailing began to cry while she stammered out her woeful experience. Ying Ying was aghast and enraged upon hearing her story.

"How could a police officer be so devilishly cruel? How could he just leave you at this place? He should have taken you to the station with him," Ying Ying exclaimed.

*   *   *   *

The next morning, Ailing woke up feeling the weight of devastation pressing on her. The calamity of the day before replayed again and again. Ever since she left the hell of her abusive mother-in-law's grip, she regained her sense of dignity and respectability. She lived a decent and useful life. She paid back the society that allowed her to build a good life.

I am not able to bear any more humiliation that I don't deserve. I refuse to bear the humiliation imposed on me by the cop. She felt ashamed of not having the power to protect herself, having to endure such a grave insult. She needed to cleanse out the shame, to restore her dignity.

What can I do? Should I seek legal justice?

She regretted that she had not taken down the policeman's badge number or the plate number of his cruiser.

I have no evidence even if there is an outlet for me to speak up.

She was lost in the haze of injustice.

314

There is no justice in the world. That was a remark of an attorney.

Newspapers! I should give the story to the newspapers. But would the papers pay attention to it? Would this be newsworthy to the papers? No! Police brutality was ten times worse. One time there was as a report on the newspaper about a Chinese old man being beaten severely by a policeman who accused him of soliciting a prostitute. He could not speak a word of English to exonerate himself. It was the Chinese community that hired an attorney to defend him and provided character witnesses to support his case. In the end the city apologized and paid for his damage. As for the policeman, not only was he exonerated but compensated as well. How could the accuser and the accused be innocent at the same time? And why would the police be compensated too?

The newspapers sneered at the case and gave the story this caption: "The only loser is the city."

Ailing had always held that law would be on one's side if he did not break it; the police would not harass an innocent person. That view was seriously in doubt now.

She lived in an area in Newton, far from the subway station. Without her car she must take a taxi to the station, then the subway to the studio in Boston. She and Sidney taught one class together. He taught the women and she the men. She told Sidney about the incident and asked him to understand that if she was absent he had to teach the class by himself.

"Can you get your car today instead of next week?" Sidney asked.

"I am afraid they won't let me take the car. The police wanted to make sure that I don't have the car before I have a valid license. He also said that he would tell the Registry to revoke my license for good so that I would never drive again," Ailing stated.

"This policeman should be revoked so that he would never be on the street bullying motorist again. His behavior is making my blood boil. As for your car, of course you can have a licensee driver to pick it up with you any day.. They can't say that if you don't have a license you can't have a car in the garage." Sidney argued. "Call the towing company. Tell him you will go with a friend to pick up the car."

Ailing was doubtful but called the towing company nevertheless.

"I would like to come with a friend and pick up my car."

"We are closed," the man said abruptly.

"You are? On your business card it says 24-hour towing service." *If you wanted to lie in order to keep my car for extra days you should not have given me your business card.*

"When are you coming?" The man was irritated. "You have to have two drivers with valid licenses to come with you. And you must pay in cash. Hear?"

"I will come at 4pm." She thought one hour and six minutes might be enough. She did not dare ask any more questions. She called Ying Ying and Kang Wei. Kang Wei was out of town. Ying Ying would be coming. She needed another licensed drive.

"I will get someone for you. Don't worry." Ying Ying called several people but they were away for the weekend. An Kai was the only one in town. Ying Ying told An Kai to go directly to McQuin's towing service. She went to pick up Ailing at her studio. When they arrived at 4:01pm the guy had already left.

"He must have left deliberately in order not to let you pick up your car," an Kai offered his surmise.

There was a gentleman, Anthony, who was a student of Ailing's ballroom dance, heard about her calamity. He said she should have called him when she was stranded on the street that night.

"It was very late, Anthony. And you live in Peabody. I couldn't call you," Ailing explained. In fact she never thought about him.

"No, it wouldn't have mattered. When you are in such a situation any hour would not be too late to call me. And it would not be too far for me to come to you. Remember that. Any time, when you are in need, call me." Anthony, a thirty-five-year-old engineer and a divorcee, had long been an admirer of Ailing's but had not expressed his feelings to her in so many words.

"Did you get the cruiser's plate number? Was he a Newton police?" he asked.

"I don't know. It was dark and the lights on the cruiser were flashing. I couldn't see the plate. And I had no way to know the policeman's badge number."

"You need to have someone to take care of you, Ailing, my dear. It's a dangerous place out there. I am not being chauvinistic but you need a man to protect you unless you know how to protect yourself." Anthony sounded like a big brother. "The policeman was excessive. You should seek justice by reporting the incident to the police commissioner, by sending him a well-written letter. Let him know that you are a minority and the police might have treated you more harshly because of that. I know you don't believe race is a factor. But it may be very true."

Influenced by Ying Ying's belief that the American society was the least discriminatory, that race issue was exaggerated, Ailing also detested people playing the race card.

She thanked Anthony for his concern.

On Monday Ying Ying and An Kai were going to take Ailing to the Registry to renew her license. But Anthony insisted that it would be "an honor and a pleasure" if he could take An Kai's place. That afternoon they went to McQuin's to pick up the car. She paid for the towing and three days of storage, all in cash.

As they were leaving the parking lot Ailing casually asked the towing guy:

"The officer who stopped me was a Newton police, wasn't he?"

"A state police," he said.

After they left the towing service Ailing said to Anthony: "I wonder if I should ask the IRS about McQuinn's practice, and call the Attorney General's office too, just to get a sense about whether there might be something shady going on between the police and the towing service. I'd like to hear from the Attorney General's office if the police should have given me the option of having a friend drive my car home."

"I doubt you will get any information," Anthony said.

People at China Society couldn't believe Ailing's dreadful saga.

"I think the police was angry as hell. That's why." Keith, a new staff member, made his point unemotionally.

"But was Ailing's little mistake enough for him to raise hell of wrath? Anger is an emotion aroused by personal reasons, usually," Ying Ying retorted in ire. "An expired license is a careless mistake. Especially this year when no notices were sent to motorists and Ailing was out of the country. It certainly does not qualify as a personal reason for the police to get mad as hell. If she had assaulted him physically or verbally that would have constituted a personal reason for him to get angry. An invalid license should not arouse anger in the police. The police should be cool-headed."

"There are born bullies. This police was just that," staff #2 added. "They like to display their power whenever there is a chance."

"It's a professional hazard. Those guys are desensitized, callused. They treat everybody as criminal," Staff #3 added his opinion.

"What about detective Cunningham?" Staff # 4 questioned. Apparently as a joke. The others were lost and asked:

"Who?"

Staff #4 laughed and said: "Detective Cunningham. You know. Clint Eastwood's movies. Mel Gibson in Lethal Weapon, Richard Burgi in Sentinel. They are passionate cops. They always protect the good people and punish the bad guys."

"Come on. Those are idealized characters. You watch too many movies and TV shows," Keith criticized.

"Honestly. I took those as realistic depictions of our law enforcement personnel. It has never occurred to me that the majority of the cops are like that jerk, probably," Ying Ying fumed.

*   *   *   *

The police bullying and humiliation were not the end of Ailing's misfortunes. A week later she received two notices in the mail. One was from the Registry of Motor Vehicles. Another was from the state police department. The RMV letter stated in the first paragraph:

Your are hereby notified that effective d/m/y your license/right to operate a motor vehicle is revoked for an indefinite period for IMMEDIATE THREAT.

Under that were four paragraphs that read:

When your license or right to operate motor vehicles has been suspended or revoked, you must immediately cease to operate all motor vehicles until your license or right to operate has been reinstated.

If the above applies to the registration of your motor vehicle, operation of such vehicle must cease at once and the registration certificate and plate(s) must be surrendered to me immediately. You may request a hearing concerning this matter at the Driver Control Office at the Registry of Motor Vehicles, located at 630 Washington St., Boston, MA.

If your revocation is the result of a court conviction for driving under the influence of alcohol, pursuant to Massachusetts General Laws Chapter 90

Section 24, you may appeal your conviction to the superior court. In all cases, it you are aggrieved by a decision or order of the Registrar you may, within ten days of the effective day or the Registrar's order, appeal to the Board of Appeal on Motor Vehicle Liability, Policies and Bonds, One South Station, 5th Floor, Boston, MA 92119. You can also download an appeal application from their website at WWW.STATE.MA.US/DOI or call them at 617-351-9710. No appeal will stay the suspension or revocation order and you must still comply with the above directive.

Note: At the time your license or right to operate is reinstated you will have to pay a $100 - $1,200 reinstatement fee. Make check payable to RMV.

Susan Arnold, Registrar

The notice from the state police department was a citation of two counts of criminal offense and one count of civil offense. The criminal offenses were "unlicensed operation of MV" and "Stop for police, fail." The civil offense was "marked lanes violation."

This citation showed the name of the policeman who sent the wretched fate to
Ailing. Like thunderbolts exploding on her head, Ailing was crashed and stupefied. She understood that the police charged her with criminal offenses; her license was revoked indefinitely. But she did not understand what the RMV had demanded her to do? She did not belong to the first category because her registration was valid. She also did not belong to the second category because she was not convicted by a court for driving under the influence of alcohol. What should she do to have her license reinstated, if possible? Without transportation how was she going to get around?

She needed someone to explain the letter to her. It was not an issue with the English language. She was fluent in English. The letter was confusing. It took her a while to understand the small print on the back of the police citation too. It stated that within four days from the time the citation was issued she must submit the citation to "the court on the front of the citation." In a moment of distraught and haste she read the printed words on the front of the citation but failed to find the address of a court. Four days!!. Two had been used for the traveling of the mail. She had two days left. If she mailed it back it might miss the deadline. What would happen in that case? More worry singed her.

She called Ying Ying. Ying Ying had gone to a meeting. She called Pei-hua. *Pei-hua is a lawyer. She should be able to help me.*

"The RMV letter sounds confusing to me too. I think you need to find out which court is handling your criminal offense and go there in person to give them the citation. You don't want to pass the four-day limit." Pei-hua gave her an advice. "And you need to get a criminal defense lawyer. This is a serious matter. I have no experience in handling such cases." She did not have a magic wand to wave the baleful event away.

Ailing thought Pei-hua might not be as resourceful as a white attorney. So she called the dance studio's legal counsel, Earnest. His reply was no better than Pei-hua's. He said:

"I am a corperate lawyer. I think you need a trial lawyer. If you want me to represent you, I will. But I don't know how much good that will do. I don't really know the criminal court's procedures. Besides, the police, the court and the defense lawyers are all meshed together. It's a sort of a fraternity brotherhood, a good-ol'-boy club. They speak the same language. They may know one another. They can get things resolved easily among themselves. I am an outsider. I don't belong to that club. But I can recommend an excellent lawyer to you."

The two attorneys' words sent Ailing to deeper distress. She carefully read the citation several times, from the front to the back. Then she saw a few words hand scribbled at the lower right corner-- Dedham district Court.

How could I not have noticed it earlier? She blamed herself. She needed to make a call to that court and ask some questions. She checked the phone book. Her phone book did not include the town of Dedham. She called 411 and got the number.

She listened to the recorded message twice before choosing the Criminal Department. She reached a clerk instead of a recording. *Thank God.*

"Thank you so much for taking my call. Please help me." She must beg the lady so that the latter would not hang up. "I got this citation and a letter from the Registry of Motor Vehicle. I don't understand what is said in the letter. I don't now what to do."

"What do you mean you don't understand the letter? Do you read English?" the clerk asked. Ailing's slight accent gave her away as a non-native speaker.

"I do read English. But the letter sounds confusing. And the citation said I must submit it to your court in four days. I have only two days left and I just got the letter." Ailing spoke in a pleading voice.

"What was said in the letter?"

"It said that my license and right to drive was revoked indefinitely. But the reasons for the revocation do not fit my situation. I really don't know what to do."

"I don't have time to talk on the phone. We are very busy here. But if you come in with your citation I can explain the letter for you." She sounded normal, not cold and harsh. She even offered to explain the letter. It was more than Ailing could hope for. She thanked the clerk.

She asked if Anthony would drive her to the Dedham district court.

"I can't believe that the event has developed to this level." Anthony was enraged. "I think we should first go to the RMV and ask what the letter tells you to do, then go to the court with the citation. But it's too late now. Let's do it first thing tomorrow."

The next day they went to the RMV at 9am, got a number, and waited to see the personnel in the Appeal's office.

"You need to get a hearing to find out if your license can be reinstated," the appeal's Officer said.

She made an appointment to go back another day and went to the Dedham court to drop off the citation. The criminal department clerk she had spoken with on the phone was not there.

Two days later she appeared at the RMV for the hearing. The woman officer said there was nothing she could do. She encouraged Ailing to see the Appeal Officer. She paid fifty dollars and made another appointment to go back for that. She paid another $15 to get a copy of her driving record that would support her claim as a good driver. It puzzled her to see the record showing only the present year with her "Immediate Thread," and "criminal offense. She went back to ask for a complete record a few days later. The clerk told her that she already had the complete record. The record only showed her current violations because the previous years were clean.

She went to the RMV's Appeal's Officer on the day of the appointment. The large and rough-looking man read the police report and said:

"You must get your doctor to fill out these questions. We have to see if you are fit to drive. You need to get a court judgment. Then you must take a road test."

"Sir, I have been driving for years. I was a step 9 driver, never had any violation. Look at my driving record. I can't see why I am not fit to drive."

"It doesn't matter how perfect your driving record was or how good a driver you have been. The police officer said you were not fit to drive, you are not fit to drive." *The police have omni power just like God.*

Ailing asked her doctor to fill out the questionnaire and went back to see the Appeal's Officer. This time it was a woman.

"Wait outside. You will be called," the stone-faced woman ordered. She waited for two hours before the woman called her in.

"There is nothing we can do here. You must get a court judgment to resolve the criminal offense case first before the Registry can do anything. If the court confirmed that you are guilty you will end up in jail and your license will never be reinstated." The woman's visage was stolid. Her tone was glacial. And she would not allow Ailing to ask a question.

Where is justice, fairness, and humanity? What crime have I committed? Missing the date of license renewal is such a huge crime that I should be home arrest for months, or even indefinitely, even be thrown in jail? her heart shouted. But she did not speak up.

"Just do as I've said," she commended.

A court judgment will determine whether I can ever drive a car again!!! Or go to jail? A person can lose his freedom or mobility for life just because of a small mistake. What kind of law is that? Why does the justice system not confer proper punishment to the hard criminals, the rapists, murderers, financial criminals, illegal immigrants who inflict serious harm to the citizens and the society? Why is punishment not fitting the crime? In despondency these thought swelled in Ailing's mind.

Sidney drove Ailing to the Dedham District Court.

"Could you tell me when will a court date be assigned to me?" Ailing asked the clerk.

"It may take months."

"Oh." Ailing was distressed. "This will be extremely difficult for me. I live in an area where there is no public transportation. It is nearly impossible for me to go on with life without transportation. How do I get to work? How do I go to the market? I cannot afford to use taxis all the time."

"You can drive. The police complaint was that you had no license that day. If your license is renewed you are allowed to drive. The criminal issue is separate from your driving right," the clerk said. She did not show any sign of contempt to a "criminal." Her job must have desensitized her. Beside, there must be innumerable people being labeled as "criminal" who in fact were not. She understood that. At this moment her noncommittal face and voice alleviated Ailing's self consciousness.

"Really? You mean it? That is great." Ailing felt the day just became brighter. Her main concern was regaining her mobility. The court clerk's words were different from what the RMV people had told her. The latter said that reinstatement of her license relied upon the court's judgment in favor of her. Yet the court clerk gave her a glimmer of hope. If she were allowed to drive as the court clerk had said then defending her criminal charges would be less urgent. She believed she could win.

"I still wish to have an earlier court date though. May I get one?" she asked.

"There is nothing I can do about that. Maybe your lawyer can ask the court to move the date up."

These obvious conflicting statements from the court clerk and the Registry of Motor Vehicle were unsettling to Ailing after her initial elation.

"Who should I believe? It was confusing," she said to Anthony.

"We'd better make sure," Anthony said. He and Ailing read the RMV letter again and believed that the court clerk's information was wrong. Ailing's hope was snuffed out. Anthony tried to console her.

"Don't worry too much about driving. I will drive you wherever you need to go."

"Thank you for your kind offer. But that is a huge inconvenience to you and I have no right to impose that on you."

"Ailing, no such talk, please. You know it's my pleasure, and honor."

A few more days passed. Ailing received a notice from the Dedham Court giving her a date to appear. That was two months away. Her traveling expenses, $40 taxi fee to and from the bus station every day, was considerable. She could not ask Anthony to drive from Peabody to Newton to take her to work and shop. But two months were better than "several" months of waiting. She should feel somewhat relieved.

She re-examined her mistakes. She regretted about her oversight in the license renewal business. From this point on she would make it a habit to check the expiration date every year. As for not pulling over for the police in a dark street at 2 o'clock in the morning under drizzles, she would not have done it differently. Safety was more important than obeying a policeman especially when there had been many instances when villains masqueraded as police. Even if he was a bona fide police as in this case, she could not be sure. So why take the chance? She was tormented by the havoc wreaked on her by this petulant policeman. But it beat being raped and killed.

She had heard on the radio, read in newspapers, and saw reports on TV about police brutality. Usually she was sympathetic to the police who carried out grave duties to protect the society. Very often they faced dangerous elements. Many got shot at, lost their lives or were severely injured. Police were heroes in her regard. Did these professional hazards callous their minds, harden their feelings, and make them hate all people and treat them as enemies?

While she was musing on the issue, a TV news report caught her attention. It was about a policeman who captured a driver trying to run a red light. In normal cases, the police would write a citation and let the driver go. But this policeman, much like the one who resolved to destroy Ailing, yelled and threatened the motorist. He was caught by a hidden video camera. The tape was played on TV. Ailing saw that policeman harshly silenced the driver who attempted to speak. The wife in the passenger's seat cried and said:

"Please just write a citation and let us go. My mother is dying in the hospital. We have to rush there to see her before she dies."

The police yelled at her: "You are a goddamn liar. You think I will let you off so easily?"

The husband tried to tell the police that he did stop at the red light. The light seemed to stay red for longer than usual. There was no car at the intersection and they must get to the hospital in a hurry. So he drove through the red light.

The police did not let him talk. He yelled:

"Shut your mouth, I don't care who is dying. You just listen to me. I will throw you both in jail. I can do that."

The woman cried harder and pleaded with him: "Please let me have the chance to see my mother for the last time. Please just write the citation quickly."

The police yelled more and said, "shut your mouth" six more times while using scurrilous language at them. When the husband tried to plead again the police pulled out his gun and pointed it at him and said:

"You shut your mouth. I am going to throw you in jail for running the red light and arguing with me. I can do that." Little did he know, his actions and verbal abuse were all recorded. The couple did not argue with him. They pleaded with him.

It went on for a long while. When the couple got to the hospital the mother already died.

Ailing felt rankled for the woman whose final chance to be by the mother's side before she died was robbed by that heinous policeman. Her own hope for justice was quelled. Her case was insignificant in comparison to that woman's. And both their cases must be much paled in comparison to numerous others.

*   *   *   *

If the police bullying happened to her when she first came to America she would not have given it one thought. She would have taken it as a matter of course. Because she came from a communist country, she was used to not having freedom, democracy and human rights. In Mao Zee Dong's era people lived in constant fear. Police force aside, there were civil reconnaissance troops that infiltrated all levels of the society, roaming the streets, entering homes, sending reports to party authorities on anyone they deemed deserving. Ailing was born during that era. Although she was too young to be victimized, she knew how it was from her family's experiences. Even while growing up when things had lightened up, fear pervaded people's lives. The first thing that struck her when she first came, like it did to most others from China, was the liberation from fear, the freedom to make decisions for oneself. She remembered when the post office clerk asked what was in the package she was sending, she replied without thinking:

"Please open the package and check it."

The post office clerk was dumfounded and said: "Why would I open your package?"

Why wouldn't he open it? In China it was the most natural thing to do. Being checked and searched were normal.

After so many years of living in America she had forgotten the life under constant surveillance. Freedom and human rights were basic desiderata of any person. When they were compromised the America people would not tolerate it.

Yet, there were dark sides in any society.

It was revealing to Ailing too how widely apart one person's view might be from another. A certain Mr. Chao voiced his opinion upon hearing her wretched ordeal:

"You were wrong. The police were right. Because at any time, under any circumstances if you did not obey a policeman you are at fault and the court would convict you. They can put you in jail. There is no other way about it. If you have a powerful attorney he may be able to get a reduced sentence for you. If you don't you are already showing a contempt of court. You are going to get a very heavy sentence."

That categorical statement vexed her and propelled her to make up her mind against bringing a lawyer to the court.

On April 29th Anthony drove Ailing to the court. After waiting for an hour and half she was called to the courtroom. There was one state police beside the presiding magistrate. The magistrate read the incriminating report from the police. The last paragraph of the report described Ailing as "an immediate threat to the police, to the other motorists and to the society."

Ailing asked if she could speak. The magistrate said "of course." Ailing calmly stated:

"I apologize for making a mistake. I knew that I should have immediately pulled over when the police cruiser flashed his lights behind me. I failed to stop. That was a serious mistake. But I did have a good reason for that. I have heard and read many reports about fake police pulling over female drivers at night...."

The magistrate interrupted her and said: "Yes. I know all about those reports."

That was good. Ailing prepared eight pages of such reports to show him if necessary. Now she did not need to expatiate on this point.

"Did you tell it to the trouper?" he asked.

"No, I was afraid it might sound stupid and might infuriate him. So I did not say anything."

"He reported that you were crossing the white line back and forth by four or five feet. What do you have to say about that?"

"I probably did. But it was drizzling and very foggy. In some sections the lines were obliterated. And there were very few cars on the road. So I probably drifted across the demarcation lines without knowing."

"Your license was expired on December 25. It was ..." He turned the papers, trying to find out the date of the incident.

"February," Ailing informed him.

"Two months," he muttered. Then he asked: "Why didn't you renew it?"

"In the past I always received a renewal notice from the Motor Vehicle Registry. This time I did not and I over looked it."

"Because the state has no money to send the notices. It was in the news. It's your responsibility to know when to renew your license," he said.

"I know now. But I was out of the country for a while; I have probably missed the news."

"When were you out of the country?

"From November of last year to January of this year."

"Where were you?" he asked.

"I was in China for over two months."

"What did you do there?"

"I was there for a cultural exchange program. I brought dance students to China to attend an international dance exposition and to participate in

324

workshops with Chinese students. After that, I was invited by several schools to give talks and demonstrations."

"The dance students came back by themselves?"

"No, we had a program coordinator and two other staff members accompanying them. It was a program of China Society's. I was the director of the program."

"I see," The magistrate said. He flipped the papers in front of him, looked at some of them and asked:

"You got out of your car to speak to the trooper. Do you know that you should never do that? That's why the trooper called you a threat to him."

"I did not know that rule."

"You can only leave your car when ordered by a police."

"I know it now."

"Did you drive during these two months?"

"No, I relied on friends to drive me or used taxis. The taxis have cost me more money than I could afford. But I have a job. If I miss my work I would be fired. So even if I don't have money to buy food I have to hire a taxi." She added: "I am not a criminal. I am no threat to anyone. I am a useful member of the society." She spoke with confidence and uprightness.

"Have you ever broken any law?"

"No," Ailing smiled.

"I can see this is a case of misunderstanding on the part of the police. But you should understand that the police face all kinds of people everyday. It is stressful. They don't know what kind of a person you are. They treat all people the same way. I am going to dismiss this case. There will be no record of any kind on you. You have no fault."

"Thank you very much." Ailing held back the tears that were brimming. These were the first kind and just words she had heard from a government worker since that night she was condemned by the police.

Ailing was very pleased with his judgment. She thought he had stopped short in admitting that the police were wrong in making excessive accusations, over blowing the case out of proportion. She believed justice had prevailed. The state police in the courtroom, a female, representing the trooper who accused ailing, said:

"The trooper's car was not marked. It was understandable if you had suspected it to be a fake."

Ailing was surprised and happy at the same time to hear that. She had no idea about the trooper's car being unmarked because she was completely unnerved and the drizzling foggy night was very dark that she did not know if the cruiser was marked or not.

On Friday, May First, Anthony drove Ailing to the RMV in Worcester early in the morning. They spent several hours there waiting in line. First, Ailing spoke with a woman in the Appeals Office. It was the same woman Ailing spoke with two months ago. The woman asked Ailing what was the court's judgment. Ailing told her she was completely exonerated; the magistrate had declared her innocent and the policeman's misunderstanding; she was at no fault. She handed the paper from the court to the woman.

The woman told Ailing to wait outside while she processed the case. After a long while she came out to tell Ailing to get a number and pay the fee to reinstate her license. About three hours later came Ailing's turn to pay her fee. The clerk said:

"Pay $500."

"What? Why? The court dismissed the case and said I was at no fault. Why do I have to pay $500?"

The man asked: "Did you explain it to the officer in the Appeal Office? She is the one to decide whether you have to pay this fine or not. Go talk to her."

She went to ask why she was charged a steep fine when the court had declared her innocent and had dismissed her case? The stone-faced, glacial voiced woman said:

"That was the court's decision. The court has no jurisdiction over the Registry. You are an immediate threat to the police, to other motorists and to the society. That was what the police officer complained. You must pay the fine. That's $500."

What? The court's judgment does not count? Then the police can accuse anyone of any crime and the accusation would stick, even the court cannot overturn it? Would this system aggrandize the police's power to infinity and throw the door of abuse wide open? Would people in this democratic society ever see a flicker of justice? Anger permeated Ailing's chest. It was not the $500 fine that upset her. The money was not the issue. The principle was everything. This made no sense to her. Did the court and the Registry not belong to the same country? How could a court decision mean nothing to an agency in the same state?

She had no other recourse but to pay the fine. She went to the window again and gave the man her credit card.

"Cash only."

"I don't have $500 on me." Most transactions were by credit card. People did not bring that much cash any more.

"Go get the cash from the bank."

She left and went home. She had to wait three more days without a car. The following Tuesday Sidney drove her to Framingham. She filled out a license reinstatement application form and waited for her turn. Before she paid the $500 she asked the clerk:

"May I ask a question?"

"Sure." The woman said, in a nonabrasive manner and voice. Ailing was almost not used to that after her experiences with the bureaucrats at the RMV.

"I was pulled over by the police. My case was resolved in the court. The court said I was at no fault and exonerated me completely. Why do I still get a $500 fine?"

The woman asked: "The court gave you a piece of paper? Can I see that paper?"

"The Appeal's Officer in Worcester took it and did not give it back to me."

The woman checked the record in her computer and said:

"I cannot do anything for you now because they already decided that you have to pay $500. The only thing you can do is go back to Worcester and talk to the same person; explain that the court already dismissed your case, there is nothing against you anymore. You shouldn't have to pay this charge."

"I will pay. I cannot do without a car any longer. I will lose my job." Ailing succumbed to the unjust situation. It was apparent that charging the exorbitant fee or not depended on that stone-faced woman's mood rather than by the book. What use would there be to go back and plead to that woman? She might even be further annoyed and do something worse. It was hard to predict.

"Don't pay yet. Once you pay you can never get the money back even if you appeal and win," the woman warned her, not knowing what was on Ailing's mind.

"I will just pay. I don't believe I can convince that woman to change her mind. She would not do that for me."

Ailing was acutely aware that if she had any connection with people in the Registry this unwarranted fine would have been removed without a question. She would not want that kind of a favor under any circumstance. She only wanted to see justice and fairness. She used to believe justice and fairness did exist in the country.

The woman behind the counter at the MVR in Framingham happily took the $500 and gave Ailing a receipt.

"Now you can drive," she said.

The application form was left on the counter. She did not need it.

*   *   *   *

Sidney was very upset about the whole thing. He said: "You had no fault yet you had to pay. Now, paying the fine is admitting that you are at fault. It makes no sense."

"This is called Government official's heavy-handed treatment of innocent and helpless small people," Ailing commented.

Brooding over her experience Ailing wrote to her friend in China:

> It has been a distressful and revealing experience to me, one that makes me feel being oppressed, unfairly treated, and that justice is nowhere to be found. For the first time since I came to America I clearly realized the similarity between this wonderful country and the totalitarian communist countries such as my motherland where petty, corrupt officials used their omnipotent power to overrun helpless people. Even here, people can live in fear and misery too.

She was contemplating whether she should just leave the whole calamity behind her, or seek retribution, to get even. But she had no recourse. She wrote to a few more friends in the States just to vent her grievance. Her friends' reactions and opinions on what she ought to do varied. One Chinese friend said:

"Though I heard about changes in China, it was no different from before in many ways. Police terrifying people is a normal way of life. People are used to it, never think of it as harassment or something to grumble about."

Another good friend wrote:

> It was an outrage. I couldn't believe that such a thing would happen in Massachusetts. In MS, AK or AL maybe it could happen, but in the liberal MA? I'm very angry for you. Just thank God that you got a just/fair judgment. Do you still have contact with the press? It'd make a great article and give many folks a platform to tell their grievances too. Then again, I don't want you to be a target of the bad cop, since he knows and could get your profile easily, you don't know what he will do. For your own safety, swallow the incident and move on. Life after all is unfair, as we all already know.
>
> Just thinking of you being left alone in a closed gas station, on a February night brought tears and anxiety to me. May nothing like this ever happen to you or anyone again!

Yes, the danger of the police seeking revenge would be terrifying if I would successfully expose his excessive abuse of power. Maybe I should just swallow the bitter reality, Ailing thought in despondency.

Another friend uttered a different voice. He wrote:

> If something like this happened to someone before and that person had taken action within the given procedure of the law, this behavior may well have been stopped, curtailed or at least not condoned. There are countries where all police are crooked and you must work within their law, but that is not the case here, especially in affluent neighborhoods where the citizens are more educated and less tolerant of blind injustice. That's why exposure is the greatest ally you have, this search for justice. If you are unsure, make sure that you talk to people that can give you an assessment of how widespread this abuse is. Write to the Boston Phoenix paper, it might be called a bad Paper but I think it's still the Phoenix. They are an independent paper and they have a good investigative staff.

Occasionally a desperate situation would lead to a turn of destiny. Anthony's helpfulness, attentiveness, patience, and care during the period of Ailing's hardship deeply touched her. Her sense of gratefulness developed into affection. Anthony had long been a silent admirer of Ailing's. He saw his opportunity to propose and seized it. Ailing accepted without hesitation. They had an intimate wedding at a small church with the blessings from their best friends. Ailing was very happy. But she had been happy since she was freed from the stranglehold of her former mother-in-law to find herself in her work. She wrote to her friends:

> Happiness comes from within oneself, when one feels content. No amount of money and fame can bring happiness if one does not have the feeling of contentment and gratitude. I am very content with what I have. I am grateful to the society and the country. I feel blessed to be in the U.S.. I feel fortunate that I can do some good for the society in terms of teaching school children how to dance, and volunteering for the elders. Of course I am especially happy that I have married a good man.

Chapter 11

It was near Mid-Autumn Festival.

A symbol of completeness, togetherness was attributed to the fullness of the moon. Family members near and far would get together to enjoy the moon and eat moon cakes.

Meilan, having no family, felt lonelier at this time than ever. While sitting by her desk, looking out of her office window listlessly, her secretary knocked and entered.

"Boss, there is a Mr. Wang to see you. He said he was an old friend of yours and he just came from America," the secretary announced.

"Mr. Wang, from America. Who could it be?" Meilan muttered. She knew many Mr. Wangs in America. *Who would drop in without a phone call?*

"Invite him in," she told the secretary.

A grizzled gentleman was led in.

Meilan looked at him in surprise. She had never expected to see him. He was older, a middle-aged man. His hair had turned gray and he had put on a few more pounds. But the overall change was small.

"Kai-de, it's you?! When did you come to Beijing? How did you find me?"

This is the Taiwanese man who had a flaming love affair with Meilan in Beijing fifteen some years earlier. Because of his wife's severe mental illness he could not divorce her or abandon her. He had begged Meilan to forgive him.

"I arrived two days ago. How did I find you? Everyone can tell me where Miss Liang Meilan is. Look at your office building," Kai-de uttered. Meilan smiled.

"*Hai*, just a little something to do, to pass the time. Otherwise I would have rotted away idling at home." It was the Chinese people's habitual humility. It had no meaning. She continued:

"Have a seat please. How are you doing these years?" She gestured him to take a seat on the sofa. As she spoke her secretary brought in tea and snacks and set them on the coffee table. She poured the tea in two cups, offered one to Kai-de and put one in front of Meilan's seat and left. Meilan sat in an armed chair and picked up her tea to slowly sip it.

"I retired," Kai-de said.

"So early?"

"Yes, I was tired. Tired of working, tired of living. I was tortured by life for

330

too long. My late wife had a few extremely bad years before she passed away, two years ago."

"I see." The image of Kai-de's wife screaming, crying, laughing, biting her caretaker, pulling her own hair, throwing things around was still fresh in Meilan's mind.

"I took an early retirement before my wife's passing."

For two years Wang Kai-de lived a reclusive life. Meilan occupied his mind and heart during the years of their separation. He heard about business tycoon Hemmingway being in love with Meilan, and Meilan's success in business. He knew she was single and wondered if he might still have a chance. He owed Meilan so much. Would she still want him, a broken man?

Although Meilan had married and divorced once before meeting Kai-de, he was her first true love. For the longest time she tried to put him out of her mind, but a misty, vaporous image of him always followed her in her sub-consciousness. Those layers of mist and vapor faded away when the real figure appeared in its full solidity.

At the night of the Autumn Moon Kai-de and Meilan went to a nice restaurant for dinner. Then they came back to Meilan's home, sipping wine and listening to music.

It only took a few get-togethers--strolling in the Bei-hai Park, spending a few quiet evenings in her living room, to revive her feelings and emotions for him, hard to believe as it was. For a long time tender romantic feelings were far removed from her. She had become a cold and hard person, tyrannical, tough as a nail. Expanding her empire, defeating her competitors, and making more money had been her sole focus. She had assumed and accepted the reality that she would be alone for the rest of her life. But now, she was reliving the moments of her most happy times.

Kai-de felt the opportunity was ripe. He proposed marriage. Meilan accepted.

They had the wedding in Beijing. It was a headline in the papers and a news item on the television. Meilan always made the news. It was her strategy to keep her fans from forgetting her. She had a superb ability to make small mundane things about her into colorful news. She spared no expense on the wedding and made it a major social event. Everyone who was someone was invited.

After spending a few weeks of honeymoon touring some of the most fascinating scenic sites in China they flew to Boston to give another wedding banquet. Meilan asked Ying Ying to give her the current addresses of everyone she had met since she first came to that city. She regarded them her best friends in America. Ying Ying offered to help her send the invitations to those on the list.

At the banquet she hardly had any chances to speak to the guests. So she invited some of them to her new home on Mount Vernon Street on Beacon Hill, after she and Kai-de spent another honeymoon in Europe.

Ying Ying had not kept up the connection with Woolan and Susie. On rare occasions she would accept an invitation from Ching Ju to her parties. Woolan and Susie both apologized for not keeping in closer touch with Ying Ying. They were too busy with business and money making. The two had so much in common but they hardly contacted each other. Perhaps they were competitors of sort.

Meilan was intrigued and surprised at the financial successes of Susie and Woolan. She asked many questions trying to know how they made it so well. There was a sliver of disapproval or discrediting, due to jealousy, revealed in her eyes. Meilan never could stand seeing other people doing well as if they had taken something that belonged to her.

"You two did well. Not bad. Not bad. Heaven treated you well in leading you to meet those big wealthy people. Without them I am afraid you couldn't have got too far." She firmly planted them on the ground. Kai-de strode away to entertain the other guests. He was an amiable, seasoned host who made his guests feel right at home.

"Where is that flashy artist? What is his name, I cannot recall. You know whom I mean. The one you all regarded so highly," Meilan asked Ying Ying.

"You mean Meng Song?" Ying Ying asked.

"Yes, yes, I think that's his name. Where is he now? What is he doing?"

"He went back to Shanghai. He is a much sought-after artist, active in the international art scene," Ying Ying replied

"Don't forget to mention that he also has a thriving business, a wife and a son too. He owns a large art complex in Shanghai with art galleries, artists' studios, an arts-and-crafts store, book store, music store, artist club house, and a café. He is no different from all the other industrious, entrepreneurial Chinese going back from Boston," Pei-hua added.

"I see." Meilan exclaimed. Her voice betrayed a shade of disbelief mixed with jealousy. "Pei-hua, remember? I said everyone liked to make money." She paused a second and said: "I wonder why I did not know his establishment."

"Did you know everything that was going on in Shanghai? Did you even pay attention to the art circle?" Pei-hua retorted.

"Meilan has so much going on in her own business empire. We can't expect her to notice everything in Shanghai," Ying Ying intervened. She did not like to see Pei-hua and Meilan bicker over a small subject again like they often did. They both understood and dropped the subject. Meilan turned to asked Ying Ying a question:

"Ying Ying, do you plan to have kids?"

"No such plan."

"You mean not now?".

"If I tell you that I have made up my mind not to have children since high school what would you say?" Ying Ying asked.

"Why?" Meilan was surprised. "Having children is a natural outcome of marriage."

"Because of that I did not want to marry. It took my mother many long speeches to change my mind about marriage. But she couldn't persuade me to have kids."

"It's a natural stage in our lives. It is how the human race perpetuates." Meilan insisted.

"I am not against perpetuating the human race. The human race will not become extinct without my contribution. The world is overpopulated already as it is." Ying Ying held her ground.

"That is a strange philosophy." Meilan shook her head.

"That is called freedom of choice. Ying Ying's philosophy will not lead to the danger of human extinction, I am sure." Pei-hua was bickering again.

"Are you going to have children?" Meilan ignored Pei-hua's argument and carried on her point.

"I don't know yet. It's not an urgent decision to make," Pei-hua casually tossed it back.

"When are you going to get married again, Pei-hua. Is there a lucky man waiting?" Meilan felt that she was in the position to ask these extremely personal questions because they were close friends.

"There are many suitors," Ying Ying answered on Pei-hua's behalf. "But I don't think she is ready for marriage yet."

"Don't wait for too long. I thought I would be a confirmed single for life and I got married. I am glad that many of you ended in happiness: Ailing has married a good man; Ching Ju has two beautiful children, Woolan has a daughter. Only Denis and Pei-hua are still unmarried. By the way where is the beautiful little Jenny?"

Ying Ying looked at Pei-hua with a meaningful smile. She answered Meilan's question:

"Jenny is in London. She went to study at the Royal Academy of Dramatic Arts there. Kevin is in London too "

"You mean that young resident doctor who played Emperor Guangxu? He went to London because of her?" Meilan asked.

"Yea. He was one of Jenny's three dedicated suitors," Pei-hua put in.

"Jenny played Lady Zhen opposite him in *The Intrigues in the Manchu Imperial Court*," Ying Ying added.

"I remember that. They looked like a perfect couple on and off stage," Meilan commented with sincerity.

"They sure did," Woolan agreed. "I suppose they will get married."

"I believe they will. Kevin has told me that they were destined to be together," Ying Ying said. "I hope they will move back to Boston."

"Meilan, do you plan to settle here permanently?" Susie asked.

The conversation returned to the subject of Meilan. Everyone was eager to know if she would be back for good. Her reply was:

"I'd like to. But I can't leave my business in China entirely without my supervision."

She and Kai-de bought a ten-thousand-square-feet Victorian house in Brookline. They worked with an architect on the renovation design. Under the architect's supervision the renovation was done in five months when Meilan and Kai-de went to Beijing. Then they hired an interior decorator to help with furnishing the rooms. The interior decorator suggested that they hire an art consultant to bring art works for them to choose. Meilan immediately thought *why should I hire an art consultant? I should ask Ying Ying to help.*

"Ying Ying, I need your help on selecting artworks. That Meng Song, should I use his paintings? Can you buy them for me?" Meilan called and asked Ying Ying.

"You didn't like his paintings as I recall."

"But you think so highly of him."

"Ha, ha," Ying Ying chuckled. "It's more important that you like it."

"Well, it's more important that I have good art to reflect good taste." Meilan tittered.

"All right, there are galleries representing him. One is in Boston. I can go with you to see which ones you can tolerate."

"You have to decide for me how many I need for all the rooms."

"You may want to have different artists instead of only him."

"You will have to select other artists for me too."

"That's easy. We have a selected artists' registry, those we have shown through the years. They are all very good or we would not have shown them. Their slides are on file. You should look at them."

"No, I don't have to look at them. I don't know art. You don't want me to pick." Meilan was downright forthright. She pondered for a second and asked: "Do you think I should have one or two portraits of me by a good artist?"

"Why not?" Ying Ying laughed. "Every rich lady has portraits of herself in her house. Ching Ju, her husband and children all have portraits."

"Are they good? I am sure they are good. Do you like their artist? Should I use him?"

"The portraits are no doubt very good. But I heard that the artist does not do portraits anymore. You asked if I liked him. I like his work. But I don't like him
as a person."

"Oh, you know him? Of course, which artist would not know you? Something wrong with his personality?"

"Too much to say. Let's not bother with it." Ying Ying paused a second and continued: "But it doesn't affect my opinion on his work. I think you can acquire one or two pieces of his. He has a big show at the Museum of Contemporary Art, if you are interested in seeing his work. "

"Ai, I don't understand art, much less contemporary art. I'll just let you decide what to get."

Thinking about the valuable service Ying Ying would be providing her, Meilan said:

"Ying, your help is invaluable. It cannot be measured in monetary terms. I wouldn't want to insult you. But please accept my remuneration."

Since when have you learned to speak in such a polite, subtle way? Ying Ying was amazed. She said: "Forget it, Meilan. We are friends. And I am not a professional art consultant."

Ying Ying studied Meilan's house, and selected appropriate artwork for the various rooms. Meng Song and Fang Kuei aside, four other non-Asian artists from New York and other regions were represented.

All six artists were invited, with traveling and hotel-room expenses paid, to the house-warming party to reveal their work. Meng Song was the only one not coming. Fang Kuei happened to be in town and accepted the invitation. Of Meilan's China Society acquaintances, Manna was the only one absent. Linda and Sally had not kept in contact with anyone at the organization ever since the Chinese New Year event in 1989. Susie, being a highly successful businesswoman, had no time or interest in the arts. Only occasionally was she in touch with Ying Ying. But all three of them were invited by Meilan to her party.

Fang Kuei saw Ying Ying speaking with someone. He had not seen her since that year at Ching Ju's party. His adverse feelings toward her had subsided especially when he knew that she had acquired his paintings for Meilan. He decided to reacquaint with her.

"Hi, Ying Ying. How are you?" He strode to her and greeted. Then he extended his hand to shake with Kang Wei's. "How are you Professor Kang?"

"Hi. I am fine," Ying Ying said. "Oh, this is Susie, Susie, this is Fang Kuei. You have seen his work here."

"Yes. Great work. Ying Ying spoke so highly of you." Susie smiled and said gently. She had not actually heard Ying Ying speak of this artist, but thinking that remark would not go wrong. Fang Kuei was pleased and somewhat surprised.

"It's very nice of Ying Ying to say that. I am always indebted to her kindness." He then turned to Ying Ying and said: "If you have some time I hope you would drop by the MCA to take a look at my show. I think it is the best of my work so far. The show has toured Europe and Asia. Boston is the final stop."

"A very ambitious show, I have seen it already. Very impressive." Ying Ying meant it but didn't want to show much enthusiasm. " Well reviewed too."

Humanity And History at the Museum of Contemporary Art was Fang Kuei's magnum opus that he had worked on for two years. During that time, with the help of his useful network of numerous important contacts, he mapped out a route from Asia to Europe to North America, for his touring exhibitions at museums. It was the answer to the question he contemplated a few years ago: *What would be the work I create that is so powerful as to exert a mighty impact on the art world and leave an indelible mark on history?* And it was intended to establish himself as a great artist in history.

Pei-hua made her way to Ying Ying and the others and said: "Hi, how are you everyone? May I interrupt your conversation?" She turned to Ying and said: "Would you go over there for a minute? Meilan needs you." She looked at Kang Wei and said: "You too, Kang Wei ."

Ying Ying and Kang Wei excused themselves and followed Pei-hua.

"She wants you to talk with George Hemmingway, Herald Schmidt and

Andrew Johnson."

Meilan was not sure that George Hemmingway would come. Though disappointed by Meilan's subtle rejection, Hemmingway's large heartedness and good breeding overcame the achy feeling gnawing at him and graciously came to the party.

*   *   *   *

Fang Kuei had the chance to chat with Susie at length about their respective backgrounds and undertakings. They developed a liking for each other. He had had too many women in his life, most of them pretty and sensuously appealing. Susie was none of that. Her years of success in business gave her that air of a professional woman. She was suave, genteel, and dignified. She had been romantically entangled with several men through the years, but not bound to any one for long. New opportunities were always welcome. Without knowing Fang Kuei's womanizing history, she thought this attractive-looking artist seemed to be a good candidate. They exchanged phone numbers and promised to get in touch.

Fang Kuei thought Susie was uniquely suitable for him to marry because of her money, power and reputation in the real estate business in Boston and surrounding towns, being comparable, he thought, with his fame and status in the art world. The marriage would boost their social status by a few notches; perhaps qualify them to rub shoulders with the Morrison's circle of Boston Brahmins. This thought delighted him.

Susie is an independent woman. She would not cling to me like the other women did. I will maintain my freedom to go anywhere and do anything I want. This thought delighted him too.

He asked her out a few times. Each time they learned more about each other. Susie was very sensible and undemanding. She even fought to foot the bills a few times. Without hesitation, he brought up the marriage proposal.

"Susie, we both have been single long enough. I think we have reached the time to think about marriage. And I think we will make a good couple. Our marriage will be good for your business and my career, and will give us a ticket to Boston's elite social circle." It was not a romantic proposal by any standard. There was no mentioning of love, or even admiration. It was for practical benefits. But it sounded just fine with Susie. She married for love once and it ended up in a divorce. A marriage brought about by mutual benefits would be solid and lasting because both would want to keep these benefits.

They quickly got married. The wedding was not grandiose. It was held in the grand ballroom of Susie's won hotel. The banquet was catered by her own restaurant situated in the hotel. Susie's house was large and classy enough. Fang Kuei needed not to do anything, but move in.

Susie's business partner Mr. and Mrs. Deng flew in to attend the wedding and gave Susie some expensive jewelry and Fang Kuei an Audi TT as wedding gifts. Mr. Deng learned much about Fang Kuei's art. He liked it, and

336

thought he should do something to make Susie happy. So he suggested:

"Susie, why don't we buy Fang Kuei's paintings for all our buildings?"

They own office buildings, apartment buildings, hotels, and a bank. There were plenty of walls for Fang Kuei's work. Beside the available pieces, Fang Kuei spent a year to create new works specifically for each spot he chose for his work. The existing artwork in those buildings were completely taken down because their inferior qualities would be heightened while juxtaposed with Fang Kuei's work. The Dengs paid Fang Kuei appropriately for his artwork. The proceeds were enormous.

"Money has no value if not used on something meaningful," Fang Kuei said to Susie.

"How would you like to use it? Do you want to invest in something?" Investment was what Susie did best. It was the first thing coming to her mind.

"Invest in something? Yes, I will invest in something. But not the kind of things you have in mind."

"What do you think I have in mind?" Susie smiled. "And what do you have in mind?"

"You are thinking of real estate or other commercial ventures. I am thinking of investing in the society, something that will benefit the public."

"You sound like Fang Ying Ying." Susie smiled some more. "What exactly are you thinking of doing?"

"I am going to build a museum of contemporary art and an artists-colony in Shanghai. The money I have is not enough. But my artwork is selling well. I can fund the project. Or maybe I will get other people to do a joint venture with me."

"That is an awesome idea. Helping the society and immortalize your accomplishment at the same time." Susie pointed out the crux of Fang Kuei's thoughts. "I will support your venture. I can provide funds." Susie's suggestion was what Fang Kuei wished to hear. And yes, that would also be a meaningful use of her funds.

He went to New York to open an account at Bank of China and deposited his money. Then he flew to Shanghai. He did not tell Ching Ju about his project. Now that the Morrisons had done all they could to help him get where he was there was no need to keep in close touch with them anymore.

Meilan and Kai-de spent half the time in Beijing and Shanghai to oversee Meilan's business. Kai-de, with his experience and expertise started doing consulting work for China and the U.S. When they were in Boston they always invited old friends to their house for dinner and shared a good time.

*   *   *   *

When Fang Keui's touring show opened in Beijing and Shanghai it made a tremendous commotion and reverberation. He generously repaid those friends in the news media whose hype brought about the commotion. The newspapers and TV reports gave him such extravagant claims as: "Fang Kuei has conquered the continents of Europe and America. He is the greatest artist of our age, and one of the greatest in human history."

Important government bureaucrats and corporate bigshots were invited to the opening reception in both cities. They congratulated him and praised him. He in turn, presented each of them with a carefully selected gift suitable for the importance of their positions. This was to pave the road for the future when he might need them for something.

This time, as soon as he arrived in Shanghai he brought presents and visited a few of those bureaucrats. They opened all the necessary doors for approval of his plan as a preferred project of the city, and acquiring the whole campus of a closed-down college at much below market price and with subsidy from the city. And he only needed to put forth a down payment and pay the rest in interest-free installments for ten years. The officials involved would have a share of the stake, under the table without mentioning. Before Fang Kuei returned to Boston, renovation and construction were well underway.

What interested those bureaucrats most was that the project was intended to be a moneymaking venture. Museum of Contemporary Art, Shanghai or MCAS, as it was called, would have duel functions. On the one hand, like any museum, it would exhibit art for public appreciation. On the other, it would be a commercial outfit that bought and sold, and held art auctions. The apartment units in the art colony were rented to artists at high rates because of "the prestige of living there" instead of providing rent-free like those in the U.S.. MCAS would nurture and promote new artists and harvest large profits from selling their works. Artists being shown would have to donate one or two pieces to the museum that in turn would auction them off. MCA Shanghai also had several adjunct divisions such as a museum store, restaurant, and a publishing department, all moneymakers. According to Fang Kuei's calculation, MCAS would be profitable as soon as it opened its door.

Susie was very pleased with Fang Kuei's project. She never realized that a cultural operation would be profitable. She did not know that Fang Kuei had a business brain even better than hers. She was more proud than ever about their marriage. *Why does Ying Ying not use her two organizations, to make money? She is so prudish.* She wondered.

In addition to his fame in the art circle and the project's potential commercial success, Fang Kuei was invited to teach in a prestigious university in Shanghai. The fact that he had no graduate degree did not matter. He was given a professorship and taught graduate students.

This news stunned Ying Ying. She thought about Professor Lian of UMass (University of Massachusetts) who had a Ph.D. in American Literature, several major publications, and chairmanship of the English Department. He offered to teach a course at his alma mater in Shanghai on a voluntary basis as his pay back to the school that educated him. The school did not accept his offer to perform this charitable service. It was apparent that Professor Lian did not tread the beaten path of bribery or wheel-greasing to open doors in China. *What an outrageous shame!!* She felt disgusted.

Fang Kuei went back and forth a couple of times to teach his course that required one month of his time each semester. The main purpose of his trips was to oversee the construction.

He never made it to Shanghai on his third trip. The plan crashed shortly after taking off from the Newark Airport in New Jersey. This blow crushed Susie. She was despondent for months. The God-made marriage was like a flash of light, a spark that went off in a wink, without warning. She did not think much about Fang Kuei's assets in Shanghai. But what would happen to those assets? Susie was not a partner in that business and her name was not in any document. Would she have any claim to it?

*   *   *   *

Dong Fei-yan was never able to develop and grow her non-profit organization, Contemporary Music New England, that Ying Ying helped her incorporate. No large ensemble was ever formed. She reorganized her small group of five members including herself and Ivanov, and went on concert tours a few times a year. It was what she wanted to do although the money they generated from these concerts was measly and they still had to share the house with Brandon. But she was content.

She got a call from her brother in Taiwan saying that their father was seriously ill and she should go home to see him. She hated to go without Ivanov yet she couldn't take him along on account of the cost. So she went by herself. Her flight from Boston was delayed and she missed her connection in Los Angeles. She was at the airport about midnight. *I should let Ivanov know what happened.* So she called. She counted twelve rings before Ivanov answered.

"Hi, it's me. I am at the Los Angeles Airport ..." She did not finish telling him why she was calling him from the airport. A loud and angry voice went through to her:

"Why are you calling me at this hour? Do you know what time it is?"

"Oh, sorry it's only 12 midnight here. I forgot it's 3:00am in Boston. But I wanted to tell you that I missed my connection and ...."

"So you missed the connection. What can I do? You have to wake me up just to tell me this?" He hung up. She felt as if being slapped. She was hoping to hear a few kind words of concern although she knew that was too much to hope for. *Brandon would have ...* She put that out from her mind. She always warned herself not to compare Ivanov with Brandon.

Three weeks later she went back to Boston. Brandon picked her up at the airport because Ivanov was not home. Brandon was also the one that took her to the airport when she left.

"Ivanov left me a note to pick you up. He said he had to go somewhere," Brandon informed Fei-yan.

"He didn't say where he went?"

"No."

She couldn't figure out where Ivanov might have gone. She called the few friends they had and the other three members of her music group. She couldn't reach that twenty-year-old girl cellist. The other two had no clue of Ivanov's whereabouts. *Could anything have happened to him?* His instrument and some other things were not in the house. Could he have gone to a music gig out of town? She was mystified and worried. She waited for his return in anxiety. He did not reappear until two weeks later.

"Where have you been? Why didn't you call to let me know? You know how worried..." Fei-yan chided. Before she finished her sentence Ivanov shouted:

"I will call you if I want to. If I don't call you that means I don't want to. You have no right to demand that I do."

"What is the matter with you? Where have you been? Are you going to tell me?"

"It's none of your business. I am not your husband. You have no right to know anything." He dashed to the room and gathered the remaining of his things and took them to the car. Fei-yan followed him.

"What are you doing? You ..." She yelled.

"Can't you see what I am doing? I am moving out. I will use the car to move my things. But don't worry I will return it tomorrow."

Like a thunderbolt exploded on her, Fei-yan gaped; no words came out. Her chest was tight. She tried hard to draw air into her lung. She watched Ivanov drive away.

*　　　*　　　*　　　*

Brandon came home late at night. The house was completely dark. He thought Fei-yan and Ivanov must have gone out. He turned the living room light on and saw Fei-yan curled up on the couch. He wondered if she was asleep. He surreptitiously walked over and peered at her. Whisperingly he asked:

"Fei-yan, are you asleep?"

Fei-yan moved, her face buried in her forearms. Lightly she shook her head.

"Why were you here in the darkness? If you are tired you should go to bed." His gentle voice broke Fei-yan's silence. She cried and stammered:

"I...I...Iva...nov ... has... has... gone."

"What?" Brandon was lost. He didn't understand what she meant by "has gone." *Is he dead? Accident?* "What do you mean he has gone?"

"He has left me. He moved out." Fei-yan cried harder.

"Come now. Don't cry. He will be back. You had a quarrel with him?"

"No. He just said he wanted to move out."

"He might be upset about something. He will be back. Have you had dinner?"

"No."

"Ok. I am going to cook something." Brandon took some things from the refrigerator and prepared to cook.

Fei-yan could not stop sobbing. But she felt some warmth from Brandon's gentleness carried in his soothing voice and subtle concern. Small wonder how these used to be the very part of her daily existence but disposed by her as being boring. All she met with from Ivanov was rough handling, constant criticism, controlling, oppressing, shouting and yelling everyday. She had forgotten what dignity, freedom, and respect was. She was submissive to the degree of servility to Ivanov. She thought she was in love with him. In fact she was fearful of him. So much so that she dared not think about leaving him. Beside, how would it be possible for her to do it? Moving out? The house belonged to her and Brandon. She should not be the one to move out. Ask him to move out? That would be out of the question. Ivanov's rage would raise the hell. And, he would have nowhere to go. Now he had left on his own will. She was released from his iron control and abuse. She would regain her lost dignity, her freedom to think, to speak and act. Were those not what she had secretly wished to reclaim for quite some time?

She lifted her head up to look at Brandon in the kitchen that was an extension of the living room. *He is a good man, always kind and patient. He has taken so much from me, and Ivanov, without ever losing his temper.*

Brandon made noodles in Chinese style and a bowl of salad.

"It's ready, a simple supper. Come." He opened the refrigerator to get the ice water, then put the kettle on the burner to boil water for tea. He always drank ice water with his meal. But Fei-yan liked hot tea. Fei-yan did not move from the coach. Brandon strode over to her. He extended his hand to her and said:

"Come on, get up. Let's eat. You must be hungry by now."

Fei-yan gave him her hand. He pulled her up. She cried and threw herself onto Brandon's bosom.

"Oh, Brandon." Fei-yan was emotion-charged. She needed Brandon more now than she had ever. "I am so sorry...."

"Come now. Don't feel bad. Ivanov will be back. I will try to find him." He patted her on her back.

"No, Brandon. Forget Ivanov. I don't need him to come back. And forgive me. If you still want me. I will come back to you."

So, Fei-yan and Brandon reunited. Brandon was not a passionate or expressive man. Yet he always loved Fei-yan even when she betrayed him and openly humiliated him. Fei-yan was not regretful about Ivanov's leaving. But she was curious. She asked if any of her friends and associates knew where he had gone. Eventually she found that he had moved in with that twenty-year-old cellist. She lost two members of her five-member music group. But she asked the other two to stay on. Her spirit and love of music did not wane. Instead, she was energized by this unfortunate and at the same time fortunate event in her life.

*   *   *   *

Mei Shan's attorney failed to extricate her from the clamps of law. She was found guilty of home invasion and fraud. Brad spent hefty legal fees in vain. He was fed up and regretted that he had married a slut and a thief. When the judge sentenced Mei Shan to ten years imprisonment he began divorce proceedings instead of appealing to the superior court on her behalf.

Manna was still on the run, a fugitive of the law. Roger vowed to fine her and retrieve his sons.

END